A
Bittersweet
Garden

Books by Caren J. Werlinger

Novels:
Looking Through Windows
Miserere
In This Small Spot
Neither Present Time
Year of the Monsoon
She Sings of Old, Unhappy, Far-off Things
Turning for Home
Cast Me Gently
The Beast That Never Was
When the Stars Sang
A Bittersweet Garden

Short Stories:
Twist of the Magi
Just a Normal Christmas
(part of *Do You Feel What I Feel? Holiday Anthology*)

The Dragonmage Saga:
Rising From the Ashes: The Chronicles of Caymin
The Portal: The Chronicles of Caymin
The Standing Stones: The Chronicles of Caymin

A BITTERSWEET GARDEN

CAREN J. WERLINGER

CORGYN
Publishing

A *Bittersweet Garden*
Published by Corgyn Publishing, LLC.

Copyright © 2019 by Caren J. Werlinger
All rights reserved.

e-Book ISBN: 978-0-9982179-3-2
Print ISBN: 978-0-9982179-4-9

E-mail: cjwerlingerbooks@yahoo.com
Website: carenwerlinger.com
Blog: cjwerlinger.wordpress.com

Cover design by Patty G. Henderson
www.boulevardphotografica.yolasite.com

Cover photo credit: Pixabay

Interior decoration: Can Stock Photo/Red Koala

Book design by Maureen Cutajar
www.gopublished.com

For Beth
Do chroí, mo chroí

Acknowledgements

Like many of my stories, *A Bittersweet Garden* has been waiting years to be told. Not until my spouse and I had the opportunity to travel to Ireland in 2015 did I have the last real pieces I needed to be able to write this book. I'm not sure I could be as brave as Nora is in this story—to live a dream, if it meant going alone and upending my life—but it was a dream come true for me to be in Ireland. I hope to get back there soon.

I need to thank many people for their help (whether they knew it or not) in bringing this book to fruition: Ray Walsh, our tour guide in Ireland, who was a bottomless source of information on all topics; the staff at Ashford Castle and its Lodge, who made our stay there most welcoming; the people of Cong, who put up with an endless stream of tourists like us, who love *The Quiet Man*; my editor, Lisa, who forces me to dig deep to answer her questions and without whom this book would not be what it is; and, always, my beloved, Beth—I couldn't write at all if I didn't have her support and encouragement.

Thank you, also, to my readers. Your loyalty and messages have meant more to me than I can ever tell you.

Sláinte!

The Lake Isle of Innisfree

I will arise and go now, and go to Innisfree,
And a small cabin build there, of clay and wattles made:
Nine bean-rows will I have there, a hive for the honey-bee,
And live alone in the bee-loud glade.

And I shall have some peace there, for peace comes dropping slow,
Dropping from the veils of the morning to where the cricket sings;
There midnight's all a glimmer, and noon a purple glow,
And evening full of linnet's wings.

I will arise and go now, for always night and day
I hear lake water lapping with low sounds by the shore;
While I stand on the roadway, or on the pavements grey,
I hear it in the deep heart's core.

~ W.B. Yeats

Chapter 1

ORA MCNEILL PRESSED HER forehead to the glass, peering through the airplane window, trying to see through the clouds below. The sun, brilliant here above the cloudbank, was blinding. The video screen built into the back of the seat in front of her showed their little plane had been flying over Ireland for the past thirty minutes as it descended toward Dublin, but she hadn't been able to see anything.

She'd wanted to come here her entire life—*maybe even longer than that,* she sometimes thought.

The flight crew had already cleared all the coffee cups and debris from the breakfast they'd served to the sleepy passengers nearing the end of their overnight flight. Most of the older people around her seemed to know one another and were apparently all part of the same tour.

She'd carried on a stop and start conversation with Iris, the grandmotherly woman beside her, who had knitted nearly the entire

1

night, her green and yellow baby blanket spilling onto Nora's lap. Nora now knew that Iris was a widow from a little town an hour west of Minneapolis, had five grandchildren—with a sixth on its way, thus the baby blanket—and had never flown outside the States. Neither had Nora, for that matter.

"And you're traveling alone? I could never do that. Don't you think you'll miss home?" Iris had asked upon learning that Nora's plans were to spend the next three months in Ireland. Iris had only been gone a dozen hours, but claimed she was already missing her grandkids.

Deciding it was probably more diplomatic not to scoff, Nora simply shrugged. "Probably, but I'll be visiting family."

Nora snugged her seatbelt as the plane bounced through a bit of turbulence. The window was suddenly obscured by white. When the plane emerged from the clouds, there was Dublin, spread out below them in the distance.

Her heart pounded at her first glimpse of Ireland. Beside her, Iris harrumphed, clearly unimpressed, but Nora ignored her. It didn't matter that it was gray and dreary and looked almost like the view of Northern Virginia around Dulles airport. She sat back with a sigh. Nothing mattered except she wasn't going to be stuck in Fredericksburg for her entire summer.

The plane quickly descended and, soon, Nora was wheeling her carry-on off the plane with her backpack slung over both shoulders, following Iris and all the other passengers through the airport toward the baggage claim carousels. She grinned at the signs, all written in English and Irish. She'd been studying and could read some of the words. Of course, being able to say "That's a yellow bicycle" or "I have a black cat" probably weren't the most practical phrases, but still.

When she'd collected her one checked bag and had her passport stamped—"my first stamp!" she'd said stupidly to the sleepy-looking agent—she made her way through the airport, bustling even at this early hour. Following the directions the customs agent had given her, she went outside to find the bus, her luggage trailing behind her.

The morning was misty, and the air smelled of diesel fumes, but nothing could dampen her excitement. She found the bus, with a uniformed driver chatting to another man in a different uniform with a reflective vest.

"This is the bus to Galway?" she asked.

The driver turned to her, looking her up and down. "American?"

She nodded and shrugged out of her backpack straps.

"That'll be a hundred fifty euro," he said.

She froze, her hand searching for her wallet inside her backpack. "A hundred fifty? I thought the website said eighteen?"

"Not for Yanks."

She stood there, her mouth open, until his buddy burst out laughing.

"Stop teasin' her."

The bus driver grinned and climbed into the bus where he punched a few buttons on his console. It spit out a ticket that he handed to her as she passed him a twenty-euro note.

"Just leave your bags," he said, pointing to a few others sitting on the pavement as he handed her change. "I'll load them."

She hoisted her backpack up the steps onto the bus and dropped into a seat, stashing her backpack on the seat beside her. She listened to the low conversations taking place around her and realized all the other passengers seemed to be either American or European—anywhere but Ireland. She supposed she'd been stupid to think anyone from Ireland would be catching a bus from the airport. Of course they'd all be tourists like her. She was also the only person on the bus traveling alone.

It doesn't matter. It's going to be like that all summer. All that matters is that you're here. She unzipped her backpack and dug out a bottle of water and a granola bar.

3

Within a few minutes, the bus was pulling away from the airport. She craned her neck, trying to take it all in. The bus passed through Dublin, pausing at a couple of stops to let more people on. She snapped photos through the bus windows with her phone, half-wishing she'd planned to spend some time here, but money was tight, and she hadn't felt quite brave enough to tackle Dublin on her own.

"I'll be back," she whispered as the bus drove along the river with its arched bridges.

She fought to stay awake and take in the views of the flat countryside outside the city, but her eyes fluttered closed and her head bobbed as she fell asleep despite her efforts.

When she woke, the bus was winding its way through Galway's streets to the bus station. She stood with the other passengers to collect her bags as the driver unloaded them from the cargo compartment, and then stumbled into the station where the pleasant young woman at the ticket counter checked the bus schedule for the next leg of her journey.

"You've just over an hour before your bus leaves," she said.

Nora paid for the ticket. "Is there anyplace close by where I can get a cup of coffee?"

"Sure there's a Starbucks just round the corner," the ticket agent said, pointing. "You can leave your bags here if you like."

Nora stashed her luggage and thanked her before going in search of caffeine.

By the time the next bus was underway, she was jazzed on a double-shot cappuccino and a scone.

Unlike the express bus, this one stopped in several towns as it made its way north. The terrain had changed quite a bit, becoming hillier and the roads much narrower. She held her breath a couple of times, wondering how on earth the bus and the oncoming vehicles—on the wrong side of the road—were possibly going to pass without scraping each other or the hedges and stone walls bordering either side

4

of the road. She whispered several prayers of thanks that she'd decided not to rent a car and drive herself.

The bus's elevated height gave her a great view of small houses with neat front yards—gardens here, she remembered—separated from the road by low walls. She chuckled at the tiny cars tucked into impossible parking spaces, sometimes seeming to have just been pulled up onto the sidewalks.

The sun came and went as clouds drifted, soft rain misting the windows and then passing to allow slanting beams of sunlight to sparkle on the drops. Passengers boarded and left at each stop along the way. She tried to catch snatches of conversation, delighting at the accent.

Her caffeine was wearing off, and the jetlag was beginning to weigh on her as the bus neared her destination.

"Cong," called the driver.

She roused herself to wheel her bags along the center aisle.

"Visiting?" asked the driver as he carried her bags down for her.

"For the whole summer," she said.

He winked. "Have a grand summer, then."

The driver waved as the bus drove away. She stood in front of the Crowe's Nest Pub, debating whether to go in for a real meal, but the day was fading and she had a ways to go yet.

She hoisted her backpack straps higher on her shoulders and took a suitcase handle in each hand, rolling them along the street. The narrow sidewalk was crowded with people, most of them part of a tour, judging by the badges they wore on lanyards around their necks and the cameras and phones they held up, snapping photos every few steps. She dropped off the sidewalk into the street, her head swiveling as she walked, trying to take in everything. Some things felt as if she'd been here before: the corner with the Celtic cross the bike flew around, Cohan's pub. She'd watched *The Quiet Man* so many times, she had the dialogue memorized. She especially loved the scenes with the villagers who'd been the extras in the movie.

"There we are," Mamma said every time, pointing.

"Oh, those were fine days," Pop said, his pipe firmly clamped in his teeth as he nodded fondly.

From the time she was sitting on her grandfather's knee, she'd listened to the stories of how the movie people had come to their tiny village, transforming it for those months, even bringing in electricity where it hadn't been before.

Nora couldn't wipe the grin off her sweaty face as she tromped along, passing the ruins of the abbey, walking past the ivy-covered cottage that had been the vicar's house in the movie. When she reached the church at the curve of the road, she paused to catch her breath. It was Church of Ireland, but it had served as a Catholic church for the movie. She leaned on the wall, panting. Behind her, a vehicle's motor drew near. She turned to see a dark green Land Rover approaching. The driver braked as he passed her and backed up. The door was emblazoned with "Ashford Castle".

"Where are you bound, Miss?" he asked.

"The Lodge."

The young man jumped out and hurried around to her. "I'll give you a lift."

"Are you sure?" she asked, but he was already loading her bags into the cargo area.

"It's my pleasure. I've just got to drop off these guests for dinner, if you don't mind."

"Not at all. Thank you."

He got in behind the wheel as she climbed into the passenger seat. She smiled and nodded at the couple in the rear seat.

He drove into the village along the way she'd just come, stopping at Cohan's. He got out to open the rear door for the woman, confirming a pickup time for later that evening.

"Your first time in Cong?" he asked Nora when he got back in.

"Does it show?"

He chuckled. "Just a bit. You've got that gleam in your eye."

She laughed. "I guess I do. My grandparents were born here. They've told me about Cong my whole life."

"Is that a fact? Who are they?"

"Brigid Cleary and Thomas McNeill. I'm Nora McNeill."

"And I'm Craig O'Toole," he said. "Do you still have family here?"

"I have cousins, second or third, I guess," Nora said. "My grandparents' siblings' grandchildren. It's so confusing. I mean to look them up while I'm here."

Craig had taken a different road out of the village, Nora realized. "Why aren't we going back the way we came?"

"One way into the village," Craig said.

He took a right and drove past a vast stretch of manicured grass with a few golfers in the distance. As if he knew what her reaction would be, he stopped the Land Rover at the curve where the castle came into view. He grinned at her gasp. It was better than her dreams, the picture-perfect stone castle with the crenellated towers and the lake just beyond.

"Do you ever get tired of it?"

"I don't, no. I keep seeing it through fresh eyes when I drive guests here." He chuckled again. "Would you like to visit the castle? I can drive you up to the Lodge after."

As tempting as it was, Nora could feel her body rebelling if it didn't get sleep soon. "That's really nice of you, but... I'll visit it tomorrow."

"Tomorrow, then."

Craig drove on, pointing out the Thatched Cottage restaurant before taking a turn that bore them left and then right again, through deep shadows and mossy trees until they emerged into golden sunlight and a different view of the lake, with small boats bobbing in the cove below.

"Here you are. The Lodge."

He opened the tailgate and insisted on carrying her bags inside for her. "Got a guest for you, Sarah. She was walking all the way from the village."

7

"Oh, you poor thing." Sarah clicked her computer keys, fingers flashing with vivid red polish.

"See you later, Miss McNeill," Craig said with a cheeky wink in Sarah's direction.

"McNeill?" Sarah stared at her screen. "Here you are. Three nights with us, right?"

"Yes." Nora sighed. "I wanted to stay at the castle, but..."

Sarah laughed. "No more need be said. We've a lovely location at a fraction of the cost."

Nora nodded sheepishly.

"How about I make you a reservation for tea at the castle tomorrow evening, if you've no other plans?"

"I don't have any other plans. That would be wonderful."

Sarah scanned Nora's credit card and handed her a key and a stack of brochures. "Just call if you need anything."

Nora found her way to her room. As soon as she got inside, all her plans to wander the grounds were forgotten when she saw the puffy white duvet on the bed. It was only mid-afternoon here, and she knew all the travel advice said to stay up and get used to the new time zone, but...

"I'll just close my eyes for a minute," she muttered as she stretched out and promptly fell asleep.

THE ROOM WAS NEARLY dark when she woke. She sat up, feeling shaky and drugged, her mind sluggish, as she tried to remember where she was.

Cong. She was at Ashford. She flopped back down with a happy sigh.

Her stomach growled, reminding her she hadn't fed it anything healthy in several hours, and that airplane meal hadn't gone down well.

She glanced at her watch, mentally moving the time ahead five hours. Almost nine o'clock here. She had no idea what would be open at this time.

She rinsed her face, patted it dry on a luxurious towel, ran a brush through her honey-blonde hair, and went in search of food, grabbing her stack of pamphlets on her way out.

A few minutes later, she was seated at a table in the bar with a bowl of creamy vegetable soup and thick slices of hearty brown bread.

Sated, she sat back, sipping her tea and letting her body settle. She leafed through the brochures. Among them was a map of the Ashford grounds and surrounding area. She scooted her chair closer and leaned over the map. She already knew the layout of the area around Cong from her grandparents, but it was cool to see it drawn out like this.

She pushed back from the table and gathered her papers. On her way back to her room, she stepped outside where a misty rain was falling.

"'Tis a nice, soft evening," she said, chuckling to herself.

Today, despite all the obstacles and opposition, she'd arrived at the destination of her dreams. Tomorrow, she'd start living her dream.

THE CHESTNUT FILLY SHIED at the white handkerchief fluttering from a tree branch, but Briana was ready. Her legs clamped tightly, keeping her arse glued to the saddle as the horse jumped sideways.

"Ginger, you silly thing," she said in a matter-of-fact voice, nudging the filly over to inspect the flapping cloth. "See? I think you just like finding things to pretend to be scared of."

The delicate ears swept back at the sound of her voice, and the nostrils quivered as the filly sniffed the handkerchief. Briana leaned over to untie it and stuff it in her back pocket.

An enormous gray wolfhound mix bounded out of the woods.

"And where have you been, Shannon?"

The dog, her coat dappled with drops of water from the underbrush, grinned up at her, tongue lolling.

Dog and horse stood nose to nose. Briana let them have their moment before they walked on, Ginger's hooves thudding on the damp, hard-packed trail as it threaded its way through the woods. Droplets of water clung to every leaf, every needle. It was all washed clean from the night's shower. Briana loved the freshness of the air after a rain.

Up ahead, an aluminum can clanked from where it was tied to a fence rail. Again, the filly jumped with a frightened snort. Again, Briana spoke quietly, using the pressure of her legs and hands to guide the horse toward the fence.

When Ginger was satisfied the can wasn't going to hurt her, Briana likewise untied it and shoved it into her saddle bag before letting the filly break into a controlled canter. The wolfhound loped beside them, easily keeping up. Other trails forked off the main one, but they continued on this path.

The calm morning suddenly exploded as a pedestrian, head bowed over a paper, unexpectedly stepped off one of the side trails directly into their path.

The filly shied in real terror this time. Shannon let out a booming bark, and the walker looked up and screamed before falling into a huge rhododendron. Ginger skidded to a halt and then reared. Briana grabbed mane, fighting to keep her seat as she brought the filly down.

"Whoa... whoa," she said soothingly. "There, now."

Ginger stood, trembling, as Briana turned her fury on the figure floundering about in the rhododendron. "What the bloody hell were you—"

She found herself looking into a frightened, pale face staring up at her from the dark green rhododendron leaves.

"I am so sorry," the woman in the bushes stammered as she tried to get up.

Every branch she grasped bent under her weight, leaving her to fall further into the greenery. She fell even deeper into the bush as she recoiled from Shannon, who had come over to sniff the stranger.

With an exasperated sigh, Briana dismounted.

"Shannon, get back," she said, using her hip to push the huge dog out of the way.

Being careful to keep a tight hold of the reins in one hand, she reached out with her other to disentangle the Yank. Tourists. No local would walk so blindly along bridle paths.

She pulled the woman to her feet, glaring up into a face a good hand higher than her own. "Are you hurt?"

"No." The woman brushed her backside off, plucking a few leaves from her jacket. "Are you?"

Briana had already turned back to Ginger to inspect her, running her hands down the filly's forelegs.

"Fine," she muttered. "You're fine."

She rubbed the filly's pretty face, marked with a white blaze. Ginger was eyeing the American warily, stretching her neck out to sniff at the stranger.

"Your hand," Briana said.

"Sorry?"

The woman stared down at her, and the height difference irritated Briana all the more. "Give her your hand to sniff so she knows you're not something to be afraid of."

The woman did as Briana instructed. Ginger's nostrils fluttered, and she snorted. The American jumped and jerked her hand back. Shannon shifted to place her enormous head under the Yank's other hand and was rewarded with a scratch.

On the ground, a piece of paper fluttered against the rhododendron, making Ginger snort again in mock terror.

"Oh, stop it." Briana gave her a pat and bent to pick up the paper. It was the map the American had dropped.

11

"Where were you headed?" she asked as she held it out.

The woman took it from her. "I was looking for the Old School-house."

Briana looked her up and down. Not a fly rod in sight. "You don't look like you're here for the fishing."

The tourist blushed. "I'm not."

Briana pointed. "Well, it's that way." She led Ginger to a fallen tree she could stand on to vault into the saddle. "But you'd best keep your head up and your ears open as you walk."

She urged Ginger onward down the path. At a bend in the trail, she twisted in the saddle and saw the American staring after her. She turned back around with a shake of her head.

"Idjit."

NORA GRUMBLED TO HERSELF as she walked. "Said I was sorry. Not like I meant to… She didn't have to be so rude."

She was a little embarrassed, remembering how she'd jumped when that chestnut mare had snorted against her hand. As much as Nora had loved horses growing up and had begged and begged for one of her own, it had been years since she'd been around any. And that had to be the biggest dog she'd ever seen, almost the size of a Shetland pony.

The rider—Nora only now realized how tiny she was—had made her feel ridiculously small. It seemed to her that she'd been made to feel small most of her life, and she was sick and tired of it. *Tired of allowing it,* she corrected herself.

Her irritation was soon forgotten as she took in the enormous trees, their trunks covered in moss and lichens. There was even one type of tree whose bark wrinkled near the base of the trunk, making it look like an elephant's leg.

"Gosh, my imagination could have run wild here." She knelt to snap a photo with her cell phone.

She remained there, just listening and absorbing the atmosphere of the woods, envying her grandparents for getting to grow up here. *Probably among these very same trees*, she realized. Sighing, she pushed to her feet and continued on her way. When she emerged from the forest, the trail continued until she found herself facing a quaint stone cottage that looked like something from a storybook. No wonder the Old Schoolhouse was such a popular accommodation. It looked delightful.

She glanced at her map again and turned to the right, following the directions she'd been given. The hedge-lined road wound and wound, and she caught glimpses of other houses, their low walls surrounding neat gardens. She came upon another lane that branched off, hardly more than a trail through the trees, looking way too narrow for a car. She wandered uncertainly down the shaded path, her heart pounding, until the trees parted to give her her first view of the cottage that would be her home for the rest of the summer. Her heart plummeted when she saw it.

"He said he's not done anything with it for a while now," Pop had warned after he'd written to an old friend of his to inquire for her. "He's a farmer, not a landlord, but the cottage is empty, and he's offering it to you for next to nothing."

Nora reminded herself of that as she took in the unkempt state of the little house, its steep slate roof covered in moss, ivy growing up the walls where chunks of the lime wash had fallen off, exposing the stone underneath. The skeletal remains of a few dead bushes sat on either side of the door.

Tilting her head, she tried to imagine what it could be if it weren't so... lonely, she decided.

Her mother had always sighed indulgently when Nora would assign personalities to inanimate objects, but Mamma had pretended right along with her, whether it was her bike becoming her horse—a gleaming black stallion, name of Coal, that no one but Nora could ride—or declaring that her favorite climbing tree was hugging her when it let her clamber up to settle contentedly in its branches, hiding from the world while she drew or read. She'd even imagined that her bed enfolded her protectively as monsters tried to peer in at her through the windows.

Later, with Amy... well, Nora had quickly learned that a vivid imagination wasn't something that everyone had. Or valued.

Now, she pictured the cottage with clean windows and cheerful flowers and the door thrown open to welcome guests.

At that, she laughed aloud. "Just what guests do you think you're going to have here, Nora Mary Brigid McNeill?"

A flash of movement caught her eye, freezing her mid-laugh.

A face. She could have sworn she'd seen a pale face, there in the upstairs window. Was someone living here?

Her entire summer was planned around having this cottage to herself. She strode to the door and banged on it, but no one answered. She stepped sideways to one of the windows, rubbing the grime off to peer inside. The furniture was all covered in sheets. Clearly no one was living here. She braced a hand on the stones to lean in for a better view, and felt a sudden wave of dizziness. She stumbled backward.

"You're seeing things," she mumbled. "Still jet-lagged."

Her face broke out in a cold sweat. The rain jacket that had been a welcome layer when she began her trek was now feeling uncomfortably warm. She took it off and tied the sleeves around her waist, mopping her face with her shirtsleeve.

Drawing her map out of her pocket, she tried to get her bearings. Her cousin's shop should be... that way. At the edge of the clearing, she glanced back at the cottage. Nothing. With a shake of her head, she headed back down the path to the road.

As she walked—remembering to watch for oncoming traffic on the right side of the road—she waved at passing cars. Within fifteen minutes, she saw a sign for The Bittersweet Garden.

A greenhouse was connected to a sprawling pergola-like structure, both filled with tiers and tiers of potted plants, hanging baskets of more flowering plants, raised beds of all kinds of herbs. She caught sight of movement through the glass walls of the greenhouse.

Going to the door, she peeked inside. "Hello?"

A woman stood, her jet-black hair bundled through the back of a battered baseball cap. "Yes? Can I help you?"

"I'm looking for Sheila Donnelly."

"Are you Nora?"

The woman beamed at her, approaching with her hand held out. "Sorry," she said as she used a rag to swipe at the dirt on her palm. "Welcome to Cong. How was your flight?"

"It was fine," Nora said, letting Sheila wring her hand.

"Come on in for some tea," Sheila said, dragging Nora toward the rambling building next to the pergola. It looked as if additions had been cobbled onto additions over the years.

Sheila toed off her muddy Wellies and left them on a brush mat while she slipped into a pair of rubber clogs. She took her cap off and shook her hair out, combing her fingers through it.

Nora found herself inside a charming shop with more shelves crammed with all kinds of gardening implements, hats, gloves, hand creams, soaps, candles, sachets. It smelled heavenly.

"Do you own this?" Nora asked. "It's wonderful. I used to garden with my Mamma when I was little."

"I guess it runs in our blood." Sheila pointed. "I make the soaps and the candles and such with my own herbs and oils and spices."

Sheila led her through the shop to a small kitchen beyond. A chubby russet-colored terrier, sleeping on a rug there, stirred himself at their entrance.

"This is Rusty," Sheila said as she filled a kettle at the tap. She plugged it in and gestured to the table. "Have a seat."

Nora pulled out a chair. The entire kitchen was inviting, with whimsically painted cupboards and hutches, everything worn and homey and mismatched, almost the polar opposite of the antiseptic white and stainless steel surfaces of her own kitchen. Through a doorway on the other side of the kitchen, she caught a glimpse of a comfortable-looking den with a mishmash of cushy sofas and chairs.

"This is so nice," Nora said. "So inviting."

Sheila raised her eyebrows. "Well, Martha Stewart will never come calling here for decorating ideas. But it's home."

"It's wonderful."

"How's everyone in America?" Sheila asked as she sorted through a tin for tea bags.

Nora looked up from where she was scratching Rusty behind the ears. "Everyone's good. Mamma and Pop are loving retirement and four great-grandchildren. They send their love."

Sheila laughed. "And we send it right back. Are they going to come for a visit home? It's been what... fifteen years at least."

"I know. I couldn't come the last time they did. I think they'd like to; they keep talking about it."

"Have you met any of the other cousins?"

"Not yet." Nora scooted her chair closer. "I just got here yesterday, but I'd love to meet them all."

Sheila set a plate of sliced almond bread on the table, along with a bowl of whipped butter. In a few minutes, she joined Nora at the table with two steaming mugs of tea.

"So," Sheila said, "my Gran says you're to be here for the whole summer. What prompted that, then?"

Nora felt trapped by the innocent kindness in Sheila's brilliantly blue eyes, and wondered how to answer. "Well..." She busied herself buttering a slice of bread. "There were things keeping me from traveling that just aren't issues any longer. It seemed like the right time."

Sheila leaned forward and touched Nora's hair, startling her. "And how did you come by this little souvenir?"

She held up a rhododendron leaf.

"Oh, that." Nora gave an embarrassed laugh. "I scared a horse and fell into a bush." At Sheila's confused expression, she added, "I wasn't watching where I was going and almost collided with a horse on one of the trails."

She frowned. "Pretty rude rider, though."

Sheila paused with her mug halfway to her mouth. "Who was that?"

"Didn't get a name. Short woman. Nasty temper. Big dog."

To her surprise, Sheila burst out laughing. "That'd be Briana Devlin and her Shannon. She's not much for people, is Bri, but she's a magician with the horses."

"Well, it was mostly my fault," Nora admitted grudgingly. "I had my nose buried in my map and wasn't paying attention."

"Briana's a good friend," said Sheila. "We'll have you both meet us down at the pub and make proper introductions. Get you off on a better foot."

She buttered her own slice of bread. "Where are you staying?"

"The Lodge at Ashford for two more nights. I just had to."

Sheila nodded. "I understand. 'Tis a treat. Then where?"

"A cottage not too far from here. I think it's called Sióg Cottage. Did I pronounce that right—*shee og*?"

Sheila choked on her bread. "Sióg Cottage?" she croaked when she could speak, pronouncing it *shee od*. "You're staying there?"

"Um... I will be. Come June first. Why?"

"Nothing. Nothing a'tall." Sheila cleared her throat and raised her mug in a toast. "Welcome home, cousin."

BRIANA FINISHED BRUSHING GINGER and led her out to the paddock. "Go on," she said, unbuckling her halter and slipping it over her ears.

The filly kicked her heels a little as she sprinted across the paddock, looking more like a yearling than a three-year-old. Briana shook her head and went back inside to muck stalls, waving to Sonya, who was giving a lesson in the ring.

She was humming to herself, her wheelbarrow half-full of horse manure and soiled straw, when a shadow fell across the door of the stall she was in.

"How'd she go?"

She didn't glance up at the man standing there. "Fine. She still likes to act the fool, as if she's scared of things, but she's only pretending."

"Doesn't matter if she's pretending if a guest comes off when she shies."

"Quinn, she's but a baby." Briana paused and leaned on her pitchfork. "She just needs more training."

He shrugged. "I'll rely on you to let me know when she's ready to go out." He eyed her. "You could take her out."

Briana scowled. "Not on your life. I told you, I don't mind shoveling shite, and I'll train. But I'd rather sit on this pitchfork than deal with silly tourists who come to Ireland and decide they've just got to ride a horse. Either they've never ridden in their lives or they think they're bloody John Wayne and can go galloping over fences."

He snorted, sounding a lot like Ginger. "You're right enough there. Jimmie called. Says Princess has come up a bit lame. When you're done here, can you take William over to the riding stables? They've got a group going out at two. Bring Princess back here if she's sound enough to walk. If not, I'll drive over later with the trailer. We'll tend to her." He turned to go but then paused. "Oh, got a text from Sheila. She wants to have dinner down the pub tonight. Said she'll stand the first round."

Briana grinned. "I'm there, then."

"Six o'clock. And be sure to scrape the shite off your boots."

She laughed as he walked away. She spread fresh straw in the stall and then wheeled the barrow down the aisle, stopping at the last stall at the rear of the barn.

She set the barrow down and rested her arms on the stall door, staring at the gray hindquarters being presented to her.

"Are you going to say hello today?"

In answer, a hind hoof shot out, striking the door hard enough to make her arms tingle.

"One day, you will." With a sigh, she picked the barrow up and took it out to dump on the dung pile.

Chapter 2

ORA SAT AT A TABLE in the Lodge's parlor, where she could see both the lake and any cars approaching. Sheila had insisted on driving her back to the Lodge after their visit. "You've walked miles today," she'd said when Nora tried to protest. "We'll pick you up this evening to take you to the pub."

"You're sure it's no problem to cancel the tea reservation at the Castle?" Nora had asked Sarah anxiously when she got back.

"Not a bit." Sarah typed a message on the computer. "You have a nice evening in the village."

Nora had peeled out of her sweaty clothing and rinsed off in the shower. After drying herself, she succumbed to the lure of her bed for an hour's nap. She still felt a bit off-kilter with the time change, but that brief rest refreshed her. She dressed in clean clothes and went to the parlor to wait.

Sheila's blue Kia SUV pulled up at the circular drive, and Nora jumped up to go out to meet it.

"Have a good evening, Miss McNeill," Sarah called from the desk.

"I will," Nora said, beaming. "I'm having dinner with my cousins!"

She hurried out to find a tall, sandy-haired man opening the SUV's door for her. His freckled face split into a grin. "Hi, Nora. I'm Quinn."

He gripped her hand and waved her into the back seat.

He got in, and Sheila put the car in gear, glancing at Nora in the rearview mirror. "Are you rested, then?"

"I am, thanks. I didn't realize how tired I was. Thanks so much for picking me up."

Quinn twisted around in the seat. "Sheila said you walked clear out to our place this morning. You'll put some miles on your legs this summer if you don't get yourself a car."

Nora realized that his pale reddish-blond eyebrows and lashes almost disappeared on his weathered face. "I think I'm safer walking. I'd hate to run someone off the road when I panic and jump back to the right side."

He laughed and turned back around. "You may be right."

Sheila navigated the winding road into the village and found a parking spot. Nora followed them into the pub, where most of the people sitting at the bar hailed them.

"I saved you a table," the bartender said, pointing.

"Thanks, Andrew." Sheila left Quinn to order the first round while she shepherded Nora to a table in the rear of the pub near the fireplace.

"A fire in May?" Nora asked, sniffing at the scent of peat.

"Nights are still chilly here," Sheila said. "And the tourists expect it."

Quinn was back in a few minutes with three pints of Guinness. Nora took a sip.

"Oh, that's good."

Sheila passed menus around. While they were looking them over, a shaggy dog head appeared on the other side of the table. Nora looked up to find the rude rider from the morning standing there beside her dog.

"Bri," said Quinn, shifting his chair over to make room for her. "Have you met our cousin from America? This is Nora McNeill. Briana Devlin."

Briana nodded. "We've met. In a manner of speaking."

She sat, and their server brought her another pint of the dark beer. Briana smiled her thanks.

"What'll you have?" the waitress asked the table, laying a familiar hand on Briana's shoulder.

Quinn and Sheila both ordered shepherd's pie, while Nora opted for fish and chips.

"I'll have a burger," Briana said.

The server left to place their orders.

"How'd Princess go?" Quinn asked.

Briana took a long drink before saying, "Her off foreleg. It's warm and a wee bit swollen. I walked her back and rubbed it down."

Nora had no idea what they were talking about, but took advantage of the opportunity to study Briana more closely. Without her riding helmet on, her short hair shone a vivid red in the firelight. Her eyes, now that they weren't scowling in Nora's direction, looked to be blue or gray. It was hard to tell exactly.

Sheila, apparently not interested in stable talk, turned to Nora. "Tell us more about your family."

Nora quickly gulped the mouthful of Guinness she had just taken and wiped the rich foam off her upper lip as Quinn's and Briana's attention turned to her. "Um... well, our family is mostly settled in Virginia. Near DC. A town called Fredericksburg."

"And you're one of four girls?" Sheila prompted when Nora paused.

Nora nodded. "Number two. My sisters are all married. The oldest has two children, and the others have one each, and one is expecting. I work at a university. In the library."

"And you were able to get the entire summer off?" Sheila asked in surprise.

Nora shrugged. "I've worked there for thirteen years and have never taken more than a couple of days off. When I asked, my supervisor said yes."

Quinn leaned his elbows on the table. "So what do you want to do with your summer in Ireland?"

Nora opened her mouth, but Briana said, "Wait. She's come here to write a book."

She chuckled at her own joke, but Nora felt the heat rise in her cheeks. Quinn gave Briana an elbow in the ribs.

"I know it sounds silly," Nora stammered.

"No, it doesn't," Sheila said, shooting a harsh glare in Briana's direction. "Tell us about it."

Nora gave a quick shake of her head, fighting a sudden sinking feeling in her belly. "It's just something I've been toying with for a while. It'll probably turn out to be nothing. I didn't have any really firm plans. I've just always dreamed of coming here and decided this was the time to do it."

"Well, good for you." Sheila raised her glass. Briana and Quinn followed suit. "Welcome to Cong. *Sláinte.*"

Their dinner arrived, and Nora busied herself eating as Sheila and Quinn chatted. Apparently, in addition to the greenhouse and nursery, they owned a riding stable that catered largely to tourists visiting Cong and Ashford, and it seemed Briana worked for them.

As she ate, Nora watched them, their easy familiarity with one another. Quinn stabbed all of the carrots from his shepherd's pie, depositing them on Sheila's plate while Briana passed over almost half of her chips to Quinn.

She glanced up and saw Sheila focused on something behind her. Nora twisted in her seat to see a family seated at the adjacent table, a proud grandmother bouncing a baby on her lap. She turned back around, but Sheila's eyes were downcast, her long lashes veiling her gaze. Under the table, Quinn reached for her hand. Briana caught

Nora's eye for just a second, glaring at her as if she'd been caught intruding on something she wasn't meant to see.

Confused, Nora blinked at her plate while Briana asked Quinn another question about one of their horses. When Nora looked up, everything was normal, the moment passed so quickly that Nora wondered if she'd imagined it.

They resumed eating, and Nora surprised herself by finishing her fish and chips. All that walking had made her ravenous.

After a second pint that Briana insisted on buying for the table, Nora was pleasantly full and relaxed. A heavy weight settled on her thigh, and she found Shannon's large head plopped there as she leaned against Nora.

"She likes you," Sheila said.

"She startled me this morning; she's so big." Nora laid her hand on Shannon's head, and the dog closed her eyes contentedly.

"She doesn't do that with many," Briana said.

Nora glanced up to find Briana eyeing her as if she were reappraising her. She gave a half-shrug. "I've mostly been a cat person, but I love dogs, too. I guess I've always gotten along with most animals better than most people."

Quinn clapped Briana on the shoulder. "Well you two have that in common." He drained his glass. "Come on, Nora. We'll give you a ride back to Ashford."

THE FIRES IN THE great hearths are banked for the night. By their glow, he can see that a few of the stable lads have snuck into the kitchen to sleep near the warmth, lying on their thin blankets for a bit of cushion from the flagstones. His own hands ache from hours and hours at the forge, but work was work. Take it and thank the gods.

The wooden tables along the walls are laden with food: baskets of apples; loaves of soft white bread; other baskets filled with onions, carrots, turnips, parsnips; tubs of creamy yellow butter; crocks of buttermilk. There are barrels of freshly ground flour and barley and oats, waiting to be baked into fresh bread and cakes and rolls.

Quietly, he creeps through the kitchen to a corridor down which is a room lit by flickering candlelight. There, her dark head bent over her work, sits a woman who leans near the guttering candles, her nimble hands sewing tiny stitches in the yards and yards of heavy satin lying upon the table.

Startled at his entrance, she nearly knocks a candle over when she jumps.

"Christ Jesus, you scared me, Donall!"

He kneels before her, grinning. "I hope I do more than scare you." He leans in for a kiss.

She playfully slaps him away, but not before she returns the kiss. He lays a gentle hand on the swelling of her belly.

"You're working too hard."

She sighs. "Ah, well. 'Tis feast or famine when the family come to Ashford."

His expression darkens. "Speaking of famine, have you seen all the food in the kitchen? It's a sin, the way the English hoard while our people can't dig a bloody potato from the ground without it's black and rotten."

"Shhhh." She looks fearfully over his shoulder toward the corridor lest they be overheard, but all is still. "They bring us work. I'll have weeks ahead, trying to finish these gowns for the Yule ball."

He sits back on his heels. "And I only now finished shoeing the last of the horses for the hunt tomorrow. And there's more needs mending. Some of the wagon wheels. Saddles and bridles and harnesses. We'll be fine. But others won't, Móirín."

She presses her forehead to his. "I know. We can't take care of everyone, *mo grá*."

He takes her by the hand. "Come now. You need to rest. You and the wee one you carry."

She blows out the candles and allows him to help her to her feet. "We'll leave the children with your sister for the night. No sense in waking everyone to take them home and put them back to bed."

He wraps her cloak around her and guides her back through the kitchen, snatching a couple of rolls for the walk to their cottage.

NORA MADE THE MOST of her next couple of days at Ashford. She walked the extensive grounds and gardens of the castle, using her camera for better photos of the formal gardens and the walls and arches separating them. She got views of the castle from every angle and could see slight variations in the stone and the architecture of different wings that had been added over the centuries.

Rob, the uniformed guard at the gate to the castle bridge, waved as she came and went. She saw Craig a few times, ferrying guests in the castle's Land Rover, and waved to him as well. She took his advice and had a wonderful lunch at the Thatched Cottage.

She learned that it was a good idea to have an umbrella or rain jacket with her at all times. The showers came and went quickly, leaving a wet gleam on the ferns and flowering shrubs that lined the groomed walks, enhanced by the slanting sunlight that peeked through gaps in the clouds. She toured Lough Corrib, enjoying the boat captain's descriptions of all the little islands that dotted the lake.

She'd never walked so much in her life, but she loved it. She hiked the footpath along the river from the castle to the village, where she toured *The Quiet Man* museum and wandered the little shops, taking tons of photos to email back home.

She had her tea at the castle, pausing to snap a few more photos of the stone hounds flanking the entrance. Inside, she was unable to stop grinning as she sat in the midst of the rich paneling and opulent furnishings. She caught her rippled reflection in one of the glass cupboards, and her grin faded for a moment as her distorted face stared back at her.

She'd done it. "No-nonsense Nora", the serious, studious one who never went anywhere or did anything exciting, she'd managed something none of her sisters had done. She shifted her chair so that she didn't have to see herself and savored her tea.

By her last morning, though, she was itching to be in her own place. She enjoyed her last breakfast at the lodge where outside, a steady rain was pouring from leaden clouds.

"I'll be checking out today," she told Sarah, who was again working the desk.

"And moving into Sióg Cottage," Sarah said.

Nora stopped abruptly. "How did you know that?"

Sarah smiled. "Word gets round a small village. Especially when someone lets a haunted cottage."

"Haunted?" Nora choked off her laugh, remembering the face in the window.

"Sure not everyone believes that. 'Tis just the stories of unexplained lights and noises. You'll have to come back and tell us if you met the *sióg*, the fairy that lives there."

Nora went back to her room to pack. She'd looked up the meaning of "sióg" and knew that it meant "fairy" in Irish, but she'd assumed that was just a fanciful name to lure gullible tourists to rent the place.

"Don't be silly," she told herself, but a little shiver crept down her spine.

By the time she had showered and repacked her bags and backpack, the steady rain had turned to a downpour. She weighed her options as she wheeled her bags toward the lobby. She'd be soaked through trying to slog through this to the cottage. Maybe a taxi...

"Good morning, Miss McNeill."

28

She entered the lobby to find Craig standing there wearing a rain jacket, the Land Rover idling outside the door.

"We can't send you off to walk in this wet," Sarah said.

"Thank you so much." Nora let Craig take her bags. At the door, she paused and turned to Sarah. "I'll let you know how it goes with that fairy."

Sarah grinned. "You be sure to do that."

Craig drove carefully through the puddles. "Have you had a good time here at Ashford, then?"

"I really have," Nora said with a sigh, as the castle's turrets seemed to disappear into the heavy clouds.

Craig had to drive the long way around. He glanced at her quizzically. "What prompted you to rent this cottage, if you don't mind me asking."

"The owner is an old friend of my grandfather's. A Mr. McCarthy. He said the key would be in the door today. Seems kind of funny to leave the key in the door. Isn't he afraid someone might just let themselves in?"

Craig burst out laughing. "Not feck— Beg pardon. Not likely, Miss."

She frowned. "You don't believe the stories about the cottage being haunted, do you?"

He just shrugged. "We're Irish. We believe all kinds of things."

He turned down the wooded lane that led to the cottage. Wet tree branches scraped the windows. "Well, here we are. Sióg Cottage."

He retrieved her bags from the back of the Land Rover while she splashed through the rain to find the key right where Mr. McCarthy had said it would be. She turned it and pushed the door open. Craig brought her bags to her, but didn't set foot across the threshold.

"Here you go, Miss McNeill."

She tried to hand him a five-euro note, but he shook his head, his boyish face splitting into a grin.

"No money between friends. It's not good *craic*. Have a grand summer. We'll see you about, I'm sure."

He jogged to the vehicle and backed it around to face the lane, waving as he drove away.

Nora stood in the doorway, peering into the dark interior.

"Don't be ridiculous," she said sternly and, taking a deep breath, stepped inside.

She stood still, waiting... for what, she wondered. Everything was quiet. There was no repeat of the strange dizziness she'd felt the last time she was there. The sheets covering the furniture stirred a bit at her entrance. She moved her bags to a corner and shrugged off her backpack.

At the base of the stairs, she found a basket filled with clean folded sheets and towels.

She inspected the cozy cottage, chuckling at the little two-burner cooker and miniscule oven set into what looked like an old fireplace in the kitchen. Upstairs were two bedrooms and a bathroom—tub, no shower.

"Well, that'll be interesting."

But it was hers. Hers and hers alone. Perfect.

"You're leaving? Just like that. For the whole summer."

Amy's accusing words still rattled around in Nora's head, stirring up all kinds of guilt.

"I'm not the one who should be feeling guilty," she reminded herself, trying to shrug off the memory like an annoying fly.

She tied her hair back and gathered the sheets covering the furniture, sneezing at the dust she raised. She paused in the front bedroom, the one from whose window she'd seen the pale face. Nothing in the room seemed to have been disturbed.

"You were imagining things," she muttered, taking the sheets downstairs.

She was just opening the door when Sheila's SUV drew up and she got out.

"Thought you might need some help getting this place ready to live in," Sheila said. "Farmer McCarthy squeezes a coin so tight, he could

30

make Brian Boru's harp sing. I figured he wouldn't have hired out any cleaning to be done here."

"You figured right," Nora said.

"Well, then." Sheila rolled up her sleeves. "Let's get to work."

BRIANA SQUATTED IN THE stall with Princess, checking the foreleg yet again to make sure it was sound. She ran her hands over the tendons above the fetlock—still slightly warm. Groaning a little as she pushed up to stand, she retrieved a bag of ice from the tack room and wrapped it in place.

"You'll get a few more days off from hauling tourists around, my girl," she murmured.

Princess rumbled her thanks, resting her head on Briana's shoulder. Bri smiled, laying her cheek against the gentle mare's neck. They stood like that for a moment. She was one of Briana's favorites. She made the most beautiful babies, all just as sweet-tempered as their mother.

Briana reached into her pocket and pulled out a carrot. "Here you go."

"Ah, there you are." Quinn appeared in the stall doorway.

Briana gave Princess a pat and joined him.

"How is she?" Quinn gave the mare a scratch.

"Another couple days off, I think."

He nodded. "I told Jimmie as much." He eyed her. "Your leg giving you trouble?"

She shrugged and rubbed her thigh. "Doesn't like the rain."

"Well, we're in the wrong country, then. If it aches now, wait till you're old and gray. Can you keep an eye on things here? Sonya has a guided at three if the sodding rain stops, and I was going to check on the yearlings in the far pasture."

"Where are you off to?"

He slid a scrap of paper from his pocket. "Sheila asked me to pick up a few things for Nora. They've been cleaning old man McCarthy's cottage all afternoon."

Briana snorted. "Sure it's just like him to rent it out so someone else'll do all the cleaning for him."

Quinn nodded. "You're right there."

She frowned. "I could do that," she said, jutting her chin at his hand.

His sandy eyebrows rose. "You'd do this?"

She gave a half-shrug. "I was kind of rude to her the other day when she spooked Ginger."

He grinned and thrust the list into her hand. "I won't argue. Thanks."

"I may regret this," she grumbled, but he was laughing as he hurried away.

She whistled for Shannon, who came galloping from the indoor ring where she'd been playing chase with Dilly, the stable mutt. Together, they got into the SUV and headed to the market. The rain hadn't stopped completely, but had tapered off to a drizzle.

As she had no idea what the American might like above and beyond the things on Sheila's list, she stuck with those items.

A few minutes later, she returned to the car, where Shannon waited for her, sniffing eagerly at the bags.

"You stay out of the eggs," she said sternly.

The stout tail thumped against the door.

Briana knew exactly where the cottage was, but had only been by on horseback. She drove down the wooded lane to find Sheila's car still parked there. The cottage door was ajar. She parked and gathered the bags while Shannon trotted right in.

"What the—"

She heard Sheila's voice before she could get to the stoop.

"Look at my clean floor!" Sheila stood, her fists on her hips.

Briana saw a telltale trail of wet paw prints leading straight across the wooden floor boards to where Shannon now sat, grinning up at Sheila.

"Sorry," Briana said.

"Ah, well. You've brought food, so you're forgiven."

Shannon gave a low woof.

Sheila smiled and patted the giant head. "And so are you."

Nora came down the stairs, carrying a bucket and rag. "Oh, hi." She stumbled, her foot missing a step.

Briana's heart leapt, and she nearly dropped the bags to lunge forward and catch her, but Nora regained her balance.

"Bit of a klutz," Nora mumbled, her cheeks blushing scarlet.

"I'm beginning to see that," Briana said.

Nora had a streak of grime across her nose that, oddly, made her more appealing. So the blonde American princess wasn't afraid to get dirty.

Briana hoisted her bags. "Quinn was busy, so I got drafted."

Nora's cheeks pinked up again, and Briana mentally kicked herself as she realized what that sounded like. "Actually, I volunteered. Sorry about our first encounter."

Nora's face immediately broke into a smile. "Thanks for this." She swung her bucket toward the bags.

"Well, I'm starving," Sheila said, leading the way into the kitchen.

She and Nora washed up while Briana laid out bread and meat for sandwiches, along with a bag of crisps. Nora put the rest of the groceries away, and Sheila plugged the kettle in for tea.

Nora glanced at the receipt and went to her backpack, still sitting in the corner. She returned to the kitchen holding out some bills.

"Any sign of the ghost yet?" Briana asked, pocketing the money.

Nora shook her head. "Not a peep so far, but we've been making so much noise, maybe we just missed it."

She found a cupboard with some chipped dishes and quickly washed three plates. A couple of minutes later, Sheila plopped three mugs of tea on the table.

"Ghost or no, let's eat."

By THE TIME THE sun was setting, Nora was exhausted. She filled the tub with warm water—the water heater didn't rise to the level of truly hot water—trying to remember how long it had been since she'd taken a bath.

She yawned. It had been a good day. She smiled, picturing Briana grudgingly admitting she'd volunteered to go to the market. Nora was glad she hadn't argued about being repaid. Craig not taking a tip was one thing, but if she couldn't repay someone for a trip to the store, things could get awkward very quickly. She needed to remember to ask Sheila the rules about money and what the heck *craic* was.

She changed into her pj's and brushed her teeth before crawling between the clean sheets on the bed. She'd chosen the front room, telling herself no fabled ghost was going to dictate where she slept while she was here.

As she closed her eyes, she whispered, "If you're here, just stay quiet."

Almost immediately, she drifted off to sleep.

Chapter 3

NORA'S FIRST WEEK IN her cottage flew by, filled with more cleaning and rearranging of furniture. Old Farmer McCarthy stopped by a couple of times, first to collect June's rent, then again, a few mornings later with his wife, who brought Nora a loaf of soda bread and a small crock of their own butter.

"Thank you so much," Nora said. "Would you like to come in?"

Mrs. McCarthy's eyes widened. "You'll never find me setting foot in that cottage." She quickly made the sign of the cross.

Farmer McCarthy rolled his eyes. With his short, stocky frame and his weathered face, he reminded Nora of a leprechaun. He pushed his ragged tweed hat back on his head. "How's Tommy?"

She grinned. "He's good. He and my grandmother send their love."

He laughed, relighting his pipe. "The shenanigans we got into as boys. Give them our best."

"I will."

They got back into their old truck. She waved them off as it rumbled away and carried the bread and butter into the kitchen.

All her work was done. The little cottage was as she liked it. No one else coming into her space to tell her things weren't set up efficiently, or that this would be better off there, or that those pillows didn't go with that chair, or...

She laughed at herself. "Let it go, Elsa."

Outside, the sun shone and birds were noisily flitting about. She put on her walking shoes and set out for Sheila and Quinn's place.

It was a glorious morning, clean and bright. She strode along, remembering to keep an ear tuned for hoof beats.

She found Sheila working in the greenhouse, her cheeks rosy with the humid warmth under the glass panels. *Maybe that's the secret to her wonderful skin.*

"Good morning!" Sheila said.

Nora held up a bag. "Made you and Quinn some cookies, to thank you for all your help."

"There was no need to do that," Sheila said, tugging off her gardening gloves to reach into the bag and sample one.

"Well, I was hungry for some oatmeal cookies. This is the second batch," Nora said ruefully. "That little oven is going to take some getting used to, and the oatmeal here is different."

"Mmmm. Second batch was the charm. You'll be a hit around here, baking like this."

Nora glanced around. "What are you working on?"

"Transplanting those nasturtium. I thought I'd hired teenage help for the summer, but as she's not bothered to show up one blessed day this week, I'm guessing she's got better things to do."

"I could help you."

Sheila paused with a trowel full of dirt ready to dump into a new pot. "You're after spending your holiday working?"

Nora shrugged. "I'm after spending my holiday enjoying Ireland. I don't mind working some. You'll have to teach me, though. I gardened some with Mamma, but I'm sure different things grow here."

Sheila held out a spare pair of gardening gloves. "You're hired, and I'll admit I'm happy to have someone old enough to have a work ethic. How old are you by the way, if you don't mind my asking?"

"I don't mind. I'll be thirty-five this September."

"Just behind us. Quinn and I are thirty-six."

She put Nora to work repotting the little plants, using rich compost mixed in with the dirt for the new pots.

"How long have you and Quinn been married?" Nora asked as she shoveled some of the mixture into several lined-up pots. She sniffed. "This smells a bit like..."

Sheila grinned. "Like shite? That'd be because it's mostly horse manure. A natural by-product of the stables. And twelve years. But we've known each other all our lives. We lost touch after school until I went to a party when I was attending uni in Galway, and one of his mates had dragged him to the same party. And that was that."

They worked in companionable silence for a while.

"How are things at the cottage?"

Nora smiled. "Just grand."

Sheila laughed, somehow sounding hearty and lovely all at the same time. Nora wondered how anyone could simultaneously look so practical and so beautiful. Sheila wore her familiar ball cap holding her thick black hair back, her trouser legs stuffed into her Wellies, but there was a grace to her movements that Nora was completely lacking.

I can't even shovel shit gracefully, Nora thought as some of the compost mix spilled over the sides of a pot.

"Mr. and Mrs. McCarthy stopped by this morning, brought me a loaf of bread and some butter."

"They're nice people. Salt of the earth types. Tight with a penny, but generous with their time."

Nora reached for a new pot and caught Sheila's sideways gaze trained on her. "What?"

"I'm being nosy, I suppose, but the day we met, you said there were things that had kept you from traveling that weren't a concern any longer. I'm wondering what those were?"

Nora felt the heat rise from her neck to her cheeks. "Well, I had an old cat. Twenty-two when she died. I couldn't leave her the last few years."

Sheila nodded, glancing at where Rusty lay stretched out in the sun on a warm flagstone. "I understand that. They're so good to us, we've got to be good back." She resumed digging. "Anything else?"

Nora refused to meet those piercing blue eyes and focused instead on spreading a layer of soil in the bottom of the pot. "There was someone. Now there's no one."

"Ah." Sheila's voice was sympathetic.

"No, don't get me wrong." Nora knocked a nasturtium loose from its shipping container to plop it into the new pot. "It was eleven years of weekends only. Thank God we both had the sense to know we didn't belong living together."

"She met someone else?"

Nora's head snapped up. Either it was a lucky guess or Sheila was much shrewder than Nora had expected. "Yes."

"I'm sorry."

"I'm not." Nora considered. "I guess I should be, shouldn't I? Eleven years of mediocre, of settling. That's the sad part. No more. I'm not settling for anything ever again. Even after Amy met what's-her-name, she expected me to be available any weekend she wasn't otherwise occupied."

"She did not!"

Nora nodded. "She did. And I did it. For a while. It's not like I had other plans or someone else I wanted to spend my weekends with. But once Willa—"

Her throat got too tight to speak for a moment. She cleared it. "Anyhow, once I didn't need to stay for my cat, I started making plans."

"Good for you, cousin."

Sheila carried the tray of newly planted nasturtium out to sit in the sunshine. "These'll be part of an edible display."

"You can eat these?"

"Oh, yes. Leaves and flowers. They're delicious in a salad. As I'll prove to you when we take a break for lunch."

They worked on, watering and tending the plants and shrubs Sheila had sitting outside. Nora closed her eyes, breathing in the scent of an Irish summer day. A few customers came by. Sheila left her to go tend to them. Rusty roused himself to waddle over and say hello, lapping a bit of water from her hose. His stub of a tail wagged as she scratched his back.

"Time for some lunch," Sheila said when the customers left.

In the cheerful kitchen, she pulled the leftovers of a roasted chicken out of the refrigerator. "You make us a couple of sandwiches out of this chicken while I put together a salad."

"If I can be nosy in return," Nora began hesitantly as she sliced chicken. "The other night, in the pub, that baby...?"

Sheila's shoulders tensed at the sink where she was washing lettuce and nasturtium and other things for their salads. "You noticed that?"

"Well, yeah. I'm sorry. It's really none of my business. If you don't want to talk about it..."

She reached for a tomato and began slicing it.

"No." Sheila's shoulders dropped as she took a breath. With her back still to Nora, she said, "Quinn and I had a baby. Five years ago. She was born with a heart defect that they couldn't repair. She lived three days."

Nora stood, stricken, kicking herself for being so insensitive. She remembered her grandmother telling her mother about it but, never having met any of this side of the family, she hadn't made the connection to Sheila. "I'm so sorry."

"Thank you." Sheila blotted the wet produce on a towel and put it in two bowls. "There have been three miscarriages since. All the same heart problem."

Nora didn't know what to say.

"Most of the time, we're fine," Sheila said, looking at Nora for the first time. "But now and again..."

"I didn't mean to pry."

"You're family," Sheila said, pulling out a chair and sitting. "It's not prying as we get to know each other. The good and the bad."

Nora was glad to have something to occupy her mouth so she wouldn't ask any more stupid questions.

"This is delicious," she said a few minutes later. "Can't believe I'm eating flowers."

Sheila smiled. "You've worked up an appetite being outdoors." She touched a finger to Nora's cheek. "Too many years in a library."

"You're right. I'm after fixing that now."

She eyed the wall of bookshelves in the room beyond. "Speaking of library, may I borrow some of your books? I have a few hundred on my iPad, but I didn't pack many physical books."

"Of course you can. Anything you like."

Nora munched on her sandwich. "How many days will you need me here?"

"How many days do you want to spend working?"

Nora considered. "How about three days a week? That will give me something to do and still have enough free time to spend wandering and exploring."

Sheila nodded. "That's generous of you. I'll be grateful for the three days. I don't know that I'll be able to pay you the regular way, as you're not here on a work visa. But I'm sure I can slip you some cash and then make up the difference by buying your groceries and paying your rent."

"I can't let you do that," Nora protested. "I brought enough euros to get me through the first part of my summer, and I've got my credit card for the ATM."

"And I can't let you work for free," Sheila insisted. "We'll take it out in trade. You'll let me know if it feels like more than you want to do."

"I will. But it won't." With a happy sigh, Nora dug into her salad.

STRIPPED DOWN TO A T-shirt and jeans, Briana sang softly while she scrubbed a saddle with saddle soap. Working the thick lather into the leather, she cleaned away layers of sweat and oils. After wringing out a clean sponge in a different bucket of water, she rubbed the soap off the leather, leaving it to dry a bit. While it did, she returned to another saddle she'd already cleaned to massage in a coat of oil. The stable saddles got lots of wear, with no time usually to clean them between guided rides, so every now and then, on a slow day, they took advantage of the opportunity to tackle these chores.

"Hey, squint."

She scowled and turned to the tackroom door, brandishing her oily rag. "What do you want, Jimmie?"

Despite the teasing, his pale face wore a serious expression. "Butler has a bit of a stable cough. The vet wants him on an antibiotic for a week. I couldn't get him to take his medicine. Could you give it a shot when you've a minute?"

Briana immediately draped her rag over the saddle and washed her hands. She went to the big bay gelding's stall where he stood, looking disconsolate. His head was down, and he had a slight wheeze. She laid her hands on his ribs, feeling the rattle.

"What's the matter, big guy?" she crooned, smoothing her hands over his neck and combing her fingers through his black mane.

He nickered pitifully and gave an asthmatic cough. Jimmie handed her the medicine ball of antibiotic crushed with some molasses and rolled with some oats.

"Come on," she said, picking Butler's head up. She pried open the corner of his mouth enough to scrape a bit of the oats and molasses on his teeth. Immediately, his tongue started working to lick the sweet mixture off. "Here you go." She got him to eat the rest of the sticky mass.

She gave his face a kiss. "You'll feel better soon."

"They always take their medicine for you, Bri," Jimmie said, closing the stall door behind her as she exited.

"Do you want me to take him to the private stables later? Quinn said he was going to need Stubbs for a lesson this afternoon, so I'm already going that way."

"I think it'd be best." Jimmie paused to pat another head nosing him over the next stall door. He consulted his ever-present clipboard to check the roster of reservations. "We've plenty of horses here for the rides we've got scheduled for the next couple of days."

"I'll do it when I'm done with the tack."

"Leave it," Jimmie said. "I'll get Sonya to take over here."

"Get Sonya to take over what?" Sonya asked, coming in with an empty wheelbarrow from the day's mucking.

The tall Swede wheeled the barrow into the equipment room and stood it on end.

"Quinn needs Stubbs, and Butler has a stable cough," Briana said. "I've just a couple more saddles to finish."

"I don't mind."

"Thanks, Sonya." Jimmie's head was already bent over his clipboard as he walked away. "Call it a day when you get him settled, Bri. You were here at dawn. We'll finish what needs doing here."

"Okay." Briana reached for a lead rope and halter.

"We'll see you tomorrow, squint."

She went on down the aisle to another stall and led out a fat Connemara pony. He stood placidly while she brushed and saddled him. When he was tacked up, she slipped the halter onto Butler and led both horses outside to mount Stubbs. Shannon appeared from wherever she'd been napping.

Briana kept the pace slow so as not to get the bay gelding winded. Stubbs didn't complain, as he preferred to plod along, taking every opportunity he could to snatch a flower here or a mouthful of grass there. Shannon loped alongside, jumping at a rabbit every now and again.

Briana enjoyed the quiet, only the birds and squirrels and the occasional fox keeping her and the horses company. She often wondered if there was something lacking in her, something that drove others away to bigger places like Galway or Dublin or even America.

It was true that she was now thirty-three and didn't own a bloody thing beyond her car and dog. Her house belonged to Quinn, as did her horses. But everything she wanted and needed was right here—work she loved with people she considered a second family, enough pay to get by, a village and countryside that were her very heartbeat.

She said hello to the people out and about in the gardens she passed. One woman was putting a bicycle out for sale, an old-fashioned one with panniers behind the saddle and a rattan basket attached to the handlebars.

"Fancy switching from hooves to wheels, Briana?" the woman asked as Briana and the horses ambled by.

"Not on your life, Tessa. I like my saddles wider than my bum."

"Well, that doesn't take much as your bum's the size of my ten-year-old's." Tessa's laugh followed her for quite a while.

A thought occurred. Briana reined Stubbs to a halt and twisted in the saddle.

"Hey, Tessa! How much for that bike?"

Stubbs took advantage of the pause to snatch another mouthful of lush grass from the roadside.

"A bargain at fifteen euro!" Tessa hollered back.

When Briana arrived at the other stables, Shannon plopped down in some shade to tussle with Dilly, the two of them play-growling as the smaller dog crawled all over her.

She found Quinn in the office. "I unsaddled Stubbs and turned him out in the little paddock. I'm going to settle Butler in the box stall if you don't need it. He's feeling poorly."

Quinn didn't glance up from his computer, where he was pecking at the keyboard with his two forefingers. "That's fine."

She knew he hadn't heard a word she'd said, so she just shook her head and took Butler to the empty box stall. She spread some fresh straw and filled his water bucket, leaving a measure of oats in the feed bin for him.

"There you go," she said, giving him a pat.

He snorted and closed his eyes.

She left him and went back to the food bin to grab a few carrots before walking down the aisle, stopping to visit with the horses who poked their heads over their doors to say hello. She gave each of them a chunk of carrot.

At Princess's stall, she went in to check her foreleg. "I think you're all set to go." Princess nuzzled the back of Briana's T-shirt, plucking at it with her lips, careful not to nip. Briana stood and cradled the gentle face in her hands, her heart melting at the look in the soft, brown eyes. "Maybe another day or two's rest for you."

Princess snorted her agreement with that plan, nudging Briana in the chest. Bri obliged by pulling one more carrot from her back pocket. She snapped it in two, giving Princess half.

"I think some sunshine'll do you good."

She led Princess out of her stall and down the aisle, turning her loose in the same paddock as Stubbs.

Back inside the barn, she went to the last stall. The outside door at the far side of the stall was open and a gray head was visible, cautious eyes watching her from that enclosure.

"Do you like carrots?" Briana held the carrot in her hand.

The mare stamped her foot and tossed her head with her ears back, but refused to come any nearer.

Briana dropped the carrot into the feed bin and went back to Quinn's office. He was done with whatever he'd been doing on the computer.

"Butler is in the box stall," she said. "Needs a few days of medicine. Princess is sound but is asking for another couple of days off. She's grazing with Stubbs."

Quinn grinned. "She deserves a rest."

He was as soft on the horses as she was. She couldn't have worked for him otherwise.

"I'm heading out then, if you don't need me for anything else today."

"I don't, no."

She turned to go and then paused. "Sheila's cousin, Nora. Is she planning on getting herself a car this summer?"

Quinn laughed. "She says no. Afraid to drive on our side of the road. Why?"

"Tessa O'Rourke has a bike for sale. Might be something for her instead of walking everywhere."

"I'll mention it, thanks."

"See you tomorrow."

She got in her SUV, whistling for Shannon. With the couple hours of daylight left, she had her own errands to run.

"WHY ARE YOU DOING this, Móirín? We should be taking care of our own."

Móirín swings her cloak about her, fastening it under her chin. "Niamh, Ashford gave us permission to take what we needed to feed our families. We've been blessed with more than enough. The food in the larder won't keep forever. How can we not help those we can?" She hands baskets to Callum and Rowan. Four-year-old Una cries to go along.

"No, my love." Móirín bends awkwardly to kiss her. "You stay with your Auntie Niamh. We'll be back soon."

The babies, Séan and Teafa, play with the dolls Móirín made of leftover bits of material from the ball gowns that will most likely be left behind in wardrobes at the castle when the family goes back to England after Yule. Worn once. She tries not to think of the waste. It makes her heart hurt.

Just as her heart hurts knowing there is no shortage of food in Ireland, only for the Irish.

Niamh, her own baby on her hip, takes Una's hand to prevent her following. Despite Móirín's words, she stares resentfully at the baskets.

The air is bitterly cold when they set out. Rowan takes her mother's hand, her basket swinging from the other. Callum, too old now at seven to hold his ma's hand, strides alongside, a proper little man.

"Who are we going to, Mam?" Rowan asks, the cold air making her cheeks rosy.

"The Gallaghers and the Foyles," Móirín says, huffing a little. "I hear they've had a hard time of it."

The children chatter as they walk, anticipating Yule in a few weeks. The Gallagher cottage stands alongside fallow fields, fields that should have produced enough potatoes to keep the family fed. Matthew Gallagher is walking across the field, a basket strapped to his shoulders, filled with wood from the scant trees remaining. He waves his axe.

"We've brought a few things," Móirín says, noting the way his coat hangs more loosely when he shrugs off the basket to set it down.

"Come in," he says. "Mary had the baby just last week. She'll be happy to see you."

He carries an armful of sticks inside to feed the small fire burning in the hearth. Mary Gallagher is sitting on the bed, trying to nurse the baby, who is crying weakly. Two other children are huddled near her, their faces gaunt, their eyes big.

"Callum, Rowan, why don't you butter a bit of bread for the children?" Móirín herself uncorks a crock of stew, dishing out a small bowlful. "Just a small portion to start."

She sits on the bed next to Mary. "This probably isn't warm any longer, but here. You eat."

"I can't," Mary says, her gaze shifting to the children who have moved to the table where Rowan and Callum are reaching into their baskets to produce two loaves of bread and a crock of butter. Matthew's expression has darkened as he watches.

"You must," Móirín says in a low voice. "If you have nothing inside, you can't feed this one."

She takes the baby, too light, too thin. Mary spoons up the stew, a little at a time, and Móirín recognizes the signs of a stomach already too shrunk to take much in. She herself undoes the buttons of her dress and tucks the baby to a breast swollen with milk for the one she carries. The baby nuzzles and feeds, his eyes locked on hers, and she knows this one meal will not keep him alive. Her heart breaks as she strokes his soft cheek and downy hair. His eyes gradually close and his suckle slows. When he is asleep, she sets him on the bed and buttons her dress again.

Mary has finished, too, leaving more than half the stew in the bowl.

"You'll have more later," Móirín says. "Lie down now. Sleep with your baby."

Matthew walks them out. "Thank you." He can't meet Móirín's eyes as he says it.

"Matthew," she says, laying a hand on his arm. "Mary and the baby... She needs to eat to be able to feed him. Is there nowhere you can go? Family in Galway or Belfast?"

"Do you think they're better able to provide for my family than I can?"

She glances back inside. "I could take the baby, feed him—"

"We'll be fine," he says. "It was two bad crops, but it can't last. We'll be in fine shape when the spring comes and the fields are planted anew. God bless."

He steps back into the cottage and closes the door.

"Come, Ma."

Callum takes Móirín by the hand. He and Rowan lead her away. After what feels like a long walk, they reach a stretch of one-room tenant cottages, little more than hovels. It's too cold for the children to be outside playing, but even for that, it's too still, too quiet.

"No smoke, Ma," Callum says, eyeing the crumbling stone chimney of the last cottage in the row.

Móirín has seen it, as well. Her heart beats faster in fear as they approach. No one answers a knock. Callum hands his basket to Rowan and pushes hard to open the door. Móirín grips Rowan's shoulder.

"Stay outside a moment."

She steps into the dark cottage, clapping a hand to her mouth to cover a scream. Five children, one not yet old enough to walk, lie lifeless on a bed next to their mother's corpse. The cold, thankfully, has kept the bodies.

She crosses herself and turns to find Rowan and Callum standing behind her, their eyes wide. As much as she hates for them to see death, it's important they know.

"We're too late. They're beyond the cares of this world now."

The children join her as they pray the *Pater Noster*.

"Where's their Da?" Rowan asks as they tug the door shut, tying a rag to the door handle as a warning, and turn for home.

"I don't know. He might have left to find work." Móirín hopes that was the case, and not that he'd simply left the poor souls behind to fend for themselves.

"When we get back, we'll tell your Da. He'll come with some men and give them a proper burial."

There is no chatter now. They walk in silence. Móirín wishes she could spare them, keep them innocent. She shivers with a premonition that none of them will be spared.

NORA SAT AT HER little table in the kitchen, the front and back doors both thrown open, letting a nice morning breeze blow through. She'd fried a couple of eggs to eat with the last of Mrs. McCarthy's soda bread. Propped on the sugar bowl was one of Sheila's books on gardening basics.

"You'll learn more by doing than reading," Sheila had said when Nora borrowed it, but Nora had just laughed and said, "Librarian. Gotta do my research."

Her washing flapped gently on the clothesline strung outside the back door. The cottage had a washer, but no dryer.

When she was done eating, she marked her page and quickly washed her dishes. The only thing she was really missing so far was a coffee maker. The cottage only had a kettle. Tea was all right, but she was craving coffee.

She went to the living room where she had left a half-written letter she'd started the evening before. With no internet since she left Ashford, she was writing her grandparents to let them know she'd moved into the cottage and gotten settled. She'd need to find internet access soon to take care of some banking and bills back home, but it was kind of nice, communicating this way. She sat back down at the table serving as her desk to finish the letter, filling them in on the last few days, including the visit and greetings from Mr. and Mrs. McCarthy.

She was telling them about her semi-employment with Sheila when she heard a thump from upstairs. She sat for a moment, her heart pounding. The upstairs windows were all open, and she wondered if an animal had gotten in. A cat maybe. Or a raccoon. Did they have raccoons in Ireland?

I need to borrow a book on Ireland's fauna.

She got up and found a broom in the kitchen. As quietly as she could, she crept up the stairs, clutching her weapon. Nothing looked out of place in the wide hall—the table and lamp there were undisturbed. She moved on to her bedroom and, at first, everything there looked normal as well. But then, she saw that her pillow was lying on the floor. She'd made the bed when she got up, fluffing the pillows and placing them neatly. There was no sign of any animal. She crossed to the bed to lift the pillow back into its place, and she smelled it—a hint of something like lilac.

Immediately, the scent triggered a memory, a dream she'd had—a woman, searching and searching for... she wasn't sure what. Only the sadness and despair that she couldn't find whatever it was... Nora closed her eyes.

As quickly as the memory had come, it vanished, like smoke. So had the scent of lilac. Nora dropped to the bed, shaken.

"That was weird."

Outside, a horn sounded with a couple of quick beeps.

"Anyone up?" called a voice.

She ran downstairs to find Quinn and Sheila getting out of a pickup truck.

"Good morning," said Sheila. "We didn't wake you, did we?"

"I've been up for ages," Nora said. "What brings you here? Want some tea?"

"No, we can't stay." Quinn reached into the bed of the truck. "We just wanted to bring this by."

He set a bicycle on the ground.

"What's this for?" Nora asked.

"For you." Sheila said, holding out a helmet. "Briana found it."

"Briana did?"

"We figured you can't walk everywhere all summer. We'll still take you by the market and such when you need to, but this'll make you more mobile on other days."

"It's beautiful." Nora ran her hands over the leather saddle and the woven basket. "Just like the bike I had when I was a kid."

Quinn held up a finger. "You still have to remember to ride on our side of the road, mind you. Cars and lorries will give you the right of way here, but only if you obey the traffic rules."

"I can't let you do this," Nora said.

"Consider it part of your pay," Sheila said. "Like I said, we can't pay you what we should without a work visa, so we'll find other ways. No excuses for being late tomorrow."

Nora laughed. "No excuse. I'll be there, eight o'clock sharp."

"Come early if you want some breakfast."

"I would kill for some coffee."

Sheila nodded. "Coffee 'tis then. See you at half-seven."

"Thank you," Nora said, impulsively embracing Sheila.

"You're welcome," Sheila said with a pat on the back.

Nora grabbed Quinn before he could wiggle away and gave him a hug, too.

They got back into the truck. She waved them off and propped the bike against the cottage.

She hurriedly finished her letter and sealed it in an envelope. She folded her rain jacket into her backpack along with her wallet, then closed up the cottage and went out to try her new wheels.

She decided to stray off the paved roads and try some of the wooded trails that, according to her calculations, should take her in the direction of the village. A deep hush lay over the woods. She rode through the cool, damp air, sunlight filtering through the leaves overhead. It wasn't just that the trees in this forest were enormous; their branches stuck out at odd angles, as if they were the arms of giants, frozen and turned into trees by some ancient magic.

Don't be ridiculous. Why do you have to turn everything into some kind of fairy tale?

That voice in her head was so real that she stopped the bike. There was no one here to say those things to her, no one to chastise her for being fanciful, "or childish," she knew Amy would have said. The funny thing was, she felt like a child—in a good way. No wheels but a bike. An allowance of sorts from her savings and the bit of under-the-table cash Sheila would be passing her way. A haunted cottage in a magical forest that was more than capable of firing up her imagination. But she'd learned long ago to keep her imagination under wraps, out of the sight of others. It was only in her own head that she let it run loose. But here, there were no such constraints, no one to tell her she was silly and so, no need to be the studious, dull Nora everyone back home knew. It was kind of like being reborn. She laughed and resumed pedaling.

This time, when the huge wolfhound appeared in the trail just ahead, she was prepared. She braked to a halt and saw Briana on the same reddish horse she'd been riding at their first encounter. At least she thought it was the same one.

"Hi," she said brightly.

"Good morning, yourself," said Briana. She nodded. "Nice bike."

"It really is," Nora said. "Sheila and Quinn said you were the one who told them about it. Thank you."

Briana eyed her for a moment. "You're welcome."

"Can I ride along with you?"

Briana laid a hand on the horse's neck. "It'd be good practice for her. Would you mind walking the bike at first? You'll look like some frightful monster to her if you're riding."

She nudged the horse nearer so she could sniff the strange contraption. Shannon came over to say hello, her tongue lolling as Nora gave her broad back a thump.

Nora obliged by pushing the bicycle while Briana and the horse walked alongside. Shannon ranged ahead of them.

"She's pretty," Nora said, admiring the horse.

"She is, and knows it." Briana chuckled. "Ginger's only three, so she gets a little leeway yet for acting a fool when she sees strange things, but if we're to use her at the stables, she'll need to calm down some."

They walked on for a bit, and then Briana said, "Get on the bike now, if you don't mind. We'll trot along with you and see how she goes."

Nora mounted the bike. Ginger shied away at first, but Nora kept pedaling. Briana got the filly under control, trotting up alongside.

"Do you ride?" Briana asked, bobbing up and down in the saddle in rhythm with the horse's gait.

"I always wanted a horse, but I haven't ridden since I was a kid."

"Well, if you've a mind to give it another go, just come by the stables and we'll set you up."

Nora glanced over. "Thanks." She pointed to a fork in the path. "Is this the way to the village?"

"It is." Briana pulled Ginger up. "Stay on it till it ends, then turn right and watch for the bridge across the river at The Monk's Fishing House."

"I keep meaning to ask someone... the river. It disappears in places. I thought I got lost one day when I realized the trail wasn't next to the water anymore."

"The river is really the outflow of Lough Mask to the north." Briana pointed in that direction. "This entire area is limestone, riddled with caverns and underground streams. The river runs underground for parts of its course to Lough Corrib. Just stay on the path and sooner or later, you'll come to either the village or the river."

Nora steered the bike onto the other trail. "See you soon," she called over her shoulder.

Briana waved, and then she and the horse and dog were out of sight.

Nora rode on, grinning to herself. She had a way of getting around, a kind-of job, and, maybe, a new friend.

Chapter 4

AS PROMISED, SHEILA HAD coffee brewed and waiting when Nora arrived the next morning at seven-thirty sharp.

"Oh, thank you," Nora said as she cradled the mug and inhaled the scent. "I've missed this."

"Tea doesn't do it for you?" Sheila chuckled. "I have to admit, coffee has become my go-to drink of a morning."

"I got a cup yesterday in the village, but this is so much better." Nora took a sip. "I mailed a letter to Mamma and Pop."

"Do you not have email or text on your mobile?" Sheila placed a couple of scones on a plate and set them on the table.

"No internet at the cottage, and I didn't think an international plan was worth the money. I figure I'll find a café with internet when I need it."

Sheila sat with her own coffee. "I hadn't thought of that. Feel free to use ours."

"Really?"

"Sure. It's here. Not like you're going to use it all up. I can barely get Quinn to get on the bloody computer to take care of our orders." Nora quickly swallowed her coffee. "You do online orders?"

Sheila nodded. "Thought it might be a way to spread the word. Not so much for shipping the plants, obviously. But the candles and soaps and lotions and such. We get a fair amount of business, but with my having to tend the greenhouse and the shop, and him busy at the stables all day, we don't put enough time and energy into the website side of things."

"I can help you with that, too," Nora said.

Sheila grasped her hand. "I'd be forever grateful. You're like a gift from heaven."

"You'd be the first to ever say that." Nora covered her embarrassment with a laugh.

"I doubt it. From the way your Mamma speaks of you to my Gran, you can do anything but brain surgery, and maybe even that if you studied it in one of your books."

Nora grinned. "I'll take a look at your site later." She bit into a scone and moaned. "Forget the gardening. You should open a bakery!"

When they were done with breakfast, they headed outside to tend the tree nursery.

"We've over ten acres of trees and saplings to sell here. Let's see, I can't get used to the new system, that'd be about four hectares," Sheila explained. She pointed to a large stand of enormous, mature woods in the distance. "And over there, another fifteen acres of old-growth trees, mostly oak and beech. We let the saplings grow naturally there and harvest some of them to transplant here with the ornamental trees. Most will be leafed out now, some still in flower." She handed Nora a pair of gloves and a pruner. "Just wander down the rows, prune away any dead branches that show no sign of life."

She demonstrated the proper technique, and left Nora to it while she went to tend plants in the pergola area near the shop where she could keep an eye out for customers.

Nora made her way along the rows of trees. As she worked, she read and studied the labels tied to each sapling, trying to memorize their English and Latin names, their sunlight and watering requirements, their leaf and bark patterns. Her head was soon swimming. There was so much to learn.

The sun was gentle, but she quickly realized even here, she was going to need sun protection. Her fair complexion always burned rather than tanned. A gentle breeze stirred the leaves of the aspen sapling she was pruning, and it came to her. That scent. The same as she'd experienced in the bedroom.

Sniffing like a dog, she followed the scent upwind to a tree that was full of clusters of white blossoms. She brought one of the branches to her nose. It was like lilac, but subtly different. She snipped one branch with leaves and a cluster of flowers. Tucking it in her pocket, she continued working.

So intent was she on her work, she lost track of time until she heard Sheila calling to her. She glanced at her watch, surprised to see that it was past one o'clock.

She jogged back through the orchard toward the shop, not able to catch herself in time when she tripped on a tree root.

"What happened to you?" Sheila asked when Nora entered the kitchen, grass stains on her knees.

"Tripped."

Sheila shook her head. "You do that a lot?"

"Yeah, actually. I do. Mamma always said I was like a knobby-kneed foal, except I never grew out of it."

Sheila chuckled. "You must be starving."

"I am," Nora said, rubbing her stomach. "I hadn't realized until you called."

She took off her gloves and washed her hands at the kitchen sink.

"What's this?" Sheila plucked the white flowered snippet from her back pocket.

"Oh, I wanted to ask about this. The label said it's called bird cherry."
Sheila set the branch down and opened the fridge to pull out a ham and some stone ground mustard. "Slice that bread, will you?"

Nora sliced a fresh loaf of wheat bread. "Bird cherry?" she prompted.

"*Prunus padus.* In Yorkshire, they call it wild lilac. The bark peels and smells something awful. They used to tie the bark on doors to ward off the plague. More likely, the stink warded off anyone who might be carrying the plague. Why?"

Nora hesitated. "I smelled this. The lilac part, not the bark. In the cottage yesterday. When the pillow from my bed somehow threw itself onto the floor."

Sheila paused in the middle of cutting thick slices of ham for their sandwiches. "Say again?"

"It was just before you and Quinn came by with the bike. I heard a noise. When I went upstairs, my pillow was on the floor, and I smelled this." She pointed to the white flowers. "And..."

"And what?"

Nora flushed. "You'll think I'm crazy, but when I caught that scent, it triggered a memory of... a dream, I think. All I can remember is a woman, and such horrible sadness as she searched for something."

She gave an embarrassed laugh. "Told you it sounds crazy."

"Do I look like I don't believe you?"

Sheila scooted out a chair and sat. Nora joined her and began slathering her bread with mustard.

"Ireland is a strange country, I think." Sheila frowned as she placed pieces of ham on her bread. "We've known such tragedy—wars, famine, poverty, millions of family leaving us. Sometimes I wonder how it is we keep singing and laughing and telling stories, but then I think, if we didn't, we'd have just curled up and died off completely."

She glanced thoughtfully at Nora. "I've never seen a ghost, not to have a conversation with, but I don't think an island that's known so much sadness could not have them. Of course, Quinn would say I'm just fanciful."

Nora paused at Sheila's use of that word. She finished building her sandwich and took a bite. "Mmmm." She swallowed. "This is delicious, by the way. Quinn doesn't believe in things like ghosts?"

Sheila snorted. "Like most men, he believes in what's right in front of his eyes. If he can't touch it or see it, it doesn't exist."

"I never thought about it at all before now," Nora said. "What about Briana?"

Sheila stopped with her sandwich halfway to her mouth. "What about her?"

"I don't know, exactly." Nora pursed her lips as she thought. "From what I've seen, she's all gruff with people, but then I watch her with the horses and her dog, and she's different. Softer and gentler. And then she thought of me and mentioned the bike to you—thanks again, by the way—and I'm just like, what the hell? Sorry."

"No need to apologize." Sheila waved her sandwich. "Briana is a puzzle. As good a soul as they make, but she's had her hardships."

"What kind of hardships?"

Sheila shook her head with a cryptic smile. "A puzzle only means something if you put the pieces together yourself."

BRIANA MOPPED THE SWEAT out of her eyes with her shirtsleeve and shifted her ladder to allow her to reach a fresh window in need of cleaning. From inside, the telephone trilled for the third time. It was probably her sister again. If she didn't answer, Cara would only continue to call, leaving five messages a day.

Briana stomped into the house, stepping over Shannon who was stretched out on her side on the front stoop, and picked up.

"It's about bloody time."

"Hello to you, Cara."

Briana went to her little fridge and got out a bottle of Coke. Snugging the phone against her shoulder, she twisted the top off and took a deep drink.

"Why don't you get a mobile like a normal person?" Cara complained for the thousandth time.

"Because I've better things to do with my day than be chained to a sodding phone every minute," Briana answered for the thousandth time. Plus one. "What's up?"

"I'm calling to remind you that Kieran's birthday is next week. He'll be five, in case you've lost count since you haven't seen him in ages."

Briana closed her eyes. She had forgotten, but, "Of course, I remembered it's his birthday," she lied.

"Mum is having a party for him next Saturday. You will come?"

"Saturday... I don't—"

"Bri," Cara cut her off. "You haven't been home since Christmas. And then only for the day."

"This is my home, Cara. Just because the rest of you want to live in the middle of a million people, doesn't mean I do."

She could almost hear Cara smile. "You don't have to live here. You only have to come for a visit. Kieran will be heartbroken if his favorite auntie isn't here for his party."

Briana scowled. "That was a low blow."

Cara's laughed tinkled through the phone. "It was, wasn't it?"

"You do Mum proud, with the guilt, you know that?"

"If it works."

Briana closed her eyes and sighed. "It works. I'll be there."

"Good. Saturday week. Be here by eleven. And plan to spend the night."

Briana hung the phone up. Shannon lifted her head.

"Don't ever have sisters if you value your peace."

Shannon dropped her head back down with an exhausted groan that signified her agreement with that sentiment.

NORA WOKE TO A dark room. Everything was still, but...
"I know you're here."
She lay there, listening. There was no sound now, but there had been, in her dream. The same dream she'd had nearly every night. A woman's sobbing, a feeling of horrible loss, a voice calling... something she couldn't quite make out. Over and over the same word, but though she strained to catch it, it was always just beyond her ability to understand.

She sat up, rubbing her face, and swung her legs over the side of the bed. At the window, she gazed out at a clear sky filled with stars. Looking back at her rumpled bed, she knew she was done with sleep for now.

She went downstairs to where she had rearranged the furniture to set her desk adjacent to the window. She flipped on the lamp, squinting until her eyes adjusted. She reached for her pen and opened the notebook she'd started to use for her novel. She fumbled for several minutes, writing a few lines that she scratched out impatiently. She tried again, working from a sketchy outline. She wrote for a few more minutes, scowling as she read what she'd written, and then slid a different blank book near, the one in which she'd started writing a journal. She'd been recording a brief summary of every day she'd spent in Cong thus far. She smiled sheepishly as her pen hovered over the page, picturing herself as an old woman, reading back over this. She wanted to be able to remember everything—even these dreams.

And as she recalled this most recent dream, the words began to flow. Her pen flew over the pages, barely able to keep up with her thoughts as she recorded the scents and sounds and images in her mind. At some point, it seemed her lamplight had dimmed, and she looked up to see that dawn had started to break. She sat back, yawning. She debated making breakfast and moving on with her day, but it was a day off from working with Sheila at the nursery.

If she were home, Amy would have been planning their entire day—flea markets, a hike on the Appalachian Trail, going into DC for the day—anything but sitting around the house doing nothing.

"I can do whatever I want," Nora reminded herself.

Smiling at that, she clicked the lamp off and went back up to bed.

BRIANA STOOD IN A paddock with one of the yearlings. She had a bucket of oats and some apple slices as he crowded her, eager for the treats.

"No pushing, Tim," she said, nudging him away. "You get these when you show some manners."

She slipped a halter on and off his head, pleased when he ignored it completely as his nostrils quivered toward the apple. She rewarded him with a slice and then moved her hands, running them over his withers and down his shoulders to his forefeet. He allowed her to pick up his hoof and hold it between her knees. She gave him a handful of oats for that and moved on to his hindquarters. The colt was a little more skittish about having his hind legs handled, and she had to work patiently, talking to him, keeping her voice and hands calm.

She clipped a lead rope to the halter and led him around the paddock. He jumped, trying to yank the rope from her hands when a boisterous group of four German tourists trotted up, enthusiastically talking after a guided ride with Liam.

She calmed him, saying, "That's why you're here, to get used to the noises and the sights. Nothing's going to hurt you."

Enticed by another slice of apple, he followed her again around the enclosure.

Over near the barn, she heard Jimmie's voice with another that sounded familiar. She walked to the fence and saw Nora McNeill talking to him. The colt pushed her, nosing her pockets for more apple.

She gave him a last slice and took his halter off. "Good boy." Hanging the halter and rope on the paddock fence, she wandered to the barn in time to hear Jimmie say, "Sure we can fix you up today. Sonya's somewhere about."

"Fix her up with what?"

Jimmie and Nora both whirled around.

"Hello," Nora said with a smile.

"Nora's after taking a ride this afternoon," Jimmie said, consulting a chalkboard on the wall. "Sonya's free until a group at two, so—"

"I can take her."

Jimmie turned, his mouth hanging open.

"Close your mouth," Briana said. "You're gonna catch flies."

He closed his mouth. "You. You're willing to do a guided?"

"Well, it wouldn't really be a guided now." Briana stuffed her hands into her pockets. "I mean, she's working for Sheila and Quinn, same as we are, so..."

Jimmie grinned. "Works for me."

"Thanks," Nora said.

A telephone sounded from the end of the barn. Jimmie went inside to answer it.

Briana looked Nora up and down, taking in her jeans and trainers. "So how long has it been since you've ridden?"

Nora frowned as she thought. "Um... about fifteen years."

Briana swallowed her laugh. "Then we'll take it easy your first time out."

A half hour later, they rode side by side along a trail through the woods. Nora sat stiffly, the reins clenched in her hands as her gelding held his head up, nostrils flared.

"Relax," Briana said. "Let your body move with his walk. Feel the rhythm, and relax your hands, too. He feels the tension."

Nora loosened her stranglehold on the reins, and the gelding immediately lowered his head and settled into a comfortable ramble.

Briana studied her for a moment, trying to decide what it was about Nora that was so odd. She was long and lean but... ungainly. Kind of like the colt she'd been working with earlier. Her elbows and knees flopped about.

"Tuck in a bit," she suggested. "Snug your legs to the saddle so William feels you're a part of him." She watched Nora's body swaying with his walk. "That's better."

"William?" Nora asked.

"Yes. This is Yeats." Briana leaned forward to pat her bay's neck.

Nora laughed. "And is there a Butler?"

Briana grinned. "As a matter of fact, there is. They were all foaled the same spring and were tight as thieves. Always up to mischief. We needed three names and these worked."

They rode in silence for a while. Shannon loped tirelessly alongside the horses. Nora relaxed enough to begin looking around, tugging at the chinstrap of her riding helmet.

"It's so peaceful here."

Briana nodded. "'Tis. I love it here. I hate to leave, even for a few days."

"Are you leaving?"

"Only for the weekend, but two days in Dublin will feel like two months. My nephew's birthday," she added at Nora's questioning glance.

"I got a quick view of Dublin from the bus."

Briana stared.

"What?" Nora asked.

"I don't think I've ever met a tourist who wasn't all excited about Dublin and the bigger cities."

Nora didn't look pleased. "I don't think of myself as a tourist." She gave a little shrug. "Though I guess I am. I knew I wanted to be here. The plane landed, and I caught a bus from the airport, whirlwind view of Dublin to Galway, and then a local bus to Cong."

For some reason, that warmed Briana inside.

"I'm not much for cities," Nora went on. "We live not an hour from DC, but I can only stand going in for special shows or exhibits. A few hours, and my skin's crawling, all that concrete and all those people."

"I know exactly what you mean," Briana said.

"I'm confused," said Nora. "Did you grow up in Dublin and then move here?"

Briana twirled her finger. "Kind of the other way round. Born and grew up outside Waterford, but then my sister and her husband found work in Dublin, so my parents moved as well, to be nearer the grandchildren they were counting on."

"How did you come to be here in Cong?"

Briana weighed how honest to be with her reply. "I always wanted to work with horses. After—after my family settled in Dublin, I found Quinn. He was looking for someone. It fell into place."

Nora seemed content with that explanation.

They trotted and cantered for a bit, Briana keeping a close eye on Nora. She was still floppy, but she could stick in the saddle.

"You look like a jockey," Nora said breathlessly when they slowed to a walk. "The way you sit the horse. You look like you could fly with him."

Briana felt an old weight settle in the pit of her stomach.

Something must have shown on her face because Nora asked, "Are you okay?"

Instead of answering, Briana pointed toward another trail forking off to the right. "We'll go that way. It'll take us to the lough."

As they meandered, Briana saw movement through the trees. She signaled to Nora to pull the horses to a halt. In the clearing beyond stood a group of three people—a man and woman with one of the falconers. Suddenly a hawk came swooping down to land on the gloved arm of the man. The woman exclaimed and snapped photos with her phone.

"From the falconry school," Briana said. "It's a treat, if you're interested."

They reached a trail that followed the lakeshore.

Nora turned in the saddle to look back. "Just like the movie."

"What do you mean?"

"*The Quiet Man.* This view of the castle reminds me of the opening credits."

"Really?"

Nora gaped at her. "You've never seen it?"

"No."

"You live in Cong, and you've never watched *The Quiet Man.* Have you gone to the museum?"

At Briana's shake of the head, Nora threw up a hand. "Oh, my gosh. I just— How can you live around this and not know?"

Briana cocked her head. "Know what?"

Nora threw her hand up again in frustration. "You live it. Every day. I don't know if I can put into words how much this place called to me before I ever saw it for myself. It's just magical."

Briana snorted. "It's far from magical. You Americans romanticize Ireland so that it can never match up."

Nora thought about this as the horses walked on. "I suppose we do. I think every Irishman—and woman—who ever left here for America brought that longing with them. That's why there are so many sad Irish songs."

Briana grinned. "We are good at tugging on the heart."

They followed the path along the lake for a while.

"What did Jimmie mean, when he was so surprised that you would take me out?" Nora asked. "Which one is Sonya?"

"Sonya Lindberg. You'll know her when you see her. She's like a Valkyrie. She and Liam do most of the guided rides and the lessons. Jimmie and Quinn every now and again."

"You don't normally do these rides?"

Briana shook her head. "I'll do anything else needs doing, and there's always something needs doing around a farm. But not the guided rides."

"Then why did you offer to take me?"

"Well... you..." Briana stuttered, cursing the telltale blush she knew had risen to her cheeks. "Like I told Jimmie, this isn't a regular guided." Flustered, she asked, "Would you rather have had someone else?"

"No," Nora said quickly, but Briana could have sworn she was hiding a smile behind those eyes the same soft brown as Yeats's coat.

Out on the lough, the tour boat chugged by on its way back to the castle. Briana raised a hand as the mate waved.

"Would you like to come to Dublin this weekend?"

Where the bloody hell did that come from, Briana wondered in horror. For a moment, she hoped it hadn't actually burst from her mouth, but Nora turned to her.

"To Dublin?"

"Well, you didn't get to see any of it. I'll be busy for part of it with my nephew's birthday, but I can get you to where you can explore, and I'll join you when I can."

Nora's face broke into a brilliant smile. "That sounds nice."

"You said you're a librarian. I've a friend from school who is on the faculty at Trinity. I can call her to see if she can give you a tour if you like."

"That's really nice of you. Thanks. I think I can handle a weekend."

Briana nodded curtly. "Well, then. That's fine."

Chapter 5

ORA SAT WITH HER laptop in a busy coffee shop, catching up on email with her family. She finished a long message to her youngest sister, Amelia, and hit Send. Sitting back, she reached for her latte.

It had been an incredible day. She smiled to think of herself considering a day spent first locked in a car with Briana Devlin and then spent in the biggest city in Ireland as incredible, but... *You wanted to stretch yourself, do things differently from the way you've always done them,* she reminded herself.

Briana had arrived at the cottage promptly at seven a.m. She took Nora's carry-on bag from her and tucked it in the cargo hold of her white Hyundai.

Shannon, taking up most of the back seat, had gently nosed Nora's ear in welcome as she got into the passenger seat.

"The cottage looks nice," Briana had noted as she backed up.

"Thanks," Nora said.

Cheerful flowers and bushes bloomed in beds along either side of the door, courtesy of Sheila's nursery. Some of the ivy had been trimmed away, and the windows had had a good scrubbing.

"It doesn't look so lonely anymore," Nora said with satisfaction as they drove away.

"Lonely?"

Nora laughed self-consciously. "Nothing." The cottage had been anything but lonely, but she didn't say that.

Briana drove for a few minutes. Nora noticed she kept glancing over.

"What?"

Briana raised one shoulder. "It's... You look nice."

"Thanks." Startled, but pleased, Nora felt her cheeks warm as she tucked her hair behind her ear, glad she'd left it hanging loose about her shoulders.

For months, when she'd first started letting her hair grow, Amy had complained about it. It became a mantra every single weekend. "You look shaggy" or "Your hair's a mess" or some such thing. But Nora had already had this half-baked plan in her head—a plan to get away, to spend this summer in Cong, and she wanted her hair long enough to simply pull back without having to worry about it.

It was funny, she mused now, sitting in the coffee shop. Something as simple as her hair had been the first of many little, secret steps— getting her passport, speaking to her supervisor about an extended leave, researching Ireland's visa and citizenship regulations. She'd scrimped and saved, bringing her lunches from home for months, not shopping for new clothes or going to the movies.

She was still amazed at herself. It had been ages since she'd pushed ahead with something she wanted to do if someone else thought it was a bad idea.

When did that change? she wondered. As a child, she'd always been the stubborn one, insisting on figuring things out her own way. At some point, she'd ceded that independence for peace. It had become easier than listening to all the "I told you so" comments from Mary Fran, her older sister—and later, Amy—if her way didn't work at first. Thinking back now, she remembered exactly when it changed—the first day of classes in sixth grade. With Mary Fran only a year older and one grade ahead—but in a different school for the first time in Nora's life—her teacher, Mr. Williams, had given them quizzes to see what they'd retained from the prior year. When he saw her math and English scores, he'd said, "So, you're not a copy of your sister." Her heart had sunk at yet another comparison with Mary Fran, who was pretty and popular and athletic and had a gazillion friends. None of which Nora was good at, no matter how hard she tried. But when Nora got her papers back and saw that she'd gotten a perfect score on everything, Mr. Williams had grinned and winked. In that moment, Nora made the decision to excel in the things that Mary Fran didn't.

When her dad nicknamed her No-nonsense Nora, Mamma had said, "Leave her alone," but Nora liked it. She became the opposite of her sister—serious, studious, a loner who preferred staying in and reading on weekend nights rather than going out. Not that she'd had anyone to go out with. Until she met Amy in grad school.

At first, the happiness of their blossoming friendship had felt to Nora like a chance to start over, to reinvent herself, but somehow, even after the friendship had stumbled into a kind-of romance, she was still just Nora. Plodding, smart-but-dull Nora.

And then, the idea of this escape to Ireland had taken root, like a weed that wouldn't go away. Mamma and Pop had been the only ones Nora confided her plan to at first. They'd been delighted to help— "part of the resistance," Pop had joked. That was when Pop had contacted Mr. McCarthy and arranged her cottage. When she finally worked up the nerve to tell everyone, her family's reaction—to her surprise—had been amazement.

"I didn't want to say anything until..."

"Until it was all laid out, to the smallest detail," her mother, Mary Kate, had said admiringly.

"Until it was too late to change your plans," Amy had accused bitterly.

Nora hadn't pointed out that that was the point. She closed her eyes and sat back with her coffee cup. Here, there was no one trying to arrange her life for her. No one to tell her where to plant her flowers at the cottage or not to put her desk in front of the window because it might rain in, when she loved the way the light shone and the breeze ruffled her papers. Most importantly, there was no one to tell her she wasn't good enough to write her story. Well, almost no one. Briana's snarky comment about her coming to Ireland to write a book still stung.

Briana. What was it about her? It was embarrassing to admit—even to herself—how much she liked watching her, the way she moved, bouncing a little with the energy she could barely contain, coiled up inside that tight little body. Even in the car today, her muscular arms and lean thighs had fairly vibrated as if she couldn't relax if she tried. She could be so abrupt, to the point of being rude, and then so unexpectedly kind.

Nora's eyes opened. She set her cup down to see Briana standing outside, watching her through the window with a bemused smile on her face. It was really annoying that the sight of her made Nora's heart race in a way that could not be good.

By the time Nora had her laptop tucked away in her backpack, Briana was standing next to the table.

"How was your nephew's birthday?" Nora glanced around. "And where's Shannon?"

Briana grinned. "Probably letting Kieran ride her. He's been glued to her all day. I think he had a good time."

She took Nora's backpack and led the way outside, holding the café door for her.

"We can hide your bag in here where no one will see it," she said when they got to where she'd parked. She lifted Shannon's blanket off the back seat and folded it over the bag. "I think we'll be better off walking from here, and then I'll drive you to your guest house."

"Where are we going?" Nora asked, falling into step beside her.

"My sister, Cara, told me about a place near here that most of the tourists don't know about. It should be a bit quieter."

Briana stopped suddenly. "Unless you're after noise and crowds."

"No." Nora smiled. "I've had a day of crowds."

They continued on, weaving a path through the people on the sidewalk.

"Are you limping?" Nora asked.

"No."

And she wasn't now, but Nora could have sworn...

"How was your day?" Briana asked.

"It was wonderful!" Nora took Briana's arm without thinking. "Thank you so much for calling your friend. Gemma showed me around Trinity's campus and got me in to see the Book of Kells, which is incredible. Then I found a few other museums and spent the day going through them, just wandering around."

She realized she was still holding Briana's arm and let go. "It was nice, but I'll be ready to get back to Cong and my quiet little cottage."

When they got to the pub, Nora insisted on buying the first round, trying a Smithwick's at Briana's suggestion. They placed their food orders at the bar and carried their pints to an empty table in a back corner.

Nora watched the families with young children, mixing with older folks—all of them seeming to be locals. A few dogs were lying politely under tables, waiting hopefully for scraps of food to fall. She took a deep drink of her ale and caught Briana studying her.

"What?"

Briana tilted her head. "I just don't understand you." She looked frustrated.

73

"What is there not to understand?" Nora scoffed. "No one else has ever had any trouble."

Briana shook her head. "I don't believe that. Or they only skimmed the surface."

Nora wasn't sure how to respond to that, so just took another drink.

"You hardly said a word the entire drive here from Cong," Briana said. "But then you're fine meeting a total stranger, roaming a city you've never been, in a country you're visiting for the first time."

Briana frowned, as if maybe she could see the answers if she just glared hard enough.

Nora squirmed under the scrutiny. "I figured if you wanted to talk, you would. I enjoyed the ride, just listening to your music. And I told you, Gemma was delightful. Dublin is nice, as far as cities go."

"I could never do that."

"That I can believe." *I couldn't have done it a year ago.* But Nora chose to keep that thought to herself, as she'd then have to explain why.

Thankfully, their food arrived at that moment, cutting off any further interrogation from Briana. Nora dug into her colcannon, but out of the corner of her eye she saw that Briana wasn't eating.

Briana leaned forward, her elbows on the table, her hands hovering a fork and knife over her steak. "You know what I think?"

Nora dabbed her mouth with a napkin. "I'm not sure I want to know."

Briana's mouth curled into a tiny smile at Nora's icy tone. She cut a bite and chewed slowly.

"I think," she said thoughtfully as she cut another bite, "that you are a kind of shape-shifter, like a boggart."

"A boggart." Nora stabbed a forkful of corned beef. "I thought boggarts become the thing people fear. So that'd be a first. Thanks."

Briana seemed to ponder that as she chewed. "You're not that," she said with a firm shake of her head. "Only you become whatever the person near you expects or needs you to be." She picked up a chip and jabbed it at Nora. "I need quiet, so you were quiet in the car. Today, you met a complete stranger and were fine in her company for a few hours. Now, you're in a city full of people, and you can mix and mingle with them like you're one of them."

She narrowed her eyes as she bit into her chip. "The question is, what do you become when you're on your own. When it's just you?"

Nora stared at her. Even over the noise in the pub, she could hear her pulse pounding in her ears. How the hell had this woman—this irksome woman she'd only known for a few weeks—how had she just summed up everything in Nora's life that had led her to Ireland?

KIERAN TOOK NORA BY the hand and dragged her to his room to see his birthday presents.

"She's nice," Cara said, refilling Briana's coffee cup.

"She is that." Bri eyed her sister suspiciously. She checked that their mother was out of hearing in the dining room. "And just because you made me invite her for breakfast, don't think there's any more to it."

Cara's eyes, the same blue as Briana's, widened innocently. "I've no idea what you're talking about."

Briana snorted and took a sip of her coffee.

"Where did you say she's from?" asked their mother, Victoria, bringing a stack of plates to the sink.

"Near Washington, DC. But her grandparents were born in Cong. That's why she's visiting."

"Well, that's nice you've got a new friend, isn't it?"

Briana felt her cheeks redden and caught the wicked grin on her sister's face. Glancing at the clock, she jumped up.

"We need to get back."

"Can't you stay a wee bit longer?" Victoria asked with a little pout.

"No, Mum. I'll come back soon."

Briana ignored Cara's cough from behind her. She went down the hall to find Kieran and Nora sitting on the floor with Shannon as Kieran read one of his new books aloud. His dark head was bowed and one stubby finger traced along as he read.

Briana waited until he was finished. "Well done, little man!"

"Time to go?" Nora asked.

Briana nodded, but Kieran slapped his book shut.

"No! I have more books to read!"

She picked him up and kissed his cheek. "We'll be back so you can read the rest of your books to us."

Her eye caught Nora's, and she felt a bit nauseous at the way Nora's slow smile made her stomach do somersaults.

Nora got to her feet and followed Briana out to the kitchen.

"Thank you all for having me over," she said. "It was nice to meet you."

Victoria took her hands. "You come back with Briana any time."

It took a few more minutes for Kieran to say his goodbyes to Shannon, but at last, they were in the SUV and on their way. Shannon stretched out, exhausted, across the back seat.

"Your mom and sister are sweet," Nora said. "I'm sorry I didn't get to meet your dad and brother-in-law."

Briana shook her head. "Their Sunday tee time is sacred. Much to my mother and sister's disapproval. What my mum and sister don't know is how much money they bet every weekend."

Nora chuckled.

A light rain fell as Briana wove through Dublin's streets toward the M4 expressway. She pointed out landmarks as she drove. Nora's head swiveled to look around.

"This was nice," Nora said, settling back in her seat as they left the city. "But I'm ready to be home."

The word caught Briana by surprise. She glanced sideways at the graceful way Nora's hands rested on her thighs. In contrast, her own callused hands with their short nails were strong but hardly graceful. She double-checked and was glad to see that at least they were clean. Sometimes the deep dirt and grime of the stables was hard to scrub off.

"Tell me more about your life in the States," she said. But then she remembered the look on Nora's face in the pub last night when she'd started probing. "If you feel like talking."

Nora turned to look at her. "No quiet and music this time?"

Briana felt the corner of her mouth tug into an unwilling grin. "Not this time."

"This boggart thing is hard to keep up with, you know."

"Yeah, about that. I'm sorry—"

"What do you want to know?"

Briana couldn't bring herself to ask what she really wanted to know. "Tell me about your family and work."

"Well, you know my grandparents were born and raised in Cong. My granddad says he made a pest of himself with the film crew when they came. He was fascinated by electricity. He married my grandmother when they were just eighteen and they moved to the States in '58. He became an electrician and eventually had his own company. They got a lot of work in the building boom in DC when the Metro came along."

She paused, but Briana said, "Go on."

"Okay. My dad, Patrick, was the second oldest, like me, but he was one of six. Three of my aunts and uncles are scattered all over the country now, but two others stayed in the DC area, so we had plenty of cousins to play with when the family got together. My mom is Mary Kate. My oldest sister is Mary Fran, and I'm just a year younger. Then there was a four-year gap before Judy and Amelia came along. They're all married. I've got two nephews and two nieces so far, and Judy is due in the fall."

She stopped again, the rhythmic slap of the wipers the only sound.

Briana waited a moment and then prompted, "And your work?"

"You know I work in one of the libraries at the University of Mary Washington. I went there for my undergrad degree, then got my MLS at Catholic University. That's when I learned I could only take so much of DC. Then I went back to Mary Washington. It's a small school. I like it there." She sighed. "And that about sums up my life."

"Not all of it."

Nora's voice had a bit of an edge to it as she said, "What do you want to know?"

Briana hesitated. This was obviously cautious territory. She never did this with Quinn or the others at the stables. Of course, they knew each other's whole life histories, so no one ever needed to ask.

As if you have anything for them to ask about.

"Your sisters are all married. What about you? I mean, I know you're not married now. I suppose. But... has there... have you..."

Briana's voice trailed off. Nora was smiling at her obvious discomfort.

"You're not very good at this, are you?"

Briana squirmed. "This being?"

Nora laughed. "This whole talking to another person thing."

"No, I'm not," Briana admitted. "Dogs and horses are my usual companions."

"Okay. I'll let you off the hook." Nora took a deep breath and then spoke quickly. "I was with someone. We never lived together. She lives and works about an hour away, so it was always a weekend relationship, maybe a week or two together in the summer. Then she met someone else and decided she wanted to see if it could work. So we ended. Kind of."

Briana frowned. "What does that mean? Kind of."

Nora didn't answer immediately, and Briana wondered if she was pushing too hard, but then Nora said quietly, "Her new girlfriend has a girlfriend. So she was only available during the week. Meaning Amy still expected me to spend every weekend with her."

"Wait, wait." Briana gaped a moment as she tried to make sense of this. "She was shagging someone else who was shagging someone else, but she still expected you to..."

"Not that," Nora said quickly. "We hadn't... It had been ages since we'd been physical. It was..." She paused.

Briana waited.

"I had become just a weekly habit," Nora said. "Better than being alone. And I guess I kind of used her the same way."

Briana wasn't sure what to say. "How did you get away to come here?"

Nora reached into the back seat to scratch Shannon. "I wanted to for the last couple of years, but I had an old cat I couldn't leave. How pathetic am I? I stayed with an ex who wasn't an ex because I couldn't leave my cat."

"Not pathetic," Briana said, glancing over a couple of times while keeping her attention on the road. "Loyal, I think."

Nora smiled a little sadly. "Loyal sounds nicer. But the end result is the same. For too long, I have lived my life either in response to someone else or according to someone else's expectations. I settled for what was secure, what wouldn't lead to an argument—first with Mary Fran when I was growing up, then with Amy. I can't tell you how good it feels to be doing what I want to do for the first time in my life." She was quiet for a moment. "You were right."

Briana frowned again, thinking. "Cara would argue with you that I'm never right, but what about?"

"About my being a boggart. It felt like a slap in the face when you said it, but you're right."

She turned to look out the window, so Briana almost missed it when she said, "I didn't used to be. I was hardheaded and independent when I was little. I was just thinking about when that shifted. And that's another thing I'm after changing this summer, finding that part of myself again."

Briana didn't know what to say.

Nora shifted to partially face Briana. "Your turn."

"What?"

"I just bared my soul. Your turn."

Briana's face burned with what she knew must be a brilliant blush. "Well, there's not much to tell. I don't have an ex."

"No one?"

"No one who lasted longer than the time I was at a race meet." Briana gripped the wheel harder. "You said I looked like a jockey. I was. For eight, no, nine years."

Nora sat straighter. "That's really dangerous."

Briana snorted. "It is dangerous. But the riding isn't the most dangerous part. Crooked jockeys who stick your horse. Trainers and owners who dope the horses to hide their injuries. The horses destroyed by being over-raced and treated like machines."

Her jaw clenched. Even after all these years, it was so damned hard to think about. Harder to talk about.

"My mount that last season was an up-and-comer, a beautiful three-year-old who could have been brilliant. We'd had a bad takeoff over a big brush fence, and he strained one of his hocks—a hind leg. His next race was only two weeks later. The trainer swore to me he was sound. But I could feel it. Just a slight hesitation."

Her chin quivered. "But I asked, and he gave. He wobbled on the fourth jump. I should have pulled him up right then. At the fifth—"

Her voice broke. Nora reached over to lay a gentle hand on her shoulder. Briana angrily swiped away the tears running down her cheeks. It was a couple of minutes before she could continue.

"We'd both broken a leg, but I couldn't leave him. I'll never forget the look in his eyes." She sniffed. "I left racing after that. When my leg was healed, that was when I found Quinn and Sheila."

Nora squeezed and then dropped her hand. Briana missed the warmth on her shoulder and wished she'd put it back.

"Thank you for telling me," Nora murmured.

NORA FOUND HERSELF WATCHING Briana surreptitiously from her peripheral vision for the remainder of their drive back to Cong. They lapsed into familiar quiet, the music on the stereo the only sound. She suspected Briana had told her something she normally guarded very closely, a part of her that she didn't share with many. Sheila had said Briana was a puzzle, and it seemed a few more pieces had fallen into place over the course of this weekend.

As they approached Sióg Cottage, Nora weighed whether to invite Briana in, but she had a feeling it wasn't the right time. Briana would need to be alone after the last couple of days, and she was ready for some solitude herself.

"Thank you again," Nora said as Briana braked to a halt in front of the cottage. "It really was a nice weekend."

"You're welcome."

Briana tugged Nora's bag from the cargo hold and carried it to the door. Nora reached for her backpack and gave Shannon a parting scratch under the chin. As she turned toward the cottage, she caught a flash of movement from the upper window.

Briana stepped back and followed her gaze. "What's wrong?"

"I thought—" Nora shook her head. "It was nothing."

"Are you sure? I can come in with you."

Nora couldn't have said later what made her decline when she very much wanted Briana to come inside, but, "No. It's okay," she heard herself say.

She waited as Briana got hesitantly back into her car and reversed it, waving before she drove away. Nora turned the key in the door and cautiously pushed it open. When she stepped inside, the cottage felt chilled, and there was that scent like lilac again.

Over at her desk, where the window was firmly shut, her journal and blank book weren't where she had left them. They lay flopped open on the floor, looking as if something had whipped them off in a fury. Her loose pages were strewn all over, and her pens were likewise scattered across the room.

Upstairs, things were in similar disarray. All the pillows had been swept off her bed and were lying in the corners.

"Well, someone had a hissy fit, didn't she?"

Chapter 6

"WAIT!"

Nora called out, scrambling over roots and rocks as branches tore at her hair and clothing. Up ahead, only just visible through the trees and underbrush, was a flash of pale yellow, the only color in the forest. Behind her, a woman's voice wailed in the gloom, calling desperately.

A soft rain fell, making the roots slippery with the moss that covered them. Nora's foot jammed in between a root and a rock, and she sprawled flat-out, her hands grasping the ferns and dark soil of the forest floor.

She lay there, breathing hard. The sound of the woman's voice became fainter, and a scent came... lilac.

Nora rolled over, letting the mist fall onto her face as she panted.

Her eyes fluttered open, and she found herself staring up at her bedroom ceiling. Outside her open window, rain dripped from the roof. She pressed her hands to her eyes and realized her face was wet with tears that had run into her hair. Her hands smelled of dirt and greenery.

She sat up and clicked on the bedside lamp. The room was empty, the bed tousled as if she'd been tearing at the sheets all night. Her clothes from the day before lay in a pile, and her muddy hiking shoes sat askew in the middle of the room as if she'd kicked them off and left them where they landed. The palms of her hands were smeared with what looked like dried dirt—a familiar enough condition lately, working with Sheila at the nursery. But she hadn't gone to bed with dirty hands.

She went to the bathroom where a glance in the mirror had her looking like a raccoon, with dirt rubbed in around her eyes. She rinsed her face and scrubbed her hands till her palms were raw and pink. She dropped her pants to sit on the toilet and realized her ankle hurt. Lifting her pj leg, she saw a scrape where there hadn't been one.

Shaken, she finished in the bathroom and stumbled downstairs to put the kettle on. While it heated, she opened the back door and tried to calm the racing of her heart. There'd been other dreams—nearly every night in the week since she got back from Dublin—but none so real as this. The beautiful woman with the black hair and tormented eyes had appeared in most of them, but never had Nora woken with signs that she'd been out of her bed.

When the kettle was hot, she made herself a cup of strong tea and sat at the table, her head cradled in her hands. This was getting out of hand. She had no idea what these dreams meant or, more importantly, how to stop them.

Do you want to stop them?

That question echoed in her mind as some part of her yearned to find out what it was the woman sought, why she had come to Nora. It felt—she could barely let herself even think it—but it was almost as if she was meant to be here, that the ghost had been waiting for her to come.

"And if that's not fanciful, I don't know what is," she muttered to the empty kitchen.

She lifted her head. Maybe she hadn't only come to Nora. Maybe there was someone who did know what these dreams meant. She needed to know more about this cottage.

She waited impatiently for dawn to come. It was going to be a sloppy ride. She dressed in her still-damp clothes from her nighttime adventure and pedaled through the rain.

She was grateful to see a light burning in the kitchen window when she got to the Donnelly place. She leaned her bike against the house under the eaves and knocked timidly. Quinn opened the door.

"What in the world?" He tugged her inside.

"Who was—?" Sheila stopped mid-sentence as she stepped into the kitchen. "What's wrong? You look like death warmed over."

Nora gave them a half-laugh, suddenly feeling foolish. "I shouldn't have come. I'm making a mess all over your floor."

"Nonsense." Sheila dragged her farther into the kitchen. "You think these flagstones haven't seen their share of wet and mud? It's why we put them in."

She took Nora's dripping rain jacket and hung it on a hook alongside several others.

"Sit."

Quinn left, reappearing a moment later with a clean towel that he wrapped around Nora's shoulders. She smiled her thanks, rubbing the towel over her damp hair.

Sheila plunked a mug of hot coffee down in front of her. "What happened?"

Nora's gaze flicked back and forth between Sheila and Quinn. Sitting here in the brightly lit, cheerful kitchen, the very real feelings of her dream began to fade. She definitely felt stupid. "You know the reputation that cottage has?"

"The ghost?" The corner of Quinn's mouth quirked. "You've seen it?"

"Hush," Sheila said, flapping a hand at him. "Tell us."

In a rush, Nora described everything that she'd seen in her dreams, ending with the one from last night, the waking with dirt dried on her hands, the scrape on her ankle, all of it.

Sheila and Quinn stared at her.

"Do you sleepwalk?" Sheila asked.

"I never have," Nora said. "I mean, I know I'm kind of clumsy when I'm awake, but... It was so real. The smells, the textures of the plants and the soil when I fell. That lilac smell of bird cherry was there again."

"What was she calling out?" Quinn asked.

"I'm not sure." Nora closed her eyes, trying to remember. And she heard it. "Rowan." Her eyes opened. "She kept saying, rowan, over and over. Isn't that a tree?"

Quinn's gaze locked with Sheila's for a moment. She reached for his hand. "It's also a name. There's a legend around here, an old, old legend, of a child who was lost. A little girl. Her name was Rowan."

Nora's mouth opened and closed a couple of times. "Could this ghost be her, or her mother?"

Sheila shook her head. "I don't know, Nora. I don't remember anything else about Rowan's story. Only the name. It was a story used to scare us when we were little, playing in the woods round abouts."

Quinn tried to laugh, but didn't quite pull it off. "Yeah, but it's just a story. Like you said. Just a legend, right?"

Sheila's eyes were wide as she gazed at Nora. "I'm not so sure anymore."

"I have to know more," Nora said. "About the history of that cottage and the people who lived there."

Sheila nodded. "I'll help you."

Nora ground the heels of her hands into her eyes.

"You look exhausted," Quinn said.

Nora gave a mirthless laugh. "Apparently, I was running through the woods all night."

"You can't go back there," Quinn said. "We can fix a room up here."

It took Nora's befuddled mind a moment to process what he'd said. "No, I can't do that to you. Besides..." She frowned. "I don't think she means me any harm. She needs me... for something."

"You should get some sleep," Sheila said.

Nora shook her head. "I need something to distract me. How about we work on your website today?"

"Are you sure?" Sheila looked doubtful. "Today was to be a day off for you."

"I'm sure."

"I won't say no to your help." Sheila stood. "But first, breakfast."

BRIANA SPREAD FRESH STRAW in one of the stalls and turned to wheel the barrow of soiled straw and manure out to the compost pile. Dilly trotted in with a length of old rope. She gave him a scratch and played a little tug o' war with him. She stopped at the last stall. The gray mare wasn't inside. Briana opened the stall door and went through to the enclosure to see what she was up to. The mare stood at the fence, nose to nose with Stubbs.

Briana watched the pair of them for a moment. "I wonder."

She quickly scraped the stall clean and threw down fresh straw before going to the feed bin to get a bucket of oats.

She went to the paddock where Stubbs's ears immediately pricked at the rustle of the oats in the bucket as she shook it. The fat pony trotted over eagerly.

She fed him a palmful, leading him back over to the fence. The mare stomped her feet and bolted to the other side of her small enclosure. Briana gave Stubbs another mouthful of oats and then hung the bucket on the fencepost to give him a rubdown. He snorted in pleasure as her strong hands ran along the muscles on either side of his spine. From the corner of her eye, Briana saw the mare cautiously approaching—ears up, neck stretched forward to sniff at the oats, ready to bolt again.

Briana backed up to lean against the fence, not entirely sure this was wise, as the mare had shown every evidence of wanting to take a chunk out of anyone who came near her. Stubbs followed, allowing her to continue rubbing while she talked to him in a soothing voice.

A moment later, Briana felt a puff of warm breath on the back of her neck. The mare sniffed her, nosing her hair. Stubbs reached his muzzle up to the mare, nickering. The mare stepped closer, lowering her head over Briana's shoulder and allowing Bri to touch her for the first time. There were streaks of white crisscrossing her dapple-gray coat, scars from the beatings she'd had.

"Well, now," Briana murmured, lifting one hand to lay it along the mare's cheek. "I know they hurt you before, but you'll never have to be afraid again."

She reached into the bucket and held a fistful of oats on her flat palm. The mare's nostrils quivered and her eyes had a ring of white as she stared for a moment into Briana's eyes, but then she dipped her muzzle to take the oats.

A half-hour later, when Quinn drove up, he got out of his truck and stood, open-mouthed at the paddock fence where the mare and the pony were grazing side by side.

"What in the name of all that's holy..."

Briana grinned. "Lizzy and I are friends now. She likes Stubbs, so I thought they'd do well pastured together."

He turned to her. "Lizzy?"

Briana lifted one shoulder. "Whatever they called her, she should have a new name now. She's kind of like Lazarus, so..."

"Lizzy. I like it."

They stood shoulder to shoulder at the fence. Briana kept her eyes on the horses. "How's Nora?"

She felt his gaze sharpen but didn't look at him.

"She's fine. More or less."

She glanced up at that. "What's that mean?"

He scanned the yard, but they were alone. "I'm not quite sure what to make of it."

She frowned. "What are you talking about?"

"She came to us a couple of mornings ago, like a wet cat in the rain." He paused, scratching his head. "She'd had a dream. Says she's been having them."

"About what?"

He gave an embarrassed chuckle and rubbed the back of his neck. "The ghost. At the cottage."

Briana's mouth hung open. "You're for real?"

He nodded. "She says it's a dark-haired woman, crying out, searching for something. That morning she came to us, she'd woken with mud on her hands and a scrape on her ankle that weren't there when she went to bed."

He bit his lip as Briana stared.

"What's the woman searching for?"

"There's an old legend around here; Sheila and I both grew up hearing it. About a child, a girl name of Rowan, who went missing. They used to scare us with it when we were kids, saying her ghost would come and nab us if we misbehaved or snuck out at night." He hesitated. "That's the name Nora said the woman keeps calling. Rowan."

"But... Nora never heard these stories, did she?"

He shook his head. "Which kind of makes me believe her. She had no way of knowing. Unless her grandparents told her, but she swears they never did."

Briana thought about what he'd said. "What do they want with Nora?"

He gave her a dark look. "That's what Sheila and I are wondering."

A WINTER STORM HOWLS outside while Donall holds the children enthralled with a tale of Brian Boru. The peat fire crackles merrily, and the children gasp at all the right places. Even Callum is captivated, setting aside the new knife Donall made him.

Yule has passed—the longest night behind them—but this blustery night makes them all glad to be snug and warm inside the cottage, under the new slate roof Donall had put on in place of the thatch the summer before the crops went bad, back when work was plentiful.

Móirín rocks the baby—the easiest to come into the world of all her babies. It should have been a time of joy with this new one, but she finds herself in tears at the least little thing.

The baby herself is a delight—cheerful and smiling at her brothers and sisters. She has the most bewitching green eyes, eyes that captivate all who hold her.

Donall casts a worried eye in Móirín's direction as she rocks and stares out the window at the bitter cold night.

"That's enough for tonight," he says.

The children all moan with disappointment.

"But Da," says Rowan, "you stopped just before the big battle."

"That I did," Donall says with a grin. "Now you'll have something to dream about. Off to bed."

He takes them upstairs and gets them all changed into their night-shirts. Realizing he's missing one, he finds Teafa trying to climb back into the wooden cradle next to the bed he shares with Móirín.

"That's not yours any longer, darlin'," he says, scooping her up and tucking her in the middle of the big bed in the other room—Callum and Rowan on the outside with the little ones hemmed in to keep them from falling out.

With the children settled, he goes down to Móirín. "Come sit closer to the fire."

He helps her to her feet and shifts her chair nearer the snapping flames. For long minutes, they sit, she holding the baby, his hand on her knee.

"What is it, Móirín? What troubles you so? Are you feeling poorly?"

She shakes her head. "'Tis nothing. I'm being foolish."

"You're no such thing. Only tell me what I can do to help."

She looks at him, his eyes full of such concern, and her own fill with tears again. "I can't stop it, Donall. I keep seeing them. The Foyles. The five of them, dead in their bed, and no one to mourn them. Mary Gallagher's little baby boy, dead before he lived a month. How can God allow such things?"

"I don't know, *mo chroí*." He tenderly brushes his fingers over the baby's forehead. "All I know is my family is alive and safe. That's all I can do. All we can do."

"But what if—?"

"Shhhh." He takes Móirín's hand and raises it to his lips. "Come to bed. You're tired."

"That's the Lord's truth. Body and soul."

She follows him up the stairs and allows him to take the baby to tuck into her cradle while she gets into bed, sliding over to make room for him. When he joins her, she lays her head on his shoulder, his arm encircling her protectively. She tries to remember what he said. *Our family is alive and safe.* Over and over, she repeats those words as she drifts into a fitful sleep.

NORA OPENED THE OVEN to check on the chicken and potatoes roasting inside. She had a couple of tomatoes on the counter, ready to be sliced, thanks to Sheila's greenhouse. She heard the rumble of an engine driving up and cutting off. Going into the parlor, the sight of Briana's Hyundai parked out front made her heart leap a little. When she opened the door, Shannon was there to greet her, sitting politely on the flagstones. A wide smile split Nora's face at the sight of the two of them. She patted Shannon's shaggy head.

"Hi," she said to Briana, who was reaching into the passenger seat.

Briana shut the car door, holding a bag in one hand. "We brought you a few things."

"You didn't have to do that."

Briana shrugged. "I know. You've got your bicycle, but Quinn said he didn't remember the last time they took you to the market, so I thought I'd pick up a few basics on my way and see if you need to make a shopping trip."

She sniffed appreciatively. "Or maybe you don't."

Nora stepped back. "Come on in. Can you stay for dinner? It's almost ready."

"Are you sure? We shouldn't have come by unannounced."

"I'd love to have some company. And I don't have a phone, so you couldn't announce yourself anyhow."

"My sister would nag you to get a mobile while you're here."

Nora chuckled. "So would mine. I could have gotten an international plan for mine, but it's been kind of nice, not being chained to a phone."

Shannon trotted inside, sniffing everything. Briana looked around just as curiously as she entered.

"Has it changed that much since the last time you were here?"

"No." Briana flushed and walked through to the kitchen.

Puzzled, Nora followed.

"Just eggs, milk, bread, biscuits." Briana laid the items out on the counter. "And beer. Not that there's anything wrong with Guinness, but you need to expand your taste for Irish beer."

She produced a six-pack of mixed ales and stouts.

"Open two for us," Nora said as she put the rest of the groceries away and got plates down from the cupboard. "How've you been? How's Kieran and the rest of your family?"

"They're good. Mum keeps asking me to bring you back to Dublin." Briana popped the tops of two bottles—a Beamish and a Murphy's—and poured them into glasses.

Nora reached into the oven and set the roasting pan on the cook top. "Do you go often? You said you don't like Dublin."

"I don't. So I don't go as often as they'd like. I think that's their strategy. Get me to come more often by inviting you."

For some reason, that made Briana blush again. She glanced up and caught Nora watching her. A long moment passed as they stared at each other.

"Um," Nora stammered, redirecting her attention. She pointed at the tomatoes. "Can you slice those?"

They sat a few minutes later, the evening sun slanting through the open back door. Shannon stretched out on her side in the warmth.

Nora noticed Briana kept glancing over her shoulder into the parlor. "Is something wrong?"

To her amusement, Briana shuffled her chair around to sit adjacent to Nora rather than across from her.

"Quinn told you," Nora said, smiling.

"If a ghost is going to come at us, I'd rather not have my back to it," Briana said defensively.

"She's not like that."

Briana paused with her fork halfway to her mouth. "What's she like, then?"

Nora took a drink of her ale as she considered how to answer. "Sad. Not vengeful. Although there was a bit of a temper tantrum. I think I've seen her twice. Just quick glimpses in the upstairs room."

Briana sat up straighter. "The day we came back from Dublin. When I dropped you off, you were looking up at the window."

Nora nodded, chewing thoughtfully. "When I got inside, things had been... rearranged. My books and pens on the floor. Pillows upstairs thrown around."

Briana's eyes were wide. "And you stay here?"

"Where else am I going to go?" Nora shrugged. "And, like I told you. She's not going to hurt me. I feel that."

"She threw your things about."

"She was upset that I left, I think. She needs my help."

"Rowan."

"Sometimes I can almost feel her anguish. Her heartbreak over... whatever happened." Nora nodded again. "She's reaching out to me."

Briana set her fork down and leaned forward. "But why you? Just because you're here?"

"Maybe. How long has it been since anyone stayed here?"

Briana thought. "Farmer McCarthy had someone let this cottage two summers ago, but they only stayed a week. I remember because I rode by as they were throwing everything back into their car as fast as they could. They didn't say why they were leaving, so I never thought any more about it."

"I think I can guess." Nora picked up her glass. "Sheila and I are going to visit Mrs. McCarthy tomorrow morning. See if she can tell us anything. She won't set foot in here. When she and Mr. McCarthy came by after I arrived, she stayed outside."

They finished eating and quickly did the dishes. Nora went to the parlor to get some money.

"Not this time," Briana declined. "I just wanted to do that. Besides, you fed me."

She shuffled her feet.

"What is it?" Nora asked.

"Are you sure you're safe here?" Briana blurted.

Nora smiled. "Want to see for yourself?"

She led the way up the stairs. Briana and Shannon followed.

Nora pointed into the back bedroom. "She's never shown any signs of being in here."

She walked down the hall to the front room. Briana paused at the threshold before taking a deep breath and following Nora into the room. Shannon came in, sniffing curiously, but stopped suddenly, one paw in mid-air. A deep growl rumbled from her chest, and she leapt almost the entire distance back to the hall, where she refused to come into the room again.

Nora watched Briana looking around warily, looking ready to bolt herself.

"See?" Nora held her hands out. "Nothing. It's like this most of the time."

"But Quinn said you've been seeing her in dreams."

"Yeah. She mostly comes to me in my sleep."

Briana glanced at Shannon, who still stood out in the hall. "She's here." She scanned the room again. There was nothing visible, but she shivered.

"Let's go down," Nora suggested.

Briana led the way this time. Shannon raced down the stairs and out the front door. Nora followed them to the SUV.

"Thanks again for coming by and bringing the groceries."

Briana opened the door for Shannon to hop inside, but then stood with her hand on the door. "Would you like to go riding again?"

It took Nora a second to process the abrupt change of topic. "Uh... sure. When?"

"Your next day off. I've a horse I need to work with, but she'll go better with company. You'd be doing me a favor."

"I'd like that. Not tomorrow, but the day after?"

Briana nodded and got into the car. "You know where the private stables are?"

"Sheila showed me."

"Meet me there at eight, then. If that's not too early."

"Eight. Thursday. See you then."

Nora waved them off. She stood there for a long time, savoring the unfamiliar—and unexpected—feelings that being with Briana seemed to bring out in her.

You didn't come here for a summer fling, she reminded herself sternly. Of course, she'd never had a fling of any kind, summer or otherwise.

She went back inside. With a glance upwards, she said, "Let's have a full night's sleep with no adventures."

NORA WATCHED THE HEDGES and stone walls roll by as Sheila navigated a winding road Nora had never been on.

"Mrs. McCarthy knows we're coming?" she asked.

She'd taken care to clean her shoes of any mud and wore khakis instead of jeans. Sheila, she noticed, had done the same, ditching her gardening trousers and Wellies for clothing more suited to a social call. In a plum-colored sweater, with her hair pulled back in a loose knot, she was stunning. Nora's best couldn't compare to Sheila on a normal day at the nursery. Nora glanced down at herself. *Face it, clean and presentable is the best you can do.*

"She does," Sheila said, slowing and pulling over to let a large truck pass. "I've a loaf of almond bread for her. A little bread and tea will help to loosen her tongue."

The McCarthy farm was kind of ramshackle. The house was well kept, with cheerful flowers planted in window boxes—clearly Mrs. McCarthy's domain—but the rest of the barnyard was littered with plows and hay rakes and spare tractor tires. Cattle and sheep grazed in a nearby pasture.

Sheila parked, but before they could get out, Mrs. McCarthy was already outside, drying her hands on a tea towel.

"Good morning to you both," she called.

Sheila retrieved the bread from the back seat, and Mrs. McCarthy ushered them into her homey kitchen. Everything from the ancient-looking stove to the porcelain sink looked well-used, but it was all spotless and orderly, down to the flour and sugar canisters on the counter, decorated with roosters and chickens.

"Sit down, sit down. I've just made the tea. Oh, Sheila, you didn't have to do that."

But Nora noted she had a wooden cutting board and a crock of butter waiting on the table.

"Thanks for having us over, Mrs. McCarthy," she said.

"'Tis my pleasure," Mrs. McCarthy said. "A nice morning with women instead of the foolishness of men for a change. I told himself I had company coming, and no men were welcome. So he and his boys are off to the fields. And call me Orlagh."

She set the teapot on the table along with three pretty cups and saucers of fine china. "I never get to use these. James is the proverbial bull in the china shop, so he gets the mugs with the chips. Chips he put in them, mind."

She poured for all of them while Sheila passed around plates with generous slices of bread.

Orlagh slathered a thick layer of butter on hers and took a bite. "Oh, that's good!"

Nora agreed with a little groan. "I'm going to go home twenty pounds heavier if I keep eating like this."

"That's what your bicycle is for," Sheila said with a grin. She tucked a stray strand of hair behind her ear as she took a sip of tea.

"So how are you enjoying the cottage?" Orlagh asked.

Nora met her eyes over the rim of her cup and saw instantly that Orlagh McCarthy was a sharp one. "I am enjoying it, but that's what we wanted to talk to you about."

"I thought so." Orlagh set her cup down, her dark eyes curious. "What's been happening?"

Nora and Sheila shared a glance. Sheila gave her a small nod. Nora launched into a recounting of her dreams. She omitted the one where she'd apparently left her bed to run through the forest.

"So," she said as she finished. "I need to know what you know of the cottage's earlier inhabitants, its history."

Orlagh pursed her lips for a moment, but the slight clatter of her cup against her saucer betrayed her nerves.

"I told James we should never have bought that cottage, but he said balderdash. It had sat empty for nigh onto fifty years before we bought it from old Paddy Morahan that everyone thought was daft because he spoke of the ghost that haunted his great-grandfather's cottage. I knew he wasn't crazy, but James bought it anyhow and fixed it up, thinking to let it to self-catering tourists like you. He couldn't figure out why no one stayed longer than a few days, but I knew."

Orlagh got up suddenly and went to a wooden cupboard. She rummaged inside, searching for something tucked behind stacks of clinking china, and returned with a bottle, tipping a bit of whiskey into all three tea cups.

She took a bigger sip and closed her eyes. "I've seen her," she breathed.

Nora leaned forward. "You have?"

Orlagh opened her eyes and stared hard at Nora. "I have. Watching me as I cleaned in that front bedroom. I thought at first James had come upstairs, but when I turned..."

She shuddered and drank more whiskey-laced tea. Refilling her cup with half-tea, half-whiskey, she said, "I left that day and never went back."

Sheila patted her arm. "I'm sure that was startling. But what do you know about the cottage's history? Paddy Morahan's great-grandfather."

Orlagh's gaze focused on the distant past as she tried to remember. "I think the story goes that the cottage was abandoned, probably during the Hunger. The Morahans moved in, but there were already tales of strange goings-on there."

Nora looked from Orlagh to Sheila. "So whatever is going on is from before the Morahans?"

"I believe so," said Orlagh.

"What do you think she means, though, when she calls out 'Rowan'?"

Orlagh helped herself to more bread before saying, "We all know the stories of the little girl named Rowan who disappeared. I'm certain it has to do with that. But what, I don't know."

She took another sip of her tea and smacked her lips as the whiskey seemed to calm her nerves a bit. She eyed Sheila. "There is one who might know."

Sheila sat up straighter. "Eve?"

Orlagh nodded.

"Who's Eve?" Nora asked.

Sheila turned to her. "She's a bit odd, is Eve. Her Irish name is…" She reached for a pad of paper from near the telephone and spelled out *Aoibheann Ní Mheolchatha*, and then pushed the pad toward Nora.

Nora gaped for a moment. "How in the world do you pronounce that?"

"EE van nee mohl KAH hah," said Sheila.

"Why can't Irish be simpler?" Nora grumbled.

Orlagh chuckled. "What fun would that be?"

"We'll go see her," Sheila said.

Orlagh tipped the bottle three more times over their tea. "If anyone can tell you anything about Rowan and the ghost of Sióg Cottage, 'tis Eve."

Chapter 7

RIANA KEPT A LIGHT hand on the reins as Lizzy pranced nervously under her. Beside them, Nora straddled Stubbs's wide girth. Shannon ranged ahead, impatient with the slow pace. The fat pony nickered, reaching over to nose the fidgety mare, calming her.

"That's why I wanted him with us," Briana said. "Thanks for coming along."

"No problem," Nora said. "She's beautiful."

"She is, but she's had a hard time of it." Briana smoothed her hand along the mare's neck.

"What happened?"

"She was a racehorse. Lots of promise, blinding speed when she was alone on the track, but no drive to get in the mix with other horses. Her trainer and jockey were brutal, thinking they could whip her to the front of the pack. She got to where she wouldn't let anyone touch her much less ride her."

"That's awful."

"A friend of mine, an exercise rider for another trainer, called me. She'd reported them to the track stewards, and they contacted the owner. He's one with dozens of horses; burns through them and then tosses them. He agreed to sell her rather than face a fine, and she came to us. Underfed, open cuts from the whip."

A rabbit jumped out of a nearby hedge. Lizzy gave a wild snort and leapt sideways, crashing into Stubbs and Nora.

Nora managed to keep her seat, tightening her grip on Stubbs's reins while Briana got Lizzy under control. She used leg pressure to gently nudge the mare toward the hedge and let her lower her head to sniff at the lingering scent of rabbit. When Lizzy was satisfied that nothing there would hurt her, they walked on.

Briana gave her an encouraging pat on the shoulder. "She's been with us for four months and is only now letting me touch her."

"Do you do this often?" Nora asked, straightening her helmet.

"This being?"

"Rescue horses."

Briana shrugged. "Quinn's good about searching the auctions for cast-offs. They make good stable horses. All most of them need is a bit of kindness and gentle handling."

"What about the trainer? The one who was treating her so badly. Did he get into trouble?"

"Rafferty was his name. I heard the stewards barred him from the track. And I know he left with a black eye."

Nora twisted in the saddle. "Quinn gave him a black eye?"

"No." Briana felt herself redden under Nora's intense gaze. "I did. Bastard deserved it."

Nora laughed softly.

They ambled on, but Nora kept snorting under her breath.

"What's so funny?" Briana asked.

"I'm just picturing you punching out some big, burly guy," Nora said, still chuckling.

"Well, I would have given him more than a black eye if Quinn hadn't tossed me into the horse trailer." She waited a beat. "Then Quinn gave him a bloody nose."

Nora laughed more loudly. "I love Ireland."

She met Briana's gaze, and Bri felt her face warm again, but with an accompanying tingle in her stomach this time.

"What time did you get to the barn this morning?" Nora asked.

"About six. Time enough to get the horses turned out and the stalls cleaned."

"I didn't see your SUV."

"It's parked at the house."

Nora's head tilted. "You walked to work?"

Briana chortled. "The house is about twenty-five yards behind the barn."

"That cute little place? I thought that was the office."

"Quinn lets it cheap as part of my pay. He likes to have someone close at night, in case of fire. He does the same at the riding stables. Liam lives in a flat fixed up over the office."

"That's handy."

"It works out for all of us. Let's canter."

A few minutes later, they slowed to a walk again. With some of her nervous energy scrubbed off, Lizzy looked around with more curiosity than fear.

"How was your visit with Mrs. McCarthy?"

"Interesting," Nora said. "She's seen her. The ghost."

"She has?"

"Yep. She said the old man they bought the cottage from talked about her, and people thought he was crazy. She doesn't know anything about Rowan, though. She suggested we go talk to an old woman..." Nora screwed her face up, trying to remember how to pronounce the name. "Aoibheann Ní Mheolchatha."

"Eve?"

Nora turned. "You know her?"

"Sure," Briana nodded to the left. "I ride by her cottage a few times a month. Deep in the woods, she is. Likes her quiet and alone." Briana hesitated. "Did Mrs. McCarthy tell you anything about her?"

"Only that she's a bit odd."

Briana let out a bark of laughter. "That's an understatement."

Nora frowned. "What do you mean?"

"She's what you might call a medicine woman." Briana grinned. "Or a witch."

"You're teasing me."

"No." Briana shook her head. "I'm not. Wait till you see her place. When are you going?"

"Sheila said we'd go this weekend."

Briana chuckled. "Let me know how it goes."

"Why don't you come along?"

Briana saw the challenge in Nora's eyes, but it was the opportunity to spend more time in her company that drove her. She nodded. "All right, then. I will."

SHEILA PARKED THE SUV in a lay-by on the side of a dirt road and opened her rear hatch. "We'll have to walk the rest of the way."

Apparently, the rules for attire for visiting Eve were different from those for Orlagh McCarthy. Luckily, Sheila had warned Nora about the need to trek, so Nora was appropriately dressed in what she thought of as her nursery clothes—nylon hiking pants that shed mud and water easily, with waterproof hiking shoes. Briana was dressed similarly in patched canvas work dungarees and worn boots. Sheila handed each of them a basket, taking a third herself.

"Where's Shannon?" Nora asked.

"Thought she'd better stay at the stables today," Briana said, zipping her jacket.

An overnight rain had left the morning cool and misty, with tendrils of fog swirling about as they made their way through the ferns and mosses. The damp chill made Nora glad she'd heeded Sheila's advice and worn a sweater under her rain jacket.

"What's in these baskets?" Nora asked.

"Things Eve can use," Sheila said. "Herbs, dried flowers, roots—ingredients for her teas and medicines. Some of my lotions and soaps."

She glanced back with a grin. "Plus a bottle. To loosen her tongue."

Nora returned the grin. "Did you think of that because it helped with Orlagh McCarthy?"

"Well, it reminded me, let's say."

Sheila pushed through a patch of undergrowth that left them soaked with water droplets. Overhead, the trees were so dense that they walked through a green twilight. Nora wondered what trail Sheila was following, because there was no path she could see. Behind her, Briana kept pace silently.

It seemed they walked for an hour, though it probably wasn't that long.

"How in the world does she exist this far from everything?" Nora panted.

"People bring her things," Briana said, not even breathing hard from the sound of it. "She barters."

Nora turned to her. "For what?"

But just then, a cottage came into view through the trees. At least, Nora thought it was a cottage. It looked almost as if it was just another feature of the forest. Partially dug into a hill, the cottage's roof of slate was covered in moss like the forest floor. The ferns and other plants grew right up to a rough wooden door. Only the wisps of smoke rising from a squat stone chimney gave any hint that a human lived there.

Sheila stopped so abruptly that Nora almost walked into her.

"Eve! Eve, it's Sheila Donnelly."

For a moment, nothing happened. Nora wondered if anyone was there. Then the door creaked open and Nora gasped.

She was... *ethereal*, Nora decided. Hair of silver-white cascaded over shoulders cloaked in a kind of gown of deepest blue that was at once shapeless and elegant, girded at her slender waist by a twisted braid of green cloth or vine—Nora wasn't sure. Her feet were clad in boots or slippers of brown. Leather? Somehow, Nora had a hard time imagining her wearing animal skins.

She would wonder later how she noticed all those other things because she could have sworn her eyes never left Eve's. Eve's gaze immediately focused on her, and Nora felt ensnared.

She was vaguely aware that Sheila had continued toward the cottage and Briana had nudged her from behind, but Nora didn't really remember taking any more steps. Suddenly, she found herself standing before Eve, staring into eyes as green as the mosses and ferns of her forest, eyes that were at once guileless and ancient.

"Dia duit," Nora managed to say.

Eve's beautiful face broke into a smile at the greeting. She reached for Nora's hand, her grasp warm and soft. It seemed to Nora that there was a spark of light at the contact. Eve smiled more broadly. *"Fáilte."*

She led Nora into the cottage. Sheila and Briana followed.

"Aoibheann Ní Mheolchatha, this is my cousin, Nora McNeill," Sheila said, setting her basket on the table where four cups sat. "I'm sorry, Eve. Are we interrupting? Were you expecting company?"

Eve chuckled softly and released Nora's hand. "No and yes, Sheila. I saw you coming."

She went to the stone hearth, where a kettle hung over a peat fire. "Please, sit."

While she poured hot water into a teapot, Nora gazed around open-mouthed. She felt she had stepped back in time to another era.

The entire cottage was filled with a hodgepodge of books—some looking to be very old—along with shelves crammed with pots and jars. Judging from the candles and oil lamps scattered about, the cottage didn't seem to have electricity. One candle on the mantel was lit, sitting inside the protection of a glass vase, like a hurricane lamp.

From the wooden beams supporting the roof hung bunches of dried flowers, hanks of different grasses tied together, twisted roots that Nora couldn't identify. She caught Briana watching her with an "I told you so" expression.

"We brought you some things I thought you could use," Sheila said, opening the lid of her basket and setting its contents on the table.

"That was so thoughtful of you," Eve said. She set the teapot on the table and picked up one of the bars of soap, inhaling its scent. "You know I love the things you make."

She poured the tea and passed the cups around.

Sheila reached into the basket that Briana had carried. "We also brought some other things." She produced two loaves of her almond bread and a bottle.

Eve laughed, and the sound was musical to Nora's ears.

"That was kind of you," Eve said. She reached for a knife. "One to share with new friends."

She nodded at the bottle. "If you'd tip a bit of that into our tea, Briana, it'll help ward off this chill morning."

Briana poured the whiskey while Eve cut the bread. Nora found a container of eggs and a crock of fresh butter in her basket and placed them on the table.

"This is quite a feast," Eve said. "What's the occasion?"

"Oh, we were in the mood for a bit of *craic*," Sheila said casually.

"What does that mean?" Nora asked. "Someone else mentioned *craic* to me."

Sheila opened and then closed her mouth.

"It's hard to explain," Briana said.

"It's conversation," said Eve. "A bit of gossip."

"A good time," Sheila offered. "You know it without words." She waved her hand at Nora. "Nora's visiting us for the summer, and Bri and I thought it'd be nice for her to meet you."

"I see."

Eve's eyes met Nora's as she slid a plate across the table to her, and Nora was certain that Eve knew why they were really there.

"From America, is it?" Eve asked conversationally. "But your family's from here."

It wasn't a question.

"Yes," Nora said. "My grandparents—"

"Brigid Cleary," interrupted Eve. "She married Thomas McNeill."

"Yes," Nora said again. "How did... Do you know them?"

Rather than answer, Eve took a bite of bread. Nora nibbled on hers.

"Nora's staying in Sióg Cottage," Sheila said, but Nora again had a feeling that bit of information was unnecessary.

She followed Sheila's lead and let the silence stretch out as they all ate and drank. Eve set her cup down and focused those hypnotic green eyes on Nora again.

"I take it you've met Móirín."

"Maureen?" Nora repeated.

Sheila found a scrap of paper and pen in one of the multitude of pockets in her trousers. "In Irish, it's spelled like this."

She wrote it out.

Nora glanced at Eve. "The ghost has a name."

Eve's eyes flashed. "Of course she has a name. Just because she's dead doesn't wipe her existence from memory." She lowered her lids, veiling her eyes for a moment, as she seemed to collect herself. "Móirín Ní Ceallaigh was a real woman who deserves to be remembered."

She got up and went to one of her shelves, sifting through stacks of leather-bound books. She found the one she sought, smaller than the others, and set it on the table, raising a little puff of dust from its brittle pages. Its leather cover was scuffed and curled around the edges, as if it had been handled a lot. She flipped it open and leafed through the fragile sheets.

"We know a little of her." Tracing a finger along faded squiggles of ink, Eve read, "Móirín was married to Donall O'Heaghra in 1839. He was a blacksmith and she a skilled seamstress." She paused. "From these records, that's all we know. When the Hunger came, the western parts of Ireland, all of Connaught—including Mayo—were affected horribly. It's likely Donall and Móirín's skills would have remained in high demand, and they might have been able to sustain their family through their trades if they could find people who could afford to pay them. But that probably wouldn't have been here. Except for Ashford, there weren't many people who were well off in these parts. Another source tells us that Donall and the children went to America."

Eve closed her book and folded her hands over top of it.

"What other source?" Nora asked, eyeing the book, wishing she could leaf through its pages. But Eve's fingers tightened protectively, and she didn't answer.

"Only him and the children?" Sheila asked.

"From what we know."

Nora glanced from Sheila to Eve. "Then what happened to Móirín? Why is she haunting the cottage? What about Rowan?" She sat back. "And what does she want with me?"

"Have you asked her?" Eve asked.

Nora opened and closed her mouth. "No."

Eve's ageless face creased into a cryptic smile. "Don't you think you should?"

BRIANA AND SHEILA EXCHANGED a worried look as Nora sat silently in the back seat, staring out the window. Sheila pulled up to Sióg Cottage and turned the car off.

"Are you all right?" she asked, turning in her seat to look at Nora. "You're pale."

Nora didn't respond.

"Nora?" Briana prompted.

"Hmmm?" Nora blinked. "Sorry. Just thinking about everything Eve said."

She opened the door and got out. Sheila and Briana followed her into the cottage. Both of them paused in the parlor, listening, waiting.

Nora noticed and snorted. "I don't think she'll come floating down the stairs at us."

"I don't know," Briana said uncertainly. "After everything Eve said, I remembered how Shannon reacted—there's not much spooks her, but whatever's here did."

Sheila pointed up the stairs. "Mind if we go up and have a look around?"

"No." Nora led the way. She gestured toward the bedroom at the back of the cottage. "Like I told you, I've never seen her in here. Nothing's ever been disturbed."

They stepped into the front room. Everything was in place.

"Shannon wouldn't come into this room," Briana told Sheila.

"That would tell me something right away," Sheila said, walking around the room. "Móirín? Móirín, are you here?"

They stood still, but there was no sound, no whisper of movement, nothing at all.

"Why don't you come stay with us for a few days?" Sheila suggested. "You," she added, pointing at Nora. "Not..." She waved her hand at the empty room.

"That's silly," Nora said. "She hasn't hurt me. I don't think she means me any harm at all. I still think maybe she needs help."

110

"Help to do what?" Briana asked.

Nora shrugged. "If we knew that, we'd have half the puzzle solved."

"I... I could stay here with you," Briana offered.

She felt her face grow hot as both Nora and Sheila stared at her. She shoved her hands into her pockets and shuffled her feet.

"Just a thought. In case you didn't want to be alone with... you know."

Nora's face relaxed into a smile. "Thanks, but I think I'll be okay. I appreciate the offer, though."

"Fine. Good."

Sheila's chuckle followed Briana as she stomped back downstairs and out to the car.

Chapter 8

NORA GAVE UP TRYING to bicycle the narrow streets of Cong. Between the tour buses off-loading tour groups near the Quiet Man Museum and the hordes of tourists roaming the streets of the village, it was nearly impossible to ride without hitting someone or getting knocked off her bike. She dismounted and walked her bicycle to the shops she'd been planning to visit, tucking her purchases into her backpack. It had been hard at first to trust that she could leave her bicycle leaning against shops or parked in bike racks and find it still there waiting for her when she came back outside.

"You mean you wouldn't do that back in the States?" Sheila had asked in astonishment.

The day was gorgeous, sunny and pleasantly warm. Rather than taking the river trail, she decided to ride the long way out to Ashford and take some photos. She pedaled her way out of town, past the abbey ruins and the old church where more tourists congregated, taking selfies. She wheeled along the tree-lined road and saw a familiar Land Rover approaching. It braked to a halt, and Craig leaned out the open window.

"Hello, Miss McNeill," he called cheerfully. "How are you enjoying your summer?"

"It's been wonderful," Nora said. "I can't believe a whole month has gone by already."

"Heading to the castle?"

"Yes. I want to get some more photos for my family."

"'Tis a grand day for it," he said. "We'll see you soon."

She rode the rest of the way to the castle. Crossing the bridge with a wave to Rob, the uniformed guard, she spent the next few hours wandering the gardens. Here, too, many more tourists were out, making it nearly impossible to get images that didn't have people in them. She focused on shots of plants and trees. Despite the increased numbers of tourists, the castle was spectacular, as always, pennants flying from the stone towers.

Deciding to treat herself, she rode back across the bridge to the Thatched Cottage for lunch.

She placed her order and tugged her iPad out of her backpack to check her most recent emails. About once a week, she brought her laptop to the nursery to connect to the internet and catch up, but she hadn't done it yet this week.

She smiled as she saw five messages from her family. The smile slid off her face as she saw the sixth message.

Amy.

Nora hesitated, not really sure she wanted to open it. At last, she clicked on the message.

Hey, you must be having a good vacation, since you haven't had time to write. Thought I'd hear something from you after four weeks. A postcard or an email.

I've been thinking I might come over to see you. Spend a couple of weeks. Let you show me around.

What do you think? Write back when you can. I've been looking into flights.

Love, Amy

Nora slumped back against her chair, staring at the tablet.

"More water?"

Nora jumped and quickly flipped the cover over the screen. "Sorry, what?"

Her server stood next to her with a pitcher of iced water. "A refill?"

"Sure. Thanks."

"You're Nora McNeill, right?"

"Um, yes. How did you know?"

The young woman grinned. "I'm Liam's sister, Mary. He said he's seen you around the stables and that you're working with Sheila at the nursery."

"I am."

"That's nice." Mary looked for a moment as if she was going to ask a question but just said, "I'll leave you, then. Have a good day, Miss McNeill."

Nora opened her iPad again and dashed off replies to her family, giving her parents and sisters the same updates about working at the nursery and the price of groceries at the market and going for another ride with Briana. But with her message to her grandparents, she hesitated. After some thought, she typed,

Mamma and Pop,

I met a woman named Aoibheann Ní Mheolchatha. Do you remember her? She remembered you. She's fascinating. Seems to know a lot of the history of this area. I'm particularly interested in the history of my cottage. Sure wish I could see you both face to face.

Love you, Nora

She hit Send and bit her lip, pausing a few moments over Amy's email. She had time to think about it. *Coward,* she chided herself as she closed her iPad case and stuffed it back into her bag.

BRIANA SAT AT THE computer in the office at the private stable, scowling at the monitor. Vaguely, she was aware of boots clomping by outside, then heard them stop and return.

"You know, computers are like horses, they can tell when you're afraid of them," Liam said, leaning around the doorway.

She turned her scowl on him. He just laughed, coming in and folding his lanky frame to sit in the chair next to the desk, crossing his freckled arms over his chest.

"What are you trying to do, squint?" he asked.

Not accustomed to explaining herself—*when was the last time you had anything to explain?*—she belatedly tried to close the browser, but Liam's quick eyes caught the image.

"The Cliffs of Moher? Are you taking a sightseeing tour, then?"

She felt that cursed telltale heat creep up her neck to her cheeks. "I just thought, since Nora McNeill hasn't seen anything but Cong and a bit of Dublin, she might want to take a couple of days and..."

Liam's freckled face split into a wide grin. "That's a grand idea. Mary said she waited on Nora at the Cottage yesterday. She was on her tablet, I suppose getting messages from home. Said she looked upset."

Briana's eyes left the computer to focus on him. "Upset? About what?"

"No idea. Bad news? Mary didn't think it was her place to ask." He pointed at the computer as he got to his feet. "Anyway, this sounds like it might be a good distraction."

He left her to check some other websites, printing off a few pages.

Absently, she chewed on a fingernail, wondering what kind of bad news Nora might have received. Someone sick back home, maybe. But she had a feeling in her gut that told her it wasn't that. She turned the computer off and went to her cottage. Leafing through the pages she'd printed, she wondered why she was even doing this. It was stupid to let herself care about someone who was going to leave in a couple of months. The whole reason she'd never let herself get involved with anyone when she was racing was the unpredictable gypsy lifestyle they all led. It had never been worth the heartache to let herself care for someone who wasn't going to be around.

If her gut was right, if Nora's bad news had to do with the woman she'd been involved with, then this idea was for naught. That thought brought her to an abrupt stop.

Why are you doing this?

What had started as a good-natured gesture had begun to change into something else in the shadows at the back of her mind, and she wasn't ready to stare at the something else in the light.

She tossed the pages onto her table and headed back outside to work with another of the yearlings.

AN AROMATIC STEAM ROSE from a pot on the stove. Nora crushed lavender with a mortar and pestle while Sheila added other oils to a large pot, stirring the thick, creamy concoction inside, as it bubbled sluggishly like white lava.

"This smells so good," Nora said.

"It works as good as it smells," Sheila said. "If I say so myself. Nothing better for your skin."

The shop bell rang.

"Give this a stir every minute or so, will you?"

Sheila left to tend to the customers, while Nora continued grinding and stirring. Steam from the pot moistened her face. The warmth felt good, chasing away the chill from a damp ride to the nursery that morning.

When the customers left, Sheila came back and peered into the stone mortar. "I think that's fine enough."

"Do you only sell your products here? I thought I saw some in town."

Sheila took over the stirring and added Nora's crushed lavender to the pot. "Several of the gift shops in the village stock them. I thought about opening a shop of my own, but it'd be one more thing to juggle. This works best."

They worked in silence for a bit, letting the mixture distill. At some point that was evident to Sheila, she slid the pot off the burner.

"We'll let that cool and then put it in the jars there."

They went to the sink to wash their implements.

"Any sign of Móirín?" Sheila asked.

"Nothing," Nora said glumly. "I finally have a name, and she's not shown herself once in these past few nights since we talked with Eve." She paused. "I've wondered if I should ask Eve to come to the cottage. She seems to have a way about her."

Sheila chuckled, tucking some loose strands of hair behind her ear. "She does that."

"How old is she?"

"I've no idea." She flicked a glance in Nora's direction. "My Gran remembers her from when she was young. Says Eve hasn't changed at all."

"That's impossible." Nora stared. "But somehow it doesn't surprise me. I just wrote my grandparents that I met her. Can't wait to hear back from them."

"It is a bit eerie, how she never seems to age." Sheila filled the kettle. "Time for a break."

Rusty stirred himself from his nap to sniff hopefully as Sheila placed a jar of cookies—biscuits, Nora remembered—on the table.

"How are your family?" Sheila asked.

Nora retrieved a couple of mugs from the cupboard. "They're fine. Getting ready for a Fourth of July picnic at my mom and dad's house this weekend."

"Can't believe you've been here more than a month already. Do you miss them?"

"I do, but I've loved every minute here."

"Then what's wrong? You sound... not quite happy."

"I got an email yesterday. Well bunches of emails. But one in particular."

Sheila lifted one eyebrow. "From what's-her-name?"

Nora sighed. "Yeah. Amy. Wants to come here for two weeks. Have me show her around."

Sheila's eyes flashed, but then she carefully composed her face. "What do you want to do?"

Nora snorted. "I don't want to waste any of my precious summer with her."

"Then tell her so."

Nora's doubt must have shown on her face because Sheila said, "Not in those words. Look, you told me you waited and planned a long time for this summer. To get away and do what you wanted for a change. Don't lose that."

She poured the hot water in the mugs and joined Nora at the table. Opening the jar, she took a couple of biscuits, giving one to Rusty who was now sitting at her feet.

"You're right." Nora broke a ginger cookie in half, taking a bite. "I've got to find a way. It just feels selfish. I feel guilty even thinking that it would waste my summer to have her here, but I know what it would be like. She'd take over, plan everything. And I would let her."

Sheila tilted her head as she regarded Nora. "Why would you?"

Nora huffed out a breath. "Because that's what I do. It's easier than arguing. Everyone around me is better at making decisions. Better at everything."

"Bollocks. That can't be true."

"Well, it feels true. It's not just my lack of accomplishments compared to them." Nora frowned at her cookie, deliberately avoiding Sheila's gaze.

"My dad took over my grandfather's electrical business and grew it into this big company. He's still handsome. My mom has this gorgeous head of silver hair and produces amazing pottery. My oldest sister looks just like her—beautiful now, and she'll still be beautiful as she gets older and continues showing her watercolors. The two younger ones are like pixies— cute and petite—and they're both teachers. One teaches music and the other art. And then there's me, all clumsy and—"

"Don't say you're ugly," Sheila cut in. "Because you're not a'tall."

"Thanks for saying that," Nora said, though she didn't believe it. "But it's not only looks. They're all artistic and creative, or have built something. My life is dull. I'm dull."

"You're nothing of the sort," Sheila insisted.

"But I am," Nora said firmly. "And I've realized I kind of set my life up that way. I'm just a librarian." She ignored Sheila's scoff. "Work and my cat and my books. It was safe and predictable. Amy liked it well enough because I never had anything else more exciting to do than hang with her every weekend. But I don't want to any longer. I want my life to be different."

"You could tell her you've met someone," Sheila suggested. "Isn't that what she did to you?"

"Well, yeah, she did, but..."

"Haven't you?"

Nora felt her cheeks burn. "What do you mean?"

One corner of Sheila's mouth twitched. "What's with you and Briana?"

"Nothing's with me and Briana." Nora hid her face behind her mug.

It was Sheila's turn to snort. "Not that I'm an expert in lesbians and their mating rituals..."

Nora sputtered as her tea went down the wrong way.

"...but it sure seems to me, judging from the way you look and then don't look at each other, that there's something going on."

Nora covered her mouth, coughing to clear her airway. "Briana…" she rasped when she could talk. "She… she drives me crazy!"

Sheila grinned. "So does Quinn. Maybe that's the best kind. He's down-to-earth, not one for romance. There's no poetry or roses. He comes in with horse shite on his boots, smelling of hay and horses, most times not until after dark. He works his tail off at the stable and then hauls mulch for me. He fills my car with petrol and inflates the tires when they run low. I've learned to be content with those more practical signs of his love."

She hesitated. "And he got me through the worst time I've ever known when Annie died." She couldn't continue for a moment. "Just when I think he hasn't a romantic bone in his body, he'll bring me a wildflower he spied on the side of the road that made him think of me. I can't help but love that man. My guess is Bri would be much the same if you gave her that chance."

Nora ducked her head, staring hard at the cookie crumbling in her fingers, wishing she could stop blushing.

"Are you telling me you don't feel anything for her?" Sheila pressed.

"No. I'm not saying that." Nora felt as if the words were being dragged out of her. "Sometimes, I think she likes me, and then other times…"

Sheila leaned forward, her elbows on the table. "But how do *you* feel?"

Nora cocked her head as she struggled to answer. "I'm only going to be here for a few months. I wasn't looking for… anything."

"Sometimes that's when it comes," Sheila offered sagely. "When we're not looking."

Nora gave a half-laugh. "I couldn't manage a full-time relationship with Amy who was only an hour away. How can—"

"You knew better than to try a full-time relationship with her," Sheila interrupted. "There's a difference."

Nora frowned as she slowly spun her tea mug around and around. "I don't think I can love the way other people do. The way you and Quinn do. All in, holding nothing back."

"Bollocks again," said Sheila firmly. "Since the day you got here, you've been one of the most open, giving people I've ever met."

"That's different," Nora protested. "You and Quinn are family. Romance is different."

"You just have to meet the right person," Sheila insisted.

"I don't know," Nora countered. "I'm not sure I'm built that way."

Sheila helped herself to another biscuit. "When did you become such a cynic?"

"Am I?" Nora pursed her lips as she considered. "Maybe I am. I've read about love all my life, in thousands of books. I've wished for it. Thought I'd found it once, but it didn't feel the way everyone says it should."

She reached for another cookie, and Rusty quickly repositioned himself, resting his paw on her foot to remind her he was there. She broke a bite off and offered it to him.

"If this summer has given me anything," she mused, "it has been time to think." She slid one of Sheila's candles near, tracing a fingertip over the vines on the label. "A bittersweet garden. That's what I think the heart is. Everyone writes about love and joy and hope with flowery language, and all of it lasting for the rest of our lives. But how often does that happen? I think there's more pain and loneliness and heartache when you wish and pine for something that isn't there. We pray the lovely things will bloom, but so often the thorns take over, obscuring everything else."

Sheila reached across the table and clasped Nora's hand. "But does it follow that the thorns choke out the beauty? Even bushes with thorns bloom. And when the thorns are carefully cleared away, who knows what you might find?"

Nora felt a sudden tightness in her throat. She stared hard into Sheila's eyes, demanding the truth. "Do you really believe that?"

Sheila smiled. "I do. Truly."

A LOUD CRACK OF thunder shook the eaves, startling Nora awake. She lay for long minutes, listening to the lashing of the rain and the rumbling echoes of the thunder even as new forks of lightning strobed through the night. She got out of bed to close the windows. Though they'd been lowered, a bit of rain was blowing in. When she turned around, the lilac-like scent of bird cherry filled the room.

"Móirín?" she said softly. "Móirín Ní Ceallaigh, are you here?"

In response, the fragrance grew stronger, enveloped her.

Nora sat cross-legged on her bed. "What do you need? How can I help you?"

Faintly, so faint under the continued rumbling of thunder that Nora wasn't certain at first she'd heard it, came a whisper.

"*Rowan.*"

Nora gasped. "Who was Rowan? Móirín, what do you want from me?"

The air suddenly reverberated with the sound of weeping, and a gust of wind swept the curtains. Nora held her breath, but everything became still inside the room. Only the rain and the receding thunder could be heard.

She lay back down, listening through the fading sounds of the storm. The rolling rumbles of thunder in the distance lulled her back to sleep. And in her dreams, a child laughed.

BRIANA PACED BACK AND forth, all of ten strides from her tiny kitchen out to her sofa and back again. Shannon, tired of watching her human act so strangely, lay with her head resting on her paws. Only her eyes moved, following Briana's trek to and fro.

"It's just a kindness," she said to Shannon. "Like our trip to Dublin, right?"

Shannon's tail thumped in response.

"I'm just offering to take her to see a bit of Ireland while she's here."

Only it didn't feel like just a kindness. It felt like a date. A date with a potential for overnights together somewhere. Not that Briana knew what that actually felt like. She'd never spent a night with a lover. There were precious few female jockeys, but plenty of women who were grooms and exercise riders. Back when she was racing, it was easy enough to scratch that itch. Furtive glances, lingering smiles—a kind of secret communication that led to quick grapples in an empty stall or a caravan, but she'd always left immediately after.

Maybe the invitation to accompany her to Dublin had been a casual suggestion to allow Nora to sightsee, but the conversation on the way home, the things they'd shared with each other...

Briana stopped and squeezed her eyes shut.

It's different now, and you know it is, said an annoying voice in her head. *And what happens if you ask her and she says no?*

That stopped her in her tracks.

"Ah, Briana, you're a fecking idjit."

A sudden ruckus from outside jolted her from her thoughts. She sprinted through the door, Shannon on her heels, to find utter chaos. The first thing that registered was that Lizzy was going berserk. The gray mare was bucking and racing around her paddock, neighing wildly. Not even the presence of Stubbs was calming her. She had a split second thought that the mare might accidentally kick him as he tried to follow her.

She barely had time to notice that Nora McNeill was there, standing beside her bicycle near the barn where an unfamiliar pickup had just driven up. The man who got out of it—a balding, unshaven man with a cigarette hanging from his lips—made for the paddock gate, weaving as he walked. He was soft, gone to seed, but underneath that, he was thick and heavily muscled.

Lizzy flattened her ears and rushed the fence with her teeth bared. The man fell back, cursing.

"You worthless sack of shite," he growled.

Briana ran to the enclosure. "Get away from my horse, Rafferty."

Rafferty turned on her, swaying. The long ash from his cigarette dropped onto his stained shirt, but he seemed not to notice. "Your horse?" He peered at her with his bloodshot eyes. "I remember you, you little runt."

Briana's nostrils flared at the combined stench of sweat, alcohol, and cigarettes. She positioned herself between him and the fence, Shannon at her side. "I was big enough to give a black eye the last time we met."

"You cost me my job!" he roared.

Liam appeared at her other side. "Clear off."

"Where's Quinn Donnelly?" Rafferty demanded. "I want my god-damned horse back!"

"We bought her," Briana said. "She's not yours. Never was."

Only then did she see the thick riding crop in the brute's hand. Behind her, Lizzy's terrified neigh went through her like a knife. His knuckles tightened on the crop's handle. Before he could raise his arm, she launched herself at him, throwing all of her weight into a punch that landed in his soft gut. When he doubled over, gasping for air and grabbing his belly, she yanked the crop out of his hand and planted her other fist in his face. The stub of his cigarette went flying and blood poured from his nose. He lurched forward, bellowing like an angry bull, throwing a ham-fisted punch.

Briana ducked but not fast enough. His fist caught her cheek, knocking her sideways.

Liam seized her from behind, plucking her up as easily as a sack of potatoes. Rafferty put his hand to his nose, his lip curling as he looked at the blood.

"You bitch!"

Shannon leapt in between them, a fierce growl vibrating from deep within her chest. Dilly raced from the barn to stand between her front legs, his hackles up, barking furiously. Rafferty staggered back a step.

"I suggest you clear off," Liam said again. "Before we loose the dogs on you."

By this time, Nora had joined them, though she hadn't said a word. Rafferty glared at them, but retreated to his truck, wiping at his bloody nose and keeping a baleful eye on Shannon, who continued to growl menacingly.

"Put me down," Briana said as the pickup lurched down the drive.

Liam set her on her feet. He tried to take a look at her face, but she wrenched free and went to the horses. She easily wriggled between the fence slats and stood, her arms open. Stubbs trotted to her immediately, but Lizzy stood back, trembling. Briana crooned meaningless words to Stubbs, patting him. He followed her as she slowly approached the mare.

"You're all right now," she murmured. "He's gone. He won't hurt you. We'll never let him hurt you again."

Lizzy took one step and then another, until she could press her pretty face into Briana's chest. Slowly, under Briana's soft strokes, her trembling ceased.

Briana turned at the sudden sound of truck tires on the gravel, afraid the bastard had come back, but it was Quinn.

He jumped out. "I saw Rafferty just now. What the hell happened?"

Briana gave the horses a final pat and climbed back through the fence.

Quinn gaped at her. "And what the hell happened to you?"

He took her chin and tipped her face to inspect the cheek that Briana only now realized was throbbing like a toothache.

"She was brilliant," Nora said, her eyes shining.

Briana forgot her bruised cheek as Liam and Nora both babbled about the encounter. Quinn turned to her with a grin.

"You gave him a bloody nose?"

Briana lifted one shoulder. "You got to last time. Bastard didn't learn the lesson."

Quinn burst out laughing. "I'm guessing he won't try for a third." He pointed to her face. "We'd better get some ice on that."

"I'll do it," Nora offered.

Briana thought she heard a muffled snigger from Liam as Nora took her by the hand and led her back to her cottage.

"Sit down," Nora said when they entered the kitchen.

Briana reluctantly let go of Nora's hand and sat.

"This place is cute," Nora said as she went to the refrigerator and got a few ice cubes from the freezer. Wrapping them in a towel, she joined Briana at the table, gently placing the cold compress on her cheek. Briana winced.

"I'm sorry," Nora said. "I didn't mean to hurt you."

"It's okay," Briana responded, putting her own hand over Nora's when she started to pull away.

Nora was so close, Briana could see herself in those brown eyes. For a long moment they sat like that, Nora cradling the ice to Briana's cheek with Bri's hand over top of Nora's.

Nora's eyes shifted as she reluctantly tugged her hand free. "Your knuckles, too."

She got another towel and some more ice to apply to Briana's swollen knuckles. Briana lost track of time as Nora held her hand, leaning dangerously close, close enough to—Shannon pawed at the door with a loud bark.

Nora jumped and got up to go let Shannon in.

"I'm okay," Briana said as Shannon laid her head in her lap with a soft whine. "You were brilliant."

"You both were," Nora said. "You were fantastic."

"Not so fantastic. I should have ducked faster."

Nora laughed. "But that jerk got the worst of it."

"He did that."

An awkward silence followed.

"Why are you here?" Briana asked at last.

"I was coming by to see if you wanted to take Lizzy and Stubbs for another ride, but I guess today isn't such a good day for that."

"Probably not." Briana's heart sank.

"I work with Sheila tomorrow. How about Thursday?"

"Thursday would be perfect."

"Okay." Nora stood. Her gaze flicked to the printouts from the computer, still lying on the table. "Taking a trip?"

"No," said Briana. "I mean, yes. Maybe."

Nora frowned in bewilderment.

Briana took a deep breath. "I was doing some research on places, just in case..." Her words came all in a rush. "Do you want to see some other parts of Ireland while you're here?"

A slow smile spread across Nora's face. "I'd like that. Very much."

"Okay." Briana remembered to breathe. "Okay."

DESPITE THE CHILL FEBRUARY day, Callum's face glistens with sweat as he pumps the forge bellows for his da. With each heave, the air blasts the coals, shooting sparks up and making the flames surge. Donall withdraws the white-hot metal out of the fire and lays it on the anvil, striking it with his hammer, over and over until the iron begins to cool too much to beat. He shoves it back into the flames.

"Take a rest, boy."

He dips into a nearby bucket of water, handing the cup to his son, who drinks deeply. Then he drinks.

"How much longer?" Callum asks, dropping to a bench to rest.

"Till the work is done," Donall says. "We're lucky to have the castle sending work our way. The plowshares we're repairing here, plus the hay rakes and pitchforks. We've enough to keep us busy into the summer. Hopefully, the family will be back in the fall for another hunting party, and we'll be needed again. Never turn down work, Callum."

The boy scowls. "Rowan's not working."

"Your ma is just starting to make new liveries for the butler and the footmen. She needs help, and Rowan is working with her."

"She's not. I saw her out there." He points toward a nearby field.

Donall shields his eyes and searches the tall grass for any sign of movement. "Rowan? Rowan!" He shakes his head when he receives no answer. "That girl. Sometimes I swear the *sióg* switched our babe for an impostor."

He tousles his son's hair. "Come. That iron should be ready to strike again."

Out in the field, Rowan giggles when she hears her da calling to her. Ducking down so she's out of sight, she picks flowers. Flowers for Mam, so she won't be sad. She sees her mother cry when she thinks no one notices, and she hears her weeping at night, hears her da comfort her. There's so much sadness everywhere lately.

But flowers make Mam smile. She's gathered so many, she can't hold them all. She uses her skirt as a basket, plucking still more.

She roams far across the fields, so far that she can no longer hear the strike of the hammer in the forge. Beyond the fields of waving grass and wildflowers, there are the woods, with flowers of their own. Snowdrops and blackthorn. And more. There are the little lights that beckon, that call to her.

She carefully sets her flowers down and wanders into the forest shadows.

Chapter 9

NORA SAT AT THE table that had become her makeshift desk, her pen flying over the paper before her. Lamplight spilled across scattered pages, all dated and numbered. What she had intended to become her breakthrough novel—she rolled her eyes even to think it now—all of her plot points and notes and outline, that had been set aside. Somewhere along the way, the details from her journal had turned into a new story. Prompted by her dreams and the bits and pieces she knew thus far, her imagination was running wild. She had no idea how it would end or what twists and turns it might still take as she learned more, but she'd churned out dozens of pages.

Outside, an owl hooted. She'd borrowed a book on Ireland's birds from Sheila and Quinn. She was pretty sure this was a barn owl. She'd caught a glimpse of one, with its heart-shaped face, but she hadn't heard its hoot, so she couldn't be certain it was the same bird she was listening to.

At the moment, she was recounting her latest dream. They had been shifting a bit over the last few nights, ever since the storm, when she had tried to speak with Móirín. The child's laughter was becoming clearer, and sometimes she thought she heard two voices. But always, always there was the searching, the bottomless grief.

Her lamplight faded as dawn broke. More birds began their morning chorus—wrens and doves. She thought she'd seen a kingfisher near the river with its brilliant flash of blue.

She sat back and rubbed her eyes. Her stomach growled. She checked the clock. Time for breakfast before meeting Briana for their ride.

Yesterday at the nursery, Sheila naturally had wanted full details of the kerfuffle at the stables.

"She did not!" she'd exclaimed when Nora told how Briana had gut-punched Rafferty and then given him a bloody nose.

"Yeah, she did," Nora said, grinning. "It was great. I wouldn't normally approve of punching someone, but he came there with the intention of making trouble. You should have seen that poor mare. She was terrified of him."

Sheila's blue eyes flashed, and Nora got a hint of the temper that could rise inside her. "Good thing he met Bri and not Quinn then. If Quinn had been there, he wouldn't have driven away."

Nora hummed to herself as she toasted some bread in her little oven. She hadn't told Sheila about the invitation to go sightseeing with Briana. She'd keep that between them for now.

By the time she got to the private stables, Briana already had Stubbs saddled and waiting. Shannon ambled to her, escorting her to the paddock fence where Stubbs's reins were loosely tied.

"Hi," Nora said, leaning on the fence beyond which Lizzy stood quietly as Briana saddled her.

"Morning."

For a long moment, they simply gazed at each other, but then Stubbs gave Nora a hard nudge with his nose, mouthing her jeans.

"He's looking for treats," Brian said. "The bin in the barn has apples and carrots. Get a couple of each, would you?"

Nora returned a minute later and gave Stubbs half a carrot. "Will she let me come to her?"

"Try and see." Briana moved aside as Nora climbed through the fence with the other half of the carrot in her hand.

She approached slowly.

"Talk to her," Briana suggested when the mare threw her head and backed up a step.

Nora spoke soothingly. "You don't need to be afraid. You know you want this carrot."

Lizzy's ears pricked and her nostrils fluttered as she sniffed. She stretched her neck out, but Nora stopped.

"You have to come to me if you want this."

She waited patiently. Lizzy snorted and took a step nearer. Nora made her come all the way, patting her soft neck as the mare munched on the carrot.

"Nicely done," Briana said.

Nora felt her face grow warm with the praise. "Thanks."

She reached out to touch gentle fingers to the swollen bruise on Briana's cheek. The surprise in Briana's eyes reflected her own at her boldness. "Does it hurt much?"

"Not too much," Briana said, looking ready to bolt herself. She cleared her throat and Nora dropped her hand. "Riders up."

They mounted and walked the horses into the green shadows of the woods. Nora breathed it in, enjoying Stubbs's steady amble next to Lizzy's prancing beside them.

"Where to?" Briana asked.

An idea came to Nora. "You said you've sometimes ridden by Eve's place. Could we go there?"

"Sure. Any particular reason?"

"I need her help."

"You need a ghostbuster?" Briana asked with an impish grin.

Nora laughed. "Something like that. She said to ask Móirín what she needs, but she won't speak to me. Maybe she'll talk to Eve."

Briana shook her head. "I never thought I'd be talking so humdrum about a ghost. I never really believed in them."

Nora tilted her head. "I thought the Irish were superstitious."

"Maybe we are. But it doesn't mean I've ever lived with a spirit." She gave Nora a sideways glance. "I don't know how you stay there."

Nora considered. "If anyone had told me beforehand that I'd have to share the cottage with the ghost of a woman who used to live there, I'd have said no way. But, like I told you and Sheila, I think she needs something. It's not like a horror story about a vengeful spirit."

Briana guided them along narrow paths where tree branches hung close and low, forcing them to duck along the horses' necks. Shannon trotted ahead of them, apparently knowing where they were headed.

"I emailed my grandparents that I'd met Eve," Nora said when the trail widened again and they could ride side by side.

"Have you heard back?"

"Yeah. I got a reply from them yesterday."

"What'd they say?"

"It was weird. My grandmother warned me to stay away from Eve. That surprised me."

Briana turned to her. "Why did she?"

"I don't really know. She just said she wasn't to be trusted and that I should steer clear."

"And so, we're going to see Eve now. Do you always listen this well to your elders?" Briana teased.

Nora grinned. "I'm working on my rebellious side."

Briana frowned, seeming to be trying to decide whether or not to say something.

"What is it?" Nora prompted. "Should we not be going to see her?"

"No," Briana said quickly. "It's not that."

"What then?"

"Well, speaking of emails, Liam told me his sister waited on you at the Cottage a few days ago, and that you looked upset, maybe by some emails you received."

"Oh." Nora had almost forgotten. *You're trying to forget.* "I got an email from Amy."

"Your...?"

"I guess she's my ex." Nora shrugged in resignation. "Never lived together or made a real commitment, but I suppose that's what she is. Anyway, she wants to come here. For a couple of weeks."

Briana didn't say anything for a long time. The horses walked on through the dappled shadows. All around them, birds sang and red squirrels chattered down from tree branches. Bri tugged one of the apples from the bag strapped to her saddle and slipped a knife out of her pocket. She cut a couple of thick wedges out of the apple.

"Give these to the horses," she said. "I don't normally like to feed them when we're riding, but I want to reinforce for Lizzy that this is something nice, and I want her to trust other people."

Nora took the apple wedges and leaned forward. Stubbs was already eyeing the apple greedily, but he plucked it gently from her palm. Lizzy did the same. Briana cut the remainder of the apple in half, handing one portion to Nora. They all munched as little rays of sunlight filtered through the trees to ripple over them.

"When is she coming?" Briana asked at last.

Nora had almost forgotten where the conversation left off. "I don't know." She quickly swallowed the bite of apple in her mouth. "I mean, I haven't answered her."

"Do you want her here?"

"No." Nora was surprised at how much easier it was to say that. "I don't. Sheila says I should just tell her so, but I've been too wimpy to do it. I haven't answered her at all."

"Would you have done it? Back when you were still a habit for her?"

Nora studied her, but Briana was carefully avoiding her eyes. "Yeah. Well, I wouldn't have been here in the first place back then, so..."

Briana's face brightened. "So the rules have changed."

Nora smiled. "The rules have changed."

"Canter?"

AGAIN, AOIBHEANN APPEARED TO have been expecting them. Shannon loped into the clearing ahead of the horses, and they found Eve outside her cottage, tending to some of her plants. Her silver hair was in a loose braid hanging down her back, and she wore her familiar robe, this time a dark, mossy brown. Briana had never given it much thought, but now she did, it seemed that nearly every time she'd wandered by this cottage, Eve had been waiting to greet her.

Eve came to the horses and, to Briana's surprise, Lizzy didn't shy away from her. She murmured to them in Irish, tugging their forelocks.

"You can tie the horses to that downed tree there. They'll be able to graze."

Eve and Shannon went inside, leaving Briana and Nora to follow. They took their riding helmets off and set them near the door. Nora's blonde hair was long enough that it looked just fine. Briana ran a self-conscious hand through her short hair, mussing it more on purpose, wishing she'd stuck a cap in her pocket.

Eve was laying out three mugs of tea for them. "Nora," she said, "would you slice that bread there?"

"We don't mean to put you to any trouble," Nora said. "I just wanted to ask you something."

Eve lifted the kettle off the hook over the fire and poured hot water into her teapot. "We'll have a bite of bread and some tea, and you can ask your something."

Briana saw a pot—or was it a cauldron—steaming over the fire. And she noticed for the first time that the hearth had a separate oven built into the stone for baking.

"Eve, why have you never gotten a proper oven?"

Nora paused as she cut the bread. "Do you even have electricity?"

Eve smiled. "I'm used to doing things a certain way. Slow and steady is best for most of my work."

She laughed at the expressions on their faces. "I'm sure you can't imagine life without your modern conveniences, but they're just tools. I prefer antique tools, you could say."

She went to the hearth to stir the contents of the cauldron. She lifted the spoon to smell and taste it. Apparently pleased, she swung it back over the low fire.

"Now, let's sit with some tea and bread, and you can tell me what's brought you here on this fine morning."

Briana, curious as well, took a bite of the heavy brown bread, spread with creamy butter. She broke a bit off and offered it to Shannon, who lay near her chair.

"Móirín won't talk to me," Nora blurted. "She's there. I can smell her and sense her, and I'm still having the dreams, but she won't tell me what she wants. And I... I wondered if she would if you were to come and speak with her."

Bri wasn't certain, but it seemed a shadow passed over Eve's face. Just for a second and then it was gone. She decided it must have been a flicker of the candle that burned inside the glass lantern on the table.

Eve considered as she sipped her tea. "Have the dreams changed?"

Nora stared, her mug suspended halfway to her mouth. "How did you know?"

"What's changed?"

"There's a child." Nora frowned as she remembered. "I haven't seen it, but I can hear a child laughing in my dreams. And Móirín still cries and calls out."

Briana leaned forward. "Is it Rowan she's hearing?"

"Possibly." Eve's green eyes studied Nora. "How's your grandmother?"

Briana was caught just as wrong-footed as Nora apparently was by the abrupt change in topic.

"She's fine," Nora said, but Bri noticed her slender fingers tightening around her tea mug.

Eve was still staring intently at Nora, who was staring back.

"What did she say?" Eve asked.

"She said to stay away from you. Why would she do that?"

Eve's mouth lifted in the tiniest of smiles, but a little shiver ran down Briana's spine.

"Because she didn't like what I told her," Eve said.

"And what was that?" Nora asked, her eyes big.

But Eve raised her cup, eyeing Nora, regarding her as she sipped.

"How willing are you," she asked at last, "to see this through? To find out what happened?"

Nora looked apprehensively from Eve to Briana and back. "What do you mean? I thought she might talk to you—"

"It's not me she's reaching out to," Eve cut in sharply. She set her cup down. "Would you be willing to go to their realm to find out?"

"Now wait a minute," Briana said. "This is getting creepy."

Eve's eyes flashed green fire. "This is no different than trying to help someone here in our realm who's in trouble. Móirín and Rowan are separated and can't find each other. There is no peace for either of them until they do."

"But," Nora's brow creased, "if they're in the same realm, why can't they find each other?"

"They may not be in the same realm," Eve said. "They're simply not in ours any longer."

Nora appeared to be just as confused as Briana felt.

"There are many realms of... consciousness, let's say," Eve explained. "Some are still tied to this world, while others allow us to move on. What some call heaven or an afterlife."

Eve glanced from one of them to the other. "Haven't you ever been in the same room with someone, and you still couldn't connect, couldn't say what was in your heart?"

Nora's eyes met Bri's, and Briana was trapped, unable to look away. Eve broke the impasse.

"I'll come to help you. Tonight. Ask Sheila and Quinn to be there. At sundown." She reached for a squat jar sitting on the table and slid it toward Briana. "This salve will help with that cheek. Apply some three times a day."

She rose. "I've things I need to prepare. I'll see you both tonight."

NORA PUTTERED AROUND THE cottage for the rest of the day. At the stables, she and Briana had found Quinn.

"Tonight?" he'd asked, looking skeptical when they told him of Eve's instructions. "What, are we doing a kind of séance?"

"I've no idea what she has in mind," Briana had said. "But she wants us all there."

He'd shrugged. "Okay. I'll tell Sheila."

Briana offered to spend the rest of the day with Nora, but she had declined.

"That's silly. You have your work to do. But I'll see you tonight?"

Briana had looked, for a moment, as if she wanted to say something, but all she said was, "Tonight."

Nora dusted and swept, gathered up her papers and pens into a neat stack, arranging and then rearranging her few books. She wasn't sure what Eve had in mind or what they'd be doing or, come to think of it, where they'd be doing it.

She briefly considered going to Sheila's to send her grandmother an email, hoping to catch her online for a real-time chat. Whatever was between her Mamma and Eve she felt had now caught her up in its decades-old web. A voice seemed to whisper, *It's much older than that.*

She remembered the feeling she used to have growing up—the feeling that her ties to Ireland went back longer than she'd been alive. She'd figured it was her grandparents' fanciful tales of growing up here. For some reason, those stories had always captured her imagination much more than any of her sisters'. She shook herself and resumed her cleaning and straightening.

She made herself eat some supper, watching the sun sink lower in the west. She jumped up when she heard an engine from outside the open front door. Before she got to the door, Shannon trotted through to greet her. Sheila and Quinn parked behind Briana.

"Hi," she said to them. "Thanks for coming. I'm really nervous."

"Don't blame you," Sheila said.

"Is Eve here yet?" Quinn asked.

Nora shook her head.

"Listen, are you sure about doing this... whatever she has planned?" He took her by the elbow. "We all like Eve, but..." He glanced at Sheila.

"She told me ages ago," Sheila said, "that many people who come to her don't understand that the things she can do—I can't bring myself to call it magic—but they come with a cost. They're never free."

"What kind of cost?" Briana asked, voicing what Nora had been thinking.

"I'm not sure, exactly," Sheila said. "I don't think it's payment as we normally think of it. I got the feeling, it's more in terms of, be careful what you ask for."

Shannon's ears lifted, and Eve was suddenly there, a bulging pack hanging from her shoulders, her lantern in one hand. Nora hadn't seen her approach, couldn't have even told which direction she came from. In her gown of deep green, Eve could have blended into the forest and been almost invisible. In fact, Nora had the feeling that maybe she had been, listening to them before she made herself known.

"Good evening," Eve said.

She stood, staring at the cottage. Nora couldn't read the expression on her face but, for a moment, it seemed to her that Eve's face changed, looking almost familiar in its sadness. It only lasted a second, and then it was gone.

"Since you're all here, let's get started."

She led the way into the cottage, walking around the parlor, looking about as if she were sniffing out which way to go.

"Upstairs, I think. Bring four chairs."

The others followed her up the steps, where Shannon again refused to enter the front room. She whined from the hallway. Briana gave her a hand signal, and she lay down, her paws just over the threshold of the room.

The candle in Eve's lantern flared, flickering wildly for a moment. She nodded. "Yes. This is the place."

The room was growing dark as the twilight deepened.

Nora went to click on a lamp, but Eve said, "No. Leave it off."

She set the lantern on the bedside table and shrugged the pack off her shoulders. Squatting down, she reached into her bag. "If you four will slide the bed to the middle of the room, I'll get things ready."

They did as she asked, shoving the bed into the center of the room and positioning the chairs around it while Eve laid a dozen candles out in a circle around them on the floor. She moved the bedside table into the circle and set out jars of various sizes and shapes.

"Briana," she said. "Could you get a glass of water, please?"

Briana shrugged in response to Nora's puzzled frown and went to the bathroom, returning a minute later with a glass. Eve took it from her and uncorked one of her jars. She dropped three pinches of the green powder inside into the water and then set the glass on the table.

"We'll let that dissolve. All of you step inside the circle."

They moved closer to the bed while Eve lit the candles. Only later did Nora recall that she hadn't seen any matches in Eve's hands. Eve reached into her bag again, this time retrieving a collection of stones and crystals. Several of these, she laid on the bed.

"Nora, drink this." She held out the glass of murky green liquid.

"What is it?" Nora asked.

"Something to open you."

"Wait," Quinn said. "Before you do that. Eve, what's this about? What's going to happen?"

Eve turned to him. "We're going to guide Nora, her consciousness, to a place where she should be able to communicate with Móirín and maybe Rowan as well. If this goes to plan, she may be able to learn what happened to Rowan and why they're both still bound to this world."

"But how does that work, exactly?" Briana asked with an anxious glance in Nora's direction.

"This tea will relax Nora's mind," Eve said, offering the glass to Nora again. "It will release her inhibitions and guards, so that she can be more open."

Nora withdrew her hand. "What if I don't want my inhibitions and guards released?"

"Worried?" Sheila grinned. "We promise not to spread your secrets."

"Gee, thanks," Nora said.

"We'll be here," Eve insisted, "gathered round, to ground you to this plane and pull you back if needed."

"Pull me back?"

Eve's sharp eyes focused on her. "You'll be moving through a realm a corporeal being doesn't normally inhabit. There are... things that might try to drag you deeper in. You'll need to be able to find your way back." She offered the glass again.

Nora took it and drank. She made a face. "It tastes like grass."

Eve smiled unsympathetically. "Lie down."

Nora stretched out in the middle of the bed, trying to settle comfortably atop the stones. She felt very silly as she looked up into the others' worried faces. Eve placed more stones and crystals on her chest and stomach. She handed one last white crystal to Nora.

"Take this. Keep hold of it, no matter what."

Nora clutched the crystal to her chest.

"Now close your eyes and let your mind go."

Nora was certain that letting her mind go was the last thing she would be able to do. She closed her eyes, though, as Eve daubed some kind of aromatic ointment on Nora's forehead, eyelids, mouth, and hands. She softly intoned something in Irish. The stones and crystals began to feel warm; the scent from the ointment was pleasantly musky. The crystal in Nora's hand felt as if it was pulsing with energy. She tried to open her eyes, to roll them at Briana, but she found them to be too heavy. Her lids were weighed down, and it seemed her whole body was sinking into the softness of the mattress. The last thing she remembered was Eve's hand on her forehead.

THE AIR WAS BITTERLY cold. All the colors seemed slightly off, as if Nora were looking through strangely tinted sunglasses. She was in the bedroom, looking down at herself lying on the bed. Briana had placed a hand on her knee, while Sheila and Quinn sat on the other side, looking on anxiously.

Across the room, standing near the doorway where Shannon lay, was Móirín. She beckoned, moving into the hall. Shannon whined and scrambled out of the way. Nora followed, kind of gliding along, as if her feet weren't actually touching the floor.

Down the stairs they went, to the parlor. Móirín was clearer than she had been in Nora's dreams—her black hair gleamed, her eyes were a clear gray, her dress a deep blue. Even through the other distorted colors, these were sharp.

"Rowan," she called out the door. "Time for tea."

Her voice was soft, melodious—not torn with grief and worry as it had been in the dreams. She moved into the kitchen where Nora saw a fire burning in the stone hearth where her stove now sat. Other figures, more shadow-like, moved about—a tall man and other children. Here, there was laughter and love.

A flash of yellow caught Nora's eye. She turned and saw movement through the front door. She glanced back, but Móirín hadn't seen it. She was busy stirring a pot on the fire.

Nora hurried outside and caught a glimpse of a girl, a scarlet ribbon tying the black hair that hung down the back of her yellow dress. Here, though, the other colors around them had shifted, as if Nora had put on a different pair of glasses. Inside, Móirín and the other shadows still moved about and talked. Nora tried to call out, but her voice didn't carry here. She trailed after the girl, following the sound of her laughter.

The girl ran through the forest, pausing here and there to pluck wildflowers, gathering them into a bouquet. It seemed to Nora that there were faint lights in the shadows of the forest, as if a prism were scattering a beam of sunlight. The red ribbon in the girl's hair caught the light as she moved into a clearing with a circle of squat stones.

From behind them, Nora heard, "Rowan!"

The girl giggled, running on to gather more flowers. Móirín's cries became more urgent. Rowan stopped at the far edge of the clearing and looked at Nora. She ran into the shadows of the forest again, but by the time Nora got there, she had disappeared, as had the glowing lights.

"Rowan?" she called tentatively. Her voice echoed slightly, but there was no response.

Suddenly, the air was filled with the scent of lilac, though Nora couldn't see a bird cherry tree. She strained to move forward, but the crystal in her hand burned, glowed white as something began pulling her backward, tugging and yanking...

She gasped and opened her eyes to find Quinn and Sheila leaning over her, while Briana gripped her knee hard.

Eve was still intoning something in Irish with her palm pressed to Nora's brow.

"What happened?" Nora rasped.

"Sit up and drink this," Eve said, helping her to sit and holding a glass to her mouth.

The cool water helped clear her head. Nora realized she was still clutching the white crystal. She dropped it, expecting to see her palm scorched and blistered, but there was nothing.

"How long was I... under?" She wasn't sure what to call this experience.

"Over an hour," Briana said, a slight tremor to her voice.

Nora shifted to rest against the headboard. "That can't be. It was only a few minutes."

"Tell us what you saw," Eve said.

The others scooted their chairs closer as Nora described what she'd seen.

"I think you're right," she said to Eve. "Rowan was right there, just outside the door, but Móirín couldn't see her."

Eve leaned forward, grasping Nora's hand and squeezing painfully. "And when Rowan disappeared into the trees, that's when you smelled the bird cherry?"

Nora nodded.

Eve released her hand and sat back, her eyes closed. "We've assumed all this time that the lilac scent was Móirín, but it may have been Rowan, trying to reach out to you in her own way."

"What about that clearing with the stones?" Nora asked. "Do you know where that is?"

"I think so," Quinn said. "It's all overgrown now. Most people don't even know they're there."

He scrubbed his hands over his face. "Bloody hell. I need a drink."

Eve reached into her bag yet again, producing a bottle this time.

"Briana, go get some glasses from the kitchen while we put Móirín's room to rights." At Nora's stare, she said, "Sorry. I meant Nora's room."

Briana jumped up and went to where Shannon was wagging her tail in the doorway. She paused and looked back at Nora for a moment, and then she was gone.

"Are you all right?"

Nora looked up into Sheila's concerned face. She climbed off the bed, her legs still a bit wobbly. "I'm fine."

She helped Sheila and Quinn slide the bed into position against the wall while Eve gathered her candles and jars, putting everything back inside her bag.

"What about the lights I saw?" Nora asked.

"There are some plants, mushrooms mostly, that are bioluminescent," Sheila said. "Could have been that."

"Or the *sióg*," Quinn said.

When Sheila and Nora stared at him, he threw his hands up. "What? We're talking about ghosts. You think fairies are out of the question?"

Nora was tempted to giggle at the absurdity of the conversation, except it didn't feel absurd. Or funny.

Briana returned in a couple of minutes with five glasses. Eve sloshed generous measures of whiskey into each. Nora realized her hand was trembling as she raised her glass to her lips. The burn of the whiskey spread through her chilled body.

"It was so cold there," she mumbled, her lips almost too numb to form words.

Sheila rubbed her arm briskly. "I'm going to insist you come along home with us tonight."

Nora nodded, too wiped out to argue. A bone-deep fatigue had set in. She felt she could sleep a week. She drained her glass.

"We'll wait below while you gather whatever you'll need," Quinn said.

He, Sheila, and Eve went downstairs, Eve taking her lantern with her. Nora flipped on the light, blinking at the sudden brightness. She opened a dresser drawer to collect pj's and a change of clothes for the next day. When she turned around, Briana was standing there.

"That was scary," Briana murmured. "You got so white. You almost stopped breathing."

"It didn't feel frightening at the time," Nora said. "But I admit, I'm a little shaken now. I feel a little drunk, and I don't think it's from the whiskey."

Briana rushed forward and flung her arms around Nora. Startled, it took Nora a second to return the embrace. Briana's warmth felt as good as the whiskey. For a long moment, they stood, holding each other. At the sound of voices down below, they reluctantly parted. Nora hovered, her face mere inches from Briana's.

"Ready?" came Quinn's voice up the stairs.

"We should go," Nora whispered.

Briana nodded and headed toward the door where Shannon whined as she paced in the hall. Nora followed them down the stairs.

"Where's Eve?" she asked.

Sheila and Quinn looked around in surprise.

"She was just here," Quinn said.

Sheila took Nora's arm. "Let's go home."

Nora locked the cottage doors and got into Sheila's car. As they backed around, she glanced up at the window, half expecting to see Móirín's pale face watching them, but the window was black and empty.

Chapter 10

RIANA WAS A CYCLONE over the next few days. When she wasn't mucking stalls, she was cleaning tack or training Ginger and the yearlings or replacing broken fence boards.

"Is there some do I don't know about?" Sonya asked her one afternoon, coming in to hang three sets of tack from the guided ride she'd just completed, easily reaching over Briana's head to the saddle racks.

For all her fifteen years in Ireland, Sonya had kept her Swedish accent.

Briana glanced up from her scrubbing of the tack room utility sink. "No. Why?"

"Because you've been a *virvelvind*... what's the English word... whirlwind, all week." She waved at the tack room walls. "This place hasn't been this clean since I came here."

Briana scowled, brandishing her scrub brush. "I told Jimmie and I'll tell you—see that you help keep it that way. I can't stand clutter."

"Did I hear my name?" Jimmie poked his head around the corner.

Sonya waved at the tack room. "I was just wondering what was up with all the cleaning."

"Why does something have to be up?" Briana demanded.

Sonya and Jimmie just looked at each other.

"Out. Both of you."

Sonya chuckled, and Jimmie shook his head as he backed out, grumbling under his breath about "women" and "that time of the month."

But being left alone only let Bri's thoughts run uninterrupted, rampaging through her head like a hamster on a bloody wheel.

What were you thinking, hugging her like that?

It was nothing, she argued. *Just the moment—seeing her lying there like the dead. Still, you've started something. She nearly kissed you.*

Briana paused, her eyes closed, remembering the sweet smell of the whiskey on Nora's breath, the soft brown of her eyes, the way her own heart had pounded as she waited for the kiss that hadn't come...

"Damnation."

She shook herself and resumed her cleaning. She knew from Quinn that Nora had only stayed the one night, returning to the cottage after working with Sheila the next day, but Briana hadn't seen her. She'd been tempted to go by, to check on her—*to hold her again*—but the strength of the wanting was enough to make her stay away.

But staying away hadn't stopped Nora from occupying her thoughts for nearly every waking minute, and plenty of the non-waking ones, too. She'd never had so many erotic dreams about anyone in her life.

In the meantime, Cara and her mother hadn't given up. Cara left three messages a week, asking when she and Nora were coming to Dublin again.

And then there was the whole sightseeing thing she'd stupidly brought up. What if Nora pressed her on it? What if they went rambling down to Clare or Kerry or Cork and spent a few nights together?

"Jesus, it's been so long, I'm not sure I even remember how—"

"What's that?" Quinn stepped through the tack room door.

"Nothing," Bri muttered, a feverish blush heating her face.

He let out a low whistle. "When you're done here, you can go to our house." He peered into the corners. "Hey! You got rid of our spiders."

Her mouth tugged into an unwilling grin. "They're fine. Just relocated." She rinsed out her brush.

He peered at her more closely. "Everything okay, squint?"

"Fine." But she knew better than to think he believed her. "Did you need something?"

"I nearly forgot. Sheila wants to have dinner tonight. Our place. Six o'clock."

Briana briefly panicked and tried to think of an excuse, but she heard herself say, "Six. See you then."

He left her to her scrubbing. And her thoughts.

NORA STOOD AT THE sink, peeling potatoes, when she heard Sheila chuckle.

"What's so funny?"

Sheila looked up from the table where she was transferring pieces of chicken from a bowl of marinade to a roasting pan. "You, standing in my kitchen, humming as you peel potatoes. Who'd have thought six weeks ago?"

Nora grinned. "I didn't realize I was humming. And I can't believe how fast my summer is flying by. I don't want it to end."

Sheila pursed her lips.

Nora set her knife down. "I can see you're just bursting to say something. Out with it."

Sheila shrugged as she drizzled a little more olive oil on the chicken and then sprinkled her own herb mixture over top. "It doesn't have to be just the summer. You could move here permanently."

Nora stared a moment. *How did she know?* She hadn't said a word to anyone that she was thinking just that.

Sheila's eyes widened. "Oh, sweet Jesus. Are you?"

Nora turned back to her potatoes, flustered and caught off-guard. "I... No. My whole life is in the States. How could I just leave and move here?"

Sheila placed a hand on her shoulder, making Nora turn to face her. "Are you really thinking about it?"

Nora gave a half-hearted shrug. "Kind of. Just thinking, though. I haven't said anything to my family."

"Understood." Sheila let her go back to chunking up her peeled potatoes. "Have you told Briana?"

"No!" Nora jabbed her knife at Sheila. "No. And don't you."

Sheila held up her hands. "Promise."

Silence settled back over them. Nora spread her potatoes out in another pan, with generous pats of butter and diced onion. Sheila placed both pans in the oven while Nora scrubbed her cutting board and knife.

"I know you enjoy your work at your library," Sheila said nonchalantly. "But I've come to depend on you here. With the extra online orders we've generated since you updated our website, there's more than I can do alone. I've already been thinking I'll have to hire someone when you leave. You could work here with me. Just something to think about."

Before Nora could even process what Sheila had just said, the bell on the shop door tinkled and they heard, "Sheila? Where are you?"

"In the kitchen."

Nora turned to see a woman who, for just a second, she took for her Mamma.

"Nora," said Sheila. "This is my dad's mum, Fiona Muldoon."

The petite woman chuckled at Nora's expression. "Bit of a shock?" She gave Nora a kiss on the cheek. "I'm sorry it's taken me so long to get down here to meet you. Our B & B in Clifden is booked all of July. I left my Jack in charge. Heaven knows what disaster will strike while I'm away."

Nora held onto her hand. "Sorry, it's just, I can't believe how much you look like my grandmother."

Fiona laughed, and even her laugh sounded like Mamma's. "We're only nine months apart, but I'm older and better looking. Brigid and I used it to our advantage—and our mother's mortification—on more than one occasion. Skipping school and other mischief."

Nora felt sudden tears prick her eyes.

"Are you all right, dear?" Fiona asked kindly, her blue eyes—so like Mamma's—filled with concern.

Nora nodded. "I'm fine. Seeing you just made me homesick for my grandparents, that's all."

"Did you find anything?" Sheila asked.

Nora frowned at this cryptic question.

"I did," Fiona said, lifting her bag off her shoulder.

"Dinner's roasting," Sheila said. "Quinn will be home soon, but I can't wait. Let's go over what you found."

"I think this has earned me a glass of wine," Fiona said, sitting and retrieving a sheaf of papers from her bag.

"Wine it is," Sheila said. She went to the refrigerator to retrieve a bottle. "Nora?"

"Sure."

A couple of minutes later, they were all seated at the table with filled glasses and a plate of crackers and cheese. Rusty lay under the table where he was ready to pounce should any food drop.

"First," Fiona said, looking at Nora with her hands folded over top of her papers, "I think we should talk about Eve."

Nora blinked. "Okay."

"Sheila told me Brigid wouldn't tell you why she warned you to stay away from Eve."

"That's right. It all felt very mysterious."

"That's a good word for it." Fiona took a drink. "Before I begin, you need to know a little background. When we were young, I'm ashamed to admit it was a cruel kind of game for the kids to dare each other to see who could get closest to Eve's cottage without being snared. Of course the stories of what she did to those she caught scared us to death, even if they most likely weren't true."

Nora glanced at Sheila. "I've asked this before, but how old is she?"

Fiona flipped her hands palm-up. "Who knows? She's been in that cottage, looking exactly the same, for as long as our parents remembered."

"That's impossible," Nora said.

"So are ghosts," said Sheila with an impish grin.

"Touché."

"We'll get to that in a minute," Fiona said.

"Go on." Nora raised her glass and sipped.

"Well," Fiona said, "when we were maybe twelve or thirteen, a gaggle of us were sneaking up to Eve's cottage to spy on her. I saw her outside, doing something with her plants, and then she just vanished. Brigid crept a bit closer to see where she'd gone and, suddenly, she had Brigid by the arm and was dragging her inside. The others all scattered and ran, but I charged into the cottage, demanding she let my little sister go."

Nora smothered a grin, visualizing a feisty young Fiona doing just that.

"When I got in there, she had Brigid sitting at the fire and said, 'We were waiting for you.'"

Nora leaned forward. "So what happened?"

"She said she'd had a vision about one of us, but she wasn't sure which, as we looked so much alike."

"What kind of vision?" Nora asked breathlessly.

"That one who came from us would have to make a fateful choice—a choice that could take her life. Or give life to another."

154

Nora looked from Fiona to Sheila and back again. "What does that mean?"

"We've never known. Eve couldn't or wouldn't explain further." Fiona gave an embarrassed laugh. "We just chalked it up to Eve's strange behavior and tried to forget about it. But when Tommy said he'd arranged for you to rent Sióg Cottage from James McCarthy..."

She grasped Nora's forearm. "Brigid and Tom were thrilled when you decided to come here, but then you met Eve and, well... Brigid remembered Eve's... prophecy, we'll call it. She's worried about you, Nora."

Nora sat back, speechless.

"But it might not mean Nora a'tall," Sheila said.

"It might not," Fiona agreed. "I've worried all my adult life about my children and then all of you when you were wee ones. As you've grown, I'd almost forgotten it completely until Nora's coming here seemed to awaken something. Something tied to that bloody cottage."

The back door opened, and Quinn stomped into the kitchen, Briana on his heels.

"Fiona!" he said, his weathered, freckled face splitting into a wide smile.

Fiona got up to give him a hug. "How's my favorite grandson-in-law?"

"Well enough. You remember our friend, Briana?"

"Of course."

Briana sniffed. "Smells wonderful in here."

Sheila got up. "Wine or beer?"

"Beer for me," Quinn said, toeing off his boots.

Briana followed suit, and Nora noticed she seemed to be avoiding her gaze. Nora went to the refrigerator to get two bottles of Harp's and opened them. She handed one to Quinn.

"Here," she said, offering the other to Briana. When Bri tried to take it, she held on for a moment, forcing Briana to meet her eyes. She smiled, just barely stopping herself from caressing Briana's cheek to calm the near panic she saw in her face. Her heart thrummed happily as she returned to her seat.

"What's all this?" Quinn asked, pointing his bottle at Fiona's papers before taking a big swig.

"This," said Fiona, "is the result of hours of online research. Tomorrow," she eyed Nora, "you and I are going to the archives of St. Mary's."

"We are?"

Fiona nodded. "We are." She spread her papers out, and Nora could see that they were photocopies of what looked like ship manifests and census records.

"Gran is into genealogy," Sheila said.

"Mayo had such an enormous loss of inhabitants," Fiona said. "Both the Famine and the wave of emigration that followed left us hollowed out, but provides us with a treasure trove of information on people who originated from this county."

She slid two papers to Nora. Each had a line highlighted. Fiona pointed to one, saying, "This is a passenger manifest."

Briana, sitting next to her, scooted nearer, pressing her thigh against Nora's.

Nora had a hard time concentrating as she read, "Donall O'Hara." She paused. "He Americanized the spelling." Squinting at the faded writing, she continued, "He boarded with five children on 5th June, 1848, bound for Boston."

Quinn reached for the page. "But no mention of Móirín."

"No." Fiona nudged the second page over to Nora. "The census of 1850."

This was even more faded and difficult to read. Nora leaned close. "Clinton, Massachusetts." She ran a finger down the page. "Here he is. Donall O'Hara, smith. Then Callum, age ten, Una age seven, Séan age five, Teafa age four."

Nora looked up. "That's only four children. There were five on the ship manifest. What happened?"

"Again, no mention of a wife," said Sheila softly. "Did she die here and that's why he left?"

Fiona shook her head. "No idea. But maybe we'll find out more tomorrow."

Briana shifted away, and Nora immediately missed the physical contact. Raising her beer, Briana said, "Good luck with your search."

Nora gazed at her and raised her glass. "To finding what we need."

"ROWAN, SEE TO THE baby, will you?"

Móirín glances over to where the baby is fussing as she lies on a soft pile of blankets.

"Oh, I'll tend to her," says Mrs. Smythe, the head housekeeper.

She picks the baby up and takes her to a chair in the corner of the room where Móirín has a table covered with pieces of cloth, cut and ready to be sewn together for a new coat for Mr. Campbell, the butler. On the table is a jar filled with the latest bunch of flowers Rowan picked. The flowers are lovely but, dear God, corralling that girl is harder than shoeing a green horse.

"What unusual eyes for a baby," Mrs. Smythe says, as the baby stares up at her. "Enough to make you believe she was dropped on your stoop by those fairy-folk."

Not daring to cross herself for fear of setting off a rant about Papists, Móirín nevertheless uses her thumb to make a tiny cross on her forehead, her lips, and her heart. "Having carried her myself for nine months, I can tell you she's mine."

Mrs. Smythe gives the baby a finger to suckle. "How many did you say this one makes?"

Móirín, wishing very hard Mrs. Smythe had somewhere else to be, says, "She's our sixth."

"Six! It's positively indecent how you Irish breed. Civilized people would never do any such thing."

Móirín notices the frown on Rowan's face, and nudges her under the table. When Rowan glances in her direction, Móirín gives her a little shake of the head.

She bends back to her work, neat stitches creating smooth seams, as Mrs. Smythe laments her "exile", as she calls it, to Ireland from the family's other country house in Yorkshire.

"Of course, they needed someone to bring some order to Ashford, as the Irish peasants were robbing them hand over fist."

Mrs. Smythe seems oblivious to the angry flush in Móirín's cheeks or the way Rowan has turned her back as she works on the sleeve cuffs, sewing the way her mam taught her.

When at last the baby has drifted off to sleep, and Mrs. Smythe has left to see to some other things, Rowan looks up.

"Why does she say such things about us, Mam?"

Móirín tries to keep her tone even. "A lot of the English think the way Mrs. Smythe thinks. That we're no more than an island of ignorant people, breeding like rabbits. They think the famine is our own fault. That's why they won't help."

"But that's wrong."

Móirín's voice cracks and she blinks tears back as she says, "Yes, *mo chailín*. It's wrong. One day they'll realize that."

NORA SNEEZED.

"God bless you," said Fiona.

Nora grinned and dabbed at her nose with a tissue. "Thanks."

They had spent the early part of the morning wandering the church cemetery, searching out family graves. Nora counted herself blessed that all four of her grandparents were still alive—her mom's folks lived in North Carolina now and she'd never known her great-grandparents—so there was no strong sense of family roots to be found in the States. Here, though, their family went back several generations, both the Cleary and McNeill sides. Some of the old limestone markers were so pitted that the names were impossible to make out. There was no real sadness on Nora's part, as she hadn't known any of these people, but it strengthened a feeling of connection to Cong in a way that just being here hadn't. Her family's roots in this area were deep.

Now, sitting in the church basement, she bent back over the ancient—and dusty—register of baptisms while Fiona returned to her perusal of digitized records. The church secretary had told them the records in the computer were incomplete, and she'd been hesitant to give them access to the original books until Fiona assured her that Nora was a university librarian. When Nora produced a pair of clean cotton gloves for handling the books, the secretary had relented.

"You're in your element here," Fiona observed as Nora ran a finger down the page.

"Yeah," Nora said with a sigh. "I guess I am."

"You sound unhappy about that."

Nora marked her place with a gloved finger and sat back. "Not unhappy. Just... unsettled, I guess."

Fiona gazed at her, waiting for her to choose her words. It was almost like having her grandmother here.

"Don't say anything to Mamma and Pop yet," Nora began, "but I'm thinking of, maybe, moving here for good."

Fiona's raised eyebrows were her only sign of surprise.

"I mean I love my family," Nora said quickly. "I miss them, but I can visit with them online."

"What about your work?" Fiona asked.

"I'd miss library work," Nora admitted. "But Sheila has offered me work with her at the nursery. She'll have to hire someone no matter what."

"She told me what a tremendous help you've been," Fiona said. "What with the website and learning all the rest of the nursery business."

"It's been so much fun," Nora said, her face lighting up. "Learning about all the herbs and oils she uses in her soaps and salves and lotions. And everything she's taught me about plants and trees. It's been such a change from what I do every day. Been doing every day for years."

Fiona smiled. "Maybe that's the appeal. You're doing something different, something that's stimulating to you."

Nora frowned, flicking the tip of one gloved finger where the cotton puckered. "You think it won't last. Like an early mid-life crisis."

She stopped suddenly as she heard the words leave her mouth. *It's not all that early.*

"I didn't say that." Fiona turned back to the computer monitor. "And is there no one else to go back for?"

Nora, too, bent over her book, but she wasn't reading. "Not really."

"But there's someone here?"

Nora's head whipped up again, but Fiona was intently focused on the monitor. "I don't know." Her shoulders sagged. "Am I that transparent?"

"Not transparent so much as… open," Fiona said gently. "Like that book in front of you. There for anyone with the eyes to see."

"But it doesn't feel wise to make such a huge change based on something that might not work out."

"Would that be your main reason for moving here?"

"No." Nora bit her lip. "Would you think I'm crazy if I told you I've always had this feeling, like I was being drawn here?"

Fiona faced her again. "No, dear. I don't think that's crazy a'tall."

Nora bent over her book again, and Fiona returned to her computer screen. They worked in silence for several minutes, the only sound the ticking of the clock on the wall.

"How do you know when it's real?" Nora asked softly.

"When it's real, you won't have to ask."

Nora bit her lip again, trying to stem tears that suddenly stung her eyes, but then she froze, the other conversation forgotten. Bending over the brittle page before her, she gasped.

"What?" Fiona wheeled her chair over to read the line Nora indicated. "Sweet Jesus."

"I think," Nora murmured, "we need to speak to my grandmother."

Chapter 11

YEATS GRUNTED IN PLEASURE as Briana laid into the brush, running it in long strokes along his spine. Standing on a stool, she followed with her hands, massaging and kneading. His near rear hoof kicked a little.

"Found the sore spot, did I?"

The gelding had carried a heavy Swiss tourist who Liam reported had spent most of the ride twisted in the saddle, talking to the woman behind him, leaving poor Yeats to counterbalance the git's weight.

"Good thing I wasn't there," she grunted along with Yeats as she worked. "Or he'd have walked back. Then Quinn would fire me, and no one would be working on you."

Sweat beaded on her forehead and ran down her back. By the time she was finished, she felt she needed a massage her own self.

"How's he, then?"

She stepped down off the stool and turned to Jimmie. "He'll be fine, but no heavy loads for a day or two."

He nodded, making a note on his clipboard. "We've a group of five women tomorrow morning. Think he'll be okay with them?"

"Yeah." She gave Yeats a pat, and he nickered his thanks.

Reaching for the stool and her brush, she carried them out of the stall. "Where's Quinn?"

Jimmie didn't glance up. "Horse auction in Sligo."

"Well, don't schedule anything for me on Thursday. I'm taking the day off."

She felt his eyes boring into her back. He followed her into the tack room.

"A day off?"

"Yes, Jimmie. People are allowed to take a day off now and again."

"So you're 'people' now, are you? What's the occasion?"

She kept her back to him as she straightened things unnecessarily. "No occasion. Just have some things to do."

"Okay, squint. You'll have your day off. For things."

She heard him chuckling as he walked away. "Git."

But she supposed she couldn't blame him. She almost never took a day off, so taking one for any reason other than to go to Dublin to see her family would naturally raise his curiosity.

Now that part was taken care of, she needed to see if her plans for her day off would come together. Maybe she should have seen to that part first… She hurried to her cottage to shower.

A few minutes later, smelling much better and wearing clean jeans and a T-shirt, Briana whistled for Shannon and got into the SUV.

A light rain misted the windshield as she drove. Her heart fell when she found Sióg Cottage dark, the door shut, no sign of Nora's bicycle. She drummed her fingers on the wheel for a moment.

"I wonder."

She drove on to the nursery. The shop was shut up for the day, but she parked and followed Shannon around back to the kitchen door. The kitchen was empty, but the lights were on. She let herself in, scuffing her shoes on the mat.

"Sheila?"

There was no answer, but she heard voices coming from the den. Following the sound, she found Nora, Sheila, and Fiona all gathered around the computer where a familiar face peered out at them.

Sheila turned and waved Briana in as Nora was saying, "But you never spoke to her again after that?"

"No," said the woman in the monitor. "I steered clear of her, and I wish you would, too, Nora."

"I can't," Nora said.

"We'll keep an eye on her, Brigid," Fiona said. "But you see what you can find out on your end, will you?"

"I will. Take care, all of you."

"I love you, Mamma," Nora said. "Love to Pop. I'm sorry I missed him."

She ended the video call and sat back.

"What in the world is going on?" Briana asked.

Nora whipped around. "Hi."

"Is this a bad time?"

"Not a'tall," Sheila said.

They all went back into the kitchen. Briana was very aware of the way Nora's face had lit up. Shannon plopped on the kitchen floor to get on Rusty's level.

"What's all this?" Briana asked, taking in the papers scattered on the table. She sniffed. "What's baking?"

"Our research," Nora said, taking a chair and nudging the one beside her for Briana. "The papers, not the baking part."

"That'd be the soda bread," said Sheila. "To go with the Guinness stew in the pot. You'll stay and have supper with us."

"Gladly." Briana sat. "What did you find?"

"Some very interesting things," Fiona said.

"Tea?" Sheila asked. "The kettle's still hot."

"Yeah, thanks." Briana craned her head to read one of the pages. "What are these?"

"Copies of baptismal records," said Fiona.

"And these are death records." Nora pointed to another sheet.

"Anything of Rowan?" Briana asked, sliding one paper near.

"Yes." Nora leaned closer, pressing her shoulder to Briana's. She traced a finger down the faded lines on the page. "She was baptized in 1841, on five September."

"So she was probably born in July or August," Fiona said.

Sheila set a steaming mug in front of Briana. "The church didn't have complete birth records. We're guessing with babies being born at home, and people living too far away to get to church regularly, a lot of them most likely only went for things like baptisms, marriages, funerals."

"And remember," said Fiona, "a lot of babies were stillborn or died as newborns and didn't live long enough for a church baptism, especially after the first few bad crops of the Famine. I'm thinking the ones that did live were baptized as soon as the parents could manage, in case the worst happened."

She leafed through other pages. "We found a record of Móirín and Donall's marriage, and the baptisms of their other children. It seems Rowan was their second-born, and the oldest girl."

"But look at this." Nora passed another paper to Briana.

Briana's mouth fell open. "Holy sh—" She bit the word off. "Beg your pardon, Fiona."

"No need. Holy shit, indeed."

"But it can't be." Briana looked around from one of them to the other. "Aoibheann? Their fifth child was Aoibheann? You're not suggesting..."

"We don't know what we're suggesting," Sheila said.

166

"That's why we needed to talk to my grandmother," Nora said. "But she doesn't remember anything more than Fiona does about Eve."

"I thought on the census forms you brought," Bri said to Fiona, "it only had four children listed with Donall."

"But there were five on the ship manifest," Nora reminded her.

"That's right," Fiona agreed, sorting through her papers to find that one. "We don't know what it means."

"It's just a coincidence," Briana said firmly. "I mean, it's not a common name, but it's just coincidence, right? And her name is Aoibheann Ní Mheolchatha, not Heaghra."

"Which in America, would be Mulcahy, I think," Nora said. "Did she marry?"

"Listen to what you're saying," Briana said. "You're talking as if she could be one and the same."

Fiona lifted her hands with a shrug. "I've always been intrigued by the stories from my parents and grandparents that Eve never changes."

Nora gave a nervous laugh. "This puts her up there with leprechauns."

Fiona pointed a finger. "Don't joke about the wee folk. Or the *sióg*. 'Tis an invitation for them to work their trouble and mischief. And worse."

"What do you mean?"

"In Irish folklore, the fae and other creatures aren't cute or kind, like cartoon movies would have you believe. They could be vengeful and possessive of those who crossed their path."

"And on that note," said Sheila, "we need something stronger than tea."

Two hours later, fortified by a fine supper of wine, stew and fresh bread, they cleaned up the kitchen. Sheila had scooped enough kibble for Shannon and Rusty's dinner as well.

"I'll keep some stew on the warmer for Quinn," Sheila said. "Hopefully that man will be home soon, and no new horses with him."

Briana grinned. "Don't count on that. You know him."

Sheila sighed. "I do. And I'm not counting on it."

"At least they earn their keep," Nora said.

"Some of them do."

The worry in Sheila's tone pricked at Briana's conscience. It had been at her instigation that Quinn had rescued Lizzy and a few other horses that they knew weren't suited for the riding stable. Quinn's margins were tight, and what with extra mouths to feed and vet bills for those horses that didn't earn their keep, it was a stretch for his budget.

"I should be going," she said heavily. "Thanks for dinner."

There'd been no opportunity to speak with Nora, so now there was that on top of everything else. She patted her thigh for Shannon.

"Would you mind giving me a ride home?" Nora asked.

"No." Briana's heart lifted. "We don't mind at all."

They said good evening to Sheila and Fiona and stepped outside into the soft rain. Briana loaded Nora's bike into the boot of the SUV and got in.

"Thanks," said Nora. "Not a good night to bicycle."

"They wouldn't have let you ride in this."

A tense silence filled the car as Briana drove through the murky evening, trying to think of how to broach the thing she wanted to say.

"Is something wrong?" Nora asked.

"No," Briana said quickly. She turned onto the narrow drive to the cottage. "Not wrong. I was just wondering... I asked for Thursday off, if you've no other plans, just for a day of rambling about Connemara, since you've seen so little of it."

Nora's face, in the lights from the dashboard, broke into a delighted smile. "That sounds lovely. Thank you."

Briana braked in front of the cottage and hopped out to unload the bicycle. Under the cottage eaves where they were sheltered from the rain, she and Nora stood awkwardly, neither seeming to want to say goodnight, but neither brave enough to take the next step.

"Well," Briana said at last, "I should—"

Nora's hand moved. Briana reached out to take it, but Nora pulled her key from her pocket and unlocked the door. Briana took a step back and stuffed her hand in her own pocket.

"I'll let you go," Nora said, but she sounded reluctant. "See you Thursday?"

"Thursday. Early. And wear your walking shoes."

Briana jogged around the car to climb into the driver's seat. Nora gave a last wave as Briana drove down the lane. Shannon leaned forward from the back seat and nosed Bri's cheek.

"I know, I know." She gave Shannon a rub. "I'm a fecking chicken."

NORA PACED FROM WINDOW to door and back again on Thursday morning, dressed in her hiking pants and waterproof shoes. Her backpack was stuffed with a rain jacket, an extra fleece, snacks, and bottled water for them. Her camera was charged and packed as well.

Fiona had left Wednesday morning. "I've got to get back or who knows what Jack will have done."

She made Nora and Sheila promise to call her if they learned anything more of Móirín and Rowan.

As soon as they were alone, Nora told Sheila about Briana's cryptic plans. Sheila's curiosity had been piqued as much as Nora's. All day long, she'd peppered Nora with questions as they tended plants in the greenhouse.

"Do you think she'll take you to Ballintubber Abbey?"

"No idea," Nora said. "I've read about it, but don't think I've said anything."

An hour later, "Have you expressed any interest in Clew Bay?"

"No."

At one point, Sheila jabbed her trowel at Nora. "I wonder if she and Gran cooked up a plan to visit Clifden?"

It sounded like something Fiona might do, given Nora's conversation with her during their research session at St. Mary's.

But Nora was as clueless as Sheila. The anticipation was kind of fun. And she knew, though she would never have admitted it to Sheila, that part of the anticipation was the prospect of spending an entire day with Briana. It would be a nice break from the mystery of Móirín and Rowan, which was a constant shadow looming over her lately.

The dreams had taken a decidedly darker turn in the last week or so. Rowan's laughter—if indeed it was her—had turned to screams and cries for help. But when Nora tried to call to her, tried to figure out where the cries were coming from, she woke, sweating and breathless.

When Briana drove up, Nora was out the door before the SUV had come to a full stop.

"Hi," she said as she opened the passenger door.

Briana pointed at Nora's backpack. "You've got rain gear, in case we run into a bit of wet?"

Nora stowed her bag behind her seat. "I do. Plus some snacks and water."

"All right, then. We're off."

"Where are we off to?"

Briana shook her head. "'Tis a surprise."

Shannon rested her shaggy head on Nora's shoulder for a moment, earning a scratch before stretching out across the back seat.

Nora tried at first to keep track of which direction they were headed and try to guess their destination, but she soon found herself simply sitting back and enjoying the passing scenery.

"How's your family?" Nora asked when it seemed Briana wasn't going to initiate any conversation.

"They're fine. We will have to go back to see them before you leave or I'll never be forgiven. Kieran hasn't let me forget that we promised to let him read more books to us."

Nora smiled, but then the smile faded away. *Before you leave.* Her summer was flying by way too fast.

"How about you?" Briana asked.

"What do you mean?"

"How are your family and friends in the States?"

"They're fine. Got a chance to catch up on the news when we talked with Mamma the other evening."

"Anyone planning to visit?"

Nora bit back a laugh. "Very subtle. No. At least I don't think so."

Briana cast her a quick sideways look. "You haven't answered her."

"No." Nora let a guilty sigh escape. "I figure no reply is as good as a 'no', but... no."

Briana drove with her right hand on the wheel, her left resting on her thigh. For a moment, Nora thought about how nice it would be to reach over and take it. *Do it.*

She was just reaching over when Briana's hand moved back to the steering wheel.

"What is it?" Briana asked, her attention caught by the movement.

"Nothing." Nora quickly reached back to retrieve two bottles of water from her backpack. She loosened the top on Briana's and set it in the drink holder. "How long till we get there?"

Briana grinned. "A bit yet."

She kept glancing at Nora, looking more concerned.

"Do I have something on my face?" Nora reached up self-consciously to make sure she didn't have any leftover breakfast on her mouth.

Briana shrugged. "You look tired, that's all. More dreams?"

Nora tried to decide whether she should be offended. "You could say that," she said with a scoff. "Almost every morning, I wake up feeling as if I've been running through the woods all night long. Sometimes..."

"Sometimes what?"

Nora ran a hand through her hair. "A couple of times, I've have mud or dirt on my hands, leaves in my hair. And wet clothes in a pile on the floor."

Briana nearly drove off the road. Correcting the car, her hands gripped the wheel tightly. "You've been walking in your sleep?"

"I don't know. Maybe. I don't know how else to explain... but I don't remember doing it. I mean, I'm running through the woods in most of my dreams. Rowan is crying out for help now."

"Nora, this is getting ridiculous." Briana reached over and gripped Nora's hand. "You have to get out of that cottage."

Nora stared down at her fingers, intertwined with Briana's—exactly what she'd hoped for just moments before. "I can't."

"Why can't you?"

"I told you, they need me."

"But this is crazy," Briana insisted. She seemed to realize what she'd done and released her grip on Nora's hand to put her own back on the wheel. "If you're being dragged out of your bed in your sleep, who knows what else could happen to you?"

Nora couldn't deny the same thought had occurred to her, but she felt this irresistible compulsion to find out what happened to them.

They rode in silence. Nora wished she still had Briana's warm hand in hers.

Towering hedges of fuchsia flashed by, their red flowers brilliant against their dark green leaves, turning the road into a kind of tunnel. It was hypnotic. Nora felt her eyelids grow heavy. Despite her attempts to stay awake, she fell into a deep sleep.

BRIANA PULLED TO A stop next to a couple of other cars. She reached over to wake Nora, but hesitated. Biting her lip, she watched Nora sleeping. It was God's truth, she looked more than tired; Bri had actually been a bit shocked upon seeing her this morning. The dark circles under her eyes made her look as if she hadn't slept for days. She could probably use several hours of sleep outside that blasted cottage, but the entire day was planned around an itinerary.

"Nora." Briana nudged her shoulder gently. "Nora, we're here."

Nora jumped and her eyes fluttered open. She sat up, rubbing her eyes to wipe the sleep out of them. Briana waited as Nora frowned in puzzlement at the landscape before them.

"Where are we?"

Waves washed up onto a broad sandy beach. Grassy hillocks pushed up here and there, and the sun slanted through fast-moving clouds.

"Come and see."

Briana got out, holding the door for Shannon while Nora took a minute to get her camera out of her backpack.

"Do you recognize it?" Briana asked.

Nora turned in place. "It looks kind of familiar." She walked toward the water, looking up and down the beach. "Is this...?"

She turned to Briana. "Is this where they filmed the horse race?"

Briana grinned. "Yeah. Lettergesh Beach. I looked it up."

Her grin faded as the surprised expression on Nora's face disappeared and her eyes filled with tears. Flummoxed, Briana stood there watching Nora walk away from her.

"What the—?"

Shannon looked at Bri for a second before trotting after Nora.

Briana's heart, so light a moment ago, was now in the vicinity of her stomach as she followed. If this was Nora's reaction to their first stop, this was going to be a hell of a day.

Miserably, Briana followed and stood beside Nora, her hands in her jacket pockets as they watched the waves for several minutes. Shannon chased some gulls, splashing through the surf.

"Did I do something wrong?" Briana asked at last.

Nora shook her head, but still couldn't look at Briana. She wiped her sleeve across her eyes.

"This is the nicest..." Nora sniffed. "No one has done anything like this for me. It means a lot."

Briana stared at her in bewilderment. She gestured. "So these are good tears?"

Nora half-laughed. "Yes. These are good tears." She reached for Briana's hand. "Thank you."

She gave Bri's hand a squeeze and let go. "Let's walk."

Briana followed her down the beach, wishing she were brave enough to take Nora's hand again and hold it as they walked.

Nora stopped, frowning. "Are you limping? Your leg is bothering you, isn't it?"

Bri shrugged. "It comes and goes, like the weather in Ireland."

"We don't have to wander."

"We came here to wander," Briana insisted. "And walking is better than sitting."

They explored the dunes, climbing one of the taller hills to get a better view. Nora lifted her camera, snapping dozens of photos. Briana studied her as she climbed the tussocks, squatting to take a shot from a low angle with beach grasses in the foreground. There was something different about her now—a grace in the way she moved, unlike the clumsiness she'd exhibited when she first arrived.

They spent the better part of an hour exploring. Nora insisted on a few photos of Briana and Shannon, framed by the ocean or the dunes.

Nora sighed, strands of her blonde hair blown about by the stiff breeze coming in off the water. "This was great. Thanks again."

"We're only getting started," Briana said. "If you're ready to move on..."

Nora's face lit up. "What's next?"

Briana shook her head. "You'll have to wait and see."

They hurried back to the SUV.

"This feels like a scavenger hunt," Nora said with a giggle.

"It kind of is."

Briana followed the Connemara Loop signs, stopping a few places so that Nora could take more photos. At Letterfrack, she headed west on N59.

Nora's head swiveled as she took in the scenery. When they saw the signs for Clifden, she asked, "Are we going to see Fiona?"

"Yes and no. We are having lunch with her and Jack at their B & B, but first..."

She drove into the town center, around the roundabout, and found parking. Nora gaped as they got out.

"This was... It looks a little like... was this Castletown?"

"That's what the guidebook said."

Nora's face lit up, and she snapped several more photos before they got back in the car. "Do you know the way to the B & B?"

"Fiona gave me directions. Ready?" Briana shifted into drive, checking her mirror for oncoming traffic.

Nora wriggled into her seat. "Ready."

A COUPLE OF HOURS later, Fiona and Jack waved them off. Their B & B was charming—an old farmhouse with five comfortably furnished rooms in the main house, a large stone fireplace in the parlor, which Jack kept stocked with peat in the cooler months, and a rustic dining table big enough to seat twelve comfortably. They'd built an addition off the side of the original house so they could have some private space, but still be close for guests. The farmhouse overlooked Clifden Bay, though heavy clouds had moved in, bringing a steady rain and fog.

Jack kept them entertained as they ate a wonderful lunch of homemade soup and brown bread, followed by scones with strawberry jam Fiona had put up the summer before. Nora was hit hard with a pang of homesickness, what with Jack cracking up at his own bad jokes the way Pop always did, and Fiona looking so like Mamma.

She caught Briana watching her closely a few times, and forced herself to snap back to the present. But she couldn't quite shake a feeling of melancholy as they drove away.

"Are you all right?" Briana asked as she navigated the narrow, winding road.

Nora thought about lying to her, but that just seemed wrong. "They remind me so much of my grandparents."

"You miss them."

Nora nodded. "I do."

Briana seemed to deflate a little. "Do you want to go straight back to Cong?"

"No." Nora gave Briana's arm a squeeze without giving herself a chance to second-guess it. "What else did you have planned?"

Briana glanced at her doubtfully. "A couple more stops. Are you sure?"

"I'm sure."

For a while, the slap of the wipers was the only sound.

"What made you decide to do this?" Nora asked.

"You talk so much about that movie and how it brought you to Ireland, I just thought you might like to see a bit more of what went into making it."

"You researched this," Nora said.

Briana shrugged. "Yeah."

Even under gray skies with the rain coming down, Briana's red hair caught what light there was. Nora longed to reach out and caress it. Touching her arm was one thing, but... She stuffed her hands between her knees instead. "Why did you?"

Briana's hands tightened on the wheel. Rather than answering, she asked, "Why were you crying at Lettergesh?"

"I don't know if I can explain," Nora said softly. "Have you ever been surrounded by people, people you love and who love you, but felt you didn't quite belong there?"

"Why do you think I don't go to Dublin more often?"

Nora met Briana's gaze for a moment and saw that she did understand. "I love my family, and it's not that we don't get along or anything. It's just... I don't have a spouse or kids. I think they just expect me to be there, like a piece of furniture, but if I'm not, I'm not sure they notice. I wonder if they've missed me at all this summer."

Briana snorted. "That may have more to do with us than them."

"You're probably right," Nora agreed. "I guess I feel like my life doesn't measure up to their expectations. Or maybe it's only my expectations. Whatever. I've never reached for much. Just my job. And Amy. Kind of."

"I know mine feel the same way about working with horses. Mum always wanted me to go to university."

"I did that, but it still doesn't feel like enough."

They rode for a while, each lost in her own thoughts.

"She—Amy—wouldn't have done something like this for you?"

"No. It's not that she was mean or unkind or anything." Nora struggled to explain. "It just wouldn't have occurred to her to plan something like this. She thought I was silly for loving that movie so much." She sighed. "She thought I was silly about a lot of things."

"Aren't you angry about what happened?"

Nora pondered that for a long moment. "I was, I guess. More hurt than anything. We'd drifted into just a friendship without even knowing it had happened. I suppose she felt that spark with Tracy and needed that connection. It wasn't there with me any more. Looking back, I'm not sure it ever was."

"But Lettergesh..."

Briana wasn't going to let this go. Nora's heart pounded as she tried to force the words out. *Once you say them, you can't take them back.*

"You took the time to plan this, to do something special for me," she heard herself say. "I can't tell you how much that means."

This time, she did reach out to caress Briana's soft hair. Briana's eyes widened, but she leaned into Nora's palm. When she took Nora's hand and pressed it to her lips, Nora thought her heart might actually stop. She'd never imagined she could feel so much from such a simple gesture.

They drove on, hands clasped, neither speaking. Words weren't needed, which was good because it was all Nora could do to breathe.

The sky lightened, and the rain became a drizzle and then stopped altogether. Briana navigated for a while with one hand on the wheel but eventually said, "I'll need both hands now."

She reached for a sketched map she'd tucked into her console. Following its directions, she turned off the road, taking a series of smaller roads before finally turning onto what looked like little more than a cow track and then coming to a stop.

Nora clapped both hands to her mouth, and her eyes filled again. "The cottage."

They got out. Shannon bounded ahead of them, nose down as she tracked the scent of rabbits through the wet grass. Nora crossed the bridge, stopping to gaze at the ruins of what had been White O'Morn. The crumbling cottage looked nothing like it had in the movie, but the surroundings...

"This was it," Nora murmured. "Another name for heaven."

She reached for Briana's hand, squeezing it. Together, they wandered around the remains of the cottage. Nora stepped over the rubble into the cottage's interior. Briana picked her way across the rocks in the rambling stream to wait at the bridge, leaving Nora to her thoughts as she stood there, her arms wrapped around herself, just breathing in the wonder of standing in this spot.

When Nora went back to the bridge, Briana pointed.

A rainbow. Arching through the sky over the cottage. Perfect.

"Do you want your camera?" Briana asked, rising to go to the SUV.

Nora shook her head. She tugged Briana back down and sat next to her on the bridge. "I just want to make this memory with you."

For long minutes, they sat shoulder to shoulder. Nora tried to take it all in. Lambs bleated in a neighboring field as clouds scudded across the partially blue sky. She turned to find Briana watching her, all freckles and blue eyes and so damned adorable. *Kiss her.*

Just as she leaned in, another car pulled up and parked beside their SUV. She and Briana jerked apart and jumped to their feet as a carload of loud American tourists spilled out.

"Let's go," Nora said.

Briana whistled for Shannon, and they climbed back into the car. "Where to now?" Nora asked as Briana drove back the way they'd come.

"Just one more stop."

From the corner of her eye, Nora saw Briana glancing in her direction, but she refused to look, afraid of how much her eyes would betray the torrent of feelings tumbling inside her. The air in the car fairly crackled with the tension of that unfulfilled kiss.

"Bloody hell."

Briana braked to a hard stop and grabbed Nora by her jacket, yanking her over to mash her mouth against Nora's. What started as a furious crush of lips and tongues and teeth changed, gentled as they tasted and explored each other. Nora cupped Briana's cheek and felt Bri's hand on the back of her head, holding her in place.

A giant dog tongue joined the melee, swiping both their cheeks. When they parted, Shannon was panting at them with a doggy smile.

Nora gave Briana another light kiss and sat back. "Drive."

"THIS IS THE LAST stop?"

Nora started to unbuckle her seatbelt when Briana parked in front of Cohan's Pub in Cong.

179

"Not quite. Wait here."

Briana left the car idling while she hurried inside to pay for the fish and chips she'd ordered yesterday. She carried the bagged dinners back outside and handed them to Nora.

"Hold these. I don't trust Miss Big Teeth back there."

She drove to the private stables, parking at her front door. "This is the last stop."

She held the door for Nora, who hesitated.

Only then did Briana realize what this might look like, especially after the tussle in the car. "Dinner here seemed quieter than the pub."

Shannon quickly did her business and trotted inside with Dilly on her heels. He looked up at Briana hopefully, his tail wagging, looking too cute to ignore.

"All right, then."

She scooped some extra kibble into another bowl and went to the cupboard to get down plates.

"Open two bottles of Guinness, will you?"

Nora obliged, pouring them into the glasses waiting next to the fridge while Briana slid their fish and chips onto the plates. She wore a puzzled expression as she took her plate and followed Briana to the couch. Bri picked up a remote and clicked the TV on.

After a moment, the DVD loaded. Nora's mouth hung open.

"*The Quiet Man? We're* watching *The Quiet Man?*"

Briana grinned. "You keep talking about this blasted movie. And I just spent the whole day rambling about Connemara. I figured I might as well see what all the fuss is about."

If she thought there would be any further conversation, she quickly realized she was wrong. Nora took a deep drink of her Guinness, and shifted to sit on the floor with her plate on the coffee table. She tucked into her fish and chips with her eyes glued to the screen.

Briana sighed and followed suit. She tried to concentrate on the movie, but her gaze and her thoughts kept drifting to Nora, who sat raptly watching the telly. She chuckled to herself as she realized Nora's lips were moving.

"You do know all the dialogue, don't you?"

Nora flushed a brilliant pink. "Sorry. I'll be quiet."

The movie was charming, if unrealistic. Briana could see how Americans, especially, would be beguiled by the story and the music. What she enjoyed most was watching Nora's reaction, the way her face lit up, the way she just couldn't help humming along when song broke out, which it seemed to do every few minutes. And it was fun to see bits of Cong and Connemara showcased as they were in the 1950s. She recognized some of the scenery.

"I can't believe I've never watched this," she admitted as the closing credits ran.

"Did you really like it?" Nora asked, turning to her. "Or are you just humoring me?"

"I really liked it." Briana shook her head. "Probably not as much as you, but I liked it."

Nora took the remote and backed the movie up to the crowd shot at the end, when the vicar's car is driving through the village. She paused the movie and went to the TV.

"That's my Mamma," she pointed. "And that's my Pop. And there's Fiona."

"Which makes it even more fun for your family."

Nora crawled to sit with her back to the sofa, her knees hugged to her chest. "Thank you for one of the nicest days I've ever had."

Briana gazed down at the curve of her cheek, the way her honey-colored hair lay soft on her shoulders, and she knew something had shifted for them this day. The kiss in the car had been almost one of frustration, but now...

She moved to sit next to Nora, brushing her fingers gently over her cheek. As if she'd been waiting for some kind of signal, Nora turned to her.

This time, their lips met gently, opening, yielding as they took their time. She sifted Nora's hair between her fingers, enjoyed the sensation of Nora's hand running up her side from her hip to her shoulder, with her thumb just skimming the side of Briana's breast. The effect was electric.

Briana moaned and pushed away. "If I'm to drive you back to the cottage tonight, we'd better leave now."

Nora gazed into her eyes. "I don't want to go."

Briana smiled. "I was really hoping you'd say that."

Chapter 12

OUTSIDE THE BEDROOM WINDOW, the sky lightened and the birds began to wake. Nora lay on her side, watching Briana sleep. She hadn't slept that well in ages, which was saying something as they'd made love for what felt like hours. Sex with Amy had never been like this. It hadn't been bad, just... not like this. It felt as if she and Briana were made to fit together, which was kind of funny considering the difference in their height.

Briana's tough little body had moved with her, carrying her to one of the most intense orgasms she'd ever had as they tumbled about on the bed. And when Nora had explored Briana's body, not sure what kind of response she'd get, she'd been surprised to find all of Briana's normal control flying out the window.

"Don't stop!" she'd panted as Nora brought her to four orgasms in quick succession, each more powerful than the previous.

At last, Briana had collapsed atop Nora, gasping for air as her body continued to shudder. Remembering what Briana had told her about not spending the night with anyone, Nora had half-expected to be asked to gather her things from where they'd been tossed around the bedroom as they ripped each other's clothing off, but Briana had curled up against her, her arm draped over Nora's stomach, until they both drifted into a pleasantly exhausted sleep.

Nora eased out of bed now, searching in the dim light for her underwear and shirt. She opened the bedroom door to find Shannon stretched across the doorway with Dilly lying next to her.

"Good morning," she whispered, giving both dogs' ribs a thump when they scrambled to their feet. "Come on."

She let the dogs out the kitchen door, relieved to notice that Briana's tiny kitchen was equipped with the same nice coffee maker Sheila and Quinn had—a detail she'd not paid attention to the evening before. She quickly got coffee brewing and went into the bathroom.

A few minutes later, she emerged. No toothbrush, but she'd at least scrubbed her teeth with a little toothpaste on her finger. It always killed her how people in movies and books shared slobbery kisses first thing upon waking. Didn't anyone have morning breath?

Shannon was ready to come in—she spotted Dilly trotting into the barn—and Nora was more than ready for coffee.

"Go wake her up."

Shannon bounded into the bedroom, and Nora chuckled as she heard "all right, all right, I'm up" followed by footsteps stomping into the bathroom.

She poured two cups, suddenly realizing she didn't know how Briana took her coffee. Or what she liked for breakfast. It made her ridiculously happy to know there were so many things to learn about her lover.

My lover. She'd never had a lover, at least not that she'd thought of in that sense. She and Amy had drifted into sex almost as casually as they'd drifted out of it. There hadn't ever been any real passion, nothing like this crazy desire Nora had as Briana made a sleepy entrance into the kitchen—wearing a thin T-shirt that didn't hide the outline of her nipples—to tear that T-shirt off and make love with her right here on the kitchen table.

"Coffee first," she said, placing a cup in front of Briana as she sat. "What?"

"Nothing," Nora said, smiling. "I'll tell you later."

AN HOUR LATER, HAVING had another quick toss in bed following breakfast, Nora stood in the kitchen, kissing Briana good-bye for the day.

"Thank you again for yesterday," she said.

"You're welcome." Briana smiled shyly. "Thanks for last night. And this morning."

Nora laughed.

"You sure you don't want a ride back to the cottage?"

"The walk will do me good," Nora said. "Give me time to clear my head before I go to the nursery."

Briana flicked a thumbnail over a scratch in the paint of the door-jamb. "Don't clear it too much."

"No worries there." Nora put a finger under her chin and tilted her head for a last light kiss. "I'll be lucky to keep my mind on my work today."

They stepped outside to find Liam leaning against the paddock fence, grinning like an idiot.

"Shut it," Briana snapped, but he just laughed and sauntered into the barn.

"Later," Nora said.

She looked back once to find Briana still watching her. With a last wave, she shrugged her backpack higher onto her shoulders and strode off. She took now-familiar shortcuts through the woods, smiling to herself as she walked.

Her mind was fuzzy, happily distracted by memories of the last twenty-four hours, so she didn't notice immediately that her cottage was in some disarray. She stopped abruptly when she stepped inside. Similar to when she returned after Dublin, the desk in the parlor had been swept clean of her books and pens. But this time, the curtains had also been pulled down, so that the bent rod hung drunkenly from one end.

"Pissed I didn't come home last night?" Nora asked aloud.

She scooted her desk chair closer to the window to try and reattach the curtain rod to the window casing, but she quickly realized she was going to need tools she didn't have.

Upstairs were more signs of chaos—not just bed pillows thrown across the room, but all the bedclothes, ripped off the bed and strewn about, and another curtain ripped down.

"What the hell?"

With a frustrated sigh, Nora tossed things back on the bed to remake later.

"I'm going to work now," she said loudly as she changed clothes. "I would appreciate it if you didn't have any more temper tantrums while I'm gone. I'll be back this afternoon."

She quickly brushed her teeth, scrubbed her face, and ran a brush through her hair. Inspecting herself in the mirror, she decided that was good enough for the nursery, since she usually had to bathe after work anyway.

She pedaled along, humming happily. She felt she could have bicycled to Galway and back. When she rolled into the nursery, a couple of early customers were already there. She waved at Sheila and parked her bike near the kitchen door.

Without being asked, Nora began the morning ritual of misting the plants displayed in the greenhouse.

"So, how was it?"

Nora's head snapped up as Sheila came into the greenhouse, having finished with her customers. "What?"

"How was your ramble?"

"Oh. It was great. Briana surprised me with a whole day of visiting the locations where they filmed *The Quiet Man*. We started at Lettergesh Beach and then went to Clifden and had lunch with Fiona and Jack. They send their love."

"Do they now?" Sheila was staring hard at her.

"Yes." Nora turned her back on Sheila and resumed her misting. "What's on for today?"

"I got a delivery yesterday of autumn plants. Sea peas, alpine bistort, autumn crocus. We'll need to repot some of them."

"Okay. Just let me finish here."

She waited for Sheila to go, but out of the corner of her eye, she saw she was still standing there.

"And after lunch with my grandparents?"

She wasn't going to let this drop.

"We made one or two more stops, then came back to Cong. She had ordered takeout fish and chips from Cohan's, and we finished with watching the movie at her place."

Behind her, Sheila said nothing, but Nora knew better than to look at her. "She'd never seen the film, so it was fun." She knew she sounded lame, but...

"Oh, my God!"

Nora's shoulders slumped.

"You had sex!"

Giving up, Nora turned. "Well, let's just put it on a billboard on the side of the road."

"Sorry," Sheila said, laughing. She rushed over to give Nora a hug. "You and Bri... I'm just so happy for you."

"Really?"

"Yes." Sheila stepped back. "Aren't you? Happy about it?"

"Yes, of course."

"But? No, wait. This needs coffee and biscuits." She took the hose from Nora's hand and dragged her to the kitchen.

She quickly brewed some fresh coffee and put a plate of sugar cookies on the table. Rusty took up his usual position under the table, looking cute and hoping for tidbits.

"Now," Sheila said, plunking down two cups of coffee. "I don't need the down and dirty details—fascinating though I'm sure they are—but you and Bri. This is big. I've never known Briana to be with anyone in the years she's been here."

"That's because she hasn't been." Nora took a sip of coffee. "At least, I don't think she has. She mentioned…" Nora wasn't sure how much to say. "Liaisons when she was racing."

Sheila sat back. "So she told you about her racing days. And how they ended?"

Nora nodded.

"Well, well, well." Sheila took a cookie for herself, nibbling on it. "She doesn't share that with many. You've been allowed in where few dare to go."

"I know." Nora frowned at her coffee. She reached for a cookie and dunked it. Chewing slowly, she said, "It means a lot that she told me."

"Then why the long face? Wasn't it good?"

"It was wonderful," Nora admitted, flushing at the grin that lit up Sheila's face. "But that's the problem. I'm only here for a few more weeks. This just added a new complication to everything."

"'Tis only a complication if you don't stay," Sheila pointed out.

"But I have to make that decision without…" Nora fluttered her hands. "All of this clouding the picture."

"But, isn't this," Sheila mimicked the hand-flutter, "part of the decision? People have relocated for less than love."

Nora choked on her coffee. "Love?"

Sheila tilted her head. "Isn't it?"

"I don't know. It's only been..." Nora calculated. "Seven weeks." She slumped back against her chair. "Is it?"

Only later did she realize that Sheila let that line of questioning drop. *Let me stew in my own mess, more accurately.*

Instead, "How's Móirín?" Sheila asked.

"Oh, and that's another thing!" Nora jabbed a cookie in Sheila's direction. "This morning, I come home and the entire cottage is torn apart! Curtains ripped down, bedspread and sheets off the bed. It's a mess. All because I didn't come back last night."

"Is that the way of it? I'll drive you back to the cottage later and help you put things to rights."

"We'll need screwdrivers and screws," Nora grumbled. "I don't want Mr. McCarthy to think I tore his place apart."

"Orlagh McCarthy would know better."

Nora leaned forward. "Can we take a day and go looking for that place I saw, the stone circle in my vision?"

Sheila nodded. "I think we should. How about Sunday?"

Outside, a truck drove up to the nursery.

"I'll talk to Quinn, and you ask Bri about it when you see her tonight. Whenever you get around to talking, that is."

With a wicked grin, Sheila pushed back from the table and went out to wait on her customer.

"THAT'S NOT SO BAD, is it?"

Briana crooned softly as she ran a fuzzy saddle blanket over the withers and back of one of the yearlings. Three others crowded round her, knowing her pockets were stuffed with carrots. She took turns draping the saddle blanket on each of them, rubbing them with it to get them accustomed to the feel. She even draped an arm over each

189

back, hanging to put a little weight on them. They were too young to be ridden, but not too young to learn the feel of a blanket and, soon, a saddle. In a few weeks, she'd start the same process with the two foals born this season, beginning with halter training.

Snapping a few carrots, she offered them chunks.

"They're coming along well."

She turned to find Quinn watching her, his arms folded on the paddock fence. The yearlings took off, bucking and racing their way across the pasture while she joined him, climbing the fence to sit on the top rail.

"They are. Nice breeding, nice manners."

"The last thanks to you."

She noticed the frown on his face. "What's going on?"

He avoided her eyes. "We're probably going to have to sell three of them."

Her heart plummeted. It was part of this business—breeding the mares, raising the foals, training them, loving them, only to have to sell them—but she would never get used to it. She knew it was nearly as hard on Quinn.

"Any local buyers?"

That at least would be preferable to an auction, where God-knows-who could buy them.

"I've a few bites," he said. "I'll ask around some more."

The yearlings circled back over, nosing them, hoping for more treats. Quinn rubbed the delicate faces, tugged on forelocks.

"Maybe we can keep two to train as stable hacks."

She hid a smile. It wouldn't be the first time they'd ended up keeping an entire crop of foals. That was what happened with Butler, Yeats, and William.

"Have you talked to Nora today?" he asked.

She almost fell off the fence. She knew Liam wouldn't have missed the opportunity to pass on a juicy bit of gossip, especially when it came to Bri's previously nonexistent sex life.

"Why?"

"Got a text from Sheila. Seems Sióg Cottage sustained some vandalism last night." He scratched his chin, waiting a beat. "I hear she wasn't there."

Bri ignored that last bit. "What kind of vandalism?"

"Most likely the ghostly sort. Curtains ripped down, bed tossed. Sheila's going over later with some tools to help her straighten things up."

Briana bit her lip. "Quinn..."

"Go. We're nearly done for the day anyhow."

She hopped down and jogged to the cottage to pack a few things. She paused in the midst of stuffing some clean clothes into a rucksack. She wasn't even certain she'd be welcomed to spend the night. Dropping to sit on the side of her mattress, she stared at the floor.

You can stop this now. It was one night. It doesn't mean anything.

Except it did, and she didn't want it to be just one night. She closed her eyes and flopped back on the bed, flinging her arms over her face. She'd never lost control with anyone the way she had with Nora. She'd never wanted to sleep with anyone after the sex was over, and she'd never, ever cuddled with anyone the way she had last night.

She's leaving in just over a month, you daft moron, she reminded herself, but, "Bugger it."

She finished packing and remembered to scoop a bag of food for Shannon, who was waiting by the SUV.

"How did you know?"

Shannon gave a scolding woof.

"All right, I'm coming."

Sheila and Nora were already there when she pulled up. She turned the car off and walked into the cottage. Looking around at the mess, she let out a soft whistle.

When Nora appeared from the kitchen, Bri felt her breath catch in her chest.

"Hi," Nora said.

"Hi."

Shannon hopped up to place her paws on Nora's shoulders and nose her cheek.

"I'm fine," Nora said, giving her a hug and staring at Briana.

Sheila loudly cleared her throat. "Oh, for heaven's sake, kiss each other already and let's get to work."

Briana scowled but couldn't hide the blush that made Sheila laugh.

Shannon dropped to all fours. Briana accepted a light kiss on the cheek from Nora and set about picking up a few books and pens still scattered in the corners while Sheila dragged a chair to the window and climbed up to reattach the curtain rod. She had to drill new holes and use new screws, as the old ones were bent and stripped.

"Well, this ghost—Móirín or Rowan—has some strength behind her when she's angry," Sheila said.

"That's what worries me," Briana said, looking at Nora. "What if she directed some of this at you?"

Nora was busy shuffling loose pages she'd picked up and didn't immediately protest this time that they meant her no harm, a change for which Bri was grateful.

"I've a question," Sheila said, pausing her work for a moment. "If the ghost has been in this room, why is Shannon willing to be in here, when she won't go in the upstairs room?"

Nora and Briana both stopped what they were doing as well. When they all turned to look at her, Shannon stared up at them, her tail thumping against the floor.

"I've no idea," Briana said.

"We're going to search on Sunday for that circle of stones I saw when Eve did her voodoo on me," Nora said. "Speaking of which, have either of you seen her?"

"No." Sheila glanced down at Briana, who shook her head.

"Need another searcher?" Briana asked.

Her stomach did a slow flip at the way Nora's face lit up as she said, "That would be great."

Sheila grunted a little as she leaned in to apply pressure to a last turn of the screwdriver. "Got it. Hand me that rod, will you?"

She rehung the curtains, adjusting them along the rod. "There. Old man McCarthy will never know."

They headed upstairs where Sheila tackled that curtain rod as well while Briana helped Nora make the bed. Shannon kept a watchful eye from the hall.

Briana didn't dare meet Nora's eyes as her face burned, imagining being in that bed with Nora, tearing all those neatly tucked sheets apart again. She wondered if Nora was thinking the same thing.

When they were done, Nora straightened a last few things on the dresser. "Thank you both so much. This would have taken me ages on my own."

They all went back downstairs.

Sheila put her tools back in her bag. "Well, I should be going—"

"NO!"

Sheila looked up at the simultaneous outburst from both Nora and Bri. "Okay, then. How about some supper?"

Briana was pretty certain Sheila was fighting the impulse to laugh at the pair of them, but the thought of being alone with Nora after last night was... Nora had practically shouted "No" as well. She'd seemed fine this morning, but she'd had the whole day to think things through, just as Briana had. What if she now thought their night together was a mistake? What if she had no intention of asking Briana to spend the night here at the cottage? This felt a lot more complicated than it had an hour ago.

They cobbled together a dinner of pork chops, green beans, and sliced tomatoes drizzled with balsamic vinegar and olive oil—a bit fancier than anything Bri would have made for herself. She did go to the car to get some food for Shannon but left her rucksack. All of a sudden, she wasn't certain she'd be needing it. She wasn't certain of anything.

Sheila kept the dinner conversation going by asking lots of questions about their day of rambling, but when supper was over and the dishes were done, she said, "I am now going home."

She gave Nora and Bri each a kiss on the cheek, chuckling under her breath before getting in her SUV to drive away with a wink and a wave.

Briana stood outside in the gathering dusk, scuffing one boot into the dirt. "I suppose I should be going."

Nora stood beside her. "Do you want to go?"

Briana couldn't look at her. "Do you want me to?"

A few seconds ticked by.

"No. I want you to stay. If you want."

Briana dared a sideways glance at Nora then, her blonde hair catching the last of the evening light. "We're really not good at this, are we?"

"I suppose we're not." Nora gave a nervous little laugh. "Neither of us has had much practice."

"You're sure?"

Nora's answer was in her kiss. She wrapped her arms around Bri, pulling her to her toes as their mouths met, tentatively at first. But when Nora parted her lips and deepened the kiss with little flicks of her tongue, the doubt disappeared.

Briana drew away. "I have one request, though."

Nora smiled, tracing a finger over Briana's earlobe, something she'd discovered could almost hypnotize her. "What's that?"

Briana nearly forgot what she'd been about to say. "Can we use the other bedroom? I feel as if we'd be part of a threesome in your usual room."

Nora laughed softly. "Yes, we can use the other room."

Briana got her bag from the car and allowed Nora to lead the way upstairs.

THE WOODS WERE WET, everything soaked from the steady rain that fell. Nora's hair dripped onto her face as she pushed through the ferns and the bushes. Impatiently, she swept it back, wiping the wetness from her eyes as she strained to see. Faintly, the sound of weeping came to her over the steady thrum of the rain.

"Where are you?"

There was no answer, only the crying.

She pushed forward and suddenly found herself lying flat on the ground. Pushing up out of the grass was a half-buried stone, and she knew where she was. Squinting through the rain and the darkness, she tried to get her bearings.

Just outside the circle was a massive oak tree, its enormous canopy dwarfing the surrounding trees. It seemed the crying was coming from beyond that tree. She struggled to her feet and tried to move forward, but something was pulling her from behind.

She glanced down and saw a huge dog, teeth fastened onto her shirttail, tugging on it. Jerking and dragging her back...

Nora's eyes opened, and she found herself looking up into Briana and Shannon's faces as they both loomed over her.

"What happened?" she mumbled.

Shannon was half-lying across Nora's body, pinning her to the mattress.

"You were thrashing about, calling out in your sleep," Briana said.

Nora lifted her hands to rub her eyes. "But..." she sniffed. Her hands were clean. No mud or grass. "I didn't leave the bed?"

"No. Though you might have if it hadn't been for Shannon."

Shannon dropped her head to Nora's chest.

She rested a hand on the massive head. "She brought me back. In my dream, she was there."

"You wouldn't wake, wouldn't answer me." Briana sounded shaken. "What was happening?"

Nora closed her eyes. "I was searching. It was raining, but I could hear someone crying, and I was trying to find whoever it was. These are the kind of dreams I've had before where I wake up muddy and wet, like I've really been tromping through the woods." Her eyes opened. "I was in the stone circle. I fell over one of the stones."

She gripped Briana's arm. "We have to go there."

"We will." Briana lay back down, her cheek resting against Nora's shoulder. "Tomorrow."

Shannon wriggled further onto the bed, first one hind paw— waiting to see if she would be scolded—then the other until she was sandwiched in between the two humans.

"Why did I stay in bed tonight, I wonder?" Nora pressed her lips to Briana's forehead. "Was it because we were in this room? Or because you and Shannon were with me?"

"I don't know, but I don't mind saying, I don't like it one bit."

Nora realized they were both still naked. She chuckled. "If I had left the cottage, would I have put clothes on?"

Briana propped up on an elbow. "You don't get to go chasing after the ghost naked through the forest. I'm the only one's allowed to see that."

Nora lifted her face for a kiss. "Deal. If I did, the ghost wouldn't be the scariest thing out there."

Chapter 13

THE SPRING DAY IS as joyous as the mood. After the baby's baptism, the family exits St. Mary's to find a man waiting for them, standing beside a strange contraption.

"It's a Daguerrotype machine," Donall explains excitedly. "He's going to make a picture of us with it, so we'll always remember this day."

The man poses them, though he fights to maintain his patience with the younger children, who won't stay still. When he finally has the image he wants, he packs up his machine with a promise to deliver the plate the following week.

As they traipse home, Donall pulls a wagon holding the younger children and little Aoibheann Theresa, dressed in her white christening robe. Callum and Rowan skip alongside, joining Donall in a song.

Dropping back to hold her mother's hand, Rowan flounces along in a yellow dress given her by Mrs. Smythe. It had belonged to the youngest daughter of the family, "but she's long since outgrown it," Mrs. Smythe said, holding it up. Móirín worked her magic to make it fit, topping it off with a scarlet ribbon tying back Rowan's dark hair.

Donall glances in their direction. Móirín looks happier than he's seen her since before the baby was born. She catches his eye and smiles, as if she knows what he's thinking.

Back home, they set about making a meal to celebrate. Heaven knows they need to celebrate. With no new crops yet to harvest, more families have had deaths or moved away or left for America. There's a bleakness that hangs over every day like a cloud.

Donall mixes the dough for a loaf of soda bread while Móirín feeds the baby. Callum is put to work keeping the three little ones occupied.

"Where's Rowan?" he complains. "She should be helping."

Móirín lays the baby in the cradle and goes to the door. No sign of that girl. "Rowan? Rowan, time for tea!"

With a shake of her head, she goes back to put the bread in the oven and begin warming some lamb stew. When the food is ready, there's still no sign of Rowan.

"Go call your sister," she says to Callum.

He goes out the front door and bellows, "Rowan! Get in here. Now!"

Back in the kitchen, he says, "No sign of her, Ma."

"This is getting tiresome," Donall says. He strides outside and calls again, sternly this time.

Rowan knows that tone and always comes from playing her hiding games. But there is still no answer.

He goes back inside. "We'll eat without her. Teach her to go wandering off."

Móirín casts a worried glance out the window, but dishes out the stew while Donall tears the bread.

By the time they've finished eating, there's still no sign of Rowan.

"This isn't right," she frets. "Donall, Callum, go search for her. Please."

She prays as daylight fades and there's still no sign of them. When they return, her heart leaps—but only for a moment.

Callum looks as if he's been crying, and Donall's expression is grave. "We came home to get lanterns."

Móirín clutches the baby to her chest as they light the lanterns and go out into the night to resume searching.

BRIANA WOKE WITH A start. She stretched, enjoying the relaxed feeling of her body. Making love with Nora was so unlike anything she'd ever experienced before. Sitting up in bed, it took her a moment to remember where she was—Nora's cottage—and another moment to realize she was alone. No Nora. No Shannon. She yanked on jeans and a T-shirt and stumbled downstairs to find the two of them sitting side by side on the back stoop, Nora's arm draped around Shannon. She joined them, sitting on the cold flagstone on Shannon's other side.

"You scared me," she said. "Thought you'd gone running off into the forest in your sleep and I didn't notice."

The hand that was wrapped around Shannon opened, and Bri took it.

"No running," Nora said. "Just couldn't sleep."

Overhead, the sky was lightening to a deep rose over the treetops to the east.

Briana yawned. "If we're going to be waking this early, we need to get a coffee maker for this cottage."

"No point, is there?"

Bri leaned forward at the almost angry tone of Nora's voice to peer at her from under Shannon's head. "Are you okay?"

Nora released Briana's hand and shoved to her feet. "I'm fine."

Briana slowly followed her into the kitchen to put the kettle on for tea while Nora started making porridge.

"Sorry," Nora muttered with a deep sigh. "Just tired."

"More dreams?"

"Yeah."

Briana knew they should probably be talking about what she was pretty sure was really bothering Nora—*and should be bothering you*. In a little over a month, Nora would be leaving. Going back to the States. Briana had no idea where that left them. She opened her mouth to say so, but closed it, turning to get bowls and cups from the cupboard.

Breakfast was silent, each of them preoccupied by her thoughts.

"Briana," Nora said at last, reaching for Bri's hand again. "We need—"

"Hello! Anyone up?" came a shout from the front of the cottage.

Briana reluctantly released her hand and carried the bowls to the sink while Nora went to let Quinn and Sheila in.

"All set for our adventure?" Quinn asked as he stomped into the kitchen.

"Yeah," Briana said, busying herself with the dishes.

"Everything okay here?" Sheila asked, coming into the kitchen on his heels, her sharp eyes flicking from Nora to Briana.

"What did I miss?" Quinn whispered.

"Hush," Sheila said.

"Everything's fine," Briana said, placing the last mug in the dish drainer. "We all set?"

Without waiting for an answer, she marched out the front door.

"Drive or walk?" Quinn asked when they followed her outside.

Nora headed into the trees surrounding the cottage.

"I guess we're walking," Sheila said.

"This is the way I always go in my dreams," Nora said over her shoulder.

The others followed after her, threading their way through the trees.

"There used to be a trail here," Nora said.

"This is not normal," Briana said. "She knows where there used to be a path almost a hundred seventy-five years ago."

The forest seemed to close around them, with thick tree trunks and dense canopy shutting out the early morning light.

"I... I don't know which way from here," Nora said, turning in place. "It looks different, more trees now, and they're bigger."

"It should be this way to the circle," Quinn said, pushing past her.

He broke a trail for them through dense undergrowth until they stepped into a large clearing.

Unlike the thick greenery of the woods, the glade looked almost groomed—no trees or bushes, only knee-high grasses.

"Looks like someone's been here," Briana said, noting the trampled grass in places.

Nora went to a squat stone and knelt with a hand on it. She looked around. "It's changed so much from my dreams..."

She stood suddenly, pointing. "That oak. That oak tree was in my dreams."

She walked the perimeter of the circle, from stone to stone, touching each for a moment as the others waited for her to recognize something. When she came to the oak, she stepped out of the circle and went to it. Laying her hands on its enormous trunk, she sighed.

"I don't know what I thought. If I came here, I might suddenly remember something."

Quinn swept an arm toward the woods beyond the oak. "If you came here from the cottage in your dreams, and you remember this tree, stands to reason you might have gone in this direction. Let's walk on, see if anything else looks familiar to you."

"Makes sense to me," Sheila said.

Briana kept a close eye on Nora as they all followed Quinn back into the deep shadows of the forest. They spread out, no one sure what exactly they were looking for.

"Have a care," Sheila called out. "It's boggy here."

Bri's own foot squelched into some mud. She picked her way carefully, searching for firm footing. She watched as Nora's head swiveled, looking desperately for familiar landmarks.

"Do you have any idea what we're looking for?" she asked.

"Not really," Nora said. "No, wait. Bird cherry."

"What?" Quinn stopped and turned to her.

"Every time the ghost, or ghosts, have been in the cottage, there's been the lilac smell of bird cherry."

The problem was, there were at least a dozen bird cherry trees scattered throughout this section of forest, most of them saplings and not nearly old enough. But finding the trees didn't seem to yield any clues.

Briana marched along, cursing under her breath. The time she had left with Nora was short enough as it was. This mystery of the cottage's past seemed to be something that wasn't going away, and it had become almost an obsession for Nora—but it was embarrassing to feel she was competing with a pair of ghosts for Nora's attention.

Her stomach clenched with the tension from earlier in the morning, the unwelcome reminder that no sooner had she found someone she wanted to spend nights with, maybe have a future with, than that someone was going to be leaving at the end of the summer. And in the meantime, they were tromping around in the woods, looking for—

Without warning, the ground beneath her foot disappeared as her leg sank almost to the hip into a hole she hadn't seen.

"Damn!"

The others hurried to her. Quinn reached under her arms and plucked her out of the hole, setting her back on her feet.

"What was it?" Sheila asked. She parted the ferns that had covered the opening, prodding the edges of the hole with her shoe.

"We're not that far from Pigeon Hole cave. This area is probably riddled with springs and limestone holes," Quinn said. "You okay, squint?"

Bri gingerly tested her knee. "Yeah. I'm good."

"You sure?" Nora asked, wrapping an arm around Briana's shoulders.

Briana nodded.

Nora gave her a squeeze before releasing her.

"I think we've earned a big lunch," Sheila said. "Let's go back to our place."

"Sounds good," Nora said, pausing for one last look back into the green shadows before following the others toward the circle of stones.

"ALL RIGHT. WHAT'S GOING on?"

Nora blinked and looked up from the computer. "Well, I'm updating the website to include all of your autumn-scented creams and candles, and—"

"No." Sheila sat down beside Nora. "What's going on with you and Briana? Things seemed tense between you when Quinn and I got to the cottage this morning, and now you're here, and she's not. So what's going on?"

"Nothing. She has work to do at the stable, same as Quinn, and I need to get this done."

When Sheila simply sat there staring at her, Nora caved. "All right." She reached out to touch a finger to a small desk calendar. "In a few days, it'll be four weeks from the day I will leave here. One month. And this morning, Briana started talking about buying a coffee maker for the cottage. Like we have some kind of future together, and..."

She paused when her voice cracked. It was a few seconds before she could continue. "I guess it's just starting to feel real. I'll be going back to my job and my life."

"And leaving this one."

"And leaving this one."

They sat for a long moment.

"Which one," asked Sheila, "feels more real to you?"

Nora supposed her confusion and indecision must have shown in her eyes because Sheila leaned forward and laid a reassuring hand on her arm.

"Instead of thinking of it as only a month left, why don't you look at it as you've four whole weeks yet to enjoy everything—Ireland, your time with Bri, living your dream. See where it leads you. A lot can happen in four weeks."

Sheila stood but then paused at the door. "You know, even if you decide to go back to the States, you're a different woman now than you were when you arrived. It won't be the same."

She went to putter about in the shop, leaving Nora to think about what she'd said as she resumed her work on the website. The computer pinged a message. She'd been checking in on her sisters' posts on Facebook, looking at photos of the kids enjoying their summer trips to the beach and amusement parks. She'd commented on a few of them, her homesickness for her family adding to her almost nauseous feeling of uncertainty.

But this message wasn't from her sisters. It was from Mamma. *We sent you an email. Make sure you open the attachment.*

It was kind of funny that her grandparents had become tech savvy enough to track her down online and send emails with attachments.

She opened her email. Sure enough, there it was, among twenty other messages.

Nora,

Your grandfather and I took a little trip after our chat with you and Fiona. We went up to Clinton, Massachusetts to research the genealogy records there. We found some interesting photos in their Historical Society archives. Stay safe.

Love you,
   Mamma & Pop

Nora clicked open the attachments to find scanned copies of old photos. Enlarging the images as much as she could without making them too grainy, she saw a wooden building with a sign that read "Clinton Smithy." Standing in front of it was the man she'd seen in her vision, Donall O'Hara. Beside him was a teen boy. She guessed that must have been the oldest son. What was his name? Callum. There were other photos of the smithy in different seasons, most with horses tethered alongside wagons, then a few with early automobiles in the background. She was scrolling through the photos and stopped.

Leaning closer to the monitor, she gaped.

Standing next to one of the horses was a girl with what looked like white-blonde hair, hanging in a long braid over her shoulder. Even across nearly two centuries, the eyes were mesmerizing.

"That's impossible."

She was just opening an email to send a reply to her grandmother when Facebook pinged again.

It was Amy. *I've been trying to catch you online. Can we talk?*

Nora's first instinct was to close the window, but that was cowardly. Using her forefinger to peck her reply, she typed, *Yes.*

A second later, Amy's face filled the screen, familiar as Nora's own, but somehow different than Nora remembered, older and more tired.

"Hi," she said, smiling.

"Hi." Despite Nora's misgivings, it was good to see her.

"How are you?"

"I'm good."

Amy's eyes narrowed just the tiniest bit. "Thought I'd hear from you before now. Did you get my message about maybe coming to Ireland?"

Nora felt her face get hot and knew that Amy could read her, even through a computer thirty-five hundred miles away. "I did. But I've been busy."

"Too busy to spend some time with me?"

Her tone was just sharp enough and the barb just pointed enough to raise Nora's ire. "I would have thought you'd be spending as much time as you could with Tracy this summer. What would she think if you left to come here?"

Touché. That had hit a nerve, but Nora immediately felt guilty.

Amy's expression changed perceptibly. "Tracy and I aren't seeing each other anymore. Her girlfriend found out about us, and... She broke up with me."

Nora opened her mouth to reply but didn't know what to say. "Oh."

"I don't want to lose you, Nora."

Nora frowned. "Lose me? You're the one who broke up with me, remember? To explore things with Tracy."

"I... I know. I didn't mean to hurt you. But does that mean we have to throw away all our years together? You're my best friend."

Amy smiled again, trying hard to bridge the gap that had somehow turned into a chasm the size of an ocean. The Atlantic, to be precise.

"There's still time," Amy said. "I could come over. I've got my passport all set."

"Um... that really wouldn't work," Nora stalled, thinking fast. "I've got commitments here—"

"You've met someone." It wasn't a question. "Haven't you?" Amy demanded when Nora didn't say anything.

Why are you feeling guilty? Nora asked herself. "Yes," she admitted.

"What's the point of that?" Amy asked. "When you're only there for three months."

What was the point of getting involved with someone who was already in a relationship? But Nora didn't say it.

"What happens when you come back?"

"I may not be coming back." It was out before Nora could swallow the words. *Shit.*

"What?" Amy stared open-mouthed.

Nora took a deep breath, but felt surprisingly calm. "I said, I may not be coming back. I haven't made a firm decision yet, so please don't say anything to my family."

Amy deflated visibly. "I'm going to end up alone, aren't I?"

A wave of pity engulfed Nora. "I hope not, Amy. I mean that."

A moment later, after an awkward good-bye, Nora sat staring at the computer.

"Are you okay?" asked Sheila as she set a cup of tea on the desk. Nora jumped.

"I didn't mean to listen, but the sound carried," Sheila said, sitting next to the desk with a mug of her own.

Nora sat back, sipping her tea. "I am okay. I didn't intend to tell her that, but I'm glad I did."

"I thought you handled it well."

"I cut her out of my life."

"She'd already done most of the cutting," Sheila reminded her. "And you were kind. Kinder than I could have been, I'm thinking."

Nora reached for the mouse, but Sheila stopped her. "Enough of this for today. We'll work on it tomorrow. Go to Bri. And send Quinn home."

AS MUCH AS BRIANA loved the trails around Cong, with their views of the lough and the castle, and as much as she loved the horses, she realized almost every ride she took was with a purpose—training usually, or getting horses shuffled from one stable to the other. When work was done for the day, that was it. Rarely did she saddle up just for the pleasure of an evening ride. In fact, she couldn't remember the last time she had before Nora arrived.

Nora was becoming a good intermediate rider, even learning to jump. In the ring, Briana had set up a beginner's course for her.

"Stubbs may not look it, but he's a jackrabbit when it comes to jumping," she'd told Nora. "He knows more than you do. Let him set his stride. Grab mane and stand in your stirrups, just like I showed you. Trust it."

To her chagrin, Quinn had seen and was now after her to take on students, same as Sonya and Liam did. "You're a natural teacher," he'd said to her, but what he hadn't said was that it would be good for the stables for her to teach paying students. She was grudgingly moving in that direction.

Nora's advancing skills allowed Briana to take her on less-groomed trails, where they jumped downed trees and crumbling stone walls demarcating fields where sheep still grazed.

She'd begun looking forward to their late-day rides, sometimes returning to the barn after sunset.

The evening of their search of the stone circle, she and Nora ambled along the shore trail on Lizzy and Stubbs while Shannon romped ahead.

Nora reined Stubbs to a halt, looking out over the lough. "I don't know how you stand it."

Briana turned Lizzy around to join them. Following her gaze, she felt she was seeing things with new eyes. The early evening sunlight slanted through puffy clouds to gild the turrets and towers of the castle. A few tourists, probably castle guests, strolled the trails, but not many wandered this far out. Many more could be seen walking the gardens closer to the castle. Boat tours were done for the day, leaving the lake calm and glassy. A few ducks paddled near the shore while swifts darted through the air, seeking insects. Out on the lake, the islands were dark humps.

"It is kind of magical," Briana realized.

They continued along the path, the rhythmic creaking of leather blending with the soft lapping of the water against the rocky shoreline.

"Sorry I was so... moody this morning," Nora said softly.

So we are going to talk about this. Briana wasn't sure if that was a good thing or not, having never done this before with anyone. There'd never been anyone worth talking things through with before.

"Was there anything in particular wrong?" she asked. "Did I do or say anything?"

"No." Nora reached for her hand and kept it as they walked the horses side by side. "No, it wasn't you. It was all me. Instead of enjoying the morning, taking each day as it comes, I was already thinking ahead, counting down time. Sheila helped me see how silly that is."

Bri's heart lifted, but only a little. Time *was* counting down, like it or not. She was so lost in her own thoughts that she wasn't listening when Nora said, "I saw Amy today."

It took a second for that to sink in. "Sorry?"

Nora turned to her, deliberately keeping hold of her hand when Briana would have pulled away. "I should say, I spoke with Amy today. I was on the computer, doing some work on Sheila's website, when she found me and asked if we could talk. So we did a video chat."

She faced the trail again, leaving Briana to try and read her profile.

"And how did that go? Is she coming for her visit?" Briana tried to keep her voice even, but she wasn't certain she succeeded.

Nora smiled, though it seemed a sad smile. "No. She isn't coming here. And she doesn't have Tracy anymore. They broke up. And she knows I'm seeing someone." Nora looked at her again. "So now she knows that she doesn't have me anymore, either. That was hard."

Bri felt as if she were riding a green horse—one which was going along nicely, but could explode into a fit of bucking at any moment, trying to throw her. She needed to keep her seat. "Hard for you?"

"The hard part for me was seeing her so sad at realizing she's alone now. That's going to be an adjustment for her."

Briana relaxed and let go of Nora's hand. "But it's an adjustment you had to make."

Nora nodded. "Yeah. It was almost a relief for me. I didn't tell her that," she added quickly. "But I'm so much happier now."

Briana steered them onto a trail that veered into the woods, enveloping them in deeper shadows. She drew Lizzy to a stop and waited for Nora and Stubbs to come up beside them. When they did, she leaned over to kiss Nora, and found Nora already coming to her. The kiss lingered, soft and achingly sweet.

When they parted, Nora traced a tender finger along Bri's cheek.

They rode on. Briana thought about everything Nora had said, about how much happier she was now. For Bri, she knew what she was feeling was more than happy. Ambling through the woods, surrounded by the things she loved most—Shannon, the horses, the countryside around Cong—she knew that Nora would forever be among those. Briana had never been in love. A month ago, she wasn't sure she ever would be. It felt bittersweet that now she was, it was with someone who might not be in her life much longer.

Nora had declared her independence from one unsatisfactory relationship. And she'd just said herself, she wanted to take one day at a time. Bri had no idea what that would mean come a month from now.

Chapter 14

SOFT MISTY RAIN fell as Nora pedaled toward Cong. "Are you sure?" Sheila had asked as they loaded the basket and panniers with boxed candles and soaps and with jars of salves and lotions, covering them with oilcloth. "We can always drive this lot in later."

"One thing I've learned," Nora said, zipping up her rain jacket, "if you wait for the rain to stop to do anything here, it'll never get done. I'll drop these off to the shops on the list, and then go home for a hot bath."

She took the trails through the woods to avoid traffic. Keeping an eye out for horses—she chuckled now to think how ignorant she'd been that first morning—she took now-familiar paths toward the village.

The rain was blocked somewhat by the overhanging trees, but everything gleamed with moisture, the leaves all heavy with a steady drip of the rain that had made it through. She paused the bike, inhaling the mossy scent of the damp air. Nothing back in the States would ever compare to this for her.

She pedaled on, riding into Cong where the tourists still crowded the streets, rain or no. Mondays were as busy as weekends now they were in August. She made her deliveries, greeting the shop owners by name, accepting checks from them for Sheila. She went to the bookstore and picked up a couple of new books, carefully placing them in her basket and covering them to keep them dry.

Pushing her bike through the crowded streets—and touching the old Celtic cross as had become her habit whenever she was in the village—she crossed the river and mounted to begin her trek to Sióg Cottage. She'd started a pot of chili that morning. Briana had never had it, and Nora thought it might be fun to introduce her to something from America.

They'd been trading nights between her cottage and Bri's place at the stables. If the ghosts were upset by this arrangement, they were hiding it better. The cottage hadn't been torn apart lately. She and Briana still weren't sleeping in the front room on the nights they did stay at the cottage. The dreams had been less intense, less realistic, and she hadn't actually left her bed that she could tell.

Their last few nights together had been different—due to the start of Nora's period— but the cuddling and talking had been nice. Briana had opened up so much since Nora met her. She talked about how she used to skip school to steal away to the local track, pestering the trainers to let her do training rides until she finally got her jockey's license, and she spoke of the early days when she was excited to race, often winning. Nora told her more about her work at the university library. It sounded kind of dull and ordinary to her ears, but Briana seemed interested.

It felt as if they were settling into a routine—the routine of a couple. An actual couple.

Funny, she mused as she pedaled. *I never wanted to be a couple with Amy. Not like this. Not seeing each other every day, spending every night together.*

But with Briana, it felt so natural, so easy.

The one thing Nora didn't talk about was her writing. If Briana noticed the growing pile of paper with line after line of handwriting, she didn't ask, and Nora didn't think she'd tried to read them. On Nora's days off from the nursery, when Briana was working, her imagination had continued to chug along, filling in the gaps her dreams left unanswered—the day-to-day lives of Móirín and Donall and their family. She still burned to find out what happened to them.

So absorbed was she in her own thoughts that she nearly fell off the bike when she wheeled up to the cottage, and a figure moved in the shadows. Eve was waiting for her, a bag on one shoulder, her lit candle-lantern in the other.

"Oh, you scared me!" Nora pressed a hand to her racing heart.

She gathered her books from the basket and unlocked the door. "Won't you come in?"

Eve followed her inside. As before, she stopped and stood, as if testing the air or searching for something before following Nora through to the kitchen.

"It smells good," Eve said.

"Thanks. I got a pot of chili going this morning." Nora hesitated. She really, really wanted to take a hot bath to chase off the wet chill from her bike ride and then get into dry clothes, but it seemed rude to cut this visit off abruptly.

"How've you been?" Eve asked, setting her bag and lantern on the table. She swept off a cloak and hung it on a peg near the door.

"I've been fine," Nora said hesitantly, wondering if Eve could possibly know that she hadn't been here every night, and that on the nights she was here, she hadn't made herself as open to the ghosts as before.

"Why are you carrying your lantern in the daytime?" Nora wondered.

"It may be dark before I get back to my cottage. I've a few other stops to make."

Eve's green eyes scrutinized her, and Nora was suddenly reminded of the old photo Mamma had sent. In the confusion of her chat with Amy, she'd forgotten all about it.

Eve reached into her bag and withdrew a small jar with a cork sealed in place by wax. "I know you haven't been sleeping all that well..." She glanced over with an almost accusing look. "So I thought I'd make you a tonic to help. Just put a few drops of this in your tea each evening, and you'll sleep much better. 'Tis only for you, though."

"Thanks." Nora set the bottle on the counter.

Eve swung her cloak around her and slid the strap of her bag over her shoulder.

"Have—?"

Eve turned to her.

"Have you ever been to America?" Nora blurted.

Eve's face was as ethereal and otherworldly as ever, but there was a subtle shift in her features, her eyes.

Nora felt a slight prickle run over her skin, as if a chill breeze had filled the room. She told herself it was just the ride in the rain.

"Long ago," Eve said. She reached for the handle of her lantern.

Breathlessly, Nora asked, "How long ago?"

But Eve only smiled and turned to go. "Give Briana my best."

NORA HAD HER WARM bath and then changed into dry jeans and a sweatshirt. The chili was simmering on the cooker, and she was wishing she had thought to pick up some bread to go with it.

"Anybody home?" came a voice from outside.

She opened the door to find Orlagh McCarthy standing under an umbrella. Farmer McCarthy waved from the idling truck.

Orlagh held something wrapped in a green-and-white gingham towel. "I was making some of my soda bread, and I..." She hesitated. "I felt the urge to bring you some."

"Thank you," Nora said. "Won't you come in?"

Orlagh craned her neck to look past Nora into the cottage. "Oh, well... Maybe just for a moment, then."

Nora went back into the cottage, and Orlagh stepped onto the covered stoop, setting her umbrella down. Sliding one foot over the threshold, she hesitated, as if waiting to see what would happen. When nothing did, she stepped completely inside, looking rather breathless at her own daring.

"I don't know how you knew the bread would be so welcome this evening," Nora said when Orlagh thrust the towel-wrapped loaf into her hands. "I was in the village today and forgot to pick some up."

"Oh, this is better than even the bakery can make," Orlagh said. Her brow creased. "And I'm not sure, either, what got into me. Usually, when I bake, it's first thing of a morning, but this urge just came on me..."

She glanced around. "You've fixed the place up nice."

"Thanks." When Orlagh stood there, Nora asked, "Was there something else?"

Orlagh's eyes got big. "Well," she began, turning to peer back toward the truck where her husband waited. "I haven't told himself about this, but I had a dream, two nights back."

"Yes?" Nora prompted when Orlagh paused.

"It was about this cottage," Orlagh whispered. "I saw you, and a woman with black hair, and... and a little girl, also with black hair, wearing—"

"A yellow dress."

Orlagh's eyes got even bigger as she nodded.

"What about them?"

"That was the odd part," Orlagh said, frowning again. "They each took you by a hand, and they led you from here, through the fields and the woods. And all of a sudden, you all disappeared, like smoke. I woke up with my heart pounding." She laid a hand on her ample bosom.

A beep from the truck startled both of them. Orlagh jumped.

"I'd best be going or James'll have a fit that his supper is late."

"Thank you again for the bread."

Orlagh reached for her umbrella and stepped back out into the rain. "You'll have a care."

"I will."

Nora waved them off. That made two unexpected visitors so far this evening. She put the bread in the oven to warm and made herself a cup of tea, pondering what Orlagh McCarthy's dream meant. Was Móirín reaching out to others now? Trying to prod Nora back on track? She picked up Eve's tonic, wondering what it would do exactly. She wiggled the cork, cracking the dark red wax. She held the little bottle away, half-expecting a cloud of vapors to escape when she tugged the cork free, but there was nothing. A cautious sniff provided no more information about what was in it, as the liquid inside didn't smell of anything. She carefully tipped just a few drops of the clear concoction into her tea. She took a small sip, but it hadn't changed the taste of the tea at all that she could tell. She drank her tea as she moved about the kitchen, setting the small table with a crock of butter and plates for their bread.

Outside, the rain continued to come down softly. The front door was open, with an old towel spread on the floor. When Shannon stepped inside, she obediently stood on the towel until Nora could wipe her big paws dry. Briana followed, smiling at them.

"Hi," Nora said, giving Shannon a last rub and Briana a long, lingering kiss.

"Hi, yourself." Briana inhaled deeply. "Oh, that smells good. I'm near to starving."

"Come on in," Nora said, leaving Bri to hang up her rain jacket.

Shannon followed her into the kitchen, where a bowl of kibble waited.

Nora dished out two bowls of chili. "I can't take credit for the bread. Orlagh McCarthy—"

As she reached into the oven for the bread, she had a forceful image of others having done this same thing, here in this room, when the bread was baked by a wood fire. It was like her vision, the one she'd had upstairs, guided by Eve.

She swayed, and the bread dropped onto the counter with a clatter. She braced herself with one arm.

"Are you all right?" Briana asked, hurrying over to wrap an arm around her.

Nora nodded. "I'm fine. Just... just hungry, I think. Let's eat."

They sat, but Briana kept casting worried glances in her direction. Nora waited for Bri to take her first spoonful of the chili.

"How do you like it?" she asked. "I didn't make it hot. I wasn't sure if you like spicy food."

"I've never had this," Briana said, smacking her lips as she tasted it. "It's almost like Mexican, but different. I like it. It's brilliant."

She reached into her back pocket and slid a piece of paper across the table before buttering a slice of bread.

"What's this?" Nora picked up the paper and unfolded it.

Inside was a colorful drawing of a stick figure reading a somewhat lopsided and enormous book.

"Kieran?" she asked, grinning.

"We've been commanded to go to Dublin this weekend."

"Really?" Nora put the drawing down and spooned up some chili. "Sure."

She ate and realized Briana was frowning. "What's wrong? You don't like the chili."

"No, I like it." Briana stalled by eating some more before saying,

"Well, I all but promised you Kerry and Dingle and the Cliffs of Moher, didn't I? And we've yet to do that."

Nora didn't answer immediately. She busied herself buttering her own slice of bread, but inside, her guts were churning—and not from the chili. She was shaken—and a little thrilled—by the calm, the certainty she'd felt at Briana's words, the knowledge that they'd have a lifetime to do those things.

But all she said was, "It doesn't matter. We'll go to Dublin and see your family this weekend."

THE BABY WAILS PITEOUSLY as Donall carries her to his sister. "I'm sorry," he says helplessly. "I don't know what else to do."

Niamh turns her back and unbuttons her dress, tucking the babe to her breast. "The poor wee thing is starving."

In the month since Rowan disappeared, Móirín has become a ghost of herself. She who couldn't stop crying after Aoibheann's birth now can't shed a tear. She won't eat or speak. And her body can't give over any milk.

For days, she wandered the woods and fields herself, calling and searching. But now, she has taken to her bed, numb to the world, leaving Donall and the children adrift, almost as if she has died.

"Still no sign?"

He shakes his head and squats to poke at the fire. "Nothing. We've searched every day. Asked any travelers we've seen. Left notices in the village. It's as if the *sióg* have taken her into a *sídh*, leaving no sign of her in this realm."

He watches his little sister, but a child herself at nineteen, her red head bent as she croons to comfort the baby as she feeds her. How did she grow up so fast, a mother herself now? He remembers pulling her hair and teasing her mercilessly when they were children.

The past feels so much more welcoming than the present—with five children looking to him to make things right. Tears sting his eyes. He angrily swipes them away.

She glances up at Donall. "I don't know what I'd do if one of mine died—"

"Don't say that!"

She purses her lips, silenced by his reprimand, but it's clear her thoughts continue. He drops to a chair, his head in his hands.

"I'm sorry, Niamh. Only I don't know what to do."

She doesn't respond immediately. For long minutes, they sit in silence. Niamh's own baby gurgles from her cradle while her two-year-old plays with a stick, whacking it against the floor. Donall picks him up to bounce him on his knee.

"Keith has had a letter from his brother in America," Niamh says at last.

Donall stares at her. "You're not thinking of going?"

She avoids his startled gaze. "There's nothing in Ireland for us, Donall. If it hadn't been for you and Móirín and your ties to Ashford, we'd've starved this past winter."

"It's not that bad," he says stoutly but then places a hand on her shoulder. "Is it?"

"Keith hasn't had paying work since Samhain. We've no land to farm, even if potatoes would grow. We've got to make a decision soon."

A bit later, when he heads home alone, having left the baby with Niamh for now, he wonders how much longer they can go on as they are. Something has to shift soon.

MOONBEAMS APPEARED AND DISAPPEARED with the shifting of the clouds, blending with the lamplight on the desk. Nora bent with her nose almost touching the pages as her pen scrabbled furiously, recording her latest dream. She closed her eyes, trying to hold onto it— dark, pitch-black darkness. And wet. Water everywhere. And still the crying. No more laughter, only the crying and screams in the dark.

"What are you doing?"

She jumped at Briana's voice behind her. "Nothing." She splayed her hands to cover the page.

Briana rubbed her eyes. "It's the middle of the night." She laid a hand on Nora's shoulder. "Come back to bed."

Nora shook her hand off impatiently. "Not just yet. I need to finish this."

"What do you need to finish?"

"It's none of your business!" Nora snapped.

Briana withdrew her hand. A moment later, Nora heard footsteps on the stairs. A niggling voice in the back of her mind said, *you hurt her feelings.*

"I'll apologize later," she muttered, bending back over her page.

THOUGH SHE WAS ANXIOUS to be done for the day, Briana stepped back and took a deep breath. Her anxiety was transmitting itself to her work, which right now was the training of the yearlings. Tim in particular was becoming more boisterous and harder to work with, requiring greater patience on her part to train him and keep him thinking this was fun. She was grateful Quinn had had the colts gelded in the spring or this would be even harder.

"Come on now, you little git," she crooned when he tossed his head to avoid accepting the bridle and taking a bit.

Prepared for this, Bri warmed the metal bit in her hands and then smeared a little honey on it. This time, he accepted it readily, his tongue working to get all the honey off as she slipped the bridle over his ears and fastened the straps.

"See?" She rubbed and patted him. "Nothing to be afraid of."

She led him by the reins around and around the paddock before slipping the bridle off and on again a few times, until he accepted it without honey.

"All right," she said, taking it off for the last time at the gate to a larger field and giving him a little slap on the rump. "Go play."

He galloped off, his tail high, to join the other yearlings in a race across the pasture.

She trotted to the barn to clean the bridle and hang it up before going in search of Quinn. She found him in his cluttered office, Dilly curled up under his chair.

"Done for the day," she said.

He glanced up from the computer. "Off to Dublin?"

"Yeah." She scuffed her heel against the wooden floorboard.

He sat back in his chair. "Everything okay?"

"Yeah."

He reached for a stack of papers sitting on the only other chair in the cramped space. "Have a seat, squint."

She dropped into the chair. Dilly wriggled out from under Quinn's chair to jump up and place his paws on her knees. She scratched his ears.

"What's up?" Quinn asked. When she didn't answer, he said, "I didn't see Nora leaving here this morning, but your windscreen had dew all over it, so I'm guessing you stayed here alone last night."

He did her the favor of doodling on a scrap of paper so that he wasn't looking directly at her. She likewise kept her gaze trained on Dilly's soft brown eyes, half-closed as she continued to rub his ears.

"As you know, we've been alternating nights at her cottage or here," she began, feeling foolish for having this conversation with her boss. She realized she rarely thought of Quinn as her boss. "But for the last couple of nights, she hasn't wanted to leave that damned cottage. And I don't like to be away from here too many nights. I know you like to have someone about in case something happens."

He gave an impatient wave. "That's the least of my worries. Did you have a quarrel?"

"No." Dilly dropped to all fours, and Bri leaned down to continue rubbing him. "We've been good. She cooked dinner a couple of nights ago, and we made plans for Dublin. Everything was good. Then the next night, she didn't want to come here. So I stayed there again, but last night, I had to come back to my place. She wouldn't come with me."

She kept her eyes downcast but could feel Quinn studying her.

"And no disagreements or arguments? Any bad news from home?"

"No." Briana tried to think if she'd missed anything, but she'd been thinking hard ever since this started. "She had a funny spell in the kitchen that night, like she was going to pass out or something, but then she seemed fine. Other than that..."

"Only..." Quinn hesitated. "Sheila called me. Nora didn't come to work at the nursery today, so we thought maybe something happened between you."

Briana sat up at that. "She didn't go to work? But why? That makes no sense."

Quinn shrugged. "No idea."

She stood. "I'd better get over there."

He nodded. "Let us know if there's anything we can do."

She hurried to her cottage to pack a bag for the weekend. Shannon was already waiting at the SUV when she emerged. They both got in, and she hurled down the road to Sióg Cottage, her mind a whirl as to what was going on.

She racked her brain, trying again to think if she could have done or said anything to upset Nora, but she couldn't think of a thing. Maybe the bit about not going rambling to the southwest counties, but Nora hadn't acted as if she was upset about that. But that was the night she'd awakened to find Nora downstairs, writing feverishly and as snappish as a mare in season. Part of Briana wondered why she was putting up with this. She never would have before.

Then Wednesday, the last night Briana had spent at Sióg Cottage, Nora had been unusually restless, tossing and whimpering in her sleep for what felt like hours. At one point, Briana had actually shaken her to wake her. Nora had moved into her arms, burrowing in for comfort. The next morning, Nora hadn't remembered any of that.

When Briana had asked about coming by to pick Nora up to take her back to her cottage at the stables on Thursday, Nora had irritably said she didn't want to stay at Bri's place that night.

"I have things I need to do," she'd said. Her abrupt tone stung, and the hurt must have shown in Briana's face because Nora said in a more conciliatory tone, "A night apart won't do us any harm."

That much was true, Briana had to admit. There was such a thing as too much togetherness. It was just such a sudden change from the way Nora had been—the way they had been together—just a week ago.

Her worries only multiplied when she arrived at the cottage to find Nora outside, digging in the flowers. She looked up in surprise when Briana and Shannon got out of the car.

"What are you doing?" Briana asked.

"Weeding. What are you doing here?"

Briana stared at her for a second. "It's Friday. We're meant to be going to Dublin tonight."

"Oh." The blank look on Nora's face indicated she'd completely forgotten. "I'm sorry, but—"

"Kieran's expecting us," Briana said, squatting down next to her. "He'll be really disappointed if we cancel now."

Nora brushed back a strand of hair from her forehead, leaving a streak of dirt. "But you could—"

"He's expecting both of us. He invited you especially. And my mum as well." Briana sensed she needed to handle this carefully and hoped the gentle application of guilt would help. Feeling as if she were treading on very thin ice, she took Nora's elbow. "Come get cleaned up and packed, and we'll be on our way."

Nora let herself be helped to her feet. Bri guided her inside and up the stairs, into the bathroom, while Briana went to the front bedroom to get Nora's smaller suitcase from the closet. She immediately saw from the unmade bed that she'd slept in this room last night.

Shannon whined and paced nervously out in the hall, peering into the room. Briana looked over her shoulder and imagined she felt a malevolent chill emanating from the corner.

"You'll not get her," she said to the empty room.

Chapter 15

USIC, FAINT AND BEAUTIFUL—fiddles and pipes and guitars—joined with voices singing songs of longing, songs of home. Slowly, as if she were emerging from a fog, Nora became more aware of the music, the hum of tires on pavement. She blinked and looked around to see Shannon's huge head resting on her shoulder. Briana was behind the wheel, and they clearly weren't in Cong.

"Where are we?"

Briana's face was pinched, hard. Her hands gripped the wheel tightly. "We're on our way to Dublin. Don't you remember?"

Nora leaned back against the headrest, her eyes closed as she tried to do just that. It was like waking from a dream. Or was this the dream?

Briana pointed to a cup in the holder. "Coffee. Drink."

Nora took the cup and inhaled. Strong and black. The first sip was like life itself seeping back into her. She drank, and Briana's hands unclenched a little.

Shannon gave Nora's cheek a little lick and then stretched out across the back seat.

Nora felt foolish as she asked, "We're really on our way to Dublin?"

"Yes. Monday night you made the chili, and I brought you a drawing from Kieran, asking us to come. We promised when we were there, and he is holding us to our promise. We agreed to go this weekend."

Her tone sounded as if she was forcing herself to patiently explain something very simple to someone very dense.

Nora closed her eyes again. She remembered that day, but it seemed weeks ago. "What day is today?"

"Friday. That was just Monday of this week. What's going on, Nora?"

The setting sun behind them threw long shadows onto the highway ahead. The tires' hum was hypnotic in its own way. She drank more coffee, trying to clear the fog in her mind.

"I'm not sure," she said at last. "If this is Friday, these last few days have been a blur." She turned to Briana. "I don't remember you being around. Much."

"That would be because you haven't wanted me around."

The quiet of her voice contrasted with the way her hands were once again strangling the steering wheel.

Nora was almost afraid to ask. "What do you mean?"

Briana glanced over again, an expression of disbelief on her face. "You. Waking in the middle of the night to spend hours writing, basically telling me to shove off when I came to bring you back to bed. Refusing to leave the cottage to come stay with me. Telling me we don't need to spend every night together. Not even showing up to work today. Look, if you don't want to be with me, I wish you'd just say so."

Nora gaped at her. "Wait. What do you mean, I didn't show up at work today?"

"It's Friday. Sheila was expecting you. No word. You just didn't show. She was worried. She and Quinn thought maybe we'd had a fight, but I didn't know anything about it. I looked a right git when Quinn asked me."

Nora sat, stunned. How could she just not show up for work? She had vague memories of Briana coming to her, but...

"What is going on, Nora?" Briana repeated, her voice tight. "Before we have to spend the weekend pretending around my family, you've got to tell me."

Nora reached over to lay her hand on Briana's arm, but Bri didn't relinquish her hold on the wheel to take Nora's hand. Nora withdrew, shifting closer to the door.

"I honestly don't know."

"What do you mean? How can you not know?"

Sudden tears stung Nora's eyes. *What the hell is wrong with you?* She turned to look out the passenger window.

Briana startled her by reaching over to lay her hand on Nora's thigh. Nora stared at it for a moment before taking it, squeezing tightly.

"The dreams have shifted again."

"In what way?"

"They're dark."

Briana frowned. "You mean scary? Dangerous?"

"No. Yes." Nora closed her eyes again, trying to recall. "It is scary and dangerous. But it's literally dark. Pitch black. And wet. I'm trapped somewhere dark and wet."

"You were crying in your sleep the last night I spent with you."

Nora opened her eyes and looked at Briana. "I was?"

Bri nodded. "I held you until you went back to sleep, but you didn't seem to remember the next morning." She glanced over. "Don't you recall any of this?"

Nora shook her head. "I don't."

She raised Briana's hand to her lips, then pressed her cheek to it for a long moment. "I'm sorry."

Briana's gaze flicked back and forth between Nora and the road. "So you're not wanting to break up with me?"

Nora gave a strangled laugh. "No. I do not want to break up with you." She took a deep breath, like someone gasping for air after being trapped underwater. "I'm glad to be with you, and I'm looking forward to spending the weekend with your family."

Briana sighed. Nora was relieved to see her face relax into a smile. But inside, she was still scrambling, trying to recollect the last few days, days that, to her, felt as if they'd been spent in another time, with people long dead.

BRIANA SAT CROSS-LEGGED in a chair with a cup of coffee, watching Kieran trying to teach Nora how to play his favorite video game. She was hopeless, but Bri suspected she was playing badly on purpose.

Cara and Dennis were busy in the kitchen, frying up eggs and bacon. The kitchen was too tiny for a third person, so Briana was supervising the gaming. Cara caught her eye and smiled. She'd had the guest room prepared for them when they arrived last night, not even asking if Briana would be sharing with Nora. Briana found that mildly irritating and kind of endearing at the same time.

Not that sleeping in the same bed had amounted to anything they needed to hide. After a quick kiss good night, Nora had fallen asleep holding Bri's hand, and she slept like the dead, something Briana suspected she hadn't done in a long time.

She got up to refill her coffee. Dennis took advantage of her presence to duck out of the kitchen and go join the video gaming.

"Sleep well?" Cara asked innocently.

Briana gave her sister a mocking smile. "Fine. Very subtle, that. Putting us together in the guest room."

Cara shrugged. "It was that or you take the sofa. Figured you'd rather share a bed." Her wicked grin belied her attempt at being considerate, but the grin faded as she looked more closely at Bri. "What's wrong?"

Briana twitched a shoulder, as if ridding herself of an annoying fly. "Nothing." She pointed to the toaster. "Want me to get some bread going?"

Cara opened her mouth to argue the point, but Briana turned her back and busied herself with the toast, so Cara let it drop.

By the time they were finishing breakfast, the grandparents had arrived. Briana introduced Nora to her dad, Bill.

He shook Nora's hand and then scooped Kieran up into his arms. "All set, little man?"

They took two cars to the zoo, Kieran dragging Nora to sit beside him while Briana rode with her parents.

"She's such a lovely girl," Victoria said. "I'm so glad you both made it back before she leaves to go home to America."

"How much longer is she here?" Bill asked, eyeing Briana in the rearview mirror.

Briana had to think for a moment. "Three more weeks."

That realization hit her like a splash of cold water. Less than a month left. Somehow the world beyond August loomed like a shapeless void.

Once they were at the zoo, Kieran could barely contain himself as he dragged Nora and Briana with him along the paths. Nora was like her old self—laughing, catching Bri's eye and giving her secret smiles, taking her hand for brief squeezes.

Briana stood near the gorilla rainforest, watching Nora talking with Cara, and she remembered their conversation at the pub during Nora's first visit to Dublin, the night she'd told Nora she was like a boggart. In the weeks since then, Briana had felt she was getting to know the real Nora, the one she'd speculated about that night.

Watching her now, it was as if the strangeness of the past week had vanished, leaving Briana to wonder if she'd imagined Nora's odd, moody behavior. But she also wondered if Nora was becoming a boggart again.

NORA LAY STARING AT the ceiling. Beside her, Briana was breathing deeply. The house was quiet. She knew Dennis and Bill would have left early for their Sunday golf game, while Cara and Kieran picked up Victoria to go to Mass. They'd be back here soon for a late breakfast, and then she and Briana would be on their way home to Cong.

Home to Cong.

Could it be that simple? She turned her head. A ray of sunshine wriggled between the curtain panels, striking Briana's hair, turning it to copper. Her face in sleep was relaxed, almost childlike. None of the pinching and worry that had been there lately.

Worry you caused, she reminded herself.

She felt like a woman coming back to health after a long illness. Those last few days at the cottage were a blur. It mortified her that she hadn't shown for work on Friday, and she'd not yet had a chance to apologize to Sheila. She needed to do that first thing when they got back. This evening. It couldn't even wait until tomorrow morning.

She rubbed her eyes, trying to remember just why she'd been so reluctant to leave the cottage, but here, so far away, even that strange compulsion felt dream-like.

She turned on her side, one hand lightly resting against Briana's arm, enjoying the warmth, and let herself drift off into sleep once more.

THROUGH HER HALF-CLOSED eyes, Móirín sees a figure, pale and indistinct. *Rowan?* She tries to call out, but there is no strength left. No strength to fight. No strength to mourn. No strength to live. She is hollowed out. A hull.

Vaguely, she knows there are others she loves, a dear husband and children, but the pain of losing the one—no word, no sign, no way of knowing what happened to her baby... That's the part that drags her into this abyss, the not knowing.

Her soul has been rent by the not knowing. She wants it to stop. She is ready for it to stop.

Mam.

Is that Rowan, calling to her? She strains to hear it again. *Where are you? Rowan?*

A shadow moves over her. Is it death? It has finally come for her as it did for the Foyles. For the little Gallagher baby. For her own Rowan. For so many.

But it's her Donall, trying again to get her to eat something, only she can't. She loves him, but she is broken. Broken beyond healing.

SHANNON SNORED FROM THE back seat as they drove.

"For a while, I thought we were going to have a stowaway," Nora said.

Briana chuckled. "I know. Kieran was determined to come with us."

"Have you ever had him with you, just him for a week or so?"

"No." Briana looked so shocked at the mere suggestion that Nora laughed. "What would I do with him all day while I'm working? He's into everything."

"This is true," Nora acknowledged. "He's kind of a Tasmanian devil in the form of a little boy. But he is cute."

"He is that."

Nora watched Briana as she drove. The miles rolled by on the motorway. "What were you and Cara talking about?"

"When?" Bri glanced at her.

"In the kitchen. Before we packed up and loaded the car."

"Oh, nothing. Just plans for them maybe to come our way for a weekend."

But Briana's cheeks and ears were red. It hadn't looked like nothing to Nora. The two of them had been huddled in the kitchen while Nora sat at the table with Victoria and Kieran. At one point, Cara had pulled Briana into a tight hug, which had surprised Nora.

They settled into comfortable silence, listening to music, and Nora thought again how different this was from the way things had been with Amy. Any road trip they took was spent either listening to talk radio or to Amy talking about the topic of the talk radio program.

Nora's days at the library back home had been spent with people talking to or at her—students and faculty asking for help with finding sources or doing searches, coworkers talking about their families or asking her for help with projects. She'd rarely had quiet time during the day or on the weekends, so she'd come to relish her time alone in her townhouse during the week, with only Willa for company, though Willa hadn't always been a silent companion. *Who would have thought a cat could be so talkative?* she recalled with a wry smile.

Once Willa was gone, the stillness had been harder than she'd expected. Her eyes pricked with sudden tears, and she turned away to brush her cheeks.

"Are you all right?" Briana reached over to lay a hand on her arm.

Nora gave Bri's hand a squeeze. "I'm fine. Just thinking. Not always a good thing."

Briana left her hand there, warm and comforting, but letting her be with her thoughts. Amy never would have. She would have nagged and harped until Nora confessed whatever she'd been thinking about—at which point, Amy would have told her how silly she was for thinking it in the first place. So she'd learned to keep her thoughts hidden, pretend to be interested in whatever Amy wanted to talk about, and save all of her thinking time for when she was alone.

Why in the world did you ever let things get like that?

She had no answer to that question, but here, here was someone she could be completely herself with. She studied Briana again. Wasn't this worth upending her life, moving to a new country and starting over?

"THEY'RE BOTH HOME."

Briana parked beside Quinn's truck. Before they could even get out, Sheila had rushed from the house.

"I was so worried," she said, embracing Nora.

"I'm sorry," Nora said. "I never meant to worry you, and I am really sorry about just not showing up for work."

Quinn and Rusty joined them. Rusty waddled over to greet Shannon while Quinn stood with his hands stuffed in his pockets.

Sheila held her at arm's length, scrutinizing her. "Never mind work. Are you okay?"

Nora nodded. She gave Quinn an embarrassed grin. "Guess I got wrapped up in my own projects around the cottage and lost track of what day it was."

Briana stood next to the car, sharing a worried glance with him.

Sheila hooked her arm through Nora's. "As it happens, I've dinner all prepared. Spaghetti. Come in and eat with us."

Quinn sidled over to Bri as the dogs followed Nora and Sheila into the kitchen. "Is she really all right?"

"Damned if I know." Briana ran a hand through her hair. "She was in a right state when I got there on Friday. Didn't seem to remember our plans. Barely seemed aware of the rest of the world a'tall. As soon as I got her away from that cottage, it was like she woke up from some kind of trance or something."

She checked to make sure they couldn't be overheard. "I'm telling you, Quinn, there's something not right about that place."

He frowned, scratching at the stubble on his jaw. "It's only a few more weeks. We could put her up here, easy enough." He pointedly didn't look at her as he added, "Or you could have her stay with you."

Briana scuffed the toe of her boot at the gravel of the drive. "I would. No worries. If I can get her to leave the bloody place."

Quinn draped an arm over her shoulder. "Come inside and eat, squint. We'll work on her."

But despite their combined efforts, Nora stubbornly refused to accept either proposition.

"I really appreciate your offers," she said. "But I won't be chased out of my own place."

"It's not your place," Sheila pointed out reasonably. "It's a rental. With a shady history."

"I know," Nora twirled her spaghetti around and around. "But it feels kind of like my place. I don't know how to explain it, but I should be there."

Briana fought the urge to argue the point. She didn't know all Nora had escaped when she got out of her last relationship, but she knew part of it was always being told what to do. She nearly blurted that she'd be staying at the cottage, too, if that was Nora's plan, but she suddenly wasn't certain she'd be wanted or welcome to stay for the next three weeks. Maybe she could still talk Nora into switching back and forth between places. At least get her away from Sióg Cottage on some nights.

And she'd yet to discuss with Nora the crazy half-baked plan that had come into her head, the one Cara had wheedled from her. But that could wait.

When they left, with a promise from Nora to Sheila that she'd be back for work bright and early in the morning, Briana drove them to Nora's cottage.

She eyed it warily as she got out of the car, half-expecting the windows to frown or the chimney to huff smoke, like some haunted house in a horror movie, but all was still. Inside, nothing had been tossed. Nora's papers were stacked neatly on her desk, along with her pens and books.

Shannon stood in the parlor, sniffing. When she relaxed and curled up on the floor, Bri relaxed a bit as well.

"Want some tea?" Nora asked, depositing her bag on the floor and going into the kitchen.

"Sure."

Nora put the kettle on and busied herself at the counter, laying out mugs and teabags.

"What's that?" Briana asked as Nora tipped a bottle over one mug, pouring a bit of whatever was inside.

"Just something Eve gave me to help me sleep."

Briana lifted the bottle to her nose. "Eve gave you this?"

"Yes. She knew I hadn't been sleeping well, and thought this tonic would help."

Briana bit her lip as a thought occurred to her, but it was crazy. Surely Eve would never give Nora anything harmful. She'd never been known to hurt anyone. Briana shook her head.

"What?" Nora had noticed.

Briana gave her a rueful smile. "Nothing. Just wondered if it's some kind of witch's brew."

Nora held the bottle up. "'Double, double toil and trouble; fire burn and cauldron bubble.'" She raised her eyebrows and looked at Briana.

Bri shrugged. "Something like that."

They took their mugs out to the parlor and sat on the sofa there. For long minutes, they sat side by side, sipping their tea.

"I had a nice weekend," Nora said. "I really like your family."

"I think you're a hit with them," Briana said. "In fact, they might like you better than me."

Nora laughed, and the sound of it struck Briana as if she'd not heard it before, and she knew, knew without a doubt, that that was a sound she wanted to hear for the rest of her life.

She set her tea down on the side table and turned to Nora who was watching her with soft eyes. She took Nora's cup as well, placing it beside hers, and then cradled Nora's face in her hands, gently tracing the shape of Nora's lips with her thumb. Those soft lips parted, quirking into a tiny smile.

"That tickles," Nora whispered.

Briana got on her knees and leaned forward, barely brushing her own mouth over Nora's, eliciting a bigger smile. Bri placed feather-light kisses on her brow, her eyelids, down her neck—Nora shivered at that—and finally back to her mouth where Nora was ready to meet the kiss with her own, lips parted, tongue darting into Briana's mouth.

Without breaking the kiss, Briana shifted to straddle Nora's lap as her hands tugged Nora's shirt up and she ran her hands over deliciously bare skin. Nora unbuttoned Briana's jeans, slipping her hands down over Bri's bum. In a flash, Briana had Nora's bra unhooked and was cupping her breasts against her palms, rubbing the hardened nipples, causing Nora to groan against her mouth.

"Need you," Nora panted. "Now. Upstairs."

NIGHT WAS DEEP, AND silence was heavily wrapped around the cottage like a quilt when Nora got out of bed, naked, and padded out of the room. In the hall, Shannon lifted her head to watch as Nora walked into the front bedroom and stood at the window. The dog tilted her head at this strange behavior. For a long time, the human stood like that, talking in a low voice as if someone else were in the room. Shannon growled softly. But then, Nora got in that bed. She seemed as if she was sleeping. Shannon laid her head back on her paws, but she raised it again when Nora began whimpering and crying out. Shannon turned to see if Briana was getting up, but she didn't stir. Whining, Shannon paced the hallway between the two rooms.

Eventually, both humans were quiet, and silence settled over the house again. With a sigh, the dog lay down on her side where she could keep guard over both rooms.

Chapter 16

ORA HUFFED IN EXASPERATION as she untied the ribbon around the small box holding one of Sheila's rose-scented candles—dark rose-colored ribbon for these candles, lavender for the lavender-scented ones, dark green for the pine. It had been her suggestion to color-code the ribbons to match the various candles, and the shop owners had reported back to them that customers noticed the little touch. It was her third attempt to tie this ribbon neatly, and she was getting frustrated.

"What's wrong?" Sheila asked.

"Nothing."

"Well, your nothing is really loud today." Sheila carefully stacked the boxed candles in a larger box to take to the village later. "How is Briana?"

"Why does everything have to do with Briana?" Nora snapped.

"It doesn't," Sheila said carefully. In the same measured tone, she asked, "But since we're on the topic, have you two had an argument since we saw you last evening?"

"No. No argument. She stayed last night and went to work this morning."

Nora finished tying the ribbon with an acceptable bow and handed it to Sheila.

Sheila placed it in the box with the others and then crossed her arms, leaning against the counter.

Nora scowled at the expectant look on her cousin's face. She knew she looked awful. Even she could see the dark circles under her own eyes. There was never going to be an easy time to say this.

"You know I only have a little while left before I'm supposed to leave here," she began. "I…" She twisted a bit of leftover ribbon around and around her finger. "I think I want to just spend the rest of it at my cottage. I know this is leaving you short with no notice, but…"

She felt Sheila's surprise, but wouldn't look at her.

"Of course," Sheila said. "This wasn't ever supposed to feel like an obligation to you. I'll manage until I can hire someone else. I knew I was going to have to do that after you went home anyhow."

Though the words were understanding, there was a bite to her tone that made Nora cringe.

"I'm sorry—"

"No need to apologize." Sheila gathered up the box of candles and carried it out to her SUV. Nora followed her outside.

"If you'll just keep an eye on the shop until I get back," Sheila said brusquely as she got behind the wheel. "I'll only be a few minutes and then you can be on your way."

Without giving Nora time to reply, Sheila started the engine and drove away. As she drove out, a customer motored in.

Nora was able to advise the woman in choosing several plants suitable for a rock garden she was building under some trees that would offer only intermittent sun. She rang the sale up and helped the woman load the plants into her car.

She paced like a caged lion through the shop, back outside around the tiered shelves under the pergola. Her skin felt prickly, as if she were feverish, and her eyes burned under her lids. She wondered if she was coming down with something. Getting sick wasn't something she'd considered when she planned to be in Ireland for the summer. She was rarely ill, usually nothing more than the odd cold.

She went back inside to check the nursery email account and see if there had been any new orders. A few other incoming emails downloaded. One of the little bubbles indicated it was from Fiona. Nora clicked on it.

> Sheila,
>
> Have you and Nora had a chance to look over the things Brigid and Tommy sent to Nora? I thought I'd have heard from you. Can you believe that photo? It can't be Eve, but I swear by all that's holy it's her great-great-great-grandmother.
>
> Call me when you have a chance.
>
> Love,
>
> Gran

Nora had nearly forgotten—the image of the girl with the hypnotic eyes, the one that couldn't possibly be Eve but surely looked like her. Her finger hovered for a moment, and then she clicked the mouse and deleted the message.

Outside, she heard Sheila's SUV. She got up and went out to meet her.

"Everything go okay in the village?"

"Fine." Sheila planted herself in front of Nora. "I'm sorry if I was a bit short with you earlier, only you caught me by surprise."

Nora stared at Sheila's boots. "I know. I'm sorry."

"As I said, no need to apologize. I understand if you don't want to spend the rest of your holiday working. I appreciate the time you've given me. Can we have dinner at the pub tomorrow?"

"Sure." Nora forced a smile as she reached for her bike. "Tomorrow night."

She waved as she pedaled away. Riding hard, she passed a couple of hikers on the paths. At the cottage, she dropped her bike to the ground. Inside, she pushed the door shut behind her and stood leaning against it with her eyes closed.

"I'm home. And I'm not leaving again."

WITH THE SLIGHTEST LEG pressure from Briana, Ginger did a flying lead change. She had the prettiest gathered canter, like a dancer. Her delicate hooves flicked off the ground, and she was airborne again. Together, they made their way around the ring, weaving in between the jump standards, changing leads again and again until Ginger was anticipating the signal.

"She's a beauty," Quinn said from where he was leaning on the fence watching them.

Ginger trotted over to him, fairly preening.

"She is," Briana agreed, leaning forward to give her neck a pat. She avoided looking at him, forcing herself to say what needed to be said. "Seems a shame to have her just be a stable hack."

"Jesus, you read my mind." He ran his hand through his sandy hair, leaving it sticking up in places. "She belongs with someone who will compete with her."

Ginger nuzzled his arm, and he obliged by producing an apple from his pocket. He slid a knife from another pocket and cut a generous slice for her.

"I'll put out word that we've an eventing prospect, and see if we can find someone who'll bring her along as she should be."

"I'll cool her down," Briana said, swinging Ginger around to walk around the ring. Quinn climbed through the rails and joined them.

She glanced down curiously. "What?"

This time it was him avoiding looking up at her. "You two could have said something."

"What are you talking about?"

"You and Nora. You had supper with us just last night, for Christ's sake. If Nora wanted to quit, why didn't she say something then?"

Briana brought Ginger to a halt. "What are you talking about?" she repeated. "What do you mean quit?"

He looked up at her. "Nora. Telling Sheila today that she doesn't want to work anymore. We understand, of course. This is supposed to be a holiday, but to tell her at the last minute, with no notice, and then ride off." He kicked at the dirt in the ring, raising a cloud of dust. "It's poor form."

Briana's mouth hung open.

He frowned. "You didn't know anything about this, did you?"

She closed her mouth and shook her head. "She said nothing. Not last night, not this morning." She twisted the reins in her fisted hands. "It's that bloody cottage. I told you. She's only been back in it one night, and it's started up again. I woke to find her sleeping in the ghost room this morning."

"See if you can get her to spend the nights with you here. Sheila said she agreed to dinner down the pub tomorrow night, so maybe it won't be too awkward."

He gave Ginger a final pat and went back to the barn.

Briana finished cooling Ginger down, muttering aloud the entire time, and then untacked and groomed her before returning her to her stall.

By the time she was done, she'd calmed down a bit. She sensed she was going to have to tread lightly when she confronted Nora. She whistled for Shannon and drove to the cottage.

First thing she noticed upon arriving was the bicycle lying on its side. She picked it up to lean against the cottage wall and then went to the front door, knocking as she entered.

"Nora?"

She heard an answering thump from upstairs. Shannon raced her up the steps, going to the doorway into the front bedroom. Briana followed to find Nora moving the furniture.

"What are you doing?"

Nora barely looked up. "The bed isn't in the right place."

"What do you mean? It's where it's always been."

"No." Nora shook her head. "It should be there." She pointed to the adjacent wall. "It was always there."

She braced her hands on the iron headboard and pushed, shoving the bed in an arc.

"Nora," Briana said, striding over to lay a restraining hand on her shoulder. "It doesn't matter where it used to be. We don't even use this room."

Nora shook her hand off and resumed pushing. "I need to be in this room. And the bed needs to be over here."

Briana hesitated a second then helped shove. When the bed was in place against the wall, Nora carried the bedside table over next to it and stood, contemplating the arrangement.

"Is this better?" Bri asked. "Can we talk now?"

Nora looked at her, seeming to see her for the first time. "Sure. What do you want to talk about?"

But she went to the dresser and began rearranging the small vases and decorative boxes sitting on it.

"Sheila. The nursery. You just up and quitting with no notice. Don't you think we need to talk about that?"

Nora flicked a glance in her direction. "It's not a big deal. Like I told Sheila. I just don't want to work my whole summer here."

"Okay." Briana forced a more patient tone as she said, "But you gave her no notice. I don't think you would normally do that to someone."

Briana saw Nora's frown in the mirror.

"Why don't you put a few things together, and we'll go to my cottage for the night," Briana suggested.

"No." Nora turned, bracing her hands on the dresser behind her. "No, I don't want to be anywhere else."

"Nora." Briana approached and stood in front of her. "This cottage isn't good for you. It does something to you."

Nora tried to push past her. "You don't know what you're talking about."

Briana grabbed her arm. "Please. If you won't come with me, I'll stay here."

Nora whipped around. "No! I mean, you don't need to. Really. I'm fine here. You go back to your place, get a good night's sleep."

She pulled her arm free and went downstairs, leaving Briana no choice but to follow.

In the parlor, she opened the front door. "I'll see you tomorrow."

Briana opened her mouth, ready to argue, but closed it. Out on the flagstones, she turned. "Nora—"

"I'll see you tomorrow," Nora repeated, giving her a kiss on the cheek before closing the door.

Briana stood there a moment, tempted to barge inside and—*and do what, exactly?* she asked herself. Throw Nora over her shoulder and drag her out to the car? Tie her up in the other bedroom to keep her out of the ghost room?

She stomped to the SUV and yanked the door open. Shannon jumped in, and Bri climbed in after her, spraying gravel when she gunned the engine. At the end of the drive, she stopped.

"What the hell is going on? Last night, she practically had sex with me on the sofa, and today, she's all 'see you tomorrow'."

Shannon whined, and Briana reached for her, hating the sick feeling in her belly that what she'd thought might be forever was looking more and more as if it was going to end badly.

"Let's go home."

NORA LAY IN THE dark, in the front bedroom. From the bed's new position on this wall, she knew she had the same view as they'd had—Móirín and Donall—when they shared this space, made love here, bore children here, died here. She spread her hands out over the sheets. It couldn't be the same bed, surely, but still.

All evening, she'd been lying here, staring at the spiderweb of fine cracks in the old plaster of the ceiling, imagining Móirín lying in this same place, staring at the same cracks, waiting for word of her daughter's fate.

Outside, owls hooted and moonbeams slanted through the window only to disappear as clouds drifted past, and then reappear moments later. Her stomach rumbled. She'd had no supper, only some tea with Aoibheann's tonic mixed in. She longed to drift into the sleep that brought her dreams—dreams of Rowan and Móirín.

Vaguely, her mind was troubled by how she'd treated Briana.

But she doesn't understand. None of them do. They just don't understand how important this is.

Her eyes began to close. Or were they open? She couldn't tell, but it didn't matter. Around her, shadows began to move—a pale, beautiful woman and a little girl in a yellow dress. Somehow, they were less shadowy now, more solid, more real. Beckoning to her, drawing her into dreams, into their world—a world she no longer wanted to leave.

IN HER OWN COTTAGE near the stables, Briana also lay awake, her arms flung over her face as she fought tears. She didn't cry, as a matter of course. She couldn't remember the last time she had—probably at her granddad's funeral.

No, that's not right. You cried in the car with her that day, driving back from Dublin, when you told her about the race, the day Murphy went down and had to be put to sleep. You never tell anyone about that. Why her?

Briana had carefully arranged her life as she wanted it—horses, hard work, good mates, a good dog, family only occasionally. If she was lonely now and again, well that was a small price to pay for no entanglements, no heartbreak. Too much closeness—even with family—had never been a good thing.

But her mind wouldn't stop replaying images of Nora—awkwardly bouncing in the saddle on their first ride, standing in the wind at Lettergesh beach, lying naked beside her in this very bed.

Nora coming here had changed everything. Enough so that Bri had actually confessed to Cara that she was thinking about moving to the States to be with her. If she cared about her enough to do that... She sat up suddenly and checked the clock.

Three a.m.

"Damn."

She got out of bed, pulled on jeans, slipped into trainers, and went out to the car with Shannon on her heels.

They drove back to Sióg Cottage, Briana determined to talk sense into Nora. Never mind that it was the middle of the night. She had no idea what she was going to say, only a feeling that she couldn't just let Nora disappear from her life without trying—something she had never, ever wanted to do before.

When she turned onto the lane from the main road, she braked, struck by the certainty that she and Shannon should approach the cottage unannounced. She cut the motor and turned the lights off, leaving the SUV where it was.

Shannon seemed to sense the need for stealth. She stayed beside Briana as they walked the remaining distance to the cottage. When at last the trees parted, it was just as a cloud obscured the moon, leaving deeper shadows, for which Bri was grateful.

She studied the cottage, not sure what exactly she was here to do.

The front door opened unexpectedly, and she jumped, dropping into a crouch. Nora emerged, turning toward the woods—the same direction they had taken the day they searched for the stone circle. Briana was about to follow when another movement caught her eye. A figure, moving out of the deeper shadows on the other side of the cottage, followed Nora. Even with the moon veiled by clouds, there was no mistaking that silver-white hair—Eve, carrying her shuttered lantern so that it gave no light.

Briana and Shannon trailed them, treading as quietly as they could. The clouds shifted, making it a bit easier to see Eve's hair shimmering in the night. Nora was beyond where Briana could see, but Eve seemed to know where she was going.

Dew-dampened brush soon had Briana's jeans and trainers soaking wet. They reached the circle of stones. Briana squatted down, one arm over Shannon's back, as Nora stood in the center, Eve watching her from the periphery.

"Rowan?" Nora called to the night. "Rowan, where are you?"

Nora walked through the circle into the trees on the other side, but reappeared a moment later, still calling. She walked back in their direction, passing Eve as if she didn't see her.

Briana made Shannon lie down, hunching to make herself as small as possible, while Nora traipsed by in the direction of the cottage.

When Briana raised her head to look around, Eve was nowhere to be seen. Bri pushed stiffly to her feet, limping as she and Shannon followed Nora back to Sióg Cottage and watched her go inside.

Flummoxed, Briana stood there a few minutes before going to the cottage. The door was locked. She knocked on it. No answer. She banged again.

"What the bloody hell is going on?" Briana asked when Nora opened the door.

Nora rubbed her eyes. "What are you talking about?"

"You! Walking around the forest at night."

"I haven't been anywhere except bed until you showed up and woke me."

Briana pointed to the wet trousers and shoes that Nora was still wearing. "You go to bed in those?"

Nora patted her damp thighs. "I was sleepwalking again?"

"Not just you." Briana took Nora by the hand and led her to the sofa. "Eve was following you."

In the dim moonlight, Nora stared at Briana. "Eve. Was following me."

"Yes. I saw her." Briana squirmed uncomfortably. "Because I was following both of you. I came here to... to talk some sense into you, and I saw you leave the cottage, with Eve following. You went to the stone circle, calling for Rowan."

At Nora's befuddled expression, she asked, "You don't remember any of this, do you?"

Nora shook her head.

Briana took her hand. "Please, come back to my place. You need to get out of here."

Briana felt an ominous chill fill the room, though she didn't see anything. Shannon whined and shifted to lean against Briana's leg.

Nora let Bri tug her to her feet. "I'll just pack a few things—"

"No. Let's go now."

Briana kept hold of Nora's hand and led her from the cottage. Outside, the summer night enveloped them. She took a deep breath. "The car's just down the lane."

At the edge of the clearing, she looked back. A pale face was watching them from the upstairs window.

NORA FOUND BRIANA SITTING at her table, her head cradled in her hands, staring into her coffee. Shannon glanced up from her bowl of kibble when Nora entered, gave a wag of her tail, and went back to her breakfast.

Nora poured herself a cup of coffee and sat. Briana raised her head, looking at her with bleary eyes.

"Sorry to be so much trouble," Nora mumbled.

Briana studied her as she took a sip of coffee. "You look as bad as I feel."

Nora snorted. "Then that must be pretty bad." She sobered and gripped her mug. "I honestly don't remember any of what you said happened last night—wandering through the woods out to the stones, Eve, none of it."

Briana frowned. "Something really strange is going on with that cottage. Eve and the history of that place, it's just wrong."

"Yeah."

Briana shoved to her feet and stirred the porridge she'd made for both of them. "I think," she said from the stove, keeping her back to Nora, "you should stay here."

Nora heard the hesitation in her voice and knew Briana was tiptoeing around a topic she thought Nora would object to, but after last night, she was ready to leave that blasted cottage forever.

"I agree."

When Briana turned around, her surprise was plain to see, but she looked pleased. "Good." She dished out the porridge and put a container of milk on the table.

Nora stirred milk and sugar into hers. "I don't remember too much after I left Sheila on Monday and got back to the cottage. It's all kind of a blur."

"That was yesterday," Briana said, staring hard at her.

"Yesterday?" Nora was startled. It felt like days and days ago. "Just yesterday?"

"Yes." Briana spooned up some porridge. "It's Tuesday. We're supposed to have dinner with Sheila and Quinn at the pub tonight."

Nora recoiled. "I can't. I can't see Sheila after what I did. Just quitting like that." She dropped her head to her hand. "I don't know what's gotten into me. I would never—"

Briana reached for her hand, making her look up. "You're away from there now. It's all right."

Nora took a deep breath. "You're right. I guess I should go back to help Sheila out at the nursery."

Bri tilted her head. "She wouldn't be expecting you today anyhow. And... a little space might be a good idea."

"Well, I've got to do something with my time."

Briana grinned. "If it's work you're after, you've come to the right place."

True to her word, she had Nora working steadily all day: mucking stalls and spreading fresh bedding, grooming horses, refilling water buckets, cleaning tack.

"We need to keep her," Sonya said happily when she found half her work done for her. "I'm off to give a lesson. I hope we see you tomorrow, Nora."

After she left, Nora carried one last bucket of water to a stall.

"I want to be tired enough to sleep tonight," she said, leaning on a stall door, where Stubbs reached up to nibble on her ear with his soft lips. She patted him.

"You'll have earned it," Briana said. She washed the dust and dirt off her hands at the sink and wiped them dry on the seat of her jeans.

"If we're going out to dinner in the village tonight, I'm going to need clean clothes," Nora said. "And a bath."

"I still have to dose a few horses with their meds," Briana said. "Then I'll drive you over."

"That's silly. I can walk there and bicycle back in the time it will take you to finish here. Really," Nora added when Briana looked at her doubtfully. "I'll pack a small bag, and be back in half an hour, tops."

Briana hesitated. "All right, but take Shannon with you and come back here to shower."

Nora smiled indulgently. "Come on, Shannon. You can be my bodyguard."

She set off with a wave, Shannon trotting at her side.

SUCH A PRETTY COTTAGE. Donall stands outside, holding Teafa and wondering how many times Móirín said that in their years there. It rips his heart in two to leave it, but there is nothing here for him anymore. He hugs Teafa tightly, burying his face against her warm little body.

Niamh is right. It's time for a fresh start.

He places Teafa in the wagon, adding her to the other children too young to walk, along with a satchel for each of them. One bag to hold what's left of a life. None of the furniture Donall built with his own hands. None of the dishes and pewter Móirín was so proud of. It has all been sold for a pittance. The horse and wagon they'll sell in Belfast. Only some of his tools has he kept. Those he'll need in America. For the new life he'll make for himself and his children.

He took them for one last visit to their mother's grave at the churchyard, knowing none of them would ever see it again. But there is only one grave. He failed her. Failed to find their Rowan. He feels as if he killed Móirín himself when he couldn't give her answers.

A sob of despair boils inside him, but he chokes it down. He bends to pick up Aoibheann from where she lies on a blanket, but she cries and reaches for Niamh. His own babe doesn't know him. He's lost two daughters. And his wife. How is a man supposed to accept such cruelty from God?

Niamh takes the baby from him, tucking her into the wagon while Keith checks the harness straps one last time. With a cluck and a gentle tug, he urges the horse to begin pulling. The mare leans into the collar and plods away from the cottage.

"It's time." Niamh grasps Donall's hand, drawing him after the wagon. At the bend of the lane, he stops to look back.

"Don't," she says. "We need to move on, Donall. Away from here. To something better. Better for all of us."

He and his sister follow the wagon, leaving their old life behind forever.

"NORA! SHOWER'S YOURS." Briana stopped toweling off her wet hair to listen. No answer. "Shannon?"

Still nothing. She poked her head out of the bathroom. Everything was quiet. She quickly dressed in some clean clothes and went out to check. No sign of Nora or her bike. She opened the kitchen door and called again for Shannon.

Cursing under her breath, she sat down to lace up her trainers and stormed out to the stables where she found Liam scooping oats from the large bin into a bucket.

"Have you seen Nora come back with Shannon?"

He looked up in surprise. "No. I didn't know she left."

Bri ran to the car and raced to Sióg Cottage. When she turned onto the cottage's lane, everything was shrouded by sudden fog. She had to turn on the headlights to see through the mist.

She hadn't driven through any fog coming from the stables. It all seemed to be gathered near the cottage and was so heavy that she almost rammed into a tree. She parked the SUV and made her way on foot, feeling with her feet, her hands extended out in front of her, until she touched the cottage's stone wall. Groping for the door, she bashed into it when it didn't open. She wiggled the knob, but the door was locked.

"Nora? Shannon!" She went to the front window, accidentally stepping on what felt like Nora's flowers, and peered inside.

There, she made out Shannon's still form, lying on her side in the middle of the floor.

Panicking now, she returned to the door and pounded. "Nora! Nora, answer me!" When there was no answer, she stumbled to the back, tripping on flagstones she couldn't see. The kitchen door was also locked.

Going around to the front of the cottage again, she knelt down, fumbling about until she found a fist-sized rock.

"I owe you a window, Farmer McCarthy." She cocked her arm and heaved the stone at the glass. A split-second later, the stone rebounded, hitting her in the shoulder when it ricocheted off the window without breaking it.

"What the hell?" She rubbed her shoulder.

Overhead, she heard an upstairs window open.

"Nora!"

She strained to see through the fog, but she couldn't make anything out in the thick gray haze.

"Go away, Briana."

"Eve? Eve, what is going on? Let me in!"

"I can't do that. Did you think I didn't know you were following us last night? I can't let you interfere. I've waited too long."

Briana stepped back, waving a hand to try and clear the fog obscuring her view. "Waited for what?"

Goosebumps erupted all over Briana's body as Eve laughed, sounding slightly maniacal.

"Waited for what?" she echoed. "Waited for everything. I've been waiting my entire life. Nearly two centuries. My past, my future, my death. It has all come down to this."

Bri stood there, half-tempted to scoff at the impossible absurdity of what she was hearing, but she became aware of tendrils of mist wrapping about her legs like hands, reaching inside the legs of her jeans, sending a deep chill stealing into her bones. Her heart raced, and she became more afraid, imagining all kinds of horrible things happening inside that cottage. The silence was more frightening than screams.

"What have you done to them?"

"They've not been harmed." Briana thought she heard a note of sorrow in Eve's voice. "But I haven't much time. I need to know. Go away."

The window slid shut.

Briana scrabbled on the ground for her rock, ready to heave it at the window again to break in, but she hesitated for a moment.

"Think, think, think," she muttered aloud. "They've never wanted to hurt her. She's probably safe."

She dropped the rock and made her way to where she'd left the car. When she found it, she turned around carefully, having to creep down the lane until she drove into sunshine and warmth. She tried to tamp down her panic as she drove. When she got to the McCarthy farm, she saw Orlagh in her garden.

"Well, Briana," said Orlagh, setting down her bucket of green beans. "What brings you this way?"

"Nora asked me to come," Briana fibbed. "She's too embarrassed to tell you she locked herself out of the cottage and asked me to see if you've an extra key."

Orlagh chuckled. "Himself did that with his truck just the other day. 'Keep a spare key hidden,' says I, but does he listen? He does not."

Bri followed her into the kitchen, where several keys were hanging from a board screwed to the wall. Briana tried not to shout impatiently as Orlagh sifted through them, continuing to chatter before finally choosing one.

"Here 'tis. Just bring it back whenever you've a moment."

"I will." Briana pocketed the key. "Thank you."

At the end of their lane, she paused a minute, then turned the opposite way of Sióg Cottage.

"I need reinforcements."

Chapter 17

THERE WERE MORE. ROWAN was there. And Móirín. But there were others—Donall and the other children—just as they had been in Nora's vision. All happy, laughing together. Móirín held a baby, sleeping in her arms. Nora basked in the warmth of the family gathered round the hearth.

But some part of her didn't want to be there. Knew she shouldn't be there. She fought, and a hand settled on her brow. Whispered words in Irish tickled her ear. She sank back into the warmth, but it had shifted. There was a girl with white-blonde hair and striking green eyes, standing apart from the others, watching them with an intensity that was almost greedy, but a moment later, she was gone.

The words in Nora's ear changed. They might have been in Irish still, but she understood them now.

"Daughters. Sisters who should have been. A mother to one, but not both. An old woman who has never been mother, never been sister to that one."

Nora struggled to open her eyes, and the scene around the hearth dissolved. Eve— Aoibheann—leaned over her as she lay in her bed.

"I need you, Nora McNeill," Aoibheann murmured. "Nearly three lifetimes have I waited for you."

Nora tried to speak, to ask what was happening, but her mouth wouldn't work.

"Why?" Aoibheann asked for her. "Because I need to know. Need to know why my mother mourned my sister so deeply that she died of her grief. I need to know why she couldn't have stayed alive for me. I must know what my mother never did—what happened to the sister I never knew. I cannot die without knowing what robbed me of the family—of the life—I should have had."

Heartache, a bottomless pain and grief—it all seeped into Nora's mind along with the words, and she understood. She felt the weight of Aoibheann's despair, the depth of her longing. A sob ripped from Nora's throat, and tears streamed from her eyes into her hair and pillow.

Aoibheann took her by the hands. "Come now. We haven't much time. They are coming. This time, we cannot fail. We must know."

She guided Nora to her feet and reached for her lantern. Nora moved without the power to resist. Móirín waited for her, pale and beautiful as ever, smiling sadly. When they descended the stairs, Rowan was there—her yellow dress, the scarlet ribbon in her hair, her laughter.

Nora's gaze went to the still, shaggy form of Shannon, lying on the floor.

"She's not harmed, I promise you," Aoibheann said.

She waved her hand, and the door opened. She led Nora outside. Nora shivered, her skin cold and damp, as if she walked through fog, but ahead of her, Rowan stood in sunshine and beckoned to her.

"Follow," Aoibheann said in Nora's ear. "Follow her this last time."

BRIANA RECOGNIZED A FAMILIAR car in the nursery's lot, near the house. There was no sign of Sheila in the greenhouse or the shop, so she went on through into the kitchen.

There she found Sheila at the table with Fiona.

"Briana!"

They both looked up from the papers covering the entire table.

"Wait till you see—"

"Nora's in trouble," Bri cut in. "We need to go get her now."

Sheila pushed to her feet. "What do you mean?"

Briana swung her arm in the direction from which she'd come. "Eve has her trapped in that blasted cottage. Shannon is—" But her voice failed her. She couldn't say the words. "We have to get to them."

Sheila wrapped an arm around Briana's shoulders, guiding her to the table. "We will. I'll text Quinn now, but the information Gran found will help us to know what we're dealing with. Please, sit down."

She sent a quick text and poured a mug of tea, pushing it into Briana's trembling hands before sitting back down beside her.

Fiona reached across the table to pat Briana's arm. "Eve won't hurt Nora. She needs her, more than we realized. And I don't think she's harmed Shannon. She probably gave her a sleeping draught."

She scooted her chair around the table so they could examine the images and charts on the papers together. "Brigid and Tommy—Nora's grandparents—took a wee trip to Massachusetts to see what they could find. They sent it all to Nora, but never heard back and got worried, so they sent it to me. I forwarded it all to Sheila."

"And I found it in the deleted file in my email," Sheila said.

Briana frowned. "Nora deleted it?"

"It would seem."

"What is it?"

Fiona slid an old photo to her. "Look familiar?"

The black and white image was of a smithy. "Clinton?" Briana asked in confusion.

259

"That's the town in Massachusetts where the O'Haras went after they left Cong," Fiona said.

Briana bent over the photo again. Standing in front of the building, holding the halter of a horse was— She looked up. "Is that...? It can't be Eve."

She leaned nearer. The white hair, unusual on a young girl, was odd enough, but the eyes. Even in gray tones, they were hypnotic.

"There's more." Fiona laid out more forms with lists of names. "When we found the first batch of these, we only focused on Donall O'Hara and the five children. But on the same ship manifest, there were these names: Keith and Neve Mulcahy, traveling with their children."

Sheila shoved another paper near. "This is that 1850 U.S. census form. Remember, we wondered why Donall went from five children on the ship to only four on the census. Again, we were looking for the O'Hara family, but the Mulcahys were here, too."

She indicated a few lines above Donall O'Hara and his four children. There again were Keith and Neve Mulcahy, with a five-year-old son named Hugh, a three-year-old daughter named Aileen. And a two-year-old girl named Eve.

"So?" Briana asked impatiently. "What does any of this—"

"Wait," Sheila said. "Gran went back to St. Mary's and went deeper into the records. To Donall and Móirín's birth and baptism records. Donall had a sister. Niamh."

Fiona slid another faded document over top. "Niamh—with the Irish spelling—married Keith O'Mheolchatha."

Briana stared at her with an open mouth. "That's Eve's name. Aoibheann Ní Mheolchatha."

"Exactly." Fiona grinned triumphantly. "And we found these as well."

She splayed out photos of children standing in front of the Clinton Public School, with names penned in underneath. There, sure enough, along with Callum O'Hara and other O'Haras were Hugh, Aileen, and Eve Mulcahy.

"But—"

"What if," Sheila said, glancing at her grandmother, "Eve was so tiny when Móirín died that she still needed to be suckled. And what if Donall's sister and brother-in-law took her as their own. We think they raised her and she took their name."

Fiona leaned forward. "We're only guessing, but what if her need to know turned into an obsession, driving her to do whatever she had to to find out what happened to her mother and sister."

Briana sat back. "This is crazy, but if you're right, that cottage has had nearly two centuries of people in and out of it. Why Nora? Why now?"

"That's what we wondered," said Sheila. She nodded at Fiona. "Show her."

Fiona slid one more paper near. "This, as completely as we can reconstruct it, is the family tree of Donall and Móirín's children. Follow this line."

She pointed to Una O'Hara, who married a Bernard Fogarty. Briana followed their line down to a fifth-great-granddaughter, Mary Kate Ellis who married a Patrick Michael McNeill.

She gaped at Sheila and Fiona. "That can't be—"

They both nodded, beaming.

"Nora's parents." Fiona's eyes shimmered with angry tears. "This is why Eve needs her. She closes the loop between our family and Móirín's. Brigid and I thought, all those years ago when Eve told us one who came from us would make a fateful choice, that we only needed to think about our line. It never occurred to us that there could be someone who comes from both."

Outside, a truck engine rumbled and tires sprayed to a hard stop in the gravel. A moment later, Quinn wrenched open the kitchen door.

"What's wrong?"

THIS TIME, RATHER THAN running ahead as if playing a game, Rowan seemed to wait, beckoning Nora to follow. Though dusk was falling, Rowan was clearly visible as she skipped through the woods, into the circle of stones, and beyond—past the oak.

Nora trotted to catch up. This had always been where she lost sight of Rowan, but just beyond, a flash of yellow led her onward.

Somewhere behind her, she was aware that Aoibheann followed, but she was concentrating on Rowan.

She fought her way through a tangle of brush. When she was free, there was no sign of Rowan.

"Rowan! Where are you?"

The air was unexpectedly filled with the lilac-like fragrance of bird cherry. A faint sound of crying came as if from a great distance. Nora followed the scent, pushing deeper into the woods, slipping on mossy rocks and roots until...

"There." Nora stopped.

A large bird cherry tree stood under a grove of oaks, a few white blossoms still clinging to its branches.

Nora hurried forward, but suddenly the ground gave way and her feet slipped out from under her. Scrambling madly, she scratched and grabbed to stop herself falling into a rocky hole, but everything she touched was mossy, slimy, slippery. Roots reached like claws, clutching at her hair, scratching her face. Her shirt rode up as she slid downward, leaving her ribs exposed to scrape painfully over the rocks. Her head hit something hard enough to make her see stars. She landed feet-first in a pool of icy water up to her chest. The cold was so sharp, it took her breath. Her head throbbed, but no matter how hard she blinked to clear her vision, it was absolutely black. No light at all penetrated this place.

She called out, "Help!" but her lungs couldn't take in air. What came out was barely a whisper, swallowed by the dark.

She tried to climb back up into the rocky chute down which she'd fallen, but she couldn't gain purchase on the slimy rocks. Her feet scrabbled to push her up and out of the water. A current pushed against her, but she didn't dare allow it to shift her, or she'd never find this opening again. She stuck her arms up into the shaft, trying to keep a grip on those rocks. Dimly, she knew that she wouldn't survive long in this intense cold. She was already shivering uncontrollably.

A soft light glowed as Rowan appeared, floating beside her for a moment.

"I'm sorry. I didn't want this to happen to you."

"Is this..." Nora tried to speak through her chattering teeth. "Is this where you died?"

"Yes. And my mother never knew. You must not die here. Who will tell them?"

And then she was gone, leaving Nora alone in the darkness.

Nora tried again. "Eve! Eve, help me."

But the only sound was the endless, eternal trickling of water running deep under the earth.

THE WISPS OF FOG that remained around the cottage were torn, ripped as if a wind had come through. Briana and the others tumbled from Quinn's truck to find the front door now standing ajar.

She rushed inside where Shannon still lay on her side, panting. Bri dropped to her knees, cradling Shannon's head.

"What did she do to you?"

Sheila went straight to the kitchen and returned with a bowl of water. Briana helped Shannon onto her belly so she could drink. By the time she'd lapped up half the water, Quinn was clomping back down the stairs.

"Nothing. All the rooms are empty."

Briana was crying as much from relief that Shannon was alive as frustration that Nora and Eve had left.

"Where to now?" Sheila asked.

In answer to that question, Shannon got to her feet, wobbling un-steadily. Briana supported her for a moment, but then Shannon tugged free and went outside, her nose to the ground.

"Wait," Fiona said.

Briana stopped impatiently. They'd already wasted too much precious time.

"We need torches," Fiona said sensibly. "It's getting dark. If we find them, we won't be able to see what the devil they're doing."

Quinn dug around in his glove box while Sheila rifled through the drawers in the kitchen. Between them, they came up with three torches.

Briana hurried after Shannon, with the others in her wake. They followed the wolfhound, who was still sniffing her way along in the general direction of the stones. When they arrived there, she seemed to lose the scent.

"Nora!" Briana called. "Nora, where are you?"

Shannon picked up the scent again and ran, barking, through the circle into the woods beyond. In the deep shadows of the trees, they needed torchlight to see.

"Here!" called a voice from somewhere up ahead.

Briana sprinted in that direction. Eve was standing with her arms spread wide, her face tilted to the heavens as she mouthed a chant while the lantern at her feet cast an eerie glow.

"What did you do to her?" Briana demanded, clutching Eve by the arm.

"Easy, Bri," Quinn said. "Eve, what in the world is going on?"

"'Tis what's not of this world that we need worry about," she said cryptically. "Have a care, all of you. This area has underground caverns. Nora slid down one. Over here."

She led them to the base of a spreading tree where Shannon was sniffing, her entire head shoved into a hole in the ground.

"Bird cherry," Sheila said. "This is what Nora has been smelling, every time the ghosts appear."

Eve nodded.

In between the splayed roots of the tree were ferns and mosses. Fiona slipped on a hidden root and nearly went down. Quinn caught her and steadied her.

"Where?" Briana asked, reaching for Shannon's collar and pulling her away so she could see. She remembered only too well how holes could open unexpectedly.

"Just there," said Eve. "I couldn't reach her."

Bri saw it, when she parted the ferns, a gaping hole in a little ditch filled with trickling water. Fresh scrapes in the slime indicated where Nora lost her footing. She lay down on her belly, her face at the opening to the chute.

"Nora! Nora, can you hear me?"

They all stood silently, listening for a response. Nothing.

"Take my feet," Briana said. "Hand me a torch and let me down."

Quinn and Sheila knelt, each taking one of Briana's feet and holding on as she slithered into the rocky tunnel, calling and reaching as far as her arms could stretch. Spiders and many-legged worms slithered over her hands, brushed over her face. She forced herself to ignore them, though she shuddered at the thought of Nora being covered in them. The darkness of the shaft swallowed her torchlight, showing her nothing.

"Nora, are you down here?"

Her heart nearly stopped as she heard "Briana" echoing up from what sounded very far away, but it was so faint she wasn't certain if she'd really heard it or only wished she had.

"That's as far as we can let you go, Bri." Quinn tugged her back up to the surface. "We can't reach any further. And you're not going down as you are," he said quickly, anticipating her argument. "I've rope in the truck. I'll be right back. Don't do anything daft."

He took one of the torches and ran back in the direction from which they'd come.

Sheila kept a tight hold on Briana's arm as she shivered in her wet, slime-covered T-shirt.

Briana rounded on Eve. "Why did you do this? Why did—" Her voice broke.

Eve faced Fiona. "I told you and your sister long ago, that this day would come."

"You said one who came from us would have to make a fateful choice," Fiona said hotly. "You knew. You knew she was the one."

"I... felt something in her," Eve admitted.

"What choice did Nora have when you've been manipulating things all along?" Sheila demanded.

Eve's face was placid as she said, "She had a choice. To stay or not to stay. To open herself or to remain closed." She glanced at Briana. "To love or not to love. Every choice she has made has led to this. To her being willing to sacrifice her life for another."

But after "to love or not to love", Briana hadn't heard anything. Her ears buzzed, and her legs collapsed under her. *She loves me.*

"But," Fiona was saying, "you also told us she could give life to another. How the devil is she to do that if she dies down there?"

Bri's head snapped up at those words.

Sheila saw and immediately said, "She's not going to die."

But Eve was implacable. "There is more than one kind of life."

Briana sat, her head bowed again, as Sheila and Fiona argued with Eve. Inside, she was calm, disturbingly so, considering everything that was going on, but it was a stillness born of despair. She'd never told Nora how she felt—the only woman she'd ever loved—and what if she never got the chance to?

It seemed a lifetime before Quinn got back with the rope. He tied it securely around Briana's waist and handed her his torch.

"We'll see you and Nora in a few minutes, squint." He gathered the rope in his hands and lowered her into the hole in the ground.

THIS TIME, BRIANA WENT in feet-first. One hand clutched the torch and the rope, the other shielded her face from the roots and rocks as she slid deeper into the shaft. She tried to call out once, but got a mouthful of dirt. She kept her mouth shut after that.

In the torchlight, she could see scrape marks on the rocks and the mossy slime that covered them.

After what felt like ages, her feet touched something solid. She twisted to work her arm down in the tight space, and shone the torch beam into a white, wide-eyed face.

"Nora!"

She pushed to one side and slid into the water. "Jesus!" The shock of the cold took her breath away. The water was nearly up to her chin.

"Are you okay?"

But Nora was incapable of answering. Her lips were blue, and she was shivering so hard, her jaw seemed to be locked.

Briana aimed the torch back up the chute. It wasn't wide enough for both of them to go together as they had planned. Her heart sank. She was going to have to send Nora up first.

She put the torch in her teeth and tried to untie the swollen rope from around her waist. She hadn't planned on having to do this in ice-cold water that was trying to move her deeper into an underground tunnel. She braced her feet as best she could on rocks she couldn't see while she fumbled with the knot.

At last, she got it loosened and managed to slip the rope around Nora's waist, tying a new knot as tightly as her rapidly numbing fingers could manage.

She took the torch out of her mouth. "Quinn will haul you up," she said through her own chattering teeth.

Nora still couldn't answer, but she wrapped an arm around Bri's neck.

"No. No, you have to go up without me." Briana gripped Nora's arm, forcing it loose, and placing Nora's hand on the rope instead. "Hold on. Don't let go."

She tugged three times on the rope. When it stretched taut and began raising Nora out of the water, she gripped the belt loop of Nora's jeans, trying to help boost her up, but she began to lose her own precarious footing. She had to grip the same slippery rocks Nora had been holding on to as Nora disappeared into the black hole above.

All she could do now was wait. She put the torch back in her teeth, needing both arms to keep herself from being swept away by the current. It wasn't fast or hard, but it was steady, and her body was losing feeling. She could no longer tell if her feet were touching bottom.

The seconds dragged into minutes. She had no way of knowing how much time had passed. The torch beam dimmed. Her feet slid, and she went under. Clawing back to the surface, she gasped for air around the torch, which was still clamped in her teeth, and scrabbled for a better hold on the rocks. She wedged her numb fingertips into a crack and held on for her life.

The torch, apparently not waterproof, began to go out, flickering on only for a few seconds before going out again. She almost yelled and dropped the torch from her chattering teeth when a different light appeared—a girl in a yellow dress—floating beside her with a faint glow. Every time the torch flickered on, the girl seemed to fade. Her presence in the dark was some comfort as time crept by and it seemed no help was coming.

Above her, Briana heard a scraping sound. The rope, with a rock tied to the end, clattered down the shaft and dropped on her face, hitting her in the forehead. She didn't dare let go long enough to untie the rock, nor was she certain her fingers could tie another knot if she did. She simply grabbed the rope and slung it under her arms, looping it around her chest twice, and gave a weak tug. Rowan smiled and disappeared.

When they pulled from the surface, the rope tightened painfully. Inch by inch, they dragged her out of the water. Slowly, Briana began to ascend the chute. The torch beam still switched on and off randomly. She was about to let it go from her frozen jaw when she saw a flash of color dangling from the roots beside her. She reached out to snatch it as the rope yanked her upward.

It seemed an eternity before she emerged from the shaft into the warmth of the summer night. Quinn gripped her by both arms and lifted her clear of the hole.

"Here you are, squint," he said softly, untangling her from the rope. "We've got you now. We've got you both."

Nora sat on the ground, Fiona's arms wrapped around her as Eve knelt next to them. Nora's eyes locked with hers, though it seemed she still couldn't speak.

Eve turned to Briana. "I'm sorry. I never meant any harm to come to either of you."

Wordlessly, Briana held out her hand. When Eve extended hers, Briana dropped something into it. Sheila aimed a torch to see what it was.

Eve held up a length of scarlet ribbon.

Chapter 18

HILE BRIANA WAS EXAMINED and released, the doctor insisted on keeping Nora in the hospital for two days. "You're severely hypothermic," he said. "We need to be sure there are no after-effects."

Nora lay in her hospital bed, huddled under three blankets, still unable to get warm. She was certain there would be after-effects for the rest of her life, though she didn't voice that thought to the doctor.

Refusing to turn off the harsh light over her bed—to the disgruntlement of the other patients in her six-bed ward—she tried hard not to remember the paralyzing despair of being trapped in the pitch-black of that underground cavern.

Sheila and Fiona had driven to Castlebar to spend all the permitted visiting hours with her the first day.

"Quinn covered the opening to that hole," Sheila said. "We had an old iron grate. He fastened it in place so no one else can ever—" She stopped abruptly.

"Ever die down there," Nora finished for her.

"I had to call Brigid and Tommy," Fiona confessed. "They never would have forgiven me if I hadn't, so when you're out of here, your family in America are waiting to talk to you."

Briana had come for a few hours the first day, barely saying a word. She simply sat, stonily silent, causing Nora to feel even more guilt than she already did. She apologized again and again.

"No need," was all Bri said.

Only there was. There was so much that needed to be said, but not in the crowded ward. As if they sensed all the unspoken words hanging in the air, Sheila and Fiona chatted to fill the void. When Nora couldn't keep her eyes open that evening, thanks to the sedative the doctor ordered for her, they left her to rest.

But even the sedative couldn't stop the nightmares, and she woke, crying out and scaring all the other patients. She reassured the nurse that she was okay, but fought sleep after that.

She sat up in bed, scouring the genealogy papers Fiona had brought to her. As inconceivable as it was, the truth of her ancestry rang true inside her: she was a distant niece to Aoibheann and Rowan—it made her head hurt to try and figure out what exactly—and a seventh-great-granddaughter to Móirín and Donall. It hadn't been random that the ghosts had reached so strongly for her, or that she felt such an urgent need to help them.

She was hit by another wave of sorrow and desolation so strong she thought it might suffocate her. For Rowan to have died that way— alone, terrified, in the icy bowels of the earth. She knew that horror firsthand, and it broke her heart to think of a child being trapped as she'd been, spending her last minutes in such despair. She curled up on her side, shoving her fist against her mouth to stifle her sobs and covering her head with her blankets to muffle the sound.

When the doctor finally relented on the afternoon of the second day and released her, Nora gratefully dressed in the clean clothes Sheila and Fiona had brought.

She wanted to ask where Briana was, but she thought she knew. Briana wanted nothing more to do with her after this. Her silence had told Nora all she needed to know, but she felt too fragile to think about that now. Allowing those thoughts in on top of everything else would surely tear her heart into irreparable pieces.

Fiona insisted Nora sit in the front passenger seat of Sheila's SUV.

"How's Eve?" she asked as Sheila maneuvered out of the hospital's parking lot.

"No one has seen her since that day," Fiona said from the back seat.

Sheila's mouth was set in a thin line. "We were more concerned about getting medical care for you lot. We'll deal with her later."

When they got back to Cong, Sheila drove home to the nursery without asking where Nora wanted to stay. They had gathered a selection of clothes and all of her electronics from the cottage.

"Everything you need for now," Fiona said in a tone that brooked no argument.

She and Sheila got Nora settled comfortably on the sofa in the den with orders to rest while they prepared supper. To make sure Nora stayed put, Sheila plopped Rusty on her lap.

"You let me know if she stirs," Sheila said to him.

Rusty curled up on the blanket covering Nora's legs and gave a contented sigh as she patted him.

When supper was ready, they brought her to the table and served her a bowl of piping hot potato soup, thick and creamy, along with generous slices of brown bread.

Quinn came home halfway through the meal. He helped himself from the pot on the stove and sat at the table. "How are you feeling?"

"Warm, finally," Nora said with a wan smile. "How's Briana?"

He gave a sideways nod as he buttered a slice of bread. "You know Briana. Doesn't say much. She seems okay." But he didn't meet Nora's eye as he said it.

Nora's stomach clenched with guilt again, and it was suddenly difficult to eat. It was hard not to notice that Briana was avoiding her.

After dinner, Fiona led Nora to the computer. "I've arranged a video chat with your family."

She stayed until the connection was made, waving from behind Nora to the entire McNeill clan who were all trying to crowd into the screen, speaking at once, wanting details as to what happened.

Nora choked up. It was so good to see them all, especially after having thought she might never see them again. She left out the parts about living in a haunted cottage and chasing ghosts through the forest, and made it sound as if she'd simply slipped into a sinkhole connected to the underground cavern system. Only the glance shared between Fiona and Brigid betrayed anything more.

Fiona wrapped her arms around Nora from behind, saying, "See, everyone? She'll be fit as a fiddle in a few days. Don't tire her out too much."

Fiona gave Nora a kiss on the cheek and left them to visit.

Despite Fiona's admonition not to tire her out, Nora was exhausted by the time she clicked off the computer.

"How are they, then?" Sheila asked when Nora returned to the kitchen.

She set another mug of tea and a slice of almond bread in front of Nora as she sat.

"They're fine. Gosh, it was so good to see them." Nora's throat tightened. "I thought... when I was down there, that..."

"Shhhh." Fiona shifted closer to wrap an arm around her shoulders as she cried. "It must have been terrifying. It's all right now."

She let Nora cry while Quinn muttered something about taking Rusty out.

"Sorry," Nora hiccupped, dabbing at her eyes with her napkin.

"No need to apologize," Sheila said brusquely. "I'll wager you'll be in for more of that before you're through. I know I would be. Eat your bread and drink your tea. We've a room ready for you."

"I've been so much trouble already," Nora said, feeling guilty again.

"Nonsense." Sheila stood. "And I'll have your word that you won't be going back to the cottage alone. At least one of us goes with you. Yes?"

Nora nodded. She wasn't sure she ever wanted to see that cottage again. She brushed her teeth and changed into pajamas.

After she'd crawled under the covers, Sheila came in, tugging the quilt up over Nora and sitting on the side of the bed.

"I keep thinking," she said softly, staring at the colorful pattern of the quilt. "It breaks my heart to think what it must have been like for them, Móirín and Rowan." Her chin quivered. "Even though Annie only lived three days, there wasn't a moment, not one, that she wasn't held by someone who loved her. And I held her as she died."

Tears spilled from her eyes. "For Rowan to have died like that... I can understand how it could have killed Móirín never to know. I don't know that I could have survived that."

Nora freed one arm from under the covers and clasped Sheila's hand. They stayed like that for a few minutes before Sheila swiped the tears from her cheeks and stood. She pointed to the small lamp casting a soft glow from atop the chest of drawers. "So you won't be in the dark," she said. "Good night."

BRIANA BRUSHED GINGER UNTIL she gleamed like new copper. The filly tossed her head, fully aware of how good she looked. She pranced in the crossties.

"Settle down now," Bri murmured. "We want her parents to like you, too, and they won't do that if they think you're too much horse for their little girl."

Quinn had put word out that they had a good prospect for eventing or showjumping. Of course, Ginger was too young to do any aggressive training yet, but a family with an eager ten-year-old had inquired. Filly and girl could come along together if all worked out. They were driving up from Killarney to meet Ginger and let Sally try her out.

Briana stepped back.

"You're beautiful." She went to Ginger and pressed her forehead against the filly's. "I'll miss you, but you need to fly. And you can't do that as a stable horse."

Voices outside announced the arrival of Sally and her parents. She heard Quinn greeting them.

"All set?" she asked.

Ginger snorted in answer. As if she knew how important this was, she followed Briana docilely, arching her neck and prancing only a little.

Briana noticed with a shock that they'd brought a horse trailer with them.

Sally clapped her hands, and her freckled face split into a wide smile. "Look, Mum! She's ginger, just like me!"

Sally might have looked bookish and awkward, with her glasses and braces on her teeth, but she knew how to approach Ginger, giving the filly a chance to sniff her.

"We gingers need to stick together." Briana grinned. "Want to help me tack her up?"

Together, they saddled her. Sally had no trouble getting Ginger to take the bit. Briana took her around first, showing off her paces with Sally hanging onto the fence alongside her parents.

When Sally mounted—Bri noticed with some chagrin that the stirrups didn't have to be shortened for her—she kept a light hand on the reins as she took the filly around the ring.

"She's a natural," she said to Sally's mum, who stood with her hands clasped in worry.

"That's what her instructor back home says."

The dad stood with his hands in his pockets. "And you didn't drug the horse? You know, to calm her down."

Briana bristled, but Quinn laid a hand on her shoulder. "Mr. Waldren," he said, "I know horse traders have a bad reputation, but we don't run that kind of business here. I've a copy of the report from the vet you sent here to check her. If you're the least bit worried, then we'll just keep Ginger and bring her along ourselves."

The poor man's shoulders slumped. "I'm sorry. I was told to ask that. But you look like decent people, the both of you."

An hour later, the Waldrens drove off with Ginger loaded in the trailer and Sally hanging out the car window waving at Briana.

Briana's throat burned with the effort to choke back her tears. She'd brought that filly along from the time she was foaled. It had to be done, but it never got any easier.

"Thanks, squint," Quinn said, giving her a squeeze. "I know you'll miss her, but she and young Sally will make a good pair."

Briana nodded and stalked away to her cottage. Quinn let her go. She reached into the fridge for a Coke and slammed the door. She was standing with a hand pressed to her eyes when someone knocked on the door.

"Go away," she said, swiping her arm across her face.

"Okay."

"Nora!" Briana whipped around. "I thought you were Quinn."

Nora hesitantly stepped inside. Even with deep, bruised-looking circles under her eyes, she was beautiful. Briana guessed she hadn't been sleeping well. *I know the feeling.*

When Briana only stared at her and didn't say anything else, Nora folded her arms tightly across her chest.

"Is it okay I'm here?"

"Yes. I... we just sold Ginger." Briana held out the bottle. "Coke?"

"Sure."

277

Briana handed her that bottle and got another from the refrigerator. "How are you? Are you all right?"

"I'm fine." Nora fiddled with the top, twisting it in her fingers. "How about you? You're limping more."

"I'm fine. My leg just aches a bit."

They sat, an awkward silence stretching out like a thorny hedge between them. Shannon pawed at the back door. Briana got up to let her in, and she went straight to Nora, sitting and gazing into her face.

"I would have come to the hospital to fetch you, but..." Briana said, but the rest of her thought trailed into nothingness.

"No. It was fine. Sheila and Fiona have been great." Nora nodded, scratching Shannon's ear.

They both took long drinks of their Cokes.

"Quinn said you're staying with them."

"Yeah." Nora glanced at her. "Have you been back? To the cottage?"

Briana shook her head.

"Me, either. Sheila made me promise I wouldn't go alone."

Briana looked at her warily. "Is that why you're here?"

"What? No. I mean, not entirely. I wanted to see you. To talk to you. But clearly you don't." Nora set her Coke down and stood. "I'm sorry I bothered you."

"You're not bothering me!" Briana stood, too, walking across the kitchen, wishing there was something to punch. "I've wanted to talk to you, but there's always someone about."

"I'm sorry."

"Would you stop apologizing!"

"If you want me to stop apologizing, then stop yelling at me!"

"I'm not yelling *at* you! I'm just—" Briana turned away, her fingers pressed to her eyes again. She fecking hated to cry.

"Christ." Her shoulders hunched defensively. "I love you. And I almost lost you without ever telling you that."

It seemed the air was suddenly sucked out of the kitchen, and she found it hard to breathe. Had she really said those words aloud?

Gentle hands made her turn, pried her fingers loose. Briana blinked up into Nora's eyes. Her own felt as bruised and swollen as Nora's looked.

"What did you say?" Nora asked.

Briana's eyes darted, looking for an escape, but Nora smiled and cradled her face in her hands—her warm, soft hands.

With a heavy sigh, Briana gave up. "I said I love you. And I almost lost you."

Nora crushed her mouth to Bri's, holding her tightly. She pulled away long enough to whisper, "I love you, too," and then kissed her again.

NORA STARTLED AWAKE, BUT it took her a moment to figure out where she was. Briana's couch, her head cradled on Bri's lap, as they had both apparently fallen asleep. Shannon sat up from where she'd been keeping watch and licked Nora's cheek.

She peered at the clock. These few hours had been the best sleep she'd had since that day. She gazed up into Briana's face, her head lolled to one side. Nora suspected Briana hadn't slept any better lately.

She sat up, and Briana stirred, rubbing her eyes.

"Didn't intend to fall asleep," Briana mumbled.

"I think we both needed it."

Bri noticed the way Nora was watching her. "What?"

"Nothing," Nora said. "I just love you is all."

Briana flushed. "You say that, so natural."

Nora shook her head. "I don't. It should be natural, but it's been ages since I've said it to anyone. I never thought I would again."

"I've never said it to anyone but Mum. And then hardly to her." Briana looked at her. "I love you, Nora."

It made Nora ridiculously happy to hear it. Her stomach rumbled. "I'm starving."

"Me, too, come to think of it." Briana shoved to her feet and held out her hand. "Let's go out."

"Where?"

"The Cottage at Ashford. You're still on holiday. It should feel like a holiday."

"I ought to change, but Sheila only packed a few things, and these are best I have with me."

Briana looked at her in a way that made her blush. "You look great. Let me get out of my stable clothes, and we'll go."

She paused in the doorway to the bedroom and turned. "Do you want to stay here tonight?"

Nora hesitated. Part of her wanted to be with Bri more than anything, but night was still the hardest time. The things they'd shared today had already left her feeling raw and wrung out. "I'd like to, but..."

She stole a glance at Briana, afraid of what she might see, but Bri's gaze reassured her that she wasn't angry or hurt.

"It's okay. Call Sheila and let her know I'll bring you back tonight."

As they were on the early side for dinner, the parking lot had only a few cars. Liam's sister, Mary, greeted them with a big smile. She sat them at a table near a window so they'd have a view of the castle and the lough.

They ordered wine and sat quietly, enjoying the vista.

When their fish and chips arrived, Mary asked, "How are things at the haunted cottage?"

Nora felt the color drain from her face, but Briana quickly said, "Oh, the ghost is having a ball, rearranging the furniture."

Mary looked perplexed at Nora's reaction but left them to eat.

Nora poked her fork into her fish.

"Better to make light of it, don't you think?" Briana asked.

Nora nodded and forced a smile. "You're right. No one would believe the truth if we told them."

They finished their dinner, and passed on dessert. The late summer evening lingered.

"Let's go for a walk," Nora suggested.

They crossed the bridge and wandered the garden paths, meandering toward the shore. Without speaking, they followed the undulating trail. A gentle breeze blew off the water, promising rain before morning. Soft waves lapped at the rocks.

When they got some distance from the castle and found themselves alone, Nora reached for Bri's hand. They stood, side by side, gazing back at the castle.

"I need to go back," Nora said softly.

Briana nodded. "Get back on the horse."

One corner of Nora's mouth curled. "Something like that. There is something to be said for facing the thing you're afraid of. But first..."

She looked at Briana. "I need to see Eve."

Briana nodded again. "We'll see if Quinn and Sheila will go with us. Tomorrow."

AS THEY'D DONE THE first time, Sheila parked her SUV, and they walked the rest of the way. This time, they brought no baskets of gifts, and both Quinn and Sheila had sheathed knives on their belts. In addition, Briana had a backpack stuffed with a first-aid kit, a blanket, a couple of torches, some rope, and a bottle of whiskey.

"If we don't need any of the rest," she said with a shrug as she let Shannon out of the cargo hold, "we'll just drink the whiskey."

"I'm for that," Fiona said.

She'd called Jack to tell him she'd be one more day, declaring, "We're this close to answers, I'm not leaving yet!"

The undergrowth was heavier now than it had been earlier in the summer. Thick vines blocked their path, and a few times, Sheila had to hack a way through with her knife, which was more a type of machete she used at the nursery.

The overnight rain had left everything sodden, but Nora was grateful it had stopped before dawn. Their legs and boots were still wet, but at least they didn't have to make this trek through a downpour.

When at last they approached the clearing where Eve's dwelling was, they all stopped to survey the scene from the cover of the woods. Nora wasn't certain what they expected—some kind of booby trap? But there was nothing. In fact, the entire place seemed to be deserted.

The cottage looked more than ever as if it was built into the hill. There was more moss, more vines covering it as if the earth was slowly consuming it. The plants and flowers that Eve had grown so carefully looked untended. No smoke rose from the chimney, which also had vines growing thickly up the stones.

Nevertheless, they approached cautiously. Shannon led the way, sniffing the air, but not behaving as if she sensed anything amiss. Nora noted that Quinn had his knife in his hand.

"Eve?" Sheila called out. "We need to talk to you."

There was no response.

Nora decided to try, kin to kin. "Aoibheann Ní Heaghra."

Briana looked at her.

Nora shrugged. "She's a Heaghra, not a Mheolchatha."

There was still no movement, no sign of any life. Quinn went to the oak door, which had patches of black mold growing on it. He had to cut away some ivy that had crept up and wrapped itself around the iron latch. He shoved. It wouldn't budge. He put his shoulder to the oak planks and tried again.

"It won't open."

Sheila made her way through the overgrown plants to one of the windows, rubbing the glass clean and trying to peer inside. "Maybe something's happened to her. She might be hurt. We should have come sooner."

But Fiona only said, "Nora, you try."

Nora wasn't certain how she'd be able to open the door if it hadn't given way under Quinn's weight, but she approached. When she placed her hand on the latch, it clicked, and the door swung open soundlessly.

"I'll be damned," Quinn said.

Shannon trotted inside and the humans followed.

"This is impossible," Sheila said.

Dust covered every surface. Hanks of dried herbs and flowers still hung from the beams, but they were encased in cobwebs. Motes of dust stirred as their entrance disturbed the air.

"It looks like no one's been here in years," Briana said. "Decades."

Quinn squatted in front of the hearth, poking at the ashes. "Cold."

Fiona went to a stack of Eve's books, equally dusty as she leafed through them. "Where'd she go?"

"Was she ever really here?" Sheila asked. "I'm beginning to wonder if we dreamed her up."

"We didn't." Nora was standing at the table, where Eve's lantern sat, dust-free, the candle inside snuffed out.

Next to it, a cloth-wrapped object lay, as free of dust as the lantern. Gently, she laid back the folds of cloth. The others gathered round.

Lying there was a branch of bird cherry, its white blossoms still fragrant when Nora picked it up.

"What's that?" Briana asked. "Under the branch."

"A photo," Sheila said.

"No," Fiona corrected her. "It's not a photo. It's older. It's a Daguerrotype. My grandparents had some of these."

They all leaned over to look more closely at the image of a tall, handsome man, his arm around a beautiful black-haired woman who was holding a baby, surrounded by five other children.

"It's Móirín and Donall, and their family," Nora said. "I recognize them."

Fiona tapped the glass. "Look at the christening dress. Was this the day Eve was baptized?" She pointed to a date in the lower corner. "2nd April, 1848."

Nora nodded, but she wasn't looking at the baby. "It was also the day Rowan disappeared."

"How do you know?" Bri asked.

"I just know." Nora indicated Rowan's image. "She's wearing the dress I saw her in."

Sheila pressed her hands to her chest. "If that's true, to have such joy and such tragedy all on the same day."

Quinn pointed to another object lying beside the framed Daguerrotype. "What's that?"

Nora held up the length of scarlet ribbon. "She's gone. Eve found the answers she needed. She won't be back." She looked around, certain of her conviction.

Fiona tipped the lantern. "I never saw her far from this. Somehow, this was part of it. Part of the magic that allowed her to live so long."

She wrapped an arm around Nora's waist. "She left these for you."

"I don't understand," Nora said.

"Understand what?" Fiona asked.

"The prophecy or whatever you want to call it. That Eve made to you and my grandmother all those years ago. It doesn't make sense."

"Oh, I think it does. You chose to help them and almost lost your life in the process."

"But wasn't there a part about giving life to another?"

Fiona nodded at the framed image. "Think about it. Three souls, unable to move on. You helped them find peace. It's kind of a way of giving them eternal life now, isn't it?"

Nora thought about the cottage, about how consumed she'd been for months, living with Móirín and Rowan—not just in her physical space, but in her head—and wondered if they would move on. "I'm not so sure."

"I think the unknown was more heartbreaking to them than anything," Fiona said thoughtfully. "People were dying all around them, but Rowan couldn't tell her parents what happened to her. Móirín and Donall never knew what happened to their little girl. And Eve never knew why her family had been so cruelly torn apart."

"And you really think Eve was Aoibheann?" Quinn asked dubiously.

Fiona sighed. "There are things we'll never fully understand."

Sheila asked Quinn to gather up the books while she opened some of the jars sitting on the shelves, checking to see what they contained and packing a few of them.

Nora opened the glass door of the lantern and extracted the candle inside, wiggling it loose from the mounds of wax holding it in place.

"There's one more thing we need to do. Today." She looked at Fiona. "While you're still here with us."

"YOU SURE WE SHOULD be doing this ourselves?" Quinn asked. He cast a nervous glance over his shoulder. "Shouldn't we get the priest?"

They all stood in the cemetery at St. Mary's, gathered round Móirín's grave. It had taken some time to locate it, as it was one of the headstones whose limestone was so pitted as to make it almost impossible to read.

"Since when are you all worried about rules and protocol?" Sheila asked. "And what, exactly, are we going to say? 'We were guided by a pair of ghosts and an almost two-hundred-year-old witch.'"

Fiona chuckled. "She has a point."

Sheila handed Nora her large knife. "You should be the one to do it."

Nora knelt down while the others stood in a semi-circle around her, blocking her from view of the church and rectory. Using the knife, she gouged out a patch of turf from the grass over Móirín's grave and set it aside. Then she dug more deeply, scooping out several handfuls of dirt.

She shook out the cloth Eve had left in her cottage. The Daguerrotype Nora was going to keep, but...

"Móirín, if you can hear us, this is the ribbon that was in Rowan's hair, and this is the candle that kept Aoibheann grounded in this realm long enough to find out what happened."

She wrapped the ribbon and candle up in the cloth, folding it and placing it in the hole she'd dug. "This is the closest we can come to burying them with you. Our prayer for all of you is that you will now be at peace, able to move on. Together in death as you were never able to be in life."

She scooped dirt back into the hole, covering the cloth. Gently pressing the patch of turf back in place, she got to her feet.

Briana took her hand but had to clear her throat a couple of times before she could speak. "That was good."

Chapter 19

RIANA MADE IT A point to get to the stables extra early every day, working non-stop until mid-afternoon so that she and Nora could spend the latter part of each day together, usually taking a ride. Without saying it out loud, she wanted Nora's last days in Cong to be as memorable as possible.

For her part, Nora worked with Sheila at the nursery every day. From listening to her talk about her day as they meandered the fields and woods around the stables, it seemed she took comfort in the work—whether it was among the trees, in the greenhouse, or in the shop where they brewed salves and lotions and made candles.

Nora spent her nights at Bri's place or with Sheila and Quinn. The first time Nora stayed with Briana—the day they'd buried the candle and ribbon—had been hard as they both tried to navigate this new vulnerability. Just holding each other had been as much intimacy as either of them could handle.

What Briana didn't share with Quinn or Sheila was how many times each night Nora sprang up in bed, panting and breathless, when she woke from her nightmares. Bri had them, too, but not as bad or as frequent as Nora's. She was secretly glad to not have to explain why she left the bathroom light on. She knew the two of them might never welcome complete darkness again—not after knowing the terror they'd been through. Even the shared memory of Rowan's presence in that cavern couldn't erase the horror of being trapped down there, of thinking they would both share Rowan's fate.

But, when she drew Nora back down to lie in her arms, when they held each other, there was unspoken comfort in knowing that they understood what no one else could.

All she said to Quinn was, "I want her last memories of Ireland to be happy ones."

He looked as if he was busting to say something on the matter, but he just nodded and kept his mouth shut.

Nora hadn't voiced any desire to go back to Sióg Cottage, and Briana hadn't pushed. She and Sheila had decided they'd wait for Nora to indicate when she was ready.

Inexorably, the days ticked by, and they hadn't talked about what was going to happen after Nora's ninety days were up. Whenever Briana started thinking about the fact that she only had a few days left with Nora, her anxiety transferred to the horses, especially Lizzy, and she had to push it down, focus only on what she was doing—which was a useful exercise for hiding her nerves when she was with Nora. She wanted to sear every moment into her memory, not waste it on worry, because she knew she would never feel like this about anyone ever again.

But her favorite times were when they sat on the front stoop of her cottage as dusk fell. When the work was done for the day and everything was quiet, and the horses were settled for the night in their stalls, and all the feeding and mucking and grooming was done. This was the time she loved best—Nora sitting with her arm hooked through Bri's, no words, just being together.

Briana was beginning to wonder if Nora would ever go back to Sióg Cottage. Surely, she'd have to pack up, but the thought of Nora packing hurt too much to think about, so she tried not to.

On the Friday of Nora's last full weekend, she bicycled over to the stables after she and Sheila were done for the day. She found Briana just finishing rubbing down and wrapping Princess's leg.

"Second sprain of the summer," Briana pronounced. "I'm thinking this will be her last regular season carrying tourists."

Princess snorted as if she understood and agreed with that plan.

Nora gave the mare a pat. "Will Quinn sell her?"

"No!" Bri's voice was firm. "No, she'll spend her days here. We can ride her now and again. Maybe another foal or two. She's such a good mum."

Briana stood, and Princess nudged her shoulder. Briana grinned and produced an apple from her pocket. She sliced it and offered half. The mare chomped it happily. Briana exited the stall, latching the door. When Princess looked at her with those dark, gentle eyes, Briana relented and gave her the other half.

Nora chuckled. "She has your number."

"She does. And she knows it."

Nora stepped closer and leaned in for a long, slow kiss. "You have my number, too."

A loud clearing of the throat made them both jump. Liam was standing there, holding a grain bucket, a lopsided grin on his face.

"Go away, you git," Briana said.

The sound of his laughter lingered as he walked away.

"I was wondering..." Nora began.

"Wondering what?"

"If you'd like to maybe do a bit of rambling this weekend. We don't have to go as far as Kerry or anything like that," she hastened to add.

Briana braced herself. "I can't. I'm sorry. I promised Quinn I'd do some things here this weekend."

"Oh. Okay. No problem." Nora turned away, pretending to find something interesting on the chalkboard next to the telephone.

Briana washed up at the tack room sink. "Would you like to go out to dinner tonight?"

Nora nodded, but her smile looked forced. "How about the pub and then maybe wander around the village?"

A short time later, they were in the SUV. Bri had placed a call to the pub, asking the bartender to reserve a table for them. When they arrived in the village, the tour buses were gone, but she still had to drive around before she found an empty parking space.

Briana had to laugh when Nora grumbled, "Bloody tourists."

"I think I'm rubbing off on you, and not in a good way."

Nora reached for her hand. "You've been good for me in every way."

Briana glanced over at the wistful tone in Nora's voice.

Inside, they ordered drinks at the bar, collecting their glasses of Guinness and going to the table the bartender pointed out.

"Thanks, Andrew."

They settled in a dark corner and took a drink. Nora sighed and looked around.

"What was that sigh for?" Briana asked.

Nora smiled into her beer. "I was just remembering meeting you here."

"It wasn't our first meeting," Briana reminded her. "I almost ran you down that morning."

Nora chuckled. "True. Our first official meeting, then. I complained about you to Sheila after falling into the bushes that morning. She knew immediately who I was talking about."

Briana scowled.

"That face doesn't frighten me anymore," Nora said with a grin.

"Damn."

Nora leaned forward. "If that hadn't happened, if I hadn't almost been trampled by you and your horse... My summer wouldn't have been the same." Her expression sobered. "My life wouldn't be the same."

After dinner and a second pint, they wandered the village. Nora insisted on asking a stranger to take a photo with her cell phone of the two of them standing in front of the Celtic cross in the village center and another down by the river.

"The fight scene was here?" Briana asked.

"I think so."

Bri shook her head. "I'm so glad that movie and your grandparents' childhood brought you here, Nora McNeill."

Nora took her hand. "So am I, Briana Devlin."

SATURDAY MORNING FOUND NORA pedaling from the stables to the nursery, muttering aloud and trying to tamp down her resentment.

"There's no law that says Briana has to spend every minute with me," she reminded herself. "Even if this is my last weekend here."

A weight like a stone plummeted into her stomach. Her last weekend. As traumatic as this summer had been in many ways, it had also been the best summer of her life. The best three months of her life, period.

But still, for Briana to have made plans to work this weekend, it felt like a slap in the face. When she passed a trail that would have taken her in the direction of her cottage, she briefly considered going, but she'd given Sheila her word she wouldn't go alone.

They hadn't bugged her about returning, and she knew their silence on the subject had been out of deference to her and everything she'd been through. But the rest of her stuff was there. She would have to go back soon. She needed to go back. But not today.

She sniffed at the aromas drifting from Sheila's kitchen before she even opened the door. Inside, Sheila had the table laden with two cakes, three loaves of her almond bread, and she was bent over at the oven, sliding a roasting pan with an herb-covered chicken into it.

"What's the occasion?"

Sheila looked up. "You're earlier than I expected. Well, it was going to be a surprise, but we're having a *céili*."

"A party? What for?" Nora tried to think if it was someone's birthday.

Sheila shook her head. "For you, you idjit."

Nora's heart lifted. "For me?"

Sheila smiled. "All the cousins you've not had a chance to meet are coming in for the day. Gran and Granddad are coming back. They'll be here before noon."

She set the timer on the oven. "Help me set up some tables outside. I think we're going to luck out with the weather today."

The outside tables consisted of sawhorses with boards laid over top.

"So you really didn't know?" Sheila asked. "Bri didn't slip and say anything?"

Nora must have looked like an idjit because Sheila burst out laughing. "I take it she didn't."

"She's in on it? And she kept it from me? That's why she said she was busy today." Slowly, the pieces clunked into place. Nora felt they were all clunking her in the head.

Quinn drove up with more boards loaded in the bed of his truck to set on blocks for makeshift benches. He also had three cases of Guinness that he heaved into a wheelbarrow.

The first cars began to pull in by the time they'd finished. Sheila's parents, Dan and Laura Muldoon, were the first to arrive, driving down from Donegal. They greeted Nora warmly.

"We so miss having Brigid and Tommy closer," Dan said. "Wish they'd come home for a visit."

It seemed every few minutes another car or truck rolled in, spilling out people who happily greeted one another. It turned into a kind of family reunion. Nora's head was soon swimming, trying to remember all the names and connections. Everyone brought a dish to share or more wine or beer or soda, and the tables were soon groaning under the weight of all the food.

When Briana's SUV joined the herd of vehicles in the nursery parking lot, Kieran jumped out ahead of Cara and Victoria. He ran to Nora, throwing his arms around her waist.

"Hi!" she said to Cara, giving her a kiss on the cheek.

Briana grinned guiltily when Nora turned to her.

"So you can keep a secret," Nora said.

"When I have to. Sheila threatened my life if I told you."

"Good incentive." Nora took advantage of the crowd to offer Briana one hand and Kieran the other and led them to meet everyone.

Food wasn't the only thing people brought. Guitars, fiddles, pipes, little squeezeboxes, bodhráns—all manner of instruments began to tune up together.

Fiona and Jack showed up with an instrument case and a basket of her scones.

"You can't have a proper *céili* without music," Jack said, giving Nora a hug before tuning up his own fiddle.

Soon, an impromptu band was playing a traditional Irish jig, and kids were dancing while some of the adults jumped up, clicking their heels in such a fast staccato, they were a blur to Nora. One of Sheila's brothers—Brendan, Nora thought his name was—grabbed her, whirling her into a dance, spinning her around so fast she got dizzy. Laughing, she tried to copy his footwork. Glancing to one side, she saw Sheila and Quinn dancing. On her other side, Cara and Victoria both had Kieran by the hands, twirling in a little threesome.

The music shifted, and the musicians began a sorrowful, haunting air. Giddy with the joy of the surprise *céili* and the opportunity to meet all of this extended family, Nora took Briana by the hand for a slower dance. Briana's cheeks burned a brilliant crimson, but she reluctantly glided into the lilting rhythm.

The afternoon wore into evening. Musicians rotated through the impromptu band, and the eating continued pretty much non-stop.

Fiona had the idea of contacting Brigid and Tommy for a video chat, and it seemed the entire clan crowded into the den to talk with them. With everyone talking at once, Nora figured no one actually heard a thing, but it was so nice to have the reunion extend to her grandparents.

Late in the day, Quinn got a bonfire lit. The kids had fun poking sticks in to feed the flames. As darkness fell, everyone gathered round the fire, singing along to the music.

"Happy?" Briana asked, leaning in close to Nora's ear.

Nora nodded, her heart too full for words.

"So I'm forgiven?"

Nora gave her a bump with her shoulder. "Maybe."

AN INSISTENT BEAM OF moonlight wriggled through a gap in the curtains, tickling Nora's eyelids until she woke. It was the first time in a week she'd woken peacefully without a nightmare. Beside her, Briana breathed slowly.

Nora turned to watch her for a moment. Their lovemaking last night had been wonderful. Thinking back, it was the first time since she got out of the hospital that it had been like that, unrushed and gentle and passionate in turns, rather than desperate and frantic.

She pressed the heels of her hands to her eyes to rub the sleep away and then quietly got out of bed without disturbing Briana. She reached for her underwear and a T-shirt. Shannon lifted her head as Nora walked by. She scrambled to her feet and followed Nora outside to sit on the stoop. Shannon leaned against her, and Nora draped an arm over her warm body.

Her body and mind—and her heart—were still humming with happiness from the unexpected gathering over the weekend. With Cara, Kieran, and Victoria in Cong and staying with Briana, Nora had spent Saturday night at Sheila's, which was nice, as it had given her more time to visit with Fiona and Jack.

Fiona had asked to see what Nora had found in Eve's books.

"Most of them are just classics," Nora said. "*Jane Eyre, The Secret Garden, Great Expectations, Anne of Green Gables.* All stories about orphans. Except for two. One was her book of recipes for salves and healing potions. And this one."

She opened the oldest book, the one Eve had read from the first time Nora had gone to see her.

"It was Móirín's. I'd hoped it was a diary, but it's more a ledger." She leafed through it, showing Fiona. "See? She has a page of important dates: her marriage, the birth of each child. But she also recorded each seamstress job she had, what she made and how much she got paid. Repairs she and Donall did to the cottage. But then..."

She flipped to the last page with any writing and read, "30 April, nothing. I fear my *chailín* is gone forever."

Fiona blinked rapidly with her hand over her mouth. "That was her last entry." She took Nora's hand in hers. "I'm so glad you brought peace to them."

Nora still wasn't certain she had, but she didn't say anything.

Come Sunday night, when Fiona and Jack and everyone else had gone back home and life in Cong settled back into its normal, slow rhythm, here with Briana was where she'd wanted to be.

It was funny, she mused as she rubbed Shannon's wiry fur, it wasn't until she had the contrast of this weekend that she realized how a part of her had remained trapped in that underground cavern, caught up in the misery and desolation of the ghosts of the past. It had felt for a while as if she'd never be happy again. She'd been holding to Briana like a life preserver, using her to keep her head above all the things that threatened to pull her under, into a place every bit as dark as that cavern had been.

But now... She looked up at the stars and took a deep breath. Part of her inability to decide about moving to Ireland had been questioning and wondering how much of that desire was tied to her relationship with Briana. But after the weekend, she knew.

She loved Briana—more deeply, more completely than she'd ever loved Amy. But if Briana didn't feel the same, if she walked out of Nora's life tomorrow, Ireland and Cong were still where her heart belonged. She knew that now.

Thinking back to how many times in her life she'd felt out of place, and how, listening to Mamma and Pop's stories of growing up here, she'd always had that unsettled feeling, kind of like she already knew this place, knew it from long ago. It all made sense now. Her roots were truly here, on both sides of her family.

She was ready. Ready to go back to Sióg Cottage. Ready to talk to Briana. Ready to tell her family her decision. Ready to live her life.

Giving Shannon a squeeze, she said, "Let's go back to bed."

BRIANA WOKE TO AN empty bed and the enticing aromas of coffee and bacon. She smiled and stretched. *I could get used to this.*

The smile faded. There was no time to get used to anything. She and Nora only had a few more days together. Unless Bri decided to follow her back to America.

"You should go," Cara had urged her over the weekend. "Get out of Ireland. Live a little."

The two of them had been huddled together in the kitchen when they got back here after the *céili.*

"What are you talking about in there?" Victoria, ever able to sniff out trouble, had asked.

"Nothing," Briana and Cara had said in unison, giggling like they used to when they were little.

It was odd. She and her sister hadn't been close for a long time, not since Briana had left home to try and break into racing and felt Cara had judged her choice then as foolish. It wasn't until Bri was on the cusp of leaving Ireland altogether that they'd come to understand each other. When Kieran climbed into her lap and snuggled against her, she'd nearly come undone. The thought of not being around as he grew up was almost more than she could bear.

The prospect of leaving everything she loved—the horses, the stables, Sheila and Quinn, Liam and Jimmie and Sonya, Ashford and the woods and trails she'd come to know as home—it all tore her apart. But if being with Nora meant going to America, then that was how it needed to be.

Impatiently, she brushed aside a tear that leaked out of her eye. She climbed out of bed and went into the bathroom.

When she got to the kitchen a few minutes later, Nora had a cup of coffee waiting for her.

"Good morning," Nora said with a kiss.

"Morning. This smells so good."

Nora plated eggs and bacon and toast for the two of them. She had also scrambled an extra egg for Shannon.

"She's going to be spoiled," Briana said, watching Shannon gobble the egg and lick her bowl. She prodded her eggs, wondering how to bring up everything. How the hell did you say to someone, "Guess what? I've decided to move to America with you"? What if Nora didn't want her there? She had a whole life to go back to. No matter how much she thought her family hadn't really missed her, Briana suspected they had. More than Nora knew.

"Everything taste okay?" Nora asked.

"Yeah. It's brilliant. Thanks for cooking."

Nora eyed Briana surreptitiously from under her lashes. "I was thinking... I need to go back to my cottage soon. I promised Sheila I wouldn't go alone. If you can get off work a little early today or tomorrow..."

"Yeah." Briana paused with her fork halfway to her mouth. "Today. I'll come and pick you up at the nursery, say four o'clock?"

"Sounds good."

NORA DID A LAST update of the nursery website. She'd be able to work on it remotely once she was back in the States—one of the wonderful things about the internet. But it wouldn't be the same as being here.

A ping on the computer distracted her. The little chat bubble said it was her sister. She clicked on it.

Mary Fran's face filled the screen, looking so much like a younger version of their mother that it startled Nora for a minute.

"Can't believe I caught you online." Mary Fran said. "How's the great adventure been?"

"It's been good."

"Just good?" Mary Fran frowned. "Are you hurt from your accident?"

Nora realized it had become habit to be cautious and non-committal with her responses to her sister. She took a deep breath. "It's been wonderful."

Mary Fran shook her head. "God, I admire you so much."

Nora goggled at her, certain there had been some glitch in their connection. "Sorry?"

"I said I admire you."

"For what?" Nora was still sure there had been a disconnect somewhere.

"For doing this," Mary Fran said. "For getting away. For living your life the way you want. I've always admired you."

"No, you haven't." Nora's disbelief was reflected in the small image of herself in the upper corner of the screen. She closed her mouth. "You were the most popular girl in school. You were friends with everyone. I had, what? Two friends? You're an artist. You've got two beautiful kids and a great husband. You've accomplished all kinds of things. I've accomplished nothing."

Mary Fran leaned forward, her image enlarged so that Nora instinctively drew back.

"Are you kidding? You are the bravest person I know."

At Nora's dubious expression, Mary Fran burst out laughing. "You climbed to the top of the Kennedy's tree next door."

"Only because you dared me. And I broke my arm when I fell climbing down."

A shadow darkened Mary Fran's expression. "But I never left the ground."

Nora didn't know what to say. "I'm just a librarian."

Mary Fran smiled. "My kids think librarians are superheroes. And you especially, because you're a librarian at a university." When Nora didn't respond, she added, "You have always known what you wanted to do, no matter what anyone else said. I always worried about what other people thought. You went to grad school, got your master's, built the career you wanted. And look at you now. You're in Ireland, doing what you've always dreamed of doing. I think it's great."

She sat back. "You really don't see it, do you? I'm sorry I never said this before."

"Thank you for saying it now."

A few minutes later, when Nora walked out to the pergola, Sheila did a double take at Nora's dazed expression.

"Everything all right?"

Numbly, Nora nodded. "You know those movies or books where someone misses a train and some alternate reality plays out, where their life goes in a whole different direction? I think I'm experiencing one of those moments."

At Sheila's confused expression, Nora said, "Just had a weird talk with my older sister. Turns out she admires me."

Sheila shook her head. "Told you so."

Nora set about helping Sheila repot and label a new delivery of plants as part of a colorful autumn display.

"Still a bit distracted, are we?"

"Hmmm?" Nora blinked up at Sheila, who pointed at the pots in front her.

"You're putting the wrong labels on those. The pink ones are alstroemeria, the white ones are anemones."

"Sorry." Nora plucked the small tags out of the plants and reversed them.

"Thinking about your sister?"

Feeling Sheila's probing gaze, Nora gave up. She'd learned better than to pretend around her cousin.

"I'm going to the cottage this afternoon," she said casually. "With Bri."

Sheila nodded. "That's good. It's probably time."

"Yeah. I mean, I have to pack up, don't I?" Nora heard the tremor in her own voice. "And I'm going to tell her I'm moving to Ireland."

"You're—" Sheila dropped her trowel and pulled Nora into a hard hug. "Are you really?"

Nora held her and released the breath she'd been holding. "You're okay with it?"

Sheila released her from the hug but held her at arm's length. "Why wouldn't I be? I think it's brilliant. And does it matter, if you've truly made up your mind?"

Nora grinned like a fool. "No, it doesn't matter, and it won't change my mind. I'd just feel better if I knew you're okay."

"Of course I am!" Sheila hooked her arm through Nora's. "You know this calls for tea and biscuits."

Nora laughed. "I was hoping for tea and biscuits."

They marched to the kitchen, where Nora put the kettle on and Sheila laid out a plate of her ginger biscuits.

"You make the tea," Sheila commanded when a car drove up. "I'll be back in a minute."

Rusty sat in between the stove and the table, making sure Nora saw him as she set about getting mugs and tea bags.

"All right, one cookie," she said sternly, breaking one cookie and giving him part while she popped the rest into her mouth.

It seemed half of her good memories of Ireland were connected to this kitchen and the talks—the *craic*—that had been shared here. Sheila was back soon, dropping into a chair, her elbows on the table, her blue eyes focused on Nora.

"So, tell me."

"It was the *céili*," Nora said. "And what I now know about my ancestry, and... everything. I just know this is where I belong."

"No doubts?" Sheila reached for a biscuit.

Nora shook her head. "No doubts."

"And you're going to tell Briana today? Because I'm not sure how long I can keep this quiet."

"This afternoon." Nora couldn't help a small frown.

"What?"

"One of the things I had to figure out, was would I still want to move here if Briana doesn't feel the same way about me. If she doesn't want to be together, in that way."

"And?"

Nora smiled as Sheila handed Rusty another cookie. "I would. With or without Bri in my life."

Sheila grinned broadly. "But you'd rather have her in it."

Nora nodded, grinning back.

"Then I guess you figured out that puzzle."

"Most of it." Nora sighed. "I'm hoping to have the rest of my life to learn where the rest of the pieces fit."

SUNLIGHT GLINTED OFF THE windows when Briana drove down the lane and Nora got her first glimpse of her cottage since that day. She reached for Bri's hand.

"You okay?" Briana asked worriedly. She wasn't so sure this was a good idea.

"How can it seem so foggy in my head and so ingrained, all at the same time? My memories are so clear, but I don't think they're real. At least they weren't all mine."

"You don't have to go in."

Nora took a deep breath. "Yes, I do."

Briana followed her to the door before remembering she'd returned the extra key to Orlagh McCarthy, but Nora produced a key from her pocket.

"Sheila and Fiona locked up when they came to get my stuff."

She turned the key and pushed the door open, but remained standing on the outside of the threshold. When nothing happened, she gave an embarrassed laugh.

"Not sure what I expected."

But Briana felt equally reluctant to step inside. Shannon answered by pushing in between them and striding into the parlor. They followed hesitantly.

"Do you feel anything?" Briana asked.

Nora shook her head. On the desk, her journals and papers lay, undisturbed, along with her pens. Everything looked orderly. She leafed through some of the hand-written pages.

"Your book." Briana motioned toward the stack. "Sorry I laughed at that the first night, at the pub."

"I suppose it did sound silly," Nora said. "Funny thing is, I have enough material now for five books. But none of it is mine."

"Sure it is. You lived it through them. With them. Writing their story gives them new life, doesn't it?"

"I guess it does."

They peeked into the kitchen.

"Ugh," Nora said, opening and then closing the refrigerator very quickly. "Nothing otherworldly about that. Least they could have done is take out the trash."

It was the first time in ages Briana had heard her joke about the other inhabitants of the house. She took that as a good sign and reached for the rubbish bin. "Let's get it done now."

They spent a half hour emptying out the fridge and cupboards of all the food, bagging what was still edible and tossing what was going bad.

Bri carried the bags to the car while Nora took the rubbish out back. When Briana came back in, she looked around.

"Where's Shannon?"

"Hmmm?" Nora glanced at her from where she'd been standing outside the kitchen door, staring at the woods.

"Are you okay?" Briana asked.

"I'm fine. You can't find Shannon?"

"No. She's not in the parlor. She hasn't been here with you?"

Nora shook her head, and Briana went to the front door, calling. Outside, there was no sign of her dog. Shannon never ignored her call.

"Briana," came Nora's voice from upstairs.

Bri sprinted up the steps, taking them two at a time, her heart in her throat. There in the front bedroom, sprawled on her side in the sunlight streaming through the window across the floorboards, Shannon reposed, her eyes closed, perfectly at peace. Only her tail thumped when they entered the room.

"I guess they really are gone," Briana said. "Móirín and Rowan."

"They've moved on," Nora said. "At last. Just like Aoibheann." She turned a slow circle. "It feels kind of anticlimactic. For them to just disappear without even saying good-bye."

She reached for Briana's hand. "After I leave..."

Briana tried to pull away, but Nora held on tightly. "I'll have things to take care of. Back in the States."

Why did you let this happen? You knew she was leaving. Against her will, Briana's eyes moved up, held captive by the expression in Nora's—the love there, the tenderness. Bri wasn't sure her heart could take much more of this. *Say it. Tell her you'll go to America with her.*

So preoccupied was she with her own thoughts that she almost didn't hear what Nora was saying. "Wait. What did you say?"

"I said," Nora said, smiling, "that I'll have to sell my townhouse and all my extra stuff. It may take a little time to get my family to accept my decision, but my grandparents will help."

"Your decision." Now Briana's heart galloped in her chest. She might just collapse on the floor beside Shannon if this kept up.

Nora led her to the bed. The old mattress sagged under their weight when they sat.

"Sheila and I already started the paperwork on this end for a work visa. And once I'm back, I'll start the citizenship process. I'm not sure which will be faster. The whole business might take six months before I could get back here."

Briana stared at her. Was this for real, or was Nora just having her on? Bri leaned over, her elbow on her knee. "Sweet Jesus, I think I'm going to pass out."

Nora let go of her hand. "Is that... Do you not want me to move here? I mean, I'm still going to, but it doesn't mean you're chained to me or—"

Briana sat up and silenced her with a kiss. "You silly Yank," she murmured when she could talk. "Of course I want you here. I was ready to move to America to be with you."

"You—" Nora drew away enough to look into Briana's eyes. "You would have done that? Really?"

Briana gave a non-committal sideways nod. "If I had to."

Nora laughed and pulled Briana into an embrace. For long minutes, they sat like that, Bri's head resting against Nora's chest.

"*Do chroí, mo chroí.*"

"Your heart, my heart," Nora translated, kissing the top of Briana's head. "Do you think I can talk James McCarthy into selling me this cottage?"

Briana peered into Nora's face to see if she was kidding. She wasn't. Bri lifted one shoulder. "Only if you don't tell him the ghosts are gone. If he knows that, he'll charge you an arm and a leg for this place."

Nora chuckled. "We could tell Orlagh. She'd love to be rid of this cottage."

"That she would." Briana held her breath. "Are you sure?"

"Well, this is kind of my home place. Just like White O'Morn was Sean's."

"No, I meant about... It's a big step, leaving everything you know."

"It is, but I feel as if my whole life has been leading me here."

Nora traced a finger along Bri's cheek. "As I was saying," she continued. "When I buy this place, will you move in here with me? Help me fix it up? Make it our home?"

All the panic Briana had been feeling left, just cantered away, leaving only a sense of calm. "No."

Nora's face fell, the playful expression in her eyes gone dull. "No," she echoed in a strangled whisper.

"I can't," Briana said.

Stiffly, Nora nodded and dropped her hand. Briana got off the bed and stood in front of Nora, so that she was actually the taller.

"I could never live here with you in your place," she said. "But I would buy it with you. So it would be our place. Our home."

It took a minute for her words to sink in, but Nora's face lifted, a smile once again lighting up those beautiful eyes.

"Our home. That sounds so wonderful. This cottage used to hold such love. It would be nice if it did again."

"Are you sure?" Briana asked. "Neither of us has ever lived with anyone. We'll probably drive each other mad."

Nora considered, and Bri wondered if she should have planted that seed of doubt in Nora's mind.

"I once told Sheila that I thought the heart was a bittersweet garden, filled with thorns and loneliness and heartache." Her eyes shone with tears. "I've spent the summer, feeling the pain of those who died without answers, without hope."

She looked deeply into Briana's eyes. "I don't want to go on living like a ghost, just skimming the surface, afraid to let myself love. I do love you. More than I thought I was capable of loving anyone."

Briana bowed her head. "And you know I love you, but I can't promise there won't be thorns. I wish I could, but... I know how hard I am to love."

Nora tipped Briana's chin up, forcing her to meet her gaze again. "Loving you is the easiest thing I've ever done. It's just another bar on the fence."

Briana smiled. "Trust it."

Nora nodded. "Trust it."

NORA SAT IN THE waiting area of the Dublin airport for her Aer Lingus flight, trying unsuccessfully to concentrate on her book. Saying good-bye to everyone had been harder than expected, helped only by the fact that it was temporary. Orlagh McCarthy had, in fact, told her husband that if he didn't sell that cottage to Nora and Briana, she was going for an extended visit to her sister in Sligo, leaving him to cook and clean for himself. Nora suspected her grandfather had also put a little pressure on him as they dickered on a fair price.

All of the McNeill family were planning a visit to Ireland next summer–though they didn't yet know that Nora would in all likelihood be living here by the time they came.

"I think I should tell them that part in person."

Fiona and Jack were more excited than anyone at the prospect of having Brigid and Tommy back home again.

"I'll have the kettle on and biscuits baked and waiting when you get back," Sheila had promised with a tight hug.

Briana's family, when they got to Dublin and told them everything, had been ecstatic, especially Kieran, who was looking forward to having an extra auntie. Cara was doubly excited because Briana finally agreed to shop for an iPhone so she and Nora could FaceTime.

Briana had even promised to come to the U.S. to meet the McNeill clan and spend Christmas. "I've never flown anywhere," she said nervously. "But I want to meet your family, especially your grandparents."

The ride to the airport had been silent. Nora tried to think of something to say, but words were too hard. They parked, and Briana got Nora's bags from the cargo hold. Nora had given Shannon a last hug, and then followed with her backpack and carry-on while Briana wheeled the larger suitcase.

"I'm not saying good-bye to you," Nora had said before getting in the security line, ignoring the few stares they got as she kissed Briana one last time. "I'll see you soon."

She'd looked back until she was shepherded through the security gate and lost sight of Briana. Fighting the urge to run back to her, Nora got through security and customs.

After a three hour wait, Nora was roused from her thoughts by the uniformed woman at the gate announcing boarding for her flight. She queued up and shuffled along with the other passengers. After wrestling her luggage into the overhead bin, she took her window seat and buckled her seat belt.

She sat back and tried to relax as the plane slowly filled. An older couple took the two seats next to her. She closed her eyes, sending her thoughts to Briana, hoping she could feel Nora's love. Eventually, the plane backed up and taxied to their runway. When the pitch of the jet engines changed and the airliner took off, she opened her eyes. With her forehead pressed to the glass, she watched the earth drop away, first the airport buildings and then the houses and the highways and then the fields and smaller roads—all becoming smaller and smaller.

The view from the air this time was glorious—the sun sparkled on the rivers and loughs as the jet made its way west. She tried to identify which lough was which, to try and locate Cong. It didn't matter if she couldn't see it. Her heart was there and always had been. She sat back with a smile.

"Heading home?" asked the man next to her.

Nora shook her head. "Leaving home. But I'll be back."

THE END

About the Author

CAREN WAS RAISED IN OHIO, the oldest of four children. Much of her childhood was spent reading every book she could get her hands on and crafting her own stories. She was influenced by a diverse array of authors, including Rumer Godden, J.R.R. Tolkien, Ursula Le Guin, Marion Zimmer Bradley, Willa Cather, and the Brontë sisters. She has lived in Virginia for over twenty-five years where she practices physical therapy, teaches anatomy, and lives with her partner and their canine fur-children. She began writing creatively again several years ago. Her first novel, *Looking Through Windows*, won a Debut Author award from the Golden Crown Literary Society in 2009. Since then, she has published several more novels, winning three Goldies and multiple Rainbow Awards. She recently completed her first fantasy trilogy, the award-winning The Dragonmage Saga. *A Bittersweet Garden* is her fourteenth published novel.

Made in the USA
Columbia, SC
24 February 2019